CONTEMPORARY LATIN AMERICAN SHORT STORIES

CONTEMPORARY LATIN AMERICAN SHORT STORIES

Edited by Pat McNees Mancini

FAWCETT PREMIER • NEW YORK

A Fawcett Premier Book
Published by Ballantine Books
Copyright © 1974 by CBS Publications, The Consumer Publishing Division of CBS Inc.

ISBN 0-449-30060-9

Manufactured in the United States of America

First Fawcett Premier Edition: September 1974
First Ballantine Books Edition: April 1983
Fifth Printing: November 1988

For my mother,
ELEANOR MCNEES

CONTENTS

INTRODUCTION

We in the United States are only beginning to appreciate the richness and variety of the literature Latin America* has produced since 1900. Few of us, apart from specialists in the field, were familiar with even the major works of Latin American writers until recently, and the occasional curious reader was discouraged by the scarcity of translations into English. Even the Spanish language departments in the universities continue to focus their attention on Spain, although in this century the writing of Latin America has been far more vigorous.

This state of affairs has begun to change in the past decade; perhaps the turning point came with the 1970 publication here in translation (three years after its appearance in Buenos Aires) of Gabriel García Márquez's *One Hundred Years of Solitude*. Critics, admiring the novel's brilliance and vitality, speculated that the future direction that fiction might take was perhaps being determined in Latin America. And the success of the book, both hardbound and paperback, has encouraged more publishers in this country to look for other Latin American works to offer to an increasingly interested public.** Latin American writers whose importance had been recognized in their

* By Latin American I mean all of the countries of South and Central America, Mexico, and the non-English-speaking islands of the Caribbean. Portuguese-speaking Brazil is included as well as Spanish America.

** Jorge Amado's *Gabriela, Clove and Cinnamon* had in 1962 been the first Latin American novel to make the bestseller lists and the Book-of-the-Month Club, but it never reached the wide audience that *One Hundred Years of Solitude* seems to be reaching.

own countries twenty or thirty years ago are now being read for the first time in the United States, and younger writers are encouraged by the existence of an international audience that was not available to earlier generations.

Until recently Latin American writers suffered neglect, not only in this country, but in their own; there were few publishers to print their work, and few readers to appreciate them. Jorge Luis Borges relates how when he found out one year that a book of his had sold thirty-seven copies, he felt that he should write to those people to thank them.

Until a few decades ago, literature—primarily poetry—was an upper-class diversion, written by the privileged few for the privileged few, since the majority of the population was rural and illiterate. Writers looked to Europe, particularly to France, for their models. Consequently much of their work strikes us now as imitative and derivative, although some of it is being re-examined and newly appreciated.

At the turn of the century a new literary movement began, known as *modernismo* and led by the Nicaraguan poet Rubén Darío. Purposely ignoring the political struggles that had rocked Latin America during the nineteenth century (with the notable exception was the Cuban José Martí), influenced in part by French symbolism, and determined to set themselves apart as an artistic élite, the *modernistas* experimented with language and technique. For the first time, Latin American literature commanded an international audience—because it was produced not by amateurs, however gifted, but by craftsmen. The professional writer had emerged.

Other writers, expanding on the Spanish tradition of regionalist writing, began to describe the hinterlands of their own countries, the land, the people, and their traditions, as yet relatively unknown and uninfluenced by Europe.

The early regionalists tried to portray in some detail the life and language of the rural poor; inevitably this developed into a literature of social protest, particularly when it involved the Indians. It was difficult to ignore the poverty and injustice that existed throughout Latin America, with a small number of white Europeans dominating a large, impoverished, indigenous or mixed population. Many writers felt obligated to educate their public and effect social change, and much of the fiction of the time became more and more didactic. Despite their genuine concern for the oppressed, one misses, with these writers, the feeling that they are trying to convey an experience they have felt profoundly. For all their efforts to overcome prejudice, to abandon their assumed position of racial superiority, they remain a minority writing for a minority, closer to their audience than to their subject.

After a while, these dominating trends—*modernismo* on the one hand, regionalism and social protest on the other—developed into a literary debate. Should literature concern itself with the age-old, universal themes; should it appeal (at least in America, failing a large, educated audience) to an élite; should it strive above all to be art? Or should it deal with what was uniquely American, as a literature committed to the people and accessible to them?

It was natural for a writer in a country that was only beginning to acquire a national identity to try to express that unique identity in fiction; it was also natural for writers all over Latin America, conscious that while they were now independent of Spain they were more dependent upon the United States, to stress the unity of Latin American culture as a whole. But a significant number of writers insisted that preoccupation with national or supranational identity was shortsighted, that it was the experiments of the literary avant-garde that would bring international recognition to Latin American culture.

Meanwhile, in the 1920s, many Latin American writers went to Paris, where they came into contact with André Breton and the surrealists as well as with expatriates from the U.S. The early influence of surrealism is clearly evident in the works of some Latin American writers. Conversely, the avant-garde of Paris idealized the primitive and were excited by Latin America and its indigenous cultures. Many writers who had gone abroad looked back at America with new perspective and to an extent began to shed their feelings of national inferiority. Alejo Carpentier and Miguel Ángel Asturias were two of the Americans in Paris who began to concentrate their attention on genuinely American themes in a new kind of fiction that had begun to free itself of the tendency to be documentary and picturesque. And Borges returned from Spain to Argentina to argue that it was foolish for Latin American writers to retreat into localized culture, that they were part of Western culture, in a situation comparable to that of the Jew: part of it, but not bound by any particular loyalty and therefore able to view it ironically and participate in it freely.

To be sure, regionalism and novels of social protest continued to dominate Latin American fiction during the 1920s and 1930s—often revealing the early influence of Zola's naturalism as well as more recent interest in the Russian and Mexican Revolutions. But since the 1940s Latin American writers have seemed increasingly aware that fiction, to reflect reality, must reflect its complexities as well. Many novelists (some under the influence of writers like Faulkner) have experimented with techniques that suggest the fragmentation of human experience, such as stream of consciousness, shifting time sequences, and alternating points of view. Still, it is not an introspective literature; rather, as Luis Harss and Barbara Dohmann suggest in their book, *Into the Mainstream,* it "pulls toward abstraction," and has tried on the whole to "find the point of confluence of the mythical and the personal, the social and the subjective, the historical and the metaphysical." And as David Gallagher writes in his *Modern Latin American Literature,* "sheer fantasy is a prominent ingredient of contemporary Latin American fiction (and it) takes many forms . . . Latin American novelists very often seek to create a reality that is quite deliberately *alternative* to the one they are living in." Increasingly, they do so with a sense of humor.

Latin America lends itself to writing on a grand (and a fantastic) scale. To begin with, nature is not gentle there; it is a powerful force to be reckoned with, whether in the tropical rain forests, on the Andean peaks, or on the vast plains. Much of the writing (especially early in the century) has been about the human struggle with a hostile environment. But there is another basic Latin American theme that is easier for us to appreciate: that of the Promised Land whose promise hasn't been realized, the failed ideal, the wasted dream. And if in the novels of the first three decades of this century there was a strong sense that the novel had a job to do in bringing about social change, in some more recent fiction the view of historical possibilities has been more pessimistic. There is less confidence that social problems can be dealt with in the novel, more of a feeling that history repeats itself: "Plus ça change, plus c'est la même chose." Not that Latin American writers are indifferent to politics or to social change, far from it; most of them, particularly the younger ones, are intensely committed to politics and are usually left-wing. Politics has had a decisive effect on the lives of many of the writers included in this anthology, sending them periodically or permanently into exile, and sometimes to prison. The effect of intellectual isolation on writers in countries under dictatorship is deadening. Totalitarian regimes are notoriously anti-intellectual, and in many countries the very act of writing is a protest. But increasingly Latin American writers have turned away from the "masses" as fictional subject, and have concentrated more on the personal, internal conflicts of the individual.*

Recent fiction deals more with life in the cities than with life in the country, for the simple reason that, as the world becomes increasingly urbanized, more of its problems are urban ones. Loneliness and alienation, the dehumanization of daily life, the failure to communicate—these are themes common in contemporary fiction around the world. The city has been the great leveler, for the problems created by urbanization afflict both rich and poor, and the New Yorker can appreciate the problem of the Montevidean better than either can appreciate the problems of the poor dirt farmer of the backlands.

Meanwhile, the position of the writer in Latin America has changed considerably. In this century, until very recently, unless writers were wealthy they wrote in their spare time, supporting themselves with a full-time job, traditionally as journalists, civil servants, librarians or diplomats. (And it was doubly difficult for a woman to become a writer unless she had independent means.) For half of the nineteenth and much of the twentieth century they wrote mainly for their own local literary circles, hence mainly for fellow writers and mostly those in their own country. The rate of illiteracy in most Latin American countries was (and continues to be) high; even in countries with massive immigration from Europe, the immigrants were usually poorly-educated.

But now there is the beginning of a larger reading public as the educated middle class has grown and as educational opportunities have spread to some extent. Publishers

* Much of what has been said in this paragraph does not apply to revolutionary Cuba's new literature.

are issuing larger printings, and, as communications have improved between countries, writers are no longer read only at home. The Cuban Revolution in 1959 brought about a new feeling of unity, created a bond among intellectuals all over Latin America, who sensed in it the possibilities of basic social change. This bond has been strengthened by writers' congresses, and by the efforts of several publishers and literary magazines to publish works from all over Latin America—a boon to the very small countries whose populations could not support large printings. Not only has the circulation of books among Latin American countries increased (Brazil still tends to be isolated), but an increasing number of works has been translated for readers on the Continent, and now into English (many of them with the assistance of the nonprofit Center for Inter-American Relations). With a wider audience of serious readers, more Latin American writers are now able to live by their writing alone.

1967 was a particularly dramatic year in Latin American writing. Not only was *One Hundred Years of Solitude* published with resounding success all over the world, but in the same year Miguel Ángel Asturias received the Nobel Prize for Literature, and Mario Vargas Llosa's novel *The Green House* received the first Rómulo Gallegos Award, a distinguished and lucrative new Latin American literary prize.

People speak now of a "boom" in Latin American writing, and this is justly irritating to the writers. It is not that their writing has suddenly become worthy of international attention. It is that we the readers are finally paying attention to it. This collection of stories is a response to that new interest. As a mass-market paperback, it is long overdue.

Poetry and the contemporary short story, unlike longer forms of writing, have found many outlets in Latin American newspapers and literary magazines, and even in such unlikely places as trade journals. Some of the most famous names in Latin American writing are those of poets such as César Vallejo, Pablo Neruda, and Gabriela Mistral. Only two poets are included here, Rubén Darío and Octavio Paz, but there are several Latin American poetry anthologies in print and some collections by individual poets, despite the difficulties of translating poetry.

I particularly regret that so few women are included. As opportunities for both women and writers increase in Latin America, perhaps the male writer will not so dominate the scene. Meanwhile I have included several stories by men which, I think, deal rather sensitively with themes of sexual identity and relations between the sexes.

I have purposely avoided the travelogue approach to the fiction; there are no gauchos here and no tropical rain forests. Nor is the collection meant as a course in literary history, although roughly it surveys the twentieth century; the early modern writers open the collection and some of the most promising younger writers close it. Stories don't adhere to chronological order, though; it seemed more natural to group those similar in subject, theme or approach. For example, Asturias and Icaza write altogether differently about Indians, as do Icaza and Bosch about superstition; Cabrera Infante and Norberto Fuentes are two Cubans who represent different attitudes toward the Revolution; and Vargas Llosa's story about teenage machismo seems not unrelated in concern to Puig's about romance, silver-screen style.

Not all of the Latin American countries are represented, because writers have flourished in some countries more than others. Stories were chosen primarily for the quality of the writing or the importance of the author, and not to achieve a balanced geographical representation, a national quota system. Perhaps most important, stories were chosen primarily for the reader not yet familiar with Latin American fiction. Although some stories are well-known, several are published here for the first time in English.

—PAT McNEES MANCINI

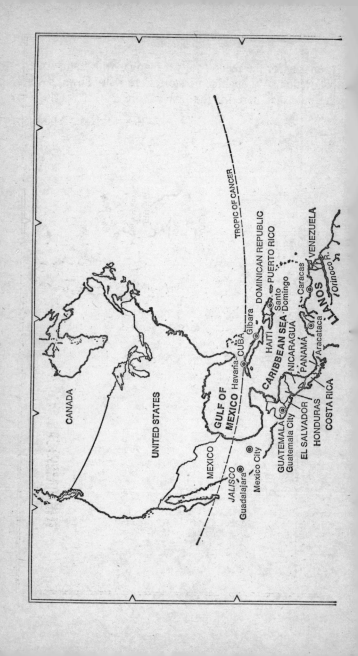

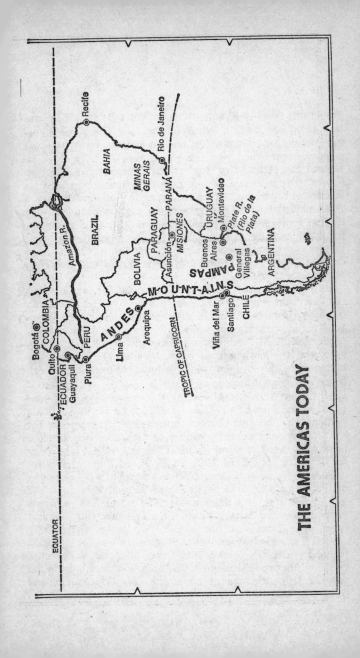

THE AMERICAS TODAY

Joaquim María Machado de Assis (1839–1908) was born in Rio de Janeiro, Brazil, of a mulatto father and a Portuguese mother. It was a humble but literate family. His first poem was published when he was fifteen. At thirty-three he entered the Ministry of Agriculture, Commerce, and Public Works, where he served for thirty-four years, eventually as director of accounting. When the Brazilian Academy of Letters was founded in 1897, he became its first president, serving diligently until his death. Despite an active life (and epilepsy), he wrote steadily and in many forms: newspaper articles, literary criticism, plays, librettos, translations from three languages, but most importantly, nine novels and over two hundred short stories.

He was an anomaly in his time. Although Zola and naturalism were the rage of Brazilian letters—Machado de Assis despised naturalism for its tendency to inventory details superficially and meaninglessly—his fiction was carefully crafted, subtle, ambiguous, and psychologically probing. Regarded now as one of the world's finest modern writers, he was literally unknown in this country until his novel *Epitaph of a Small Winner* was published here in 1952, seventy years after it appeared in Brazil as *Memorias Posthumas de Braz Cubas* (1881). Reminiscent of *Tristram Shandy,* it is the memoirs, written from the grave, of an unsuccessful picaresque comic hero. The novel was hardly noticed, and it was ten years before he finished his next novel, *Quincas Borba* (1891, *Philosopher or Dog?*), a sequel. In 1900 he published *Dom Casmurro,* considered by many his masterpiece, a novel that develops one of the author's favorite themes, love versus self-love, or the wasted potential of a human life. The novel *Esau e Jacob* (1904, *Esau and Jacob*) through the symbolism of identical twins, one liberal and the other conservative, allegorically covers the period from 1869 to 1894, a time of intense political partisanship, when the slaves of Brazil were being freed and the republic formed. The following story is from the only English collection of his stories, *The Psychiatrist and Other Stories.*

Midnight Mass

I have never quite understood a conversation that I had with a lady many years ago, when I was seventeen and she was thirty. It was Christmas Eve. I had arranged to go to Mass with a neighbor and was to rouse him at midnight for this purpose.

The two-story house in which I was staying belonged to the notary Menezes, whose first wife had been a cousin of mine. His second wife, Conceição [Conception], and her mother had received me hospitably upon my arrival a few months earlier. I had come to Rio from Mangaratiba to study for the college entrance examinations. I lived quietly with my books. Few contacts. Occasional walks. The family was small: the notary, his wife, his mother-in-law, and two female slaves. An old-fashioned household. By ten at night everyone was in his bedroom; by half-past ten the house was asleep.

I had never gone to a theater and, more than once, on

hearing Menezes say that he was going, I asked him to take me along. On these occasions his mother-in-law frowned and the slaves tittered. Menezes did not reply; he dressed, went out, and returned the next morning. Later I learned that the theater was a euphemism. Menezes was having an affair with a married woman who was separated from her husband; he stayed out once a week. Conceição had grieved at the beginning, but after a time she had grown used to the situation. Custom led to resignation, and finally she came almost to accept the affair as proper.

Gentle Conceição! They called her the saint and she merited the title, so uncomplainingly did she suffer her husband's neglect. In truth, she possessed a temperament of great equanimity, with extremes neither of tears nor of laughter. Everything about her was passive and attenuated. Her very face was median, neither pretty nor ugly. She was what is called a kind person. She spoke ill of no one, she pardoned everything. She didn't know how to hate; quite possibly she didn't know how to love.

On that Christmas Eve (it was 1861 or 1862) the notary was at theater. I should have been back in Mangaratiba, but I had decided to remain till Christmas to see a midnight Mass in the big city. The family retired at the usual hour. I sat in the front parlor, dressed and ready. From there I could leave through the entrance hall without waking anyone. There were three keys to the door: the notary had one, I had one, and one remained in the house.

"But Mr. Nogueira, what will you do all this while?" asked Conceição's mother.

"I'll read, Madame Ignacia."

I had a copy of an old translation of *The Three Musketeers,* published originally, I think, in serial form in *The Journal of Commerce*. I sat down at the table in the center of the room and, by the light of the kerosene lamp, while the house slept, mounted once more D'Artagnan's bony nag and set out upon adventure. In a short time I was completely absorbed. The minutes flew as they rarely do when one is waiting. I heard the clock strike eleven, but almost without noticing. After a time, however, a sound from the interior of the house roused me from my book. It was the sound of footsteps, in the hall that connected the parlor with the dining room. I raised my head. Soon I saw the form of Conceição appear at the door.

"Haven't you gone?" she asked.

"No, I haven't. I don't think it's midnight yet."

"What patience!"

Conceição, wearing her bedroom slippers, came into the room. She was dressed in a white negligee, loosely bound at the waist. Her slenderness helped to suggest a romantic apparition quite in keeping with the spirit of my novel. I shut the book. She sat on the chair facing mine, near the sofa. To my question whether perchance I had awakened her by stirring about, she quickly replied:

"No, I woke up naturally."

I looked at her and doubted her statement. Her eyes were not those of a person who had just slept. However, I quickly put out of my mind the thought that she could be guilty of lying. The possibility that I might have kept her awake and that she might have lied in order not to make me unhappy, did not occur to me at the time. I have already said that she was a good person, a kind person.

"I guess it won't be much longer now," I said.

"How patient you are to stay awake and wait while your friend sleeps! And to wait alone! Aren't you afraid of ghosts? I thought you'd be startled when you saw me."

"When I heard footsteps I was surprised. But then I soon saw it was you."

"What are you reading? Don't tell me, I think I know: it's *The Three Musketeers.*"

"Yes, that's right. It's very interesting."

"Do you like novels?"

"Yes."

"Have you ever read *The Little Sweetheart?*"

"By Mr. Macedo? I have it in Mangaratiba."

"I'm very fond of novels, but I don't have much time for them. Which ones have you read?"

I began to name some. Conceição listened, with her head resting on the back of her chair, looking at me past half-shut eyelids. From time to time she wet her lips with her tongue. When I stopped speaking she said nothing. Thus we remained for several seconds. Then she raised her head; she clasped her hands and rested her chin on them, with her elbows on the arms of her chair, all without taking from me her large, perceptive eyes.

"Maybe she's bored with me," I thought. And then, aloud: "Madame Conceição, I think it's getting late and I..."

"No, it's still early. I just looked at the clock; it's half-past eleven. There's time yet. When you lose a night's sleep, can you stay awake the next day?"

"I did once."

"I can't. If I lose a night, the next day I just have to take a nap, if only for half an hour. But of course I'm getting on in years."

"Oh, no, nothing of the sort, Madame Conceição!"

I spoke so fervently that I made her smile. Usually her gestures were slow, her attitude calm. Now, however, she rose suddenly, moved to the other side of the room, and, in her chaste disarray, walked about between the window and the door of her husband's study. Although thin, she always walked with a certain rocking gait as if she carried her weight with difficulty. I had never before felt this impression so strongly. She paused several times, examining a curtain or correcting the position of some object on the sideboard. Finally she stopped directly in front of me, with the table between us. The circle of her ideas was narrow indeed: she returned to her surprise at seeing me awake and dressed. I repeated what she already knew, that I had never heard a midnight Mass in the city and that I didn't want to miss the chance.

"It's the same as in the country. All Masses are alike."

"I guess so. But in the city there must be more elegance and more people. Holy Week here in Rio is much better than in the country. I don't know about St. John's Day or St. Anthony's . . ."

Little by little she had leaned forward; she had rested her elbows on the marble top of the table and had placed her face between the palms of her hands. Her unbuttoned sleeves fell naturally, and I saw her forearms, very white and not so thin as one might have supposed. I had seen her arms before, although not frequently, but on this occasion sight of them impressed me greatly. The veins were so blue that, despite the dimness of the light, I could trace every one of them. Even more than the book, Conceição's presence had served to keep me awake. I went on talking about holy days in the country and in the city, and about whatever else came to my lips. I jumped from subject to subject, sometimes returning to an earlier one; and I laughed in order to make her laugh, so that I could see her white, shining, even teeth. Her eyes were not really black but were very dark; her nose, thin and slightly curved, gave her face an air of interrogation. Whenever I raised my voice a little, she hushed me.

"Softly! Mama may wake up."

And she did not move from that position, which filled me with delight, so close were our faces. Really there was no need to speak loudly in order to be heard. We both whispered, I more than she because I had more to say. At times she became serious, very serious, with her brow a bit wrinkled. After a while she tired and changed both position and place. She came around the table and sat on the sofa. I turned my head and could see the tips of her slippers, but only for as long as it took her to sit down: her negligee was long and quickly covered them. I remember that they were black. Conceição said very softly:

"Mama's room is quite a distance away, but she sleeps so lightly. If she wakes up now, poor thing, it will take her a long time to fall asleep again."

"I'm like that, too."

"What?" she asked, leaning forward to hear better.

I moved to the chair immediately next to the sofa and repeated what I had said. She laughed at the coincidence, for she, too, was a light sleeper, we were all light sleepers.

"I'm just like mama: when I wake up I can't fall asleep again. I roll all over the bed, I get up, I light the candle, I walk around, I lie down again, and nothing happens."

"Like tonight."

"No, no," she hastened.

I didn't understand her denial; perhaps she didn't understand it either. She took the ends of her belt and tapped them on her knees, or rather on her right knee, for she had crossed her legs. Then she began to talk about dreams. She said she had had only one nightmare in her whole life, and that one during her childhood. She wanted to know whether I ever had nightmares. Thus the conversation re-engaged itself and moved along slowly, continuously, and I forgot about the hour and about Mass. Whenever I finished a bit of narrative or an explanation she asked a question or brought up some new point, and I started talking again. Now and then she had to caution me.

"Softly, softly . . ."

Sometimes there were pauses. Twice I thought she was asleep. But her eyes, shut for a moment, quickly opened: they showed neither sleepiness nor fatigue, as though she had shut them merely so that she could see better. On one of these occasions I think she noticed that I was absorbed in her, and I remember that she shut her eyes again—whether hurriedly or slowly I do not remember. Some of my recollections of that evening seem abortive or confused. I get mixed up, I contradict myself. One thing I remember vividly is that at a certain moment she, who till then had been such engaging company (but nothing more), suddenly became beautiful, so very beautiful. She stood up, with her arms crossed. I, out of respect for her, stirred myself to rise; she did not want me to, she put one of her hands on my shoulder, and I remained seated. I thought she was going to say something; but she trembled as if she had a chill, turned her back, and sat in the chair where she had found me reading. She glanced at the mirror above the sofa and began to talk about two engravings that were hanging on the wall.

"These pictures are getting old. I've asked Chiquinho to buy new ones."

Chiquinho was her husband's nickname. The pictures bespoke the man's principal interest. One was of Cleopatra; I no longer remember the subject of the other, but there were women in it. Both were banal. In those days I did not know they were ugly.

"They're pretty," I said.

"Yes, but they're stained. And besides, to tell the truth, I'd prefer pictures of saints. These are better for bachelors' quarters or a barber shop."

"A barber shop! I didn't think you'd ever been to . . ."

"But I can imagine what the customers there talk about while they're waiting—girls and flirtations, and naturally the proprietor wants to please them with pictures they'll like. But I think pictures like that don't belong in the home. That's what I think, but I have a lot of queer ideas. Anyway, I don't like them. I have an Our Lady of the Immaculate Conception, my patron saint; it's very lovely. But it's a statue, it can't be hung on the wall, and I wouldn't want it here anyway. I keep it in my little oratory."

The oratory brought to mind the Mass. I thought it might be time to go and was about to say so. I think I even opened my mouth but shut it before I could speak, so that I could go on listening to what she was saying, so sweetly, so graciously, so gently that it drugged my soul. She spoke of her religious devotions as a child and as a young girl. Then she told about dances and walks and trips to the island of Paquetá, all mixed together, almost without interruption. When she tired of the past she spoke of the present, of household matters, of family cares, which, before her marriage, everyone said would be terrible, but really they were nothing. She didn't mention it, but I knew she had been twenty-seven when she married.

She no longer moved about, as at first, and hardly changed position. Her eyes seemed smaller, and she began to look idly about at the walls.

"We must change this wallpaper," she said, as if talking to herself.

I agreed, just to say something, to shake off my magnetic trance or whatever one may call the condition that thickened my tongue and benumbed my senses. I wished and I did not wish to end the conversation. I tried to take my eyes from her, and did so out of respect; but, afraid she would think I was tired of looking at her, when in truth I was not, I turned again towards her. The conversation was dying away. In the street, absolute stillness.

We stopped talking and for some time (I cannot say how long) sat there in silence. The only sound was the gnawing of a rat in the study; it stirred me from my somnolescence. I wanted to talk about it but didn't know how to begin. Conceição seemed to be abstracted. Suddenly I heard a beating on the window and a voice shouting:

"Midnight Mass! Midnight Mass!"

"There's your friend," she said, rising. "It's funny. You were to wake him, and here he comes to wake you. Hurry, it must be late. Goodbye."

"Is it time already?"

"Of course."

"Midnight Mass!" came the voice from outside, with more beating on the window.

"Hurry, hurry, don't make him wait. It was my fault. Goodbye until tomorrow."

And with her rocking gait Conceição walked softly down the hall. I went out into the street and, with my friend, proceeded to the church. During Mass, Conceição kept appearing between me and the priest; charge this to my seventeen years. Next morning at breakfast I spoke of the midnight Mass and of the people I had seen in church, without, however, exciting Conceição's interest. During the day I found her, as always, natural, benign, with nothing to suggest the conversation of the prior evening.

A few days later I went to Mangaratiba. When I returned to Rio in March, I learned that the notary had died of apoplexy. Conceição was living in the Engenho Novo district, but I neither visited nor met her. I learned later that she had married her husband's apprenticed clerk.

Translated by WILLIAM L. GROSSMAN

Rubén Darío (1867–1916), born in Nicaragua, went to Chile in 1886 where he worked as a newspaperman and continued the study he had begun at home of Symbolism and the new techniques developing in French poetry. His own technical experiments were evident in the landmark collection of prose and verse *Azul* ["Blue"] appeared in 1888 and 1890. After a trip to Spain in 1892, he was convinced that Spanish literature needed reform. When he returned to Buenos Aires, where he also worked as a newspaperman, he became the spokesman for a new aesthetic movement that was to be known as *modernismo*. Its greatest impact would be felt in poetry. Darío urged poets to experiment with new techniques and strive for verbal perfection—above all, to avoid the common, the cliché. The emphasis of the *modernistas* on the aesthetic and the exotic seems more decorative than revolutionary now, but as Enrique Pupo-Waller points out in the Winter 1971 issue of *Studies in Short Fiction,* an issue devoted to Latin-American fiction: "A rigorous effort to perfect form in poetry as well as in the narrative produced what were the first important collections of well-structured stories in Spanish America. Fiction writers among the Modernists made use of the short story form almost exclusively. By imposing on the narrative the tensions and severe economies of poetic language, they brought about a further distillation of fictional material." Besides bringing a new richness of versification to poetry, *modernismo* brought international attention to Latin American writing. And indirectly Darío had another effect, as Luis Harss and Barbara Dohmman point out: because he lived abroad for some time as his country's diplomatic representative in Paris and Madrid, his eyes were opened to home, and he began early in the century to use American Indian lore, mostly for color, but with the effect of turning the attention of other writers to America's indigenous culture.

The Case of Señorita Amelia

That Doctor Z. is celebrated, eloquent, triumphant; that his voice is deep and thrilling; that his manner—particularly since the publication of his book, *The Structure of Fantasy* —is mysteriously compelling—you may differ with me about all these, or agree, with reservations; but that his bald spot is unique, distinguished, beautiful, solemn, poetic if you like—*that* you could never deny, I am certain. It would be like denying the light of the sun, or the perfume of roses, or the narcotic properties of certain lines of verse. Well, last night, shortly after we had greeted the stroke of twelve with a salvo of corks popping from twelve bottles of the finest Roederer, in Lowensteinger's sybaritic rococo dining-room, the doctor's head reared up proudly, like a dome of polished ivory; above it, through some trick of light, the flames of two candles, reflected in a mirror, formed something that resembled the glowing horns of Moses. The doctor's eloquent gestures, his words of wisdom, seemed to be aimed at me. As a rule my lips are silent, but on this occasion I had let fall some commonplace expression or other. For instance, "If only we could stop time in its course!"

The way the doctor looked at me, the smile that hovered about his mouth, might well have disconcerted anyone.

"Sir," he said, savoring his champagne, "if I were not utterly disillusioned about youth, if I did not know that today people who are barely beginning life are already dead, dead in mind and spirit I mean, without faith or enthusiasm or ideals, already old at heart, mere masks of life, no more . . . if I did not know all this, if I saw in you anything but a typical specimen of fin-de-siècle youth, I should tell you I have a satisfying answer to that last remark."

"Doctor!"

"Yes, but I say again that your scepticism makes it impossible for me to speak as I might in other circumstances."

In a calm, firm voice I replied, "I believe in God and in His church. I believe in the miracles. I believe in the supernatural."

"In that case I shall tell you something that will make you smile. And I hope the story will give you something to think about."

Besides Minna, the daughter of our host, there were four of us in the dining-room: Riquet, the journalist, Abbé Pureau, the doctor and I. From the drawing-room drifted the sounds of merriment, the cheerful hum of voices the occasion called for: "Happy New Year! Happy New Year!"

The doctor continued. "What wise man would dare to say, *this is so?* We know nothing. *Ignoramus et ignorabimus.* Who understands exactly the concept of time? Who knows for certain the meaning of space? Science goes groping like a blind man along the road, and when at odd moments it catches a faint gleam of the light, it proclaims its final triumph. No one has yet broken the circle formed by the symbolic serpent. From Hermes Trismegistus down to our own day, humanity has lifted barely a single fold of the veil that shrouds Isis. No one has succeeded in learning with absolute certainty the three greatest expressions of Nature: events, laws, origins. After attempting to dig deep into the vast field of the mystery, I have lost nearly all my illusions.

"In illustrious academies and in bulky tomes I have been called wise; I have devoted my entire life to the study of humanity, its origins and its ends; I have penetrated the mysteries of the cabala, of occultism and theosophy; I have passed from the material plane of the sage to the astral plane of the thaumaturge and the spiritual plane of the magus; I know how Paracelsus worked, and Apollonius of Typre; in our own time I have assisted the Englishman Crookes in his laboratory; I have delved deep into karma and into Christian mysticism; the forgotten lore of the fakirs is familiar to me, and the theology of the Roman priests; yet I say to you that the sages have not yet seen so much as a glimpse of the supreme light, and that the immensity and eternity of the mystery is the single terrifying truth."

He turned to me. "Do you know the elements that compose man? Grupa, jiba, linga, sharira, kama, rupa, manas, buddhi, atma; in other words, the body, the life force, the astral body, the animal soul, the human soul, spiritual force and spiritual essence. . . ."

I could see Minna's face growing longer and longer. Hurriedly I broke in. "But weren't you about to prove to us that time . . .?"

"Very well," he answered, "since preliminary explanations are not to your taste, let us get on with the story. It is as follows:

"Twenty-three years ago, in Buenos Aires, I came to know a French family named Revall; the founder, an excellent man, had held a consular post in Rosas' time. We lived in adjoining houses, I was young and full of enthusiasm, and the three daughters might have vied with the three Graces. Suffice it to say that few sparks were needed to kindle the flame of love. . . ."

"Lo-o-o-o-ve" was the way the portly philosopher pronounced the word, with his right thumb hooked into his waistcoat, and his agile, if chubby, fingers drumming on his impressive paunch.

"I must confess frankly that I had no preference for any one of the three, that Luz, Josefina and Amelia held the same place in my heart. Yet perhaps not quite the same: Amelia's eyes, at once gentle and ardent, her gay laughter, her childlike delight in mischief . . . yes, she was the one I preferred. She was the youngest: she was barely twelve, and I had already passed thirty. For that reason, and because the little minx had such a fun-loving disposition, I treated her like the child she was: it was the other two who had the benefit of my impassioned glances, the pressures of the hand, even serious promises of marriage, for love had turned me, in intent at least, into an abominable bigamist. But little Amelia! . . . Whenever I came to the house, she was always the first to come running, all wheedling smiles. 'Where is my candy?' she would ask. The ritual question. And I would utter the proper phrases of greeting and then sit down, in a cheerful glow, and load her little hands with rich, pink caramels and chocolate-covered sugarplums, which she would wolf down in great gulps, to the accompaniment of resounding music, palatal, lingual and dental. I can't explain what attached me so to that little girl—in short skirts still—with the lovely eyes. But the truth is that when I had to leave Buenos Aires to continue my studies, I only pretended to be moved when I said farewell to Luz, who stared at me with wide, pained, sorrowing eyes; the pressure of my hand on Josefina's was false, as she stood there with a handkerchief clenched between her teeth, struggling to fight back the tears; and on Amelia's brow I laid what is perhaps the purest and the most ardent kiss, the purest and the most passionate, that I have ever given. And I embarked for Calcutta, exactly like your beloved and admired General Mansilla when he sailed to the Orient, in the flood-tide of his youth, laden with resounding, new-minted gold coins. Already thirsting for the occult sciences I was on my way to study, among the mahatmas of India, what our poor western science is still unable to teach us. The friendship I had kept up through correspondence with Madame Blavatsky had opened up a wide field to me in the land of the fakirs, and more than one guru, knowing how I thirsted after wisdom, showed himself disposed to lead me along the path that leads to the sacred source of truth; and although my lips hoped to be refreshed in the chill, adamantine waters, my thirst was not to be quenched. Unswervingly I sought the sight my eyes longed to behold: the Keherpas of Zoroaster, the Persian Kalep, the Kovei-Ken of Hindu philosophy, the archoeno of Paracelsus, the limbuz of Swedenborg; I heard Buddhist monks in the forests of Tibet; I studied the ten sephiroth of the cabala, from the one which symbolizes unlimited space to the one which is known as Malkuth and contains the principle of life. I studied spirit, air, fire, and water, height, depth, the East, the North and the South; I came close to an understanding, even a deep knowledge, of Satan, Lucifer, Astaroth, Beelzebub, Asmodeus, Belphegor, Mabema, Lilith, Adrammelech and Baal. In my longing to comprehend, in my insatiable desire for wisdom, I would discover, just when I thought to have attained the height of my ambition, signs of my weakness, indications of what a feeble thing I was; and those concepts—God, space, time—would dissolve into an impenetrable mist before my eyes . . . I travelled through Asia, Africa, Europe and America. I

helped Colonel Olcot found the New York branch of the
Theosophical Society. And of all this"—the doctor, his
eyes fixed on Minna's, gave a special emphasis to these
words—"do you know what science and immortality come
to? A pair of blue eyes . . . or dark eyes!"

"And the end of the story?" Minna implored faintly.

More solemn than ever the doctor answered. "I swear
to you, gentlemen, that what I say is the absolute truth. The
end of the story? Barely a week ago I returned to Argentina after an absence of twenty-three years. I was fat, more
than fat enough, bald as a billiard-ball; but the flame of
love, the fire we bachelors tend like vestal virgins, was
burning still. And so my first step was to inquire as to the
whereabouts of the Revall family.

" 'The Revalls', people answered me, 'you mean Amelia Revall's people?' And they would smile a peculiar smile.
I began to suspect that Amelia, poor child. . . . After
searching and searching, I came upon the house at last.
An old negro answered the door, took my card, led me
into a drawing-room. Everything about it had a hint of
melancholy: the mirrors were shrouded in mourning-veils,
and over the piano two large portraits, in which I recognized
the elder sisters, stared at each other with sad, mournful
eyes. A few moments later Luz and Josefina appeared,

'Oh, my friend, my dear friend!'

That was all. A halting conversation ensued, full of
timid openings suddenly broken off, understanding smiles.
Sad smiles, terribly sad. From what I could understand, I
judged that neither of them had married. I could not work
up courage to inquire about Amelia . . . To these two
pathetic creatures any question might sound bitterly ironical,
might recall some irreparable misfortune or disgrace . . .
At this point a little girl came running in, the very image
of poor Amelia."

"Turning to me she demanded, in Amelia's own voice, 'Where is my candy?' "

"I couldn't find a word to say. The two sisters stood looking at each other, with pallid faces, shaking their heads mournfully."

"Blurting out some words of farewell, bowing clumsily, I left the house as if the blast of some strange wind were driving me. Later I learned the whole story. The child I had taken for the fruit of some guilty love affair is Amelia, the Amelia I left behind twenty-three years ago; she has remained a child, her life has suddenly stopped in its tracks. At a given moment some unknown god stopped the clock of time for her. With what design, who can say?"

At this moment Doctor Z. was entirely bald.

Translated by GREGORY WOODRUFF

Leopoldo Lugones (1874–1938) is less well-known outside of Argentina today than are many of his countrymen, but as a Modernist poet his influence on contemporary poetry was comparable to that of his friend, Rubén Darío, and Lugones' name crops up often when writers mention influences and literary friendships. Ever in search of the shocking image, he helped to rid Argentine poetry of the clichés made common through pale imitations of European poetry, his own writing becoming simpler as time went by. He wrote many volumes of poetry, among the best-known being *Los crepúsculos del jardín* [1897, "Twilight in the garden"], *Lunario sentimental* (1909), and *Romances del Río Seco* (1938). He is admired less for his prose, which included essays on a broad range of subjects, but some of his early stories are excellent examples of fantasy and science fiction, written with the clear influence of Wells and Poe, but at a time when such fiction was not being written in Spanish. He published two collections of stories, *Las fuerzas extrañas* [1906, "Strange forces"], from which "Yzur" is taken, and *Cuentos fatales* [1924, "Deadly tales"], and one novel, *El Angel de la Sombra* [1926, "The angel in the shadows"]. Jorge Luis Borges, a friend with whom he quarreled in the 1920s, collaborated in a study of Lugones in 1955. Lugones committed suicide in 1938.

Yzur

I bought the ape at auction from a circus that had gone bankrupt.

The first time it occurred to me to try the experiment described in these pages was an afternoon when I happened to read, somewhere or other, that the natives of Java ascribe the absence of articulate speech among the apes to deliberate abstention, not to incapacity. "They keep silent," the article stated, "so as not to be set to work."

This idea, which at first struck me as superficial, in the end engaged my mind until it evolved into this anthropological theory: apes were men who for one reason or another had stopped speaking, with the result that the vocal organs and the centers of the brain that control speech had atrophied; the connection between the two was weakened nearly to the breaking-point; the language of the species was arrested at the stage of the inarticulate cry; and the primitive human being sank to the animal level.

Clearly if this could be proved it would readily account for all the anomalies which make the ape such a singular creature. But there could be only one proof possible: to get an ape to talk.

Meanwhile I had travelled the world over with my ape, and our experiences, our ups and downs, had bound him closer and closer to me. In Europe he attracted attention everywhere, and had I chosen to I could have made him as famous as Consul[1]—but this sort of buffoonery was unsuited to a sober man of business.

In the grip of my obsession I exhausted the entire literature on the subject of speech among the apes, with no appreciable result. All that I knew, with absolute certainty, was that *there is no scientific explanation for the fact that apes do not speak*. And this took five years of study and thought.

Yzur (where he got this name I could never find out, for his former owner did not know either) was certainly a remarkable animal. His training in the circus, even though it was restricted almost exclusively to mimicry, had greatly developed his faculties; and this prompted me to try out on him a theory that seemed, on the face of it, nonsensical. Moreover I knew that of all the apes the chimpanzee (which Yzur was) is equipped with the best brain, and is also one of the most docile: my chances of success were thus increased. Every time I saw him, rolling along like a drunken sailor, with his hands behind his back to keep his balance, I felt more strongly convinced that he was a retarded human being.

Actually there is no way of accounting for the fact that an ape does not articulate at all. His native speech, that is,

[1] The reference to an animal becoming Consul is based on the action of the Roman Emperor, Caligula (12–41), who showed his contempt for the Republic by naming his horse, Incitatus, as Consul.

the system of cries he uses to communicate with his fellows, is varied enough; his larynx, although very different from a human being's, is not so different as the parrot's, yet the parrot speaks; and, not to mention that a comparison of the ape's brain with the parrot's must banish all doubt, we need only recall that, although the idiot's brain is also rudimentary, there are cretins able to pronounce a few words. As for Broca's convolution, it depends, of course, on the total development of the brain; moreover it has yet to be proved, beyond dispute, that this is the area that controls speech. Anatomy may have established it as the most probable site, but there are still incontrovertible arguments against it.

Fortunately, among so many bad traits, the ape has a taste for learning, as his aptitude for mimicry proves, an excellent memory, a capacity for reflection that can turn him into a profound dissembler, and an attention span comparatively better developed than a human child's. Hence he is a most promising subject for pedagogy.

My ape was young, moreover, and we know that it is in youth that the ape's intelligence reaches its peak. The only difficulty lay in choosing what teaching method to use. I was well aware of the fruitless endeavors of my predecessors, and when I considered all the effort expended, with no result, by so many, some of them of the highest competence, my purpose faltered more than once. But all my thinking on the subject led me to this conclusion: *the first step is to develop the organs which produce sound.*

Actually this is the method one uses with deaf mutes before getting them to articulate; and the moment I began to consider this, analogies between the deaf mute and the ape crowded into my mind. First of all, there is that extraordinary aptitude for mimicry, compensating for the lack of articulated speech, and proving that failure to speak does not argue failure to think, even though the second faculty may be impaired by the paralysis of the first. Then there are other traits, more particular because more specific: diligence in work, fidelity, fortitude—increased, certainly, by two factors which (and surely this is revealing) are allied: an aptitude for feats of balance, and resistance to dizziness.

I decided, then, to begin with a series of exercises for the lips and tongue, treating my ape as I would a deaf mute. After that his ear would enable me to establish direct communication, I should not have to resort to the sense of touch. The reader will see that in this I was planning ahead too optimistically.

Happily, of all the great apes the chimpanzee has the most mobile lips; and in this particular case Yzur, having been subject to sore throat, knew how to open his mouth wide for examination. The first inspection partly confirmed my suspicions: his tongue lay on the floor of his mouth like an inert mass, moving only in order to swallow. The exercises shortly began to produce results: at the end of two months he could stick out his tongue at me. This was the first association he made between the movement of his tongue and an idea, an association, moreover, quite in accordance with his nature.

The lips gave more trouble: they even had to be stretched with pincers. But he fully realized—perhaps from the expression of my face—the importance of that singular task, and performed it with zeal. While I demonstrated the lip movements he was supposed to imitate, he would sit there with one arm twisted behind him, scratching his rump, his face screwed up in mingled concentration and doubt, or rubbing his hairy cheeks, for all the world like a man using rhythmic gestures as an aid to setting his thoughts in order. In the end he learned how to move his lips.

But speech is a difficult art: for proof there is the child's extended period of stammering, paralleling the development of his intellect, until speech becomes a habit with him. Indeed it has been shown that the center of voice production is linked with the speech center of the brain; as early as 1785 Heinicke, inventor of the oral method of teaching deaf mutes, had guessed that this was a logical consequence. The profound lucidity of his phrase "the dynamic concatenation of ideas" would do honor to more than one present-day psychologist.

With regard to speech, Yzur was in the same situation as the child, who already understands many words before he begins to talk; but his greater experience of life made him far quicker to associate ideas and to reach conclusions. Conclusions not based on mere impressions; to judge by their varied character they must have been the fruit of intellectual curiosity and a spirit of inquiry. All this indicated a capacity for abstract reasoning and a superior intelligence which would be highly favorable to my purpose.

If my theory appears too bold, you have only to reflect that there are many animals to whose mind the syllogism, the basis of all logic, is not foreign. For the syllogism is primarily a comparison between two sensations. Otherwise, why is it that animals who know man avoid him, while those who have never known him do not?

And so I began Yzur's phonetic education. The point was to teach him the mechanics first of all, leading him on gradually to rational speech. Since the ape possessed a voice—he had this advantage over the deaf mute, besides having a rudimentary control of the organs of articulation —the question was how to train him to modulate that voice, how to produce those sounds which speech teachers call static if they are vowels, dynamic if they are consonants.

Considering the greediness of the ape tribe, and following a method which Heinicke had employed with deaf mutes, I decided to associate each vowel with something tasty to eat: *a* with *potato, e* with *cream, i* with *wine, o* with *cocoa, u* with *sugar,* in such a way that the vowel would be contained in the name of the tidbit either alone and repeated as in *cocoa,* or combining the basic sounds in both accented and unaccented syllables, as in *potato.* All went smoothly while we were on the vowels, the sounds, that is, which are formed with the mouth open. Yzur learned them in two weeks. The *u* was the hardest for him.

But I had the devil of a time with the consonants. I was sooned forced to admit he would never be able to pronounce those consonants which involve the teeth and the gums. His long eye teeth were an absolute impediment. He would always be limited to the five vowels, plus *b, k, m, g, f* and *c,* the consonants which require the action of the tongue and the palate only. Even for this much, his hearing alone was not sufficient. I had to resort to the sense of touch, as one does with deaf mutes, placing his hand first on my chest and then on his, so that he could feel the sound vibrations.

Three years passed, and I had still not succeeded in getting him to form a single word. He tended to name things after the letter that predominated in them. That was all.

In the circus he had learned to bark, like the dogs he worked side by side with; and when he saw me in despair over my vain attempts to wrest a word from him, he would bark loudly, as though trying to offer me all he had to give. He could pronounce isolated vowels and consonants, but he could not combine them. The best he could produce was a dizzying series of repeated *p*'s and *m*'s.

For all the slowness of his progress, a great change had come over him. His face was less mobile, his expression more serious, his attitudes were those of a creature deep in thought. He had acquired, for instance, the habit of gazing at the stars. . . . And at the same time his sensibilities had developed: I noticed that he was easily moved to tears.

The lessons continued with unremitting determination, but with no greater success. The whole business had become a painful obsession with me; and as time went on I felt inclined to resort to force. The failure was embittering my disposition, filling me with unconscious resentment against Yzur. As his intellect developed he withdrew into a stubborn silence which I was beginning to believe I should never draw him out of, when I suddenly discovered that he wasn't speaking because he chose not to!

One evening the horrified cook came to tell me he had overheard the ape "speaking real words." According to his story, Yzur had been squatting beside a fig-tree in the garden; but the cook's terror prevented him from recalling what was the real point, the actual words. He thought he could remember two: *bed* and *pipe*. I came near to kicking him for his stupidity.

Needless to say the profoundest agitation preyed upon me the whole night through; and what I had not done in the three years, the mistake that ruined everything was the result of the exasperation that followed on that sleepless night, and of my overweening curiosity as well. Instead of allowing the ape to arrive at his natural pace to the point of revealing his command of speech, I summoned him the next day and tried to compel him to it. All I could get out of him was the p's and m's I'd already had my fill of, the hypocritical winks, and—may God forgive me—a hint of mockery in the incessant grimaces. I lost my temper: without thinking twice, I beat him. The only result was tears and absolute silence, unbroken even by moans.

Three days later he fell ill, with a kind of deep depression complicated by symptoms of meningitis. Leeches, cold showers, purgatives, counterirritants, tincture of alcohol, bromides—every remedy for the terrible illness was applied to him. Driven by remorse and fear, I struggled with desperate energy. Remorse for the cruelty which had made him its victim, fear for the secret he might perhaps be carrying with him to the grave.

After a long time he began to improve, but he was still too feeble to stir from his bed. The closeness of death had ennobled and humanized him. His eyes, filled with gratitude, never left me, following me about the room like two revolving globes, even when I was behind him; his hand sought mine in the companionship of convalescence. In my great solitude he was rapidly assuming the importance of a person.

Yet the demon of investigation, which is only one other form of the spirit of perversity, kept urging me on to renew my experiment. The ape had actually talked. It was impossible simply to let it go at that.

I began very slowly, asking for the letters he knew how to pronounce. Nothing! I left him alone for hours at a time, spying on him through a chink in the wall. Nothing! I spoke to him in brief sentences, trying to appeal to his loyalty or his greediness. Nothing! When my words moved him, his eyes would fill with tears. When I uttered a familiar phrase, such as the "I am your master" with which every lesson began, or the "You are my ape" with which I completed the statement, to impress upon his mind the conviction of a total truth, he would close his eyelids by way of assent; but he would not utter a sound, not even move his lips.

He had reverted to sign language as the only way of communicating with me; and this circumstance, together with the analogies between him and deaf mutes, led me to redouble my precautions, for everyone knows that mutes are extremely subject to mental illness. I had moments of wishing he would really lose his mind, to see if delirium would at last break his silence.

His convalescence had come to a halt. The same emaciation, the same depression. It was clear he was ill and suf-

fering, in body and mind. The abnormal effort demanded
of his brain had shattered his organic unity, and sooner or
later he would become a hopeless case. But for all his sub-
missiveness, which increased still more as the illness took
its course, his silence, that despairing silence my fury had
driven him to, would not yield. Out of a dim past of tradition that had petrified and become instinct, the species
was forcing its millennial mutism on the animal, whose ancestral will was strengthened by his own inner being. The
primitive men of the jungle, driven into silence, to intellectual suicide that is, were guarding their secret; ancient
mysteries of the forest, formidable with the immense weight
of ages, dictated that unconscious decision that Yzur was
now making.

In the race we call evolution, man had overtaken the
anthropoid and crushed him with savage brutality, dethron-
ing the great families who ruled their primitive Eden, thin-
ning their ranks, capturing their females so that organized
slavery might begin in the very womb. Until, beaten and
helpless, they expressed their human dignity by breaking
the higher but fatal bond—speech—that linked them to
the enemy, and as their last salvation took refuge in the
dark night of the animal kingdom.

And what horrors, what monstrous excesses of cruelty
the conquerors must have inflicted upon this half-beast in
the course of his evolution to make him—once he had
tasted the joys of the intellect, the forbidden fruit of the
Bible—resign himself to stultifying his mind in degrading
equality with inferior beings; to that retrogression which
fixed his intelligence for ever, leaving him a robot, an acro-
bat, a clown; to that fear of life which would bend his ser-
vile back as a sign of his animal condition, and imprint
upon him that melancholy bewilderment which is his basic
trait.

This is what had aroused my evil temper, buried deep in

some atavist limbo, on the very brink of success. Across the millions of years the magic of the word still kept its power to stir the simian soul; but against that temptation which was about to pierce the dark shadows of animal instinct, ancestral memories that filled his race with some instinctive horror were heaping age upon age as a barrier.

Yzur did not lose consciousness as death approached. It was a gentle death, with closed eyes, faint breathing, feeble pulse, and perfect tranquillity, interrupted only at intervals, when he would turn his sad, old mulatto face toward me with a heart-rending expression of eternity. And the last afternoon, the afternoon he died, the extraordinary thing occurred that decided me to write this account.

Overcome by the heat, drowsy with the quiet of the twilight coming on, I had dozed off by his bedside. Suddenly I felt something gripping my wrist. I woke up with a start. The ape, his eyes wide open, was dying, unmistakably, and his look was so human that I was seized with horror; yet something expressive in his hands and in his eyes impelled me to bend over him. And then with his last breath, the last breath which at once crowned and blasted all my hopes, he murmured (how can I describe the tone of a voice which has not spoken for ten thousand centuries?) these words, whose humanity reconciled our two species:

"Water, master. Master, my master. . . ."

Translated by GREGORY WOODRUFF

Horacio Quiroga (1878–1937) was born in Salto, Uruguay, the son of the Argentine consul there. Influenced by the Modernists, he began writing poetry and in 1899 founded the literary journal *Revista del Salto.* He studied at the University of Montevideo, and in 1900 he made a trip to *fin-de-siècle* Paris and returned disillusioned. After a tragic accident in which he killed a close friend, thinking a gun unloaded, he moved to Buenos Aires. A visit to Misiones as the guest of the Argentine government changed his life; this tropical forest region in the north of Argentina appealed to him, as did the idea of hard manual labor, and he lived there for many years as a pioneer farmer. Nature plays a dominant role in many of his stories, some of which feature humanized animals. He knew city life well, but his stories are often a condemnation of human society's trivialities. An early collection of stories revealed a malaise that, considering the events of his life, took a justly morbid turn: besides the accidental killing of his friend, his father committed suicide, as did his first wife, a son and a daughter. He committed suicide in 1937. Influenced in his writing by Poe, Maupassant, Kipling, and Chekhov, his essays on the craft of the short story urge that every detail be part of a pattern, no word wasted. There was a wide range to his work, which included both the animal stories and Poelike horror stories, among others. His influence on Latin American fiction was decisive. Some of his best stories were collected in *Cuentos de amor, de locura y de muerte* [1917, "Tales of love, madness, and death"], *Cuentos de la selva* [1918, *South American Jungle Tales,*], *El salvaje* [1920, "The savage"], *Anaconda* (1921), *El desierto* [1924, "The desert"], *Los desterrados* [1926, "The exiles"], and *Más allá* [1935, "Beyond"].

How the Flamingoes
Got Their Stockings

Once the snakes decided that they would give a costume ball; and to make the affair a truly brilliant one they sent invitations to the frogs, the toads, the alligators and the fish.

The fish replied that since they had no legs they would not be able to do much dancing; whereupon, as a special courtesy to them, the ball was held on the shore of the Paraná. The fish swam up to the very beach and sat looking on with their heads out of water. When anything pleased them they splashed with their tails.

To make as good an appearance as possible, the alligators put necklaces of bananas around their throats; and they came to the ball smoking big Paraguay cigars. The toads stuck fish scales all over their bodies; and when they walked, they moved their forelegs out and in as though they were swimming. They strutted up and down the beach with very glum, determined faces; and the fish kept calling to them, making fun of their scales. The frogs were satisfied to leave their smooth green skins just as they were; but they bathed themselves in perfume and walked on their hind legs. Besides, each one carried a lightning bug, which waved to and fro like a lantern, at the end of a string in the frog's hand.

But the best costumes of all were worn by the snakes. All of them, without exception, had dancing gowns of the color of their skins. There were red snakes, and brown snakes, and pink snakes, and yellow snakes—each with a garment of tulle to match. The *yarara,* who is a kind of rattler, came in a single-piece robe of gray tulle with brick-colored stripes—for that is the way the *yarara* dresses even when he is not going to a ball. The coral snakes were prettier still. They draped themselves in a gauze of reds, whites and blacks; and when they danced, they wound themselves round and round like corkscrews, rising on the tips of their tails, coiling and uncoiling, balancing this way and that. They were the most graceful and beautiful of all the snakes, and the guests applauded them wildly.

The flamingoes were the only ones who seemed not to be having a good time. Stupid birds that they were, they had not thought of any costumes at all. They came with the plain white legs they had at that time and the thick, twisted bills they have even now. Naturally they were envious of all the gowns they saw, but most of all, of the fancy dress of the coral snakes. Every time one of these went by them, courtseying, pirouetting, balancing, the flamingoes writhed with jealousy. For no one, meanwhile, was asking them to dance.

"I know what we must do," said one of the flamingoes at last. "We must go and get some stockings for our legs— pink, black and white like the coral snakes themselves— then they will all fall in love with us!"

The whole flock of them took wing immediately and

flew across the river to a village nearby. They went to the store and knocked:

"Tan! Tan! Tan!"

"Who is it?" called the storekeeper.

"We're the flamingoes. We have come to get some stockings—pink, black, and white."

"Are you crazy?" the storekeeper answered. "I keep stockings for people, not for silly birds. Besides, stockings of such colors! You won't find any in town, either!"

The flamingoes went on to another store:

"Tan! Tan! Tan! We are looking for stockings—pink, black and white. Have you any?"

"Pink, black and white stockings! Don't you know decent people don't wear such things? You must be crazy! Who are you, anyway?"

"We are the flamingoes," the flamingoes replied.

"In that case you are silly flamingoes! Better go somewhere else!"

They went to still a third store:

"Tan! Tan! Pink, black and white stockings! Got any?"

"Pink, black and white nonsense!" called the storekeeper. "Only birds with big noses like yours could ask for such a thing. Don't make tracks on my floor!"

And the man swept them into the street with a broom.

So the flamingoes went from store to store, and everywhere people called them silly, stupid birds.

However, an owl, a mischievous *tatu*, who had just been down to the river to get some water, and had heard all about the ball and the flamingoes, met them on his way back and thought he would have some fun with them.

"Good evening, good evening, flamingoes," he said, making a deep bow, though, of course, it was just to ridicule the foolish birds. "I know what you are looking for. I doubt if you can get any such stockings in town. You might find them in Buenos Aires; but you would have to order them by mail. My sister-in-law, the barn owl, has stockings like that, however. Why don't you go around and see her? She can give you her own and borrow others from her family."

"Thanks! Thanks, ever so much!" said the flamingoes; and they flew off to the cellar of a barn where the barn owl lived.

"Tan! Tan! Good evening, Mrs. Owl," they said. "A relation of yours, Mr. Tatu, advised us to call on you. To-night, as you know, the snakes are giving a costume ball, and we have no costumes. If you could lend us your pink, black and white stockings, the coral snakes would be sure to fall in love with us!"

"Pleased to accommodate you," said the barn owl. "Will you wait just a moment?"

She flew away and was gone some time. When she came back she had the stockings with her. But they were not real stockings. They were nothing but skins from coral snakes which the owl had caught and eaten during the previous days.

"Perhaps these will do," she remarked. "But if you wear them at the ball, I advise you to do strictly as I say: dance all night long, and don't stop a moment. For if you do, you will get into trouble, I assure you!"

The flamingoes listened to what she said; but, stupidly, did not try to guess what she could have meant by such counsel. They saw no danger in the pretty stockings. Delightedly they doubled up their claws like fists, stuck them through the snakeskins, which were like so many long rubber tubes, and flew back as quickly as they could to the ball.

When the guests at the dance saw the flamingoes in such handsome stockings, they were as jealous as could be. You see, the coral snakes were the lions of the evening, and after the flamingoes came back, they would dance with no one but the flamingoes. Remembering the instructions of the barn owl, the flamingoes kept their feet going all the time, and the snakes could not see very clearly just what those wonderful stockings were.

After a time, however, they grew suspicious. When a flamingo came dancing by, the snakes would get down off the ends of their tails to examine its feet more closely. The coral snakes, more than anybody else, began to get uneasy. They could not take their eyes off those stockings, and they got as near as they could, trying to touch the legs of the flamingoes with the tips of their tongues—for snakes use their tongues to feel with, much as people use their hands. But the flamingoes kept dancing and dancing all the while, though by this time they were getting so tired they were about ready to give up.

The coral snakes understood that sooner or later the flamingoes would have to stop. So they borrowed the lightning bugs from the frogs, to be ready when the flamingoes fell from sheer exhaustion.

And in fact, it was not long before one of the birds, all tired out, tripped over the cigar in an alligator's mouth, and fell down on her side. The coral snakes all ran toward her with their lanterns, and held the lightning bugs up so close that they could see the feet of the flamingo as clearly as could be.

"Aha! Aha! Stockings, eh? Stockings, eh?" The coral snakes began to hiss so loudly that people could hear them on the other side of the Paraná.

The cry was taken up by all the snakes: "They are not wearing stockings! We know what they have done! The flamingoes have been killing brothers of ours, and they are wearing their skins as stockings! Those pretty legs each stand for the murder of a coral snake!"

At this uproar, the flamingoes took fright and tried to fly away. But they were so tired from all the dancing that not one of them could move a wing. The coral snakes darted upon them, and began to bite at their legs, tearing off the false stockings bit by bit, and, in their rage, sinking their fangs deep into the feet and legs of the flamingoes.

The flamingoes, terrified and mad with pain, hopped this way and that, trying to shake their enemies off. But the snakes did not let go till every last shred of stocking had been torn away. Then they crawled off, to rearrange their gauze costumes that had been much rumpled in the fray. They did not try to kill the flamingoes then and there; for most coral snakes are poisonous; and they were sure the birds they had bitten would die sooner or later anyway.

But the flamingoes did not die. They hopped down to the river and waded out into the water to relieve their pain. Their feet and legs, which had been white before, had now turned red from the poison in the bites. They stood there for days and days, trying to cool the burning ache, and hoping to wash out the red.

But they did not succeed. And they have not succeeded yet. The flamingoes still pass most of their time standing on their red legs out in the water. Occasionally they go ashore and walk up and down for a few moments to see if they are getting well. But the pain comes again at once, and they hurry back into the water. Even there they sometimes feel an ache in one of their feet; and they lift it out to warm it in their feathers. They stand that way on one leg for hours, I suppose because the other one is so stiff and lame.

That is why the flamingoes have red legs instead of white. And the fishes know it too. They keep coming up to the top of the water and crying "Red legs! Red legs! Red legs!" to make fun of the flamingoes for having tried to borrow costumes for a ball. On that account, the flamingoes are always at war with the fishes. As they wade up and down, and a fish comes up too close in order to shout "Red legs" at them, they dip their long bills down and catch it if they can.

Rómulo Gallegos (1884–1969) was born outside of Caracas, Venezuela. He studied law but abandoned it to write, supporting himself as an accountant, railroad stationmaster, and for many years as a teacher, one of the first Venezuelan writers not to be wealthy or an aristocrat. His first novel, *Reinaldo Solar*, came out in 1920, but it was for a 1929 publication that he is most famous—the novel *Doña Bárbara*, which captures the sights and sounds of cattle-raisers on the *llano*, the vast plains that run between the Andes mountains and the Orinoco River. Gallegos believed barbarism in his country could be conquered with education and literature, and *Doña Bárbara* reflects that view, with its theme of civilization (in the form of a city-educated hero) taming the lawless frontier (in the form of Doña Bárbara, the tough plainswoman he fights and whose daughter he marries). Juan Vicente Gómez, the landowning dictator who ruled Venezuela from 1908 to 1935, appointed Gallegos a senator in hopes of quieting him, but Gallegos went to the U.S. in 1931, sending back his resignation. Later he went to Spain as a salesman for National Cash Register, and there he wrote two more novels, *Cantaclaro* (1934) and *Canaima* (1935). Returning from self-exile in 1936, he became a member of the Caracas Municipal Council, served briefly as Minister of Education, and published three more novels. In 1941 he became the first popularly-elected President of his country, but was ousted by a military coup after nine months and during a ten-year dictatorship lived in exile in Cuba and Mexico. In 1958 he returned to Venezuela and devoted himself to writing and liberal politics. His last novel was about Cuba. He died in 1969, a life member of his Senate and chairman of the Human Rights Committee of the Organization of American States. His works reveal a vivid sense of the frontiers of Venezuela and a genuine desire to cope with his country's social problems.

Peace on High

In a wild mountainous region, at the edge of a steep precipice garlanded with tough creepers and bushes, a ruinous cabin huddles, above whose thatched roof no chimney-smoke has risen for a long time. A boy sits in the doorway.

He is a miserable, sad creature: a huge head held up by a scrawny neck bristled with a thin brush of filthy hairs, on a wasted body: the stomach bloated, arms skeletal, legs full of runny scabs, with enormous knees and feet deformed by malarial edema. His face is striking with its pasty skin stuck to its bones, a peeling mouth exposing its teeth. The whites of his eyes are horribly yellow deep in their staring sockets. There is a shadow of dumb, furious pain in the muddy pupils of his eyes.

He remains motionless and silent, looking over the sea of small hills that fill the immense distance of low land that stretches out before his eyes to reach a barrier of blue mountains, far off, sketched against the scudding golden cloud-background of the horizon. A bitter, stubborn grief scratches without stopping into his small heart, already scarred by a hate for everything that lives and moves around him. This feeling permanently keeps a knot in his throat, like a crying fit about to break out, but tears never come into his eyes. A wave of rage often surges in his breast and then he closes his fists and his teeth rattle in a disturbing way until, when he has torn whatever he can get his hands on, the furious feeling dies down and leaves him in a logy state. At other times, he spends whole days brooding, without talking, sitting in the doorway or lying on the hard ground, looking straight ahead, intensely, at something fascinating and terrible that seems to be in front of his eyes. During such moments of depression, the feelings of his body sapped by sickness become confused in his mind and end up by making him forget who he is. First a tickling sensation begins at the soles of his feet and slowly floods up through his entire body, and it is a horde of things that eat him up as if he were already dead. Then a horrible sensation of puffing up inside, as if his bowels suddenly started to grow big fast the way he hears the hills grow inside the precipice in the silence of dark nights, when his stomach stifles him and does not let him sleep. Finally, the emptiness inside his head: the chatter of millions of crickets approaching, a crazy whirl of stars around his eyes. And last of all, a sudden, definite silence that seems as if it will never come to an end. . . . And in the middle of all this, the obsessive vision of a man, the coalman, hugging his mother, as he himself lies in a corner of the hovel, shaking with the cold that precedes a fever. . . .

This scene witnessed by Felipe shortly after his father's death had been printed on his memory in such a way that, without knowing why—since he has never tried to figure out what it meant—, he could never look at his mother without seeing her as he had seen her that night, held close in the arms of the coalman who had placed his big black hands on her shoulders.

That is how the unswerving intense dislike for his mother had started in his small injured heart. Her efforts to prod him out of his silence from which he shut her out were useless and besides, since she never tried to do it with affection but by throwing harsh words at him or battering his broken skin with hard blows, the secret revulsion of the boy began to turn into a fierce hatred that twisted in his heart with such violence that he turned it on her blindly, fists squeezed tight, showing her his teeth grinding with a terrible sound.

In the beginning, when this happened the mother smothered his anger with a storm of blows that, no matter how hard, could never draw a single tear from him. He howled like a cornered animal and rolled about on the ground, after which he would stay there still as a corpse for hours. But then his mother adopted a different tactic that angered him even more. She stopped beating him and simply pinned back his arms until, worn out by the violence of his anger which flowed through his body like a poisonous drug, he would drop to the ground and go into his morbid condition of half-sleep. Then the woman would leave him, speaking in a low frightened way:

"Holy Mother of God!"

About this time the woman's absences from the farm began to last longer and longer. She spent whole days in the woods where she went each morning to look for a bundle of sticks or for ears of corn to steal from the cornfields and sell in the town nearby. Often she came back at nightfall with the miserable product of her sales converted into rough sheets of cassava bread and occasionally a chunk of salted fish on which Felipe would fall with voracious hunger, the excessive hunger that was never satisfied and filled his lonely days and sleepless nights with tormenting images of fantastic, delicious scenes of gluttony.

One day Felipe found a friend. From morning he had been listening to the barking of a dog as it wandered through the woods, sniffing at the footpaths as if it were looking for its lost owner. That afternoon it came toward the hut and, seeing him sitting in the doorway, stopped in front of him, wagging its tail, and then lay down at his feet panting, without interrupting its friendly stare into the horrible little face of the sick boy. Felipe, in turn, looked at it a long time, like a friend he had been expecting and had received without being surprised. He did not try to pet it or speak a single word to it. It seemed natural to him that the dog had come and settled near him. He did not think about it, just knew that he was the master the dog had been looking for all day across the farms, along the footpaths. It had found him and he was certain that the dog would never leave him. After a while an unusual thought brushed the stillness of his mind: inexplicable, nameless ideas that pass through your mind without being quite seen, the way you feel the shadow of a hand that is about to caress or harm you. He thought—without realizing that he was doing it—that the dog had come from the unknown, from the place that soared overhead, and he had not been able to see it but it had been seen by the rooster who then let out its terrible cry, stretching its neck and following its ominous flight with a frightened eye. And he thought that it had come in search of him to save him from something that was about to happen to him.

Breaking his silence, he finally said:

"I heard you barking in that cornfield this morning. I knew you were looking for me."

The dog began to bark a friendly playful bark. But it stopped suddenly and began to growl suspiciously. Felipe, who had also heard the sound of footsteps in the thicket, told him:

"It's mama. Be quiet."

Plácida was annoyed at finding the dog there and tried to scare it away, but the dog took cover between Felipe's legs, growling and looking at her with threatening eyes. She was afraid of it and stopped trying to drive it away, but you could see that she was uneasy.

She deposited the bundle of provisions for their skimpy evening meal in the hut, placing it where Felipe could not reach it, took one sheet of cassava from it, and went to eat it near the edge of the precipice.

Excited by hunger, the boy approached her greedily. She did not let him reach her, stopping him a few steps away by throwing him a piece of cassava that fell near the bushes that hung like garlands from the edge of the precipice. Felipe picked it up and sat on the ground to eat it. The dog at his side wagged its tail. The boy offered it a piece of what he was eating but, after sniffing it, the animal turned away from it and stretched out on the ground contemptuously, its head toward the woman.

Meanwhile, she could not take her eyes off her son's face, made uglier by the grotesque way it moved up and down as he chewed. He seemed more horrible than ever, and as she looked at him her heart filled more and more with a terrible grudge. That repulsive creature who was like a filthy rag already dangling in the clutch of death, yet would never stop living, was the reason for her misery. Because of him she could not find housework when she went to the town to offer her services. No one would have such a revolting creature in his house. And because of him Crisanto, the coalman, who loaded her ears with words of love, had not wanted her to move in with him. That same day he had said to her:

"Honey, if it wasn't fer that boy, you wouldna be havin'

all this trouble, 'cause I gotta house and food and if you decide to come live with me, you won't have no need to go all over the place stealin' corn or pickin' up halfburned sticks down the ravines. But that kid, I wouldn't want 'im if you covered 'im with gold. Ha, the little basta'd's a bad egg. Ya just gotta look at 'is eyes. There's badness all over him. . . . For my money, that little bast'd's the Devil's own son! Holy Mother of God! He ain't even a kid: he's like a grown man. Kids don't think about things like that one thinks. Looks to me like a man hidin' in a kid's body fer you to get careless and he c'n jump out at you. If, fer instance, I meet 'im at night on that mountain road, I c'n tell ya I wouldn't stop. . . . Ah! Sure! That's the Devil's own son. If I was you. . . ."

Their conversation had reached this point when, some distance back along the precipice where they were talking, the dog he was now used to finding there lying beside Felipe appeared. The animal, which looked as if it had lost sight of its master and was desperately searching for him, had come near them and, after sniffing around their feet, had started to bark furiously, just as Plácida was answering Crisanto:

"And if they find me out?"

"They're not gonna find ya out! The easiest thing is fer a kid that can't stay on 'is two legs to fall down that rock. . . !"

Now, gazing at the cadaverous face of her hated son, whom she blamed for her miserable life, Plácida was savoring Crisanto's insinuation:

"Who's gonna find out?"

She looked around her suspiciously. Everything seemed solitary and empty. The immense low land full of green small hills that stretched silently toward the distant horizon. Below, far off, could be seen a few farmhouses scattered among the fields and patches of wild vegetation, but they were so far away that it was impossible to make out people near them. You could just manage to see the frail smoke lifting slowly from the chimneys into the air, above the roofs.

This exploration of the lonely landscape pulled the knot in her throat painfully tighter. Over the precipice floated a heavy atmosphere that almost made you choke. Black masses of clouds rolled through the sky, filling the hollow of the low land with violet shadows. On the horizon, along the barrier of the last hilltops, you could see the bluish stain of the rain coming closer. A low rumble of distant thunder groaned in the atmosphere charged with omens.

Plácida felt herself dragged irresistibly towards the whirlpool of an evil thought.

"Don't it look like the devil 'imself's crouchin' inside that kid? Look at the way he's starin' at me! Holy Mother of God! His eyes are rollin' and 'is teeth are rattlin'! God save us from 'im! What c'n he get out of livin' like that, a rotten sack of diseases. . . ! Those worms he's got in 'is stomach are eatin' 'im alive! And the chills he gets when the fever starts to get 'im. To live like that all the time I'd rather die. . . ."

The dog stared at him, growling.

"And who could that dog be. . . ? Holy Mother of God! Look how there's things in this life ya can't explain."

Felipe had finished devouring the piece of cassava and, turning to his mother, told her roughly:

"Gimme more! I'm hungry! I want it all 'cause I'm hungry!"

The woman gave him a frightened look. The horrible whites of his eyes had flashed in an evil way. She felt that a mysterious force lurked powerfully behind the boy's words. At the same time, the imperative demand of the boy coincided with a thought that had just crossed her mind.

Trembling anxiously, she threw the piece of cassava she had left in her hand, in such a way that it fell on the bushes dangling at the edge of the precipice over the emptiness below.

Felipe stood up and fixed her with a penetrating look of fury that upset her. He had understood her intention: if he went to reach for the piece of cassava, the bushes would give under his weight and he would crash down into the ravine. There was an instant that lasted an eternity. Plácida felt that madness was whirling all around her. Felipe, with sudden resolve, took a step toward the bushes.

At the same time the dog pounced quickly on the piece of cassava caught in the bushes, letting out a strange howl. The vegetation gave under its weight and the animal's body rolled down the side of the precipice.

A dreadful night. Rain is pouring down furiously on the workfields. Crash after crash of lightning rattles endlessly like moving furniture in the solitude of the low land. You can hear the water hissing down the gullies like furious serpents. . . . For a long while you could hear the painful barking of the dog that was probably tangled in the brambles down the side of the ravine, but he stopped barking some time ago. . . .

In the hut, whose roof leaks streams of water falling from the clouds, Plácida and Felipe lie far apart, silent. By the light of the lightning flashes that brighten the place, Plácida sees the horrible whites of Felipe's eyes shining wickedly. She dare not sleep. She is afraid of the boy who carries something crouched inside, something that frightens her and at the same time holds her fascinated.

From time to time he says, with an implacable insistence that is almost driving her out of her mind:

"Mama, why do you want me to die. . . ?"

Translated by HARDIE ST. MARTIN

Miguel Ángel Asturias (1899–1974) was born in Guatemala City, Guatemala. In disagreement with the dictator Estrada Cabrera, his family moved inland to the town of Salamá. In Paris in the 1920s, he studied Mayan religion and society and helped to translate the *Popol Vuh*, the sacred Quiché book of the Mayans, which he finished in 1926. Supporting himself as a journalist, he wrote poetry and stories based on Indian and Spanish legends he had heard as a child, which were published in 1930 as *Leyendas de Guatemala*. (This collection included the following story.) At the same time, he was writing the novel that would become a masterpiece in its genre: *El señor presidente*, an indictment of the Estrada Cabrera dictatorship so vivid that publication of the novel was delayed through two succeeding dictatorships until 1946. During those years, Asturias wrote in exile. *El señor presidente* was published. In 1947, as he was representing his country at the embassy in Buenos Aires, he wrote *Hombres de maíz* [1949, "Men of Corn"], which depicts the commercial exploitation of the land of the Indians, a violation of their sacred attachment to it. Richly mythological, the novel is regarded by many as the author's finest, most ambitious work. In 1950 Asturias began his "banana-republic trilogy," (*Strong Wind, The Green Pope,* and *The Eyes of the Interred*), polemical novels showing the exploitation of Guatemala's banana plantations by the United Fruit Company. When the socialist government of Jacobo Árbenz was toppled in 1954 with United States help, Asturias was forced into exile again and wrote about the event in the stories of *Weekend on Guatemala* (1956). When he was awarded the Lenin Peace Prize in 1966 and the Nobel Prize in 1967, he was serving as ambassador in Paris, a position he renounced in 1971 with the rise to power of yet another strongman in his country. His mythological novel *Mulata de tal* was published in 1963, the tales *El espejo de Lida Sal* ["The looking glass of Lida Sal"] in 1967, and *Maladrón* in 1969.

Legend of "El Cadejo"

And El Cadejo, *who steals girls with long braids and knots the manes of horses, makes his appearance in the valley.*

In the course of time, Mother Elvira of St. Francis, abbess of the monastery of St. Catherine, would be the novice who cut out the hosts in the convent of the Conception, a girl noted for her beauty and manner of speaking, so ingenuous that on her lips the word was a flower of gentleness and love.

From a large window without glass, the novice used to watch the flights of leaves dried by the summer's heat, the trees putting on their flowers and ripe fruit dropping in the orchards next to the convent, through the part that was in ruins, where the foliage, hiding the wounded walls and the open roofs, transformed the cells and the cloisters into paradises filled with the scent of *búcaro* clay and wild

71

roses; bowers of feasting, as the chroniclers recorded, where nuns were replaced by pigeons with pink feet and their canticles by the warble of the cimarron mockingbird.

Outside her window, in the collapsed rooms, the warm shade, where butterflies worked the dust of their wings into silk, joined the silence of the courtyard, interrupted by the coming and going of the lizards, and the soft aroma of the leaves that multiplied the tender feelings of the trees whose roots were coiled into the very ancient walls.

And inside, in the sweet company of God, trimming the peel from the fruit of angels to disclose the meat and seed that is the Body of Christ, long as the orange's medulla—*vere tu es Deus absconditus!*—, Elvira of St. Francis reunited her spirit and her flesh to the house of her childhood, with its heavy locks and its light roses, its doors that split sobs into the loose seams of the wind, its walls reflected in the troughs of the fountains like clouds of breath on clean glass.

The voices of the city broke the peace of her window: last-minute blues of the passenger that hears the movement of the port at sailing time; a man's laughter as he brings his galloping horse to a stop, a cart wheeling by, or a child crying.

Horse, cart, man, child passed before her eyes, evoked in country settings, under skies whose tranquil appearance put under a spell the wise eyes of the fountain troughs sitting around the water with the long-suffering air of old women servants.

And the images were accompanied by odors. The sky smelled like a sky, the child like a child, the fields like fields, the cart like hay, the horse like an old rosebush, the man like a saint, the troughs like shadows, the shadows like Sunday rest and the Lord's day of rest like fresh washing. . . .

Dark was coming on. The shadows erased their thought,

luminous mixture of dust particles swimming in a shaft of sunlight. The bells drew their lips towards the cup of evening without a sound. Who talks of kisses? The wind shook up the heliotropes. Heliotropes or hippocampi? And the hummingbirds quenched their desire for God in streams of flowers. Who talks of kisses?

The tap of heels hurrying brought her to herself. Their sound frilled along the corridor like drumsticks.

Could she be hearing right? Could it be the man with the long eyelashes who came by late on Fridays for the hosts to take them nine towns away from there, to the Valley of the Virgin, where a pleasant hermitage rested on a hill's top?

They called him the poppy-man. The wind moved in his feet. When the sound of his goat's footsteps stopped, there he would be, like a ghost: hat in hand, tiny boots, a goldish color, wrapped in his blue greatcoat; and he waited for the wafer boxes in the doorway.

Yes, it was he; but this time he rushed in looking very frightened, as if to prevent some catastrophe.

"Miss, oh miss!" he came in shouting, "they're going to cut off your hair! They're going to cut it off!"

When she saw him coming in, livid and elastic, the novice sprang to her feet intending to reach the door. But, wearing shoes she had charitably inherited from a paralytic nun who had worn them in life, when she heard his shout, she felt as if the nun who had spent her life motionless had stepped on her feet, and she couldn't move a step. . . .

. . . A sob, like a star, trembled in her throat. Birds scissored the twilight among the grey, crippled ruins. Two giant eucalyptus trees were saying prayers of penance.

Bound to the feet of a corpse, unable to move, she wept disconsolately, swallowing her tears silently as sick people whose organs begin to dry up and turn cold, bit by bit. She felt as if she were dead, covered with dirt; she felt that in her grave—her orphan's dress being filled with clay—rosebushes of white words bloomed and, little by little, her dismay changed into a quiet sort of happiness. Walking rosebushes, the nuns were cutting off one another's roses to dress the altars of the Virgin and the roses became the month of May, a spider web of fragrances that trapped Our Lady like a fly of light.

But the sensation of her body's flowering after death was a shortlived happiness.

Like a kite that suddenly runs out of string among the clouds, the weight of her braid pulled her headlong, with all her clothes, into hell. The mystery was in her braid. Sum of anguished instants. She lost consciousness for as long as a couple of her sighs lasted and felt herself back on earth only when she had almost reached the boiling pit where devils bubble. A fan of possible realities opened around her: the night sweetened with puff paste, pine trees that smell like altars, the pollen of life in the hair of the air, formless, colorless cat that scratches the waters of the fountain troughs and unsettles old papers.

The window and she herself became filled with heaven. . . .

"Miss, when I receive Holy Communion, God tastes like your hands!" the one in the greatcoat whispered, laying the grille of his lashes over the coals of his eyes.

The novice pulled her hands away from the hosts when she heard the blasphemy. No, it wasn't a dream! Then she touched her arms, her shoulders, her neck, her face, her braid. She held her breath one moment, long as a century, when she felt her braid. No, it wasn't a dream! Under the warm handful of hair she came alive, aware of her womanly charms, accompanied in her diabolic nuptials by the poppy-man and a candle burning at the end of the room, oblong as a coffin. The light supported the impossible reality of the lover, who stretched out his arms like a

Christ who had turned into a bat in a viaticum, and this was her own flesh! She closed her eyes to escape, wrapped in her blindness, from that vision from hell, from the man who caressed her down to where she was a woman, simply by being a man—the most abominable of conscupiscences! —; but as soon as she lowered her round pale eyelids the paralytic nun seemed to step from her shoes, soaked in tears, and she quickly opened them. She tore through the darkness, opened her eyes, left their deep interior with their pupils restless as mice in a trap, wild, insensible, the color drained out of her cheeks, caught between the ster- tor of a strange agony she carried in her feet and her braid's stream of live coals twisted like an invisible flame on her back.

And that's the last she knew about it. Like someone under a spell that can't be broken, with a sob on her tongue which seemed to be filled with poison, like her heart, she broke away from the presence of the corpse and the man, half mad, spilling the wafers about, in search of her scissors and, finding them, she cut off the braid and, free of the spell, she fled in search of the sure refuge of the Mother Superior, no longer feeling the nun's feet on hers. . . .

But when the braid fell it was no longer a braid: it moved, undulated over the tiny mattress of hosts scattered on the floor.

The poppy-man turned to look for light. Tears quivered on his eyelashes like the last little flames on the black of the match that is about to go out. He slid along the side of the wall with bated breath, without disturbing the shadows, without making a sound, desperate to reach the flame he believed would be his salvation. But his measured step soon dissolved into a flight of fear. The headless reptile was moving past the sacred leaf-pile of hosts and filing towards him. It dragged itself right under his feet like the black blood of a dead animal and suddenly, as he was about to take hold of the light, leaped with the speed of water that runs free and light to coil itself like a whip around the candle which it caused to weep until it consumed itself for the soul of him who was being extinguished, along with it, forever. And so the poppy-man, for whom cactus plants still weep white tears, reached eternity.

The devil had passed like a breath through the braid which fell lifeless on the floor when the candle's flame went out.

And at midnight, changed into a long animal—twice as long as a ram by full moon, big as a weeping willow by new moon—with goat's hoofs, rabbit's ears and a bat's face, the poppy-man dragged down to hell the black braid of the novice who, in the course of time, would be Mother Elvira of St. Francis—that's how "El Cadejo" was born —while, on her knees in her cell, smiling like an angel, she dreamed of the lily and the mystic lamb.

Translated by HARDIE ST. MARTIN

Jorge Icaza (b. 1906) was born in Quito, in the Ecuadorian highlands. After graduating from the University of Quito he worked in the theater as writer and director. He had written six plays when his first and most famous novel came out in 1934: *Huasipungo* (published here as *The Villagers*). *Huasipungo* tells of the exploitation of the Indians (who, in Ecuador, form the majority of the population) by a ruling élite that moves them from their *huasipungos* (plots of land) so that they can use them as a labor force and sell the land to foreign interests. One of the first and most brutal of the social protest novels about Indians, it provoked irate attacks from those who felt it exaggerated, though others say that the conditions it described have not changed that much. Many critics consider it better reporting and sociology than it is fiction; the author expressed discouragement that it has not been more effective in bringing reform. Icaza has written several other novels and several volumes of short stories. The story reprinted below from *Odyssey Review* came from his 1952 collection *Seis relatos* ["Six stories"]. Icaza was concerned with the injustices committed by the church against the indigenous population, but with an essential pessimism he saw that the Indians' ignorance and superstition made them susceptible to oppression. In the early 1960s Icaza was running a bookshop in downtown Quito. In the mid-1970s he is attached to the Ecuadorian embassy in Moscow.

Big Precipice

At the edge of the highest of the bleak plateaus, in a shack as dwarfish as the surrounding vegetation—velvety *frailejón* plants, tough buckthorns, rachitic straws of weed—the Indian, José Simbaña, and his young woman, Trinidad Callahuazo, had been living in sin for some time. Like good *huasipungueros*,* they worked from Monday to Saturday—clearing, planting, harvesting, digging ditches, cleaning up, doing extra work on holidays for liquor—on the property of "his honor, the big boss," owner and lord of the hillside, the valley, the forest and the mountain.

On Sundays, at dawn, the pair living in sin would enter the town's church, he wearing a double poncho of Castil-

* *Huasipungueros*: Indian tenants of the *huasipungo*, a parcel of land granted to them by a landlord in return for work. They build their shacks on it and cultivate it during spare moments.

lian baize, she a dark waistband, necklaces of gold-colored beads, and a bright shawl. Lost in the anonymous crowd of Indians and *cholos*,** José and Trinidad enjoyed the Mass from a corner of the darkest nave. The liturgical pantomime of the symbolic sacrifice, the dazzling glitter of the priest's dress, the fragrance of the incense clouds, mixing in the fervent current of emotion of the country people, took on a superstitious flavor of familiar witchcraft. But when, before the Consecration, the priest spoke against wicked common law union, against violators of the holy laws, against those who neglected the sacraments of Holy Mother Church, José and Trinidad cringed in terror, a childish terror that made them look at each other out of the corner of their eyes, in anxious self-defense, with mutual accusation. A viscous dampness—the same that no doubt paralyzed their remotest ancestors in front of arquebuses, swords, armor and horses—oppressed them with this evidence of their eternal damnation.

The good preacher's realism in listing the punishments that Papa God, in His infinite power, had created for His misguided children led him into the most vulgar and exaggerated comparisons: "The indomitable fire of volcanoes, the big pot—the biggest one of all—of the old woman who sold tamales, the molten lead in the furnace of the one-eyed blacksmith, Melchor, the vipers of the forest, scorpions, spiders. . . ." The holy man lifted his hands heavenwards and, in a cavernous voice that hollowed itself in the naves of the church, gave his nightmarish picture a realistic locale, concluding:

"Like Big Precipice with the horrible crevices in its walls! Like Big Precipice with its stenches of brimstone and carrion! Like Big Precipice with its breath of moaning air and its dilated gullet of rocks! Like that . . .! Hell is just like that! Just like Precipice!"

** *Cholo*: A person of mixed Indian and European breed.

Reference to that place was enough to spread fear among the faithful. They all knew it. They all knew about the inaccessible depth that dropped three hundred meters down between sharp rocks and imprecise forms around which perennial fumaroles smoked in memory of ancient volcanic splendor. These excited the popular imagination to make the superstitious statement: "Old red Papa Devil smoked sulphur in stone pipe." Keep in mind that at one time or another they had all smelled the rotten atmosphere the swamps of the innumerable caves and windings at the bottom of Big Precipice breathed out. All of them had also heard the phantasmal wingbeats of bats, owls and large birds that rose from the heart of that abyss as night came on.

During the apocalyptic evocation of the priest, the mass of Indians and peasant *cholos* that packed three-quarters of the church shook with groans, pleas and uncontrollable trembling—reproduction of some sculpture group of clay idols in attitudes caused by a tormented subconscious. At moments like these, the priest—hands convulsed in holy anger, his eye a challenging young eagle's—dominated his work with imposing power. His work! His sculptured work of faces printed with morbid and ancestral remorses, of hands posed in humiliating supplication and degrading anxiety for pardon, of eyes clouded by unexpected and hysterical tears, of eyelids prematurely reddened by the smoke of green firewood, by rot-gut made from sugar cane, by the dirt of the wind from the bleak plateaus. A wail like that of newborn animals intimidated by torture, saturated with bad odors, would then rise with a regular beat—wave of inarticulate pleading—that rocked the multitude of sinners again and again. At such moments the good priest would almost always be overcome by nausea. Nausea after Holy Communion, sacrilege. No. He could not avoid the devil's mockery—host and holy wine in the vicinity of so much nauseating dirt. In this situation, the worried and contrite priest, his voice dripping with pardon, offered to absolve all the crimes of the Indians in exchange for Masses at one hundred rogations at thirty, and responsories for the dead at two *sucres*. Yes. All the crimes of that wretched multitude—disobeying the boss, the major domo, the political deputy, the sacristan, any idiot with shoes on, wasting minutes of work from six to six; drowning suffering with rot-gut on Monday mornings; stealing, through hunger, dead animals from the farm; telling a lie to protect the rest; mixing the fetishism and superstition of their remotest ancestors with the images of Christian saints and the Faith revealed by Papa Priest; persisting in sinful cohabitation before marrying by the Church and the law.

The offering of the cassocked one immediately reduced the swelling murmur started by the fear of punishment beyond the grave. Relief replaced the delirious anguish of the peasant mass. All trusted once more in the mercy of Dear Papa God and His minister on earth. The Indian, José Simbaña, and his young woman, Trinidad Callahuazo, were perhaps the only ones who did not draw comfort from the priest's words of pardon and hope. It was so difficult to accept their reality. Their sad reality. To defend their sinful love from the interference of the majordomo, the fines of the political deputy, the anathemas of the priest, they—he and she—had had to build their shack and fence in their *huasipungo* a few steps away from the horrifying place the reverend father compared with hell. Besides, they felt that their passion—unions interrupted and pleasures clouded by the mysterious night sounds of Big Precipice—was being consumed by the fire of silent remorse, heavy, hard as a daily bleeding of unspoken, mutual accusations. What was there to say? What to do? All the pleasure of the first carnal unions had disappeared and, especially in the woman, the thick broken thing left by portents of evil was quickly taking the dark form of guilt without pardon, a demon coiled around the throat. And so when the church was empty, after Mass and the sermon—a tombstone of peace without hopes in the air around them—, José and Trinidad—she in tears, he pale, stony with suspicion—crawled up to St. Vincent's altar, handsome and miraculous according to the country people's belief but in reality foolishly dolled up with a straw hat, trimmings of gold paper on the skirts of his cassock and a brass bugle in his right hand. Once in front of the Saint, the woman, between sniffles and sighs, pleaded for help:

"Sweet saint. Dear little St. Vincent. Help me. Papa priest says all hell is for poor ones living in sin. For . . . for us, sweet papa. All alone in big pot, mountain of fire, with devils of Big Precipice. It's not on account of badness we don't get married . . . not on account of bad love . . . not on account of sin . . . no . . . why, then? My man, my man José right here. Oh. . . ."

At the mention of his name, the latter stirred out of his bitter thought and, feeling that he played an important role in the female's complaint, nodded, thinking: "Here. . . . Yes, I'm right here, dear little St. Vincent. What my little woman says is true, holy saint. Living together like we do is necessary for Indians. Indians are stupid. How do we understand what they say . . . if it's good or bad, then . . . loving like poor little animals. There's no other way for poor Indians to live, we can't, well . . . think of it yourself, holy saint . . . like that . . . all Indians before have done it like that. Protect us from demons of Big Precipice, please . . . from wind that gives no peace whistling all night . . . from bats that make nests in ceiling . . . from all ghosts and noises that never let us love in peace. Does that make the heart stop suffering? Does it make poor Indians become better? Does it . . . defend us, holy saint. Defend us!"

The frightened woman also wrung her hands as if she were possessed, increasing the discomfiture of her lover—discomfiture of perspiring flesh, of eyes made smaller by suffering and motionless by fear, of thick hanging jaws, of trembling lips—, her lover, who out of compassion mentally took the Saint's place to answer and mentally console the lamenting, troubled woman: "Sure I'm going to defend you, sure I'm going to protect you, that's what I'm a man for. . . . A man, damn it!"

"Yes, pretty one, yes, little father. . . . When we have some eggs, little rabbits, we'll make you a present of. . . . When the earth of the *huasipungo* produces corn, too. . . ." the woman insisted.

"Yes, that's right, good little saint. Mister sacristan will take them holding them with care to the convent," the man added.

When the couple left the church, he ahead of her, and faced the indifference of people—future bleak with slave's work, private scars of repentance without forgiveness—, they both felt disheartened, sinking into a bitter depression that made them drift through the marketplace and finally, always as if by pure chance, pulled them into the street where the three bars of the town crowded together. On a Sunday or big fiesta night, lost in a fog of drink—in darkness, under the stars or the moon, in a drizzle or a storm, it was all the same—, they staggered along the haunted roads. Sometimes they slept in a ditch or among shrubbery that edged some pasture. Ah! They were happy then, with the happiness that small, confused souls experience in the sense of their own absence: far from the cruelty of the *cholo* majordomos, far from the irrevocable orders of "his honor, the big boss," far from the anathemas and sermons of the reverend father, far from the shack strangled by the noises of hell, far from the vicinity of Big Precipice.

Things became much worse with the pregnancy of Trinidad, whose fears increased until she felt death hanging over her. Overcome by a feeling of languor, she would lie down, shivering, in the middle of her work in the fields, and remain for long spells panting as if in pain. When José—accomplice, love and demon at the same time—drew near to console her, Trinidad looked heavenwards, the black abyss of her eyes burning with despair and supplication. Then she whispered in a tearful voice:

"Dearest . . . Dearest. . . ."

"What's wrong?"

"Going to spend today up there in tall clouds."

"In Papa God's heaven?"

"Yes."

"How get up there? Only flying bird."

"Flying with death."

"Hail Mary. But. . . ."

"Dearest . . . I want to. . . ."

The Indian's only answer was to make up naïvely hopeful solutions for the two of them: "When I pay big boss the debt. This year? Next year? When also . . . then we'll give reverend priest and mister deputy cash to hitch us up legally. Matrimony of the law and of Papa God. We'll change our little plot near Big Precipice for land on the hillside. We'll be in good standing with Papa God. Just be patient till then, little woman. Just be patient, woman of my heart."

"For mercy's sake, for the baby hurting in my belly, don't let . . . you won't let me end in hell, please. Give me Christian burial!" insisted the pregnant woman, anguished, filled with evil presentiments.

"Go to hell? For pity's sake, why?"

"Dearest. . . ."

"She must be bewitched to think of kicking the bucket

just like that," the Indian thought, looking with superstitious fear at the swollen body of the woman. Sometimes he forgot his prudence, his slow, cunning prudence, and instead of contemplating the pregnant woman in deceitful silence would shout in resentful anger:

"Be patient! Be patient, damn it!"

One Sunday, like all the last ones of her pregnancy, Trinidad bought one of those candles that come in one pound bundles of five at the grocery store in town. Next to her lover in the church, after Mass and the sermon, she spoke as usual to St. Vincent, holding out towards him, in a childishly threatening way, the offering she had brought:

"Look . . . look now, dear little saint . . . I have need of your charity. Are you listening?"

"Stupid woman. Talking to St. Vincent as if he was an Indian," the man mumbled, while his mate, kneeling in a corner next to the altar, facing the wall partly to hide her shamelessness, raised her blouse and waistband up to her navel and, between moans and groans, rubbed the candle over her stomach deformed by the later months of pregnancy and sinful sex. Then with feminine naturalness she placed the offering, contaminated by guilts that reeked of hell, in the large tin tray where about twenty candles of different sizes were burning. That day, while she persisted in her plea to the Saint, the woman suddenly doubled up, seized by an unbearable pain. A pain in her belly—to her it was the devil biting. With a mad look in her eyes, grasping her middle with both hands, she begged José:

"Dearest . . . Sweetest . . . I can't stand the pain of our sin any more. Here! It hurts, right here!"

"Holy Mary. What is it? What is it?"

"Dearest! I can't! I can't stand it any more! I just can't any more! Help me, please!" insisted Trinidad, pale and trembling.

Afraid that his concubine's scandalous pleas would become public, the Indian man grabbed the pregnant woman as well as he could and dragged her out of the church, speaking low:

"Hold on. Hold on hard. Just a little longer . . . until I carry you . . . until I take you. . . ."

On the road that twisted uphill, the woman realized which way they were going and, in a moment of dark despair, screamed:

"I don't want to, dearest!"

"Huh?"

"I don't want bad wind of Big Precipice. Don't want bats. Don't want vultures. Don't want mountain ghosts. Noooo! I don't want to stay with old red Papa Devil!"

"Hold on, damn it!" José ordered, pressing on. He was breathing in long, deep, wild gasps.

"Mother of God . . . sinful mule . . . my man is like sinful mule of Papa Devil . . . my man . . . my devil. . . ," thought Trinidad, seized by a vertigo of pain.

The next day the pregnant woman woke with one long groan. Instead of going to work, the man went in search of the midwife. On entering the sick woman's shack, the expert midwife—a wizened old crone with dirty hands, reddened eyelids, strings of grayish hair, an odor of cow dung —looked around her with plain suspicion. She blessed herself several times, chanted prayers she made up for her own special use against witchcraft, and then asked the Indian, dazed by his woman's condition:

"Why do you live right next to Big Precipice, next to the evil wind, next to the wind of the evil one?"

"For mercy's sake, just cure my poor woman. My poor. . . ."

"Your poor. . . ."

When the old midwife had accustomed herself to the

semidarkness of the place and warily examined the woman
tossing on her pallet of dirty goat skins and old ponchos,
she could not hide her diagnosis, her wise diagnosis:

"Mother of God! She looks bewitched!"

"Bewitched?" José said, a strange terror gripping his
veins like ice.

Without further comment, the wizened old woman undid
her hemp bag which she had brought under her arm like a
satchel of fine instruments. She drew a pregnant rabbit out
of it, which, in spite of convulsive struggles to free itself,
was handed to the Indian man. Next, the midwife stripped
the sick woman completely and ordered her to lie on her
back. When everything was set, the old woman took the
pregnant rabbit from the Indian's hands and, skilfully
sadistic, massaged the patient's body with it again and
again: over her dark shaking legs, her deformed belly, her
sex organ straining to give birth, her neck whose muscles
and veins tightened as if trying to stand great pain. Soft
and velvety at first, from the heat of constant rubbing the
animal's fur took on the painful, burning torture of mustard
plaster. The procedure lasted—long, groan-producing, useless—until the pregnant woman passed out and the rabbit
died. The midwife moved to the door to see better and so
that José too might observe, in the entrails of the bruised
animal, the mysterious and unusual illness that was killing
poor Trinidad. She slit open the rabbit's belly with the
rusty blade of a knife whose handle was a piece of stick.
She rummaged through the viscous and bloody entrails
looking for something definite and, after a few minutes of
carefully probing and separating, extracted and exhibited a
dead diminutive foetus, murmuring with consternation:

"Jesus. Sweet Jesus. Mother of God. You can see, you
can it so clear, the baby dead in her belly. Dead it is."

"Dead?"

"Can't you see? Poor baby. Sorry little thing."

"But it's only a rabbit."

"That's how the baby is inside its mother. I rubbed the animal to find out."

"You sure?"

"Possessed by the evil one, as you can see. Possessed by the Evil Wind of Big Precipice too. . . ."

"Then cure her, sweet mother. Please cure her!" José Simbaña begged, at his wit's end. But the midwife's only response was to drop the entrails and the dead animal on the floor. She wiped her hands on her waistband several times, gained the door and, blessing herself and mumbling prayers to free herself of the evil she had disclosed, fled downhill.

Discouraged by the cowardly and evasive behavior of the only one who could cure his woman, the Indian huddled up beside the pallet like a whipped dog. Something like an ancestral sense of guilt burned in his blood, something like grief filled with repressed anger. He did not, could not believe what was happening. Some evil spirit advised him to run away like the midwife. To run downhill, roam the hillside, cross the valley, through the woods, the marshes. But he did not move. He could not abandon his naked woman, twisting and trembling in the grip of fear and death—for him, these were the impalpable lashes of the Evil Wind and the Evil Spirit. Maybe he ought to wait. But wait for what? For . . . Papa God to show mercy. But hours passed and, as they passed, the poisonous fear of superstition grew in the Indian's nerves and blood like an insane and delirious power, growing with the help of the whining wind that was always flogging the shack, the cawing of birds of prey in the sky, the distant barking of dogs, the presence of bats steadily circling.

At times Trinidad, her sense of time completely lost, knelt on the tattered ponchos, her pulse feverish, in strange imploration. She appeared to be asleep . . . dead! Then the man would lean over her with bitter interest, near her face and her breasts, over the memory of the first night of their illicit love. Yes. He leaned over her to question, too. . . . Unfortunately words stuck, confused, in his throat, in a net of despair and tenderness. All they could do was rouse more affection in his blood towards that small miserable woman, that female who had managed to break the solitude.

"Damn it. Oh damn," was all José Simbaña could say then.

Later, peaceful, covered up, sweaty, she opened her eyes with their languid lids. Her breath was thin. Finding the man beside her—at the same time her accomplice and refuge in pleasure, grief, punishment, and in the great silence that surrounded them—, she persisted in the old plea for pardon and order, protection against the threat of hell:

"Swear that . . . swear, dearest."

"But what?"

"That they won't . . . the devils won't drag away poor Trinidad like the good father said."

"Damn it."

"You'll protect me. Protect me, dearest!"

"But how, little woman?"

"Burying me in a Christian manner when I kick the bucket, not like a worthless dog."

"But how, sweet woman?"

"With Mass in church, with black cloth. With large candle. With incense smoke. With bunches of white flowers. With painted box. With responsories of three *sucre*. With holy water. With. . . ."

"Only if you want to go ahead and die leaving your poor man all alone, abandoned like a grain of corn dropped on the road to town, like. . . ."

"Swear it. Swear it, please!"

The heartbreaking pleas, the pitiful tears of the dying woman, as usual tore the sincere and touching oath from the Indian:

"All right, pretty one. All right, little companion. When it has to be, we'll do it all: even if I have to rip blood from my feet and hands with work, even if I have to sink alive in the marshes, even if I have to steal cattle from the ranch, even if I have to take a whipping on my naked body. All of it, just as you say. When Papa God ordains it, I'll bury my little woman like a Christian."

Things became worse that night. The sick woman's fevered eyes glued themselves on the light from the stove, dragging themselves across the floor. Then, straying without control, they went over the cracks in the door through which the wind whistled, the dark hollows along the walls where phantoms crouched, the junctures in the straw roof where bats fluttered. And, clinging to the body of her lover who stayed next to the pallet, still fully dressed, she whispered in despair:

"They're coming for me now! Now, dearest! Now . . . now. . . ."

"Who?", the man said, pretending not to understand although he knew what she meant.

"The Evil Wind!"

"Oh Jesus!"

"The Evil One!"

"I'm here, right here to defend you, don't worry!"

"The demons reverend father talks about."

"Aaah."

"The demons of Big Precipice!"

"The demons," he echoed in a tone of fear. He felt weak and defenceless before heaven's curse.

On the third day Trinidad died. The screams, the pleading had subsided in a tide of heavy exhaustion. Then, with a slight convulsion, the body of the woman became still, eyes sunken, mouth half-open, face livid. Perhaps the man thought she was sleeping. And yet he called her in a low voice:

"Little one! Little sweetheart!"

Receiving no answer, he thought, looking for stupid consolation: "She doesn't want to answer, to speak. . . . She's pretending . . . sly . . . but. . . . Just like a dead cow or a dog. . . . Trinidad!" Realizing at last that his companion was really dead, the Indian screamed until he was hoarse, until his crazed heart, panting, strangled all possibility of lamenting. He rested a long time, crouched next to the corpse. Then, like an automaton, he left the shack. Lost, hopeless, he sat down under the agaves that fenced the *huasipungo*. Suddenly something warned him—with the intuitive knowledge of his blood—that he had to keep his sworn promise. An absurd anxiety, contempt for himself, for his impotence, made him wander over the countryside. A few hours later, quenching his thirst to regain his strength, dipping his face, like an animal, into a still pool in a shallow stream, he noticed that his face, black and blurred among the clouds of the sky, was repeating the woman's supplication: "Swear that . . . swear, dearest . . . that the devils won't drag away poor Trinidad like the good father said. Protect me, dearest! When I kick the bucket. . . ."

It was only then that he felt with certainty that someone fixed very deep in his heart had died, had disappeared forever, was nowhere to keep him company.

"No, damn it," he mumbled, rising to his feet. And scenting in the late afternoon air the only possible solution, he took the road that led to the ranch house. He found everything forbidding and impenetrable as the mind and whims of "the master, his honor, the big boss." He stayed outside the servants' quarters for a long while, not daring to make his presence known. Luckily the old woman servant, the oldest one, stuck her head out the kitchen door and asked with a haughty air:

"Well! Who are you looking for?"

"The good master, his honor."

"He's not here."

"And boss majordomo?"

"He'll be here this evening."

"Then, pretty one, I'll wait here in the corridor until he comes."

And night fell on him. At a lost hour, in the middle of the evening darkness, dogs barked. The shadow of a man on horseback crossed the yard, of a rider who hitched the horse to the milking post and approached the corridor, dragging his spurs, swaying, with heavy step. A smell of cheap liquor told the Indian Simbaña that it was the majordomo, whose arrival could solve his troubles.

"Boss," the Indian said meekly, approaching the shadow of the other who, noticing that he was being followed, arrogantly asked:

"Who the devil are you?"

"Just me, boss. José Simbaña."

"Simbaña?"

"The one from up . . . from Big Precipice."

"Ah! So! The lost Indian, the lazy Indian. You finally showed your face around here, damn you."

"My woman's dead."

"Woman? What woman? Ah! Now I know, damn you. You had a concubine. Corrupted Indian!"

"Mother of God. I come to beg you, please, boss. I beg your honor. To grant the charitable favor of giving me something in advance to bury my woman."

"You damned Indian, drunkard, dog. When you already owe so much money. . . ."

"It can't be much, boss."

"Can't be much? Almost a hundred *sucres,* over a year now."

"For charity's sake, boss. I beg your honor. For Papa God's sake. . . ."

The damns, the curses and the threats of the *cholo* majordomo crushed the perseverance of the pleading Indian. Finally, the crack of a merciless whip cut short the supplicant's voice. Satisfied and free—the ill-fated victim had scurried off like a rat—, the majordomo dragged his drunken body, excited by his show of manliness, inside the house.

José Simbaña spent the night in a deserted shed. The next morning, he had no better luck with the people he knew in town. After listening to the Indian's presumptuous request for an advance on a risky proposition of his, Eulalia Chavez, who made and sold fritters, stared at the entreating Indian as if he had gone out of his mind. Then she interrupted scornfully:

"Are you drunk or something? I've had far better propositions! Where have you ever seen people give credit to Indians, just like that, eh?"

"To bury my dead woman. . . ."

"Dead woman? What woman do you have, lying Indian?"

"For charity's sake, ma'am, your honor. I'll bring you a little pig real cheap as soon as it gets big."

"You must want the money to get drunk. No. I haven't any! Go find another fool!"

"For charity's sake, ma'am."

"Get out, pig-headed Indian!"

"Ma'am. . . ."

"Jacintooo! Come throw out this nervy, nasty Indian!"

"Get out, damn you! Drunkard, filthy Indian!"

José Simbaña knocked at well-known doors, told his

tragedy time and again, offered to do any kind of work, to hand over his animals, although he and his possessions were bound to his landlord for life. He begged with maddening persistence, with a drunkard's desperation. All, absolutely all, regarded him with as much astonishment as the maker of fritters, everyone kicked or pushed him out. And when nothing else worked they sicked their dogs on him. Thus night overtook him and he slept in a corridor. When he woke up, he remembered the *huasipungo* of his parents, Papa Luis and Mama Rosa. He would have to ask their forgiveness, shed tears of remorse for having abandoned them. Still, that was no obstacle. On the contrary, he wanted desperately to submit his bitterness to the anger and reproaches of his parents.

Grateful for the long expected surprise, the old couple gave him a big welcome. Seeing him enter their shack with downcast look, determined to ask for pardon, they thought: "Anybody that comes looking so upset must come in great suffering."

Mama Rosa spoke to him with her usual sweetness:

"My boy, my bewitched boy."

And, after scratching his head and looking him over, Papa Luis gave him a couple of light slaps on the back.

He found everything unchanged in the place of his childhood: the impertinent and mangy dog, the stunted corn, yellow as if prematurely ripe, the line of geese sunning themselves, the pigs and the chickens next to his small brothers, the corn soup in the clay pot, on the floor the bedding of rags and dry skins where he had slept his heavy animal sleep.

When Papa Luis and Mama Rosa learned the motive and the reason for their "bewitched boy's" return, they offered to give the woman a Christian burial.

"Even if we have to sell the little pigs and the lambs

the *compadre** left with us when he went away," the old
man offered.

"You go ahead, son. We'll come later with the money,"
added Mama Rosa with soothing hope.

José Simbaña ran along the zigzagging hillroads. Over-
whelming happiness pounded at the pores of his skin. He
couldn't, it was almost impossible for him to believe in the
kind, charitable solution the old ones had found for his
suffering.

Entering the path that climbed Big Precipice, the Indian
looked up at the sky with grateful fear, the sky where he
noticed about twenty vultures flying in regular circles.
"Mother of God . . . oh Lord . . . what can it mean?" he
said to himself, an indefinite, painful misgiving biting into
him. Misgiving about what? About nothing . . . about
everything. He tried talking—broken, spontaneous phrases
—with everything around him, with everything that appeared before his eyes as he ran: the stones along the road,
the mud in ditches, the green herbs, the damp cowdung,
the hard rocks, the hot sand. When he took the last turn in
the road and drew near his shack, a stench of death knotted
a violent oath in his throat. What? What? His ears fixed
on the strange flapping of diabolic wings that beat the air,
imitating the rhythms of hell, the Indian sniffed the air like
a starved dog. Evil presentiments gripped him, absurd
questions.

"Who can it be? Who can it be beating like that? Like
Devils, like. . . ."

He peered over the fence. No! He had surprised something. Something that crushed him with horror, something
to make anyone go mad. More than twenty dark, heavy,
stinking vultures moved about, crowding the *huasipungo* in

* *Compadre*: Godfather and father of the child, each with
respect to the other.

front of the shack. Someone was lying among their legs, in the middle of their quarrel and agitated wings. Someone! Satiated, some rested placidly in corners. Others more voracious and insatiable, picked at a being, a pile of human entrails. He made out legs, arms, a face without eyes. It was she. She had been dragged by the demons from the pallet, through the door, into the yard.

"Christian flesh! It's my own little Trinidad!," Simbaña screamed, not knowing just what to do. But the echo of a well-known voice, of a loving memory announced: "The very devils of Big Precipice . . . in the shape of vultures, black, stinking. The demons reverend father talks about. . . ." But the presence of what he thought were demons from hell, instead of intimidating him as usual, driving him into nightmarish flight, crammed blind strength and courage into his muscles. Her screams urged him on. The screams that boiled in his blood like a hurricane. He looked at the torn up figure of his Trinidad, like a bull about to charge, and suddenly leaped over the fence screaming:

"My woman! My little woman, damn you! My sweetheart! My big sin!"

Stunned by the flight of birds scared off by his unexpected appearance, the Indian remained motionless some seconds, as if he had been planted deep, forever, among the rags, the wrappings, the badly skinned bones, beside the eyeless face, the peeled chest, the breasts carved up by the beaks. Something like an order, a nagging, desperate need, a cry of fear, emanated from that tragic scene. Emanated and rose—warm, viscous—through the legs, the stomach, the shoulders, the throat of the disheartened Indian. Yes. It was a curse and supplication at the same time: "Swear that . . . swear, dearest . . . you'll protect me so that the devils won't drag me away like the good father said. You'll bury me like a Christian, not like an animal. Protect me, dearest. No! You won't let the devils of Big Precipice drag me away. You'll help this poor one anyway you can."

José Simbaña looked around him with despair and fury. What could he do against those fiendish, powerful birds that surrounded and then flew from him? How could he save at least what was still left of his dear woman? How?

"No, damn it! Damn you!" the Indian shouted, madly charging at the vultures every which way, into the bristling fence of agave thorns, towards the shack's roof, towards the small empty pigsty, towards skies beyond his reach.

The failure of the Indian's absurd, impossible chase increased the fury of his blind anger. He raced, leaped, dashed from side to side. But what was his senseless objective? Perhaps to rescue from the demons' bellies the pieces of his loved companion, of what had been the ephemeral delight of the pallet, his silent companion in his work, on the long roads, in his foggy sprees and punishing hangovers. His woman! Like a loose-limbed scarecrow he continued to pursue the winged demons that mocked him, flying close in and then pulling away. He followed them over the stony countryside, screaming, cursing, leaping.

Always attracted by the black, slippery birds, a knot of anger now, exuding impotent hatred, frustrated because he did not have wings, he came to the edge of Big Precipice. Beating the air with his arms and furious curses, he performed hair-raising feats of balance on rocks projecting high above the abyss, trying to catch the demons that were escaping with a deep part of himself. But they were more agile, leaping higher, and finally soared in flight to sink into Big Precipice.

"They're going down to hell like reverend father says, damn . . . with my sweetheart in their bellies. But why?" the Indian asked himself, at the peak of his despair, not daring to look down towards the bottom of the gigantic mouth of the earth formed by walls of calcined rock, while the well-known, dear voice of Trinidad urged: "Swear! Swear, dearest! Protect me . . . where are you? Now, my man, my own!" The voice of the dead woman seemed to cry out, demanding, pleading insistently from the puffed bellies, the beaks, the blood-stained claws of the birds.

"No, no, damn you! My little one! My sweetheart!" the Indian's howl ripped the air. And a blind impulse to join and obey the imagined pleas of his ill fated love forced him to open his poncho like wings and dive from the tip of the rock on which he was standing into the abyss, to be swallowed by its depths like a stone.

Translated by HARDIE ST. MARTIN

Juan Bosch (b. 1909) was born in La Vega, a medium-sized town in the interior of the Dominican Republic. The poverty he saw around him left a deep impression. Mostly self-educated, he studied literature at a college in Santo Domingo and wrote a collection of short stories, *Camino Real* [1933, "The Royal Highway"], a collection of Indian legends (1935), and *La Mañosa* (1936), a novel. In 1937 he left the Dominican Republic, appalled by the massacre of fifteen thousand Haitian squatters by order of the dictator of the country, Rafael Léonidas Trujillo. He spent 24 years in exile, traveling through Latin America, and living some time in Cuba, Chile, and Venezuela. During these years he taught, worked as a journalist, and wrote several books, including short stories and biographies. Trujillo was assassinated in 1961 and Bosch was elected president of his country in 1962, but he himself was overthrown seven months later. He lived in exile in Puerto Rico and Europe and then returned to his own country, embittered by U.S. intervention in Dominican politics. Despite a turbulent political life, he has written many books, most of them published outside his own country. Best known for his excellent short stories, many of which are fine examples of magical realism, he likes to write of the small towns and peasants of the Antilles. In any collection his bright sense of humor stands out, as in the following, the title story from *Dos pesos de agua* (1941), translated when the rate of exchange was different.

Two Dollars Worth of Water

Old Remigia clung to the saddle, and raising her tiny face, said:

"Here is a nickel for the souls in Purgatory, so it will rain, Felipa."

Felipa smoked on and made no answer. The lamentations she had heard about the drought. . . . She finally raised her eyes and scanned the sky. Clear, high, not a shadow on it. Its brightness was infuriating.

"There's not a sign of a cloud," she observed, and lowered her glance again. The brown fields showed gaping cracks. There at the foot of the hill stood a hut. The people who lived in it, and in the other, and those far, far off were all thinking the same as she and old Remigia. No rain for so many months. The men had fired the pines on the hillsides; the heat of the flames seared the limp leaves of the cornstalks; sparks flew off like birds, leaving a luminous wake behind them, and flowered in great bonfires.

All this so the smoke would rise heavenward—so it would rain. But nothing. Nothing.

"This is going to be the end of us, Remigia."

Commented the old woman: "For the years we have left—"

The drought had begun by killing off the first crop. After sucking the moisture out of the earth, it began on the brooks. Little by little their beds grew too wide for them, the stones lifted their heads covered with slime, and the little fish fled downstream. Spring after spring either dried up or turned into a swamp or mudhole. Thirsty and hopeless, many families left their little farms, hitching up their horses and setting out in search of some place where it was not so dry.

But old Remigia refused to leave. One day the rain would come, one afternoon the clouds would pile up against the sky, one night the song of the downpour would sound against the scorched palm thatch.

Ever since they had carried her son off on a stretcher and she had been left with her grandchild, old Remigia had become taciturn and saving. One by one she put her pennies in a gourd partly filled with ashes. She planted the patch of ground behind the house to corn and beans. The corn went to fatten the chickens and pigs; the beans were for her and her grandson. Every two or three months she picked out the plumpest chickens and took them to town to sell them. When a pig was nicely fattened she butchered it. She sold the meat herself and rendered out the lard. This and the cracklings she also took to town to sell. She would close the door of her cabin, ask a neighbor to look after things for her, set her grandson on a bay pony, following behind on foot. By night they would be back.

In this fashion she wore her life, with her grandson suspended from her heart.

"It's you I'm working for, son," she would say to him. "I don't want you to have to scuffle for a living or die before your time, like your father."

The child would look at her. Nobody ever heard him talk, and although he stood hardly three feet high, he was up before daylight with his machete under his arm, and the sun rose on his back bent over the garden patch.

Old Remigia hugged her hopes to her breast. She watched her corn grow, her beans ripen; she heard her pigs grunting in their sty; she counted her chickens when at night they flew up to roost in the trees. Between times she took down her gourd and counted the coppers. There were many of them, and finally silver coins of all sizes.

With trembling hand Remigia caressed the money and dreamed. She saw her grandson of marrying age, riding a fine horse, or perhaps behind a counter selling bottles of rum, yards of cloth, pounds of sugar. She smiled, put back the money, hung up the gourd, and leaned over the child, who was sleeping soundly.

Everything was going fine, just fine. Then without knowing how or why, the drought had come. A month went by without rain, then two, then three. The men who passed her cabin said as they greeted her:

"Terrible weather, Remigia."

She silently assented. Sometimes she would add:

"The thing to do is light candles to the souls in Purgatory."

But it did not rain. Many candles were burned, and yet the corn withered on the stalk. The springs dwindled away; the pig wallow grew caked and dry. At times the sky clouded over; thick gray banks formed against the horizon; a damp wind came blowing down the hillside, raising up clouds of dust.

"We're going to get rain tonight, Remigia," the men assured her as they went by.

"At last!" said a woman.

"It's almost coming down, you might say," a Negro confided.

Old Remigia went to bed and prayed. She promised more candles to the souls in Purgatory and waited. It seemed to her at times that she could hear the roar of the rain coming down from the high bluffs. She fell asleep hopefully, but in the morning the sky was as clean as fresh linen.

People began to lose heart. Everyone looked washed-out, and the ground was burning hot to the touch. All the streams in the vicinity were drying up; all the vegetation of the hillsides was burned. There was nothing to feed the pigs; the donkeys wandered off looking for locust pods; the cattle strayed to the swamps, chewing at the roots of trees; the children traveled distances of half a day for a can of water; the chickens got lost in the woods, trying to find seeds and insects.

"This is the end, Remigia. This is the end," the old women mourned.

One day in the cool of the morning Rosendo, with his wife, his two children, the cow, a dog, and a bony mule on which their household goods were loaded, passed by.

"I can't stand this any longer, Remigia. Someone has put the evil eye on this place."

Remigia went into her cabin and came out with two copper coins.

"Light this much worth of candles in my name to the souls in Purgatory," she said.

Rosendo took the coins, looked at them, raised his head, and stared long at the blue sky.

"Whenever you want to, come to Tavera. We're going to find us a little place there, and you're always welcome."

"I'm staying, Rosendo. This can't go on."

Rosendo turned away. His wife and children were disappearing in the distance. The far-off hills looked as though they were on fire from the sun.

The boy was burned as dark as a Negro. One day he came to her:

"Mama, one of the pigs looks like it was dead."

Remigia hurried to the sty. Panting, their snouts shriveled and dry, as thin as wires, the pigs were grunting and squealing. They were all crowded together, and when Remigia drove them away she saw the remains of an animal. She understood: the dead had nourished the living. Thereupon she decided to go herself to bring water so her animals could hold out.

She set out at daybreak with the bay pony and returned at noon. Stubborn, silent, tireless, Remigia kept on. Not a word of complaint passed her lips. The money gourd was lighter; but she had to go on sacrificing part of her savings so the souls in Purgatory would take pity. It was a long trip·to the nearest brook; she walked, not to tire the pony. Its flanks were as sharp as a knife, its neck so thin it could hardly support its head, and at times the rattling of its bones could be heard.

The exodus continued. Every day another cabin was deserted. The gray earth was crisscrossed with cracks; only the thorny *cambronales* stayed green. Every time she visited the brook the water was lower. At the end of a week there was as much mud as water; in two weeks its bed was like a stony old road, the pebbles giving back the glitter of the sun. The horse foraged desperately for something to nibble at and lashed its tail about to drive off the flies.

Remigia had not lost faith. She scanned the sky for signs of rain.

"Souls in Purgatory!" she pleaded, on her knees, "souls in Purgatory! We are going to burn up if you don't help us."

One morning a few days later the bay pony could not get to its feet; that same afternoon her grandson stretched out on his cot, burning with fever. Remigia went from cabin to cabin, even the distant ones, urging their inmates:

"Let us make a Rosary to St. Isidoro," she said.

"Let us make a Rosary to St. Isidoro," she repeated.

They set out early one Sunday morning. She was carrying her grandson in her arms. The child's head, heavy with fever, hung limply over his grandmother's shoulder. Fifteen or twenty women, men, and ragged, sun-tanned children, intoned mournful chants as they moved along the barren paths. They carried an image of the Virgin, they lighted candles, they knelt and raised their prayers to God. A gaunt, bearded old man, with steely, burning eyes and bare breast, marched at the head of the procession, beating his sternum with his bony hand, his eyes raised heavenward as he implored:

> St. Isidoro, Farmer,
> St. Isidoro, Farmer,
> Bring the water and hide the sun,
> St. Isidoro, Farmer.

They had all gone. Rosendo had passed by; Toribio, with his feeble-minded daughter; Felipe, and others and others. She gave them all money for candles. The last ones went by, people she did not know. They had a sick old man with them and were crushed by the weight of their sadness. She gave them money for candles.

There was now nothing to break the view from the door of the cabin across the calcined fields to the gaunt hills against which they ended. Even the bare beds of the streams were visible.

Nobody hoped for rain any more. Before they left, the old folks swore that God was punishing the place, and the young ones said it had the evil eye.

Remigia hoped. She collected a few drops of water. She knew she would have to start all over again, because there was hardly anything left in the gourd, and the little garden patch was as bare as the highway. Dust and sun. Sun and dust. The curse of God for man's wickedness had fallen there; but the curse of God could not prevail against Remigia's faith.

In their corner of Purgatory, the souls of the blessed, standing waist-deep in flames, were going over their accounts. They spent their time in the fire being purified, and, by a cruel irony, it was they who had the power to unleash the rain and bring water to the earth. One bearded old crone spoke up:

"*Caramba!* Old Remigia of Paso Hondo has spent two dollars on candles so it would rain!"

Her companions were shocked.

"Two dollars? Good Heavens!"

One asked:

"Why didn't she get any service? Is that the way to treat people?"

"We'll have to oblige her," roared another.

The order went around, the word was spread:

"Water for Paso Hondo. Two dollars worth of water!"

"Two dollars worth of water for Paso Hondo."

"Two dollars worth of water for Paso Hondo."

They were all very much impressed, almost overawed, because they had never had an order for that much water, not a half, not even a third. For two cents worth of candles they supplied a night's rain, and once they sent a small flood for twenty cents.

"Two dollars worth of water for Paso Hondo," they roared.

All the souls in Purgatory were shocked to think of the water that would have to be poured out for that much money while they burned in eternal flames until the moment when God in His supreme mercy should call them to His side.

In Paso Hondo the sky began to cloud up. Early one morning Remigia looked toward the east and saw a thin black cloud, as black as a mourning band, as thin as the thong of a whip. An hour later great masses of gray clouds were piling up, pushing against one another, scudding along. Two hours later it was as dark as night.

Full of fear, fear that such happiness might come to naught, Remigia said nothing, merely looked. Her grandson still lay on the bed, feverish. He was thin, like a rattle made of bones. His eyes seemed to peer out of two caves.

Overhead came a clap of thunder. Remigia ran to the door. Advancing like a runaway horse, a sheet of rain was coming toward the cabin from the hills. She smiled to herself, clasped her cheeks, and her eyes opened as wide as they could. It was raining at last!

Swift, pelting, singing loud songs, the rain reached the road, beat upon the thatched roof, leaped over the cabin, and began to fall on the fields. Feeling as though she were on fire, Remigia ran to the back door and saw the thick strands of water coming down, saw the earth sink to sleep and give off a dense vapor. She rushed outside jubilant.

"I knew it, I knew it, I knew it!" she cried at the top of her lungs.

The rain beat upon her head, ran down her temples, soaked her hair.

"It's raining, raining, raining!" she chanted, her arms raised to heaven. "I knew it!"

She rushed back into the house, picked up the child, pressed him to her breast, held him up and showed him the rain.

"Drink, child, drink, my son. Look, water; look, water!"

And she shook him, she hugged him, as though she wanted to fill him with the cool, joyous spirit of water.

While the storm raged outside, inside Remigia was dreaming.

"Now," she said to herself, "as soon as the ground is ready to work I'll plant sweet potatoes, early rice, beans, and corn. I've still got a little money left to buy seed. The child is going to be all right. What a pity folks left! I'd like to see Toribio's face when he hears about this downpour. So many prayers, and nobody but me's going to get the benefit of them. Maybe folks'll come back now when they hear the spell is broken."

Her grandson slept quietly. At Paso Hondo, over the dry beds of the brooks and rivers, the muddy water began to run. There was not much yet, and it eddied around the rocks. Down the hillside it ran red, thick with clay; from the sky it fell heavy and swift. The palm-thatched roof was breaking up under the pounding of the rain. Remigia dozed; she saw her field full of thriving, flourishing plants swaying in the cool breeze. She saw the patches of yellow corn, of rice, of red beans, of swelling sweet potatoes. Until finally she fell into a heavy sleep.

Outside the rain roared with never a pause.

A week went by, ten days, two weeks. The rain kept up without an hour's interruption. All the rice and lard were used up, and the salt. Through the rain Remigia set out for Camino de las Cruces to buy food. She started in the morning and got back at midnight. The rivers, the brooks, even the swamps, had taken over the world, washing out the roads, slowly invading the fields.

One afternoon a man went by, riding a big mule.

"Listen, Don," Remigia called out to him.

The man rode up to the door, and the mule stuck its head in.

"Get down and warm yourself," she invited him.

The animal stayed out in the rain.

"The sky has turned to water," the man observed after a pause. "If I was you I'd leave this low place and go up in the hills."

"Me go away from here? No, Don, this weather will soon be over."

"Look," the visitor went on, "this is a flood. I've seen some terrible ones, with the water carrying off animals, houses, plants, people. All the streams I've crossed are rising, and besides, it's raining heavy at the headwaters."

"The drought was worse, Don. Everybody ran away, and I weathered it."

"Drought doesn't kill, but water drowns, Doña. All that," and he pointed at what he had left behind him, "is flooding. I rode for three hours this morning through water up to the mule's belly."

As it was getting dark he left. Remigia begged him not to set out in that blackness.

"It's going to get worse, Doña. Those rivers will be over their banks."

Remigia went to look after her grandson who was fretting.

The man was right. God, what a night! There was a steady, menacing roar, punctuated by the crack of thunderclaps and the glare of lightning. Dirty water began to swirl through the crack at the bottom of the door and spread over the floor. The wind was howling in the distance, and now and again there was the crash of a falling tree. Remigia opened the door. A distant flash lighted up Paso Hondo. Water and more water, running down the slopes of the hills and turning the highway into a roaring river.

"Could it be a flood?" Remigia asked herself, doubting for the first time.

But she closed the door and went back in the room. She had faith, a boundless faith, greater than the drought had been, greater than the rain might be. Inside, the cabin was as wet as outside. The child was huddled in his cot, trying to escape the drip from the leaking roof.

At midnight a thud against the side of the house awakened her. As she got out of bed she felt the water almost up to her knees.

What a night, what a night! The water came in gusts; it ran everywhere, covered everything. Another flash of lightning blazed, and the thunder shook loose pieces of the black sky.

Remigia was afraid.

"Blessed Virgin!" she cried, "Blessed Virgin, help me!"

But this was not the affair of the Virgin or of God, but of the souls in Purgatory, who were shouting:

"Now, that's half a dollar's worth. Half a dollar's worth."

When she felt the water tugging at the cabin, Remigia stopped hoping and picked up her grandson. She clutched him to her breast as tightly as she could, forcing her way through the water, which hampered her as she walked. Somehow she managed to pull the door open and get outside. The water was up to her waist. She plodded, plodded ahead. She had no idea where she was going. The wind pulled her hair loose, the lightning flashed green in the distance. The water was rising, rising. She clasped her grandson still tighter. She stumbled but managed to keep her footing, pleading:

"Blessed Virgin! Blessed Virgin!"

The wind snatched her voice away and scattered it over the liquid savanna.

"Blessed Virgin! Blessed Virgin!"

Her skirt was floating. She was slipping, slipping. She felt something catch at her hair, hold her fast by the head. She thought to herself:

"As soon as this is over I'll plant sweet potatoes."

She saw the corn buried under the dirty water. She dug her nails into the breast of her grandson.

"Blessed Virgin!"

The wind howled on, and the thunder shattered the sky.

Her hair had caught on a thorny trunk. The water rolled down, down, carrying cabins and trees. The souls in Purgatory shrieked on wildly:

"Not enough yet, not enough. Two dollars worth of water, two dollars, two dollars."

Translated by HARRIET DE ONIS

Jorge Amado (b. 1912) was born on a cocoa plantation near Ilheus, in southern Bahia, Brazil. He worked as a cub reporter for a newspaper at sixteen and wrote for literary reviews. In 1930 his father sent him to Rio de Janeiro to study law; there he began his first novel, *O País do Carnaval* ["Carnival Land"], which was published in 1932. In 1933 he published *Cacau*, portraying the life of cocoa workers on the estates south of Bahia: in 1934 *Suor* ["Sweat"], about the tenements of Bahia (a selection from this is reprinted below); in 1935, *Jubiabá*, about Negro life in Bahia; in 1937 *Capitães de areia* (*Beach Waifs*), about the lives of delinquents; and in 1943 *Terrás do Sem Fim* (*The Violent Land*), about the struggle between two power-hungry cocoa planters. In 1936 he was arrested during the Getúlio Vargas regime in Brazil. In 1946 he was elected Communist deputy to the Brazilian Congress. In 1947 he went into exile in Europe when his party was suppressed in Congress. The five early novels are representative of the regionalist strain in Brazilian fiction. In the 1930s and 1940s the novel about Brazil's Northeast—its vast desert highlands and the feudal cocoa and sugar cane plantations of the lush coastal region—dominated Brazilian literature, particularly in the work of Graciliano Ramos, Rachel de Queiroz, José Lins do Rego, and Amado. Among the regionalists, Amado particularly concentrated his fiction on social protest and the class struggle. But even in the early novels Amado seems attracted by society's villains; his talent for drawing attractive rogues is more evident in his recent works, in which the element of social protest are carried more gracefully by good storytelling and high good humor. Many of the more recent works—often bestsellers—are available in English: These works include *Gabriela, Clove and Cinnamon*; *Home Is the Sailor*; *Dona Flor and Her Two Husbands*; *The Two Deaths of Quincas Wateryell*; and *Tent of Miracles*, all published within the past twenty years. Soon to be released as a movie is his most recent novel, *Tereza Batista Cansada de Guerra* ["Tereza Batista, tired of war"].

Sweat

They came down the steps together. When they reached the door, the stranger tried to engage him in conversation. His hot mouldy breath brushed the peddler's face. It was a warm night, a damp night, without any wind or sea breeze, but the stranger must have been cold because he kept his hands hidden in his overcoat pockets. He had large dull eyes and a sharp angular jaw.

"You live here, mister?"

"I live here. On the third floor."

"And is the rent high?"

"High? Yeah, it's high enough, but where can you find anything cheaper?"

"Nowhere?"

His jaw took on a sharper, a more despondent look as he asked the question. Looking steadily at the peddler's face, he repeated his query.

"So you say there's nothing cheaper, eh? Everything is high . . . ?"

"Were you in the attic yet?"

"Yeah. Nothing there. All filled up."

He stood looking out at the street. The air was still and heavy, and yet he was shivering. He removed his hands from his pockets, and rubbed them vigorously.

"Yeah, mister," he said abruptly, "that's the way it goes. Everything is high. I already owe two months' rent. . . . I live over on Captain Street. Sure, that's right. The woman comes for her rent every day. She keeps chasing us. There are four of us—I, my wife Maria Clara (she's from Serigipan), and two boys. I guess we'll have to start begging soon."

He paused wearily, spat, pulled the cap over his eyes, and continued: "I used to work for an Aurora factory till it went bankrupt. That was three months ago—and here I am now, still looking around, without a job. My wife started to take in washing, but she doesn't make enough. Well, I've got to move out today—but everything is high . . . and everybody wants money in advance. Tell me, how is it going to end?"

He thrust his hands in his pockets.

"Any rooms for rent next door?"

"I don't think so. Why don't you try the *cortico* in the back?"

"Thanks. I was there already. Everything's taken. . . ."

He eyed the street silently, spat, and scraped the saliva with his shoe. The peddler fingered the halfpenny. His first intention was to offer it to the stranger, but then he felt ashamed and rejected the idea. The coin was so small, and he did not want to offend the other. The stranger lifted the lapels of his overcoat, threw a final glance at the stairway, and walked away.

"Well, excuse me for bothering you. Good night."

For a moment he stood undecided, without knowing

whether to go up or down the hill. Finally he made up his mind and went up the ridge. The peddler watched him from a distance. The stranger was still trembling, he could see, and even though he could not hear him any more, still it seemed to him as though the sharply pointed jaw were still before him, and the tired voice were speaking plainly, and a hot mouldy breath were brushing against his face. He waved his hand despondently, and suddenly he, too, began to shiver coldly in the warm, sticky evening air.

The Italian woman, who rented out rooms on the second floor, wore clothes which covered her neck and arms. Her dresses were so long they almost dragged along the ground.

A tall woman with false teeth, she usually wore a pair of black shoes and gold-rimmed spectacles. She was very haughty and never spoke to anyone except Fernandez from the saloon, and then it was only to say hello. Sometimes when Cabaca was at the door, she would drop a nickel into his cheese box. The beggar would mumble out a mixture of thanks and insults.

"God help you break your neck on the steps some day, you bitch. . . ."

The Negress who sold *mingau* laughed heartily, but the Italian did not hear. She was already far away, walking towards the spiritualist seance which she frequented. She was a well-known medium, and when the spirit seized her, they said she danced, sang piquant songs in her own language, and gestured obscenely. She was the favorite apparition through which the spirits of corrupted priests and debauched women manifested their presence. Using her as a vehicle they related their stories, their life of perversion, in an effort to obtain mercy. Pure unsullied spirits seldom fell upon her, and when they did, generally became entangled with the foul, impure ones, which always ended up by dominating the former. That was why the seances in

St. Michael's Street were very much frequented, and why the Italian was beginning to acquire a saintly halo about her person.

The Italian woman rapped on the peddler's door with her knuckles. The knocks sounded imperious like orders, but the door remained unopened. She repeated the raps, shouting at the same time.

"Seo João! Seo João!"

A voice responded from inside the room. "Just a minute. I'm coming."

When the door opened, the Italian was standing with her hands behind her back, smiling. A face with a heavy beard stared at her from the doorway.

"Here's the bill for your rent. It was due on the fifth of the month, you know, and today's the eighteenth."

Rubbing a hand over his beard, he clutched the paper, the figures swimming before his eyes.

"Have patience, senhora! Give me a little more time. Can't you wait—say—till the end of the week? I've been promised some steady work."

The smile vanished from her mouth. Her face took on a malignant expression, as she tightened her withered lips.

"I have already waited too long, Seo João. Since the fifth of the month. Every day it's the same old story with you. Wait, wait . . . por la Madonna! I'm sick and tired of waiting! Don't I have to pay the landlord too? Don't I have to eat? I can't wait any more, do you hear? I'm *not* the mother of humanity. . . ."

Although her *not* was barely audible, the word had a tragic ring.

A baby wailed in the room. He fingered his beard.

"But surely the senhora has heard," he explained. "My wife had a boy last week. . . . The expenses, you know

how it is. . . . That's why I couldn't pay you. And then—
I lost my job. . . ."

"And what business is that of mine? Why do you get
children? Am I to blame? I want the room. Try and move
out. If not I'll throw you into the street. I'm not going to
wait any longer!"

She walked out stiffly, her dress clinging tightly to her
like glue. Shutting the door, the man buried his face in
his hands, without daring to look at his wife, who was
crying near the infant.

"I'm going to have trouble with her yet," he whispered
to himself.

He came home late now, after the Italian woman had
gone to bed. His efforts to find some money, or to get
another room and move out, were fruitless. He began to
prowl the streets, bumming a cigarette here, sponging a
few cents there in order to buy his wife some food. For
her, life had suddenly become a hellish existence. She
could hardly go to the bathroom now without hearing the
Italian shouting, "Move out! Move out! Go wash yourself
elsewhere!"

Already she had no water. To bathe the baby, she had
to go down to the *cortico* in the rear, where the women
scrubbed their laundry. Afterwards she went to the toilet.
The Italian derived a cruel satisfaction now in pursuing
her. She bolted the latrine and hid the key the moment she
spied her tenant coming. The room was filthy, undescrib-
ably dirty, and the sharp, sickening odor of human urine
and excrement was almost unbearable. João fingered his
enormous beard dejectedly.

One night he found the Italian woman waiting for him
when he arrived home. It was past midnight. She leaned
back against the wall to let him pass.

"Good evening!"

"You did not expect to meet me, eh? I want you to pay for the room and get out. If not I shall call the police tomorrow."

"But . . ."

"Give me no *buts*. I don't want to hear your excuses. All day long you sleep and when night comes, you go out and get drunk. And yet you've got the nerve to talk to me about a job. I'm not supporting vagabonds. . . . Into the street! Into the street!"

"But my wife. . . ."

"That for your wife! All she does is dirty up my room, like a pig! She doesn't know how to do anything . . . not even wash clothes. Why doesn't she go out hustling, and find herself a man, like other women? That's all she's good for, anyway."

He stared at her for a moment, goggle-eyed. Then as the impact of her words came home to him, the room turned black before his eyes, and he lashed out furiously with his fist. She crumpled to the floor and lay there moaning weakly for a minute, but when she saw his hands reaching for her throat, she stumbled to her feet and dashed down the stairs, screaming for help. João dropped his arms listlessly, scratched his beard, and went back to the room to wait for the police.

Both the commissioner and the press vindicated the Italian completely. One of the papers even published a picture of her—a portrait taken in Milan when she was eighteen years old. João was sent to prison, and the furniture—a bed, chair, and clothes rack—was seized in payment for the lodging.

Translated by L. C. KAPLAN

Roberto Arlt (1900–1942) was the first novelist to break away from traditional realism toward a more inward fiction reflecting his personal experience of life. Born in Argentina, the son of German immigrants, he revolted against a miserable childhood under an autocratic father and left home at sixteen to work in the city at blue-collar jobs that made him intimate with the life of the proletariat. Following is a quote on Arlt from *Into the Mainstream*: "He knew the life of the down-and-out, the city's lunatic fringe, its Dostoevskian underworld. What he found there he portrayed with brilliant gutter humor in a series of works—culminating in *Los siete locos* ["The seven madmen"] and *Los lanzallamas* ["The flamethrowers"] —that were at once a complete rogues' gallery of marginal characters and a map of a city's spiritual slum. . . . Working in obscurity, he discovered a city and the language that went with it. He took its pulse and introduced its sights, its sounds, its slang, sacred and profane, into literature." Arlt became a member of the Boedo group, a circle of intellectuals who, in the 1920s, strongly insisted that art should be for the people (in contrast with the more sophisticated Florida group, which included Borges and represented a more élitist attitude toward literature). He worked for a while with Ricardo Güiraldes, author of *Don Segundo Sombra*. In the preface to *Los lanzallamas*, he disclaims any pretensions to "fine writing," saying that style is the luxury of those with money and leisure time but that those are the people who rarely take the time to write real literature. His writing suffers weaknesses in narrative structure, but in the broadest sense he goes to the "root of things." In the story that follows, taken from the collection *El jorobadito* ["The little hunchback"], Arlt captures the grotesqueness of two small-time businessmen consumed by hatred for each other.

Small-Time Property Owners

One night, Eufrasia, after dinner, said to Joaquín, her husband:

"You know what? I have the feeling that this guy next door steals materials from the poor guy he's building the house for."

Joaquín frowned at her sideways with his glass eyes.

"Where do you get that from?"

"Because today as it was getting dark, he arrived with the cart loaded with brick dust and covered up with sacks, to conceal it."

"That can't be."

"But it is, because yesterday he was carrying tiles under his arm, also wrapped in a torn bag, and you could see the edge."

"Well then . . . maybe so."

"Yes. . . , I noticed it too when he was on the other job. At first he would arrive early with his cart, and then,

when he was about to finish up, much later on in the
night, and with the cart always covered. They must have
built the awning with that material."

Taciturn, Joaquín replied:

"Of course, that way it's easy to build structures and
make awnings for yourself to make others jealous."

They spoke no more. They had dinner in silence and
Joaquín, broker and small-time property owner, had his
one eye as motionless as his other glass one.

Only as she was going to bed, when Eufrasia was about
to turn out the light, did she say, without looking at her
husband, in a voice slightly unnatural because she wanted
to make it natural:

"If the owner of the house knew . . . ."

"He'd have him put in jail," was the one-eyed man's
only comment. Then they went to bed and talked no more.

The two property owners hated each other with deceitful resentment.

That feeling had ripened in the warmth of dark contemptible acts, and the dissimilarity of misfortune that they
wished on one another tinged it with different colors.

Cosme, the bricklayer, would invoke some unforeseen
catastrophe on Joaquín's property. If you asked him, he
couldn't specify what kind of catastrophe it was that he
wished on his neighbor, since only in exceptional cases
would it get as far as death. And this lack of imagination
tormented him with fleeting but stormy anger, for he was
sure that if his wish came true, he would be happy.

On the other hand, Joaquín had objectified his wish.

He wanted the bricklayer to fall into financial ruin.

He imagined his neighbor not being able to make the
monthly payments on the land which they had each bought
on credit almost at the same time, and the mere act of
picturing the auctioneer's red flag waving in Cosme's
garden made him rejoice in a perverse way. He would

grind his teeth and his glass eye would give out a more intense sparkle than the other one, peeking out from under a thin, constantly wrinkled lid.

Two events were the origin of this hatred.

When Joaquín bought his land, he requested an estimate from Cosme for the house he was planning to build, and then logically, he gave the work to another bricklayer.

But, since he had to use his neighbor's adjoining wall, his neighbor, furious, demanded a price above the usual value and Joaquín, gnashing his teeth, refused to pay. One morning when the bricklayer wasn't there, he had the roof beams placed, temporarily sustained on two posts, so that when Cosme arrived it was too late to stop the work.

But since the amount involved was less than the sum required to open a court litigation (an impossibility which made the bricklayer furious, for he wanted to ruin Joaquín), the matter came to rest at a Justice of the Peace, and in the space of a year and a half Cosme, gloomy and stormy, passed through dirty courtrooms packed with clerks and boring uncouth clowns. He became aware of all the frauds used by those who don't want to pay and for a number of months he strained his brain seeking complex systems for murdering his neighbor, but since he was quite stupid, nothing occurred to him and finally, when he was at the point of desperation with regard to the earth's justice, he collected.

Time passed and the hatred grew, no longer with the brutal energy of the first year, for now that they were in repose, the resentment ripened in the shade, distilling in their bourgeois souls a juice which fattened their marrow, pouring out fierce projects into their souls and also a particular dark and watchful enjoyment: the feeling that one day the other "would pay for this."

The first stab in the back came from the bricklayer.

Joaquín built a small room without presenting the plans to the Municipality, and the most serious thing was that he didn't have a subfloor laid down according to regulations prescribed in the Digest.

Cosme found out, chatting with Joaquín's workman at the drink counter of the corner store, and he made this very serious infraction known to the area's Municipal Inspector.

The Inspector came and the broker had to pay a heavy fine, but not without first having watched the Inspector destroy his beautiful pitch pine floor, in order to verify the infraction.

That day a tear fell from his glass eye, while in the kitchen Eufrasia cursed her husband's lack of character for not picking a fight with the bricklayer, who that night sank into his sorry little bed muttering fierce, sweet words.

Seven months later the bricklayer bought a cart and horse to transport his materials to the job site, but he carelessly failed to build the stable in accordance with the specifications in the Municipal Digest. Joaquín, under the pretext of examining his own roof, climbed up on Cosme's roof and studied the temporary stable, then the issue was turned over to an inspector, and one fine day the bricklayer was hit with a fine, in addition to the order to construct a stable, which cost him more than the cart and horse.

The success of these slashes, lubricated with jurisprudence, did not wilt the hatred.

Joaquín couldn't even look at Cosme without trembling with rage, and the other's crude looks horrified him to the point of physical repulsion, for the bricklayer was small, stocky, stoop-shouldered, and in his testy little face there were always two smiling, self-satisfied, little green eyes. H's voice would come out the side of his mouth loaded with the "ghai" sound, and when Joaquín listened to him he would get chills, to the point of being physically ill. But they would chat nonetheless.

Because sometimes they did converse. The subject was the outlandish cost of bricks, or any old thing.

Joaquín, who needed a thousand bricks for the upcoming winter, would mention:

"They say they're going up to forty per thousand."

"Forty-five."

"But that's outrageous. Do you realize? A ten-peso increase per thousand."

And because of those extra five pesos that he would have to pay within four months, he would be there for an hour protesting with the other one against the country and its laws, in solidarity because of their common misfortune regarding the cost of material.

Being miserly was pleasant for them, and contrary to people in other circumstances, instead of hiding the defect, they would exhibit it like a virtue, delighting in their penny-pinching.

And Joaquín, who was more sensitive and romantic than Cosme, when talking of their destitution, looked exactly like the owner of a Loyola Street slum dwelling, and he would thus persist in his argument, hoping to become a fat cat property owner one day, who mends the wall at his front door with a bucket full of Roman cement.

The only thing he would reproach himself for was not being stingy enough.

In spite of this apparent cordiality, whenever he talked with the bricklayer he thought he could discern an immobile soul in the other's green pupils, heavy as a monster of raw meat, which blurred Cosme's sensations, his own harsh chitter-chatter suspending him in its timid smile.

He didn't argue with him, but usually agreed with whatever the bricklayer said, while all his nerves would rise up in silent contraction, which, as the next few days passed, would be translated in his thoughts into a red spasm like skin scarred from a burn. And his thoughts, like leeches, moved about in a homicidal world of muck.

On the other hand, the bricklayer could see himself falling on Joaquín with a dagger in his left hand.

It was at the dismal corner of his house, with garbage on the dirt sidewalk, and the gas lamp with its yellow light illuminating a circle from which Cosme would spring forth whenever the one-eyed man passed by.

And while his wishes went unfulfilled, his house diminished in value, and when Joaquín tried to sell it and received a visit from a buyer, Cosme, who heard the conversation through the low wall in the back, followed the stranger, and once the man had separated from Joaquín, Cosme summoned him, convincing him that the house was made of extremely poor materials, which fact was true.

Furthermore, this hatred was cared for, fertilized, tuned like violin strings, by their respective wives.

They would wish atrocious suffering on one another, which didn't stop them from having smiling conversations, flattering one another over trifles, giving each other honey-coated smiles in their salutations, exchanging with one another a mellifluous "Yes, madame" and "No, Mrs. A," for the broker's wife, who wore a hat and silk stockings, was "madame" for the other woman, who would wear only a housedress when she went out and would never go for a haircut. And since their properties were divided by a wire fence, they would talk at siesta hour, seeking each other out in spite of themselves, going to the garden to cut roses eaten up by the ants, or to ask one another the time, pretexts which linked inexhaustible conversations together, wherein they would bring out the life of the coal dealer's wife and the possibility of a streetcar on the next street over, or, with a touching concern, give one another advice about compotes and ways to prune plants.

The reverse of what would happen with the men would occur in their dialogues, that was that Cosme's wife always agreed with Joaquín's wife, imitating the conversational mode of "Madame Eufrasia," smiling with smiles that would bend the tip of her lip toward her left eye while in turn "madame" would move her head toward her coat front, in a gesture of understanding, one of the illiterate woman's characteristics, who had developed the tic in herself so as not to show her ignorance. For such a motion was a compound of understanding and indulgence, that is, the intelligent condition raised to its highest level, an unconscious discovery but one which the bricklayer's wife used correctly.

And the hatred they couldn't throw in one another's face, the near-repulsion which separated them, would create an attraction in these dialogues, and without noticing it, whenever they conversed, they were like those children who, fearful of the void, stick their heads out of high windows.

So now Joaquín couldn't sleep.

Unexpectedly an unrest had been introduced into his consciousness. It was that strange something, that certain quickening of time throughout his nerves, so that the blood, pushed by the frenetic action of minutes, running more rapidly, made his breathing anxious.

His life had been transformed abruptly, but why didn't his wife look at him before going to bed?

Thinking back on it, the tone of her voice sounded a little strange to him, as it now came to him slightly unnatural, through wanting the thought expressed to seem like the consequence of a natural act.

And although he was agitated, he wouldn't move.

Time never passed in the darkness, but off-center because of the anxiety of waiting, he felt that the longitudinal half of his body weighed more than the other half, due to a sudden off-center shift in his consciousness.

He didn't want to look out onto his thoughts, because it seemed to him that were he to raise his head, he would hit his forehead against them.

Then, half closing his eyes, he looked through the spaces in the shutters at the yellow cylinder that sadly fluctuated in the streetlight's lamp and realized that the wind was blowing in the street.

But he didn't move; he was so motionless that his wife's voice startled him when she asked:

"What's wrong? Why aren't you asleep?"

At midnight he was still awake.

The silence was so heavy in the black cube of a room, that it sounded like the warm whisper of ghosts breaking away from the walls. There was something horrible in the situation.

He had the feeling that his wife was sitting up next to the pillow, but he didn't recognize her, because out of that pleasant daytime countenance there was left only a bony profile with a raging nose and a terrible milky look which, crossing through his flesh, etched a terrible dictum in his consciousness.

So strong was the implacable call that, frightened, he turned over in his bed, at the same time that his wife asked him in a soft voice:

"What's wrong? Why aren't you asleep?"

They couldn't sleep.

The same heavy desire had hold of them, the same picture of disaster to unleash on the bricklayer; and Cosme's shape rose up before their eyes, oversized in the solitude of their narrow street, bent over in the driver's seat of his cart, with his hair tangled across his brow and glancing out of the corners of his greenish eyes at his red load of brick dust.

Or they saw this other vision: the police sergeant arriving at dawn at Cosme's house, announcing himself by clapping and suddenly, they, hiding behind the window which opens onto the garden, would hear:

"Madame . . . your husband is under arrest for theft!"

A heart-rending cry would cross the picture and the woman would faint on the tile patio, while they, solicitous, would come running to her rescue asking:

"What's wrong, Madame . . . what's happened?"

Joaquín, unable to bear the thought any longer, said aloud:

"No, they won't convict him for that."

"Why not?"

He let his arm rest on his wife's pillow and said:

"They'll give him two years in jail . . . but conditional . . . the only thing is the headache."

"I understand."

"I'm glad of that, because you're sensitive even if you don't want to be. Yes, that's true . . . the most that'll happen is they'll auction off the house . . ."

"Who will?"

"The owner of the other job . . . for damages."

In silence the couple got flashes of ideas, looking out onto the sinister judicial prospect of a Sunday afternoon, with their little street overrun with honest property owners, excited by an auction ordered by the judge. Nice mess for the neighborhood's gluttony!

They could see the red flag waving in the bamboo while they, safe, sealed inside "their own house," conversed in turn with the coal dealer and the baker's wife about the advantages of being honorable and the misfortunes occasioned by "getting your hands dirty for one lousy penny."

Savoring his words, Joaquín added:

"No one likes to pay . . . and the owner of the job, in order to have Cosme arrested and not let go of the money

he owes him, will have an admirable pretext in the fact
that the man was stealing from him. . . ."

"But such a miserable sum?"

Joaquín answered indignantly:

"A miserable sum? You're crazy! The other day they
arrested a carpenter for carrying off some boards and a
package of nails. Where would we end up if everyone did
what he wanted? No, hon, you have to have integrity!"

"Yes, your nose clean . . . but how are you going to
manage it?"

"Tomorrow I'll find out where the job site is . . . the
owner's address. . . ."

"Hey, you're not going to write them!"

"Yes, but I'll make it typewritten and anonymous."

"Just think how that big hypocrite, his wife, will react.
You know, yesterday, with the excuse of showing me a
pattern, she says to me: 'Oh, didn't you know?, when my
husband finishes the job we're going to put shutters on all
the doors.' And all that, you know what for? Just to get
my goat."

"Beastly people!"

"And to think you have to deal with them."

"Enough for now . . . tomorrow we'll take care of
them."

Joaquín yawned for a second, and tired by then, said:

"I'm going to sleep. See you tomorrow, dear."

"Aren't you going to give me a kiss?"

"Here . . . and sleep well."

Translated by Mary Jane Wilkie

Jorge Luis Borges (b. 1899) was born into a cultivated upper-middle-class family in Buenos Aires. He spent several years in Europe. In the Twenties—a time of great literary ferment in Argentina—Borges helped to found several literary magazines. He argued that art should be international, prose free of local idiom. In the 1940s he developed the form which he calls "fictions"—a merging of essay and short story, a form which, taking on the appearance of fact, is perfectly suited to one of his major themes: that facts are not truth. Among the collections of his fictions are *The Aleph and other Stories, Ficciones, Labyrinths,* and *A Personal Anthology.* He has also written poetry and essays and in 1940 he began his literary collaboration with Adolfo Bioy Casares, whom he had met in 1930 (see Bioy Casares' biography for a description of their work together). In 1946, having signed a manifesto against the dictator Perón, he lost his job as a librarian; as an insult was appointed city poultry inspector. He resigned to teach and write. In 1955, with the overthrow of Perón, Borges was named director of the Argentine National Library, and became professor of English and American literature at the University of Buenos Aires. Unable to read at the time because of failing eyesight, he has since become increasingly blind. In 1961 he shared the International Publishers' Prize with Samuel Beckett. Writing of Borges in his study of Latin American literature, David Gallagher says, "In Latin America, and especially in Argentina, Borges is usually either revered or detested. For the apostles of committed literature he is an irrelevant, reactionary aesthete. For others, he is the stylistic genius who has taught a whole generation of Latin American novelists to write Spanish . . . liberating fiction from the duty to document 'reality.' " The "coolly cerebral" Borges consistently aims to "reveal the gap that separates our intellectual aspirations from our intellectual limitations," as in the story "Death and the Compass."

Death and the Compass

To Mandie Molina Vedia
(1942)

Of the many problems ever to tax Erik Lönnrot's rash
mind, none was so strange—so methodically strange, let
us say—as the intermittent series of murders which came
to a culmination amid the incessant odor of eucalyptus
trees at the villa Triste-le-Roy. It is true that Lönnrot
failed to prevent the last of the murders, but it is undeni-
able that he foresaw it. Neither did he guess the identity
of Yarmolinsky's ill-starred killer, but he did guess the
secret shape of the evil series of events and the possible
role played in those events by Red Scharlach, also nick-
named Scharlach the Dandy. The gangster (like so many
others of his ilk) had sworn on his honor to get Erik
Lönnrot, but Lönnrot was not intimidated. Lönnrot
thought of himself as a pure logician, a kind of Auguste
Dupin, but there was also a streak of the adventurer and
even of the gambler in him.

The first murder took place in the Hôtel du Nord—that

tall prism which overlooks the estuary whose broad waters are the color of sand. To that tower (which, as everyone knows, brings together the hateful blank white walls of a hospital, the numbered chambers of a cell block, and the overall appearance of a brothel) there arrived on the third of December Rabbi Marcel Yarmolinsky, a gray-bearded gray-eyed man, who was a delegate from Podolsk to the Third Talmudic Congress. We shall never know whether the Hôtel du Nord actually pleased him or not, since he accepted it with the ageless resignation that had made it possible for him to survive three years of war in the Carpathians and three thousand years of oppression and pogroms. He was given a room on floor R, across from the suite occupied—not without splendor—by the Tetrarch of Galilee.

Yarmolinsky had dinner, put off until the next day a tour of the unfamiliar city, arranged in a closet his many books and his few suits of clothes, and before midnight turned off his bed lamp. (So said the Tetrarch's chauffeur, who slept in the room next door.) On the fourth of December, at three minutes past eleven in the morning, an editor of the *Jüdische Zeitung* called him by telephone. Rabbi Yarmolinsky did not answer; soon after, he was found in his room, his face already discolored, almost naked under a great old-fashioned cape. He lay not far from the hall door. A deep knife wound had opened his chest. A couple of hours later, in the same room, in the throng of reporters, photographers, and policemen, Inspector Treviranus and Lönnrot quietly discussed the case.

"We needn't lose any time here looking for three-legged cats," Treviranus said, brandishing an imperious cigar. "Everyone knows the Tetrarch of Galilee owns the world's finest sapphires. Somebody out to steal them probably found his way in here by mistake. Yarmolinsky woke up and the thief was forced to kill him. What do you make of it?"

"Possible, but not very interesting," Lönnrot answered. "You'll say reality is under no obligation to be interesting. To which I'd reply that reality may disregard the obligation but that we may not. In your hypothesis, chance plays a large part. Here's a dead rabbi. I'd much prefer a purely rabbinical explanation, not the imagined mistakes of an imagined jewel thief."

"I'm not interested in rabbinical explanations," Treviranus replied in bad humor; "I'm interested in apprehending the man who murdered this unknown party."

"Not so unknown," corrected Lönnrot. "There are his complete works." He pointed to a row of tall books on a shelf in the closet. There were a *Vindication of the Kabbalah,* a *Study of the Philosophy of Robert Fludd,* a literal translation of the *Sefer Yeçirah,* a *Biography of the Baal Shem,* a *History of the Hasidic Sect,* a treatise (in German) on the Tetragrammaton, and another on the names of God in the Pentateuch. The Inspector stared at them in fear, almost in disgust. Then he burst into laughter.

"I'm only a poor Christian," he said. "You may cart off every last tome if you feel like it. I have no time to waste on Jewish superstitions."

"Maybe this crime belongs to the history of Jewish superstitions," Lönnrot grumbled.

"Like Christianity," the editor from the *Jüdische Zeitung,* made bold to add. He was nearsighted, an atheist, and very shy.

Nobody took any notice of him. One of the police detectives had found in Yarmolinsky's small typewriter a sheet of paper on which these cryptic words were written:

The first letter of the Name has been uttered

Lönnrot restrained himself from smiling. Suddenly turning bibliophile and Hebraic scholar, he ordered a package made of the dead man's books and he brought them to his apartment. There, with complete disregard for the police investigation, he began studying them. One royal-octavo volume revealed to him the teachings of Israel Baal Shem Tobh, founder of the sect of the Pious; another, the magic and the terror of the Tetragrammaton, which is God's unspeakable name; a third, the doctrine that God has a secret name in which (as in the crystal sphere that the Persians attribute to Alexander of Macedonia) His ninth attribute, Eternity, may be found—that is to say, the immediate knowledge of everything under the sun that will be, that is, and that was. Tradition lists ninety-nine names of God; Hebrew scholars explain that imperfect cipher by a mystic fear of even numbers; the Hasidim argue that the missing term stands for a hundredth name—the Absolute Name.

It was out of this bookworming that Lönnrot was distracted a few days later by the appearance of the editor from the *Jüdische Zeitung*, who wanted to speak about the murder. Lönnrot, however, chose to speak of the many names of the Lord. The following day, in three columns, the journalist stated that Chief Detective Erik Lönnrot had taken up the study of the names of God in order to find out the name of the murderer. Lönnrot, familiar with the simplifications of journalism, was not surprised. It also seemed that one of those tradesmen who have discovered that any man is willing to buy any book was peddling a cheap edition of Yarmolinsky's *History of the Hasidic Sect*.

The second murder took place on the night of January third out in the most forsaken and empty of the city's western reaches. Along about daybreak, one of the police who patrol this lonely area on horseback noticed on the doorstep of a dilapidated paint and hardware store a man in a poncho laid out flat. A deep knife wound had ripped open his chest, and his hard features looked as though they were masked in blood. On the wall, on the shop's conventional red and yellow diamond shapes, were some words scrawled in chalk. The policeman read them letter by letter. That evening, Treviranus and Lönnrot made their way across town to the remote scene of the crime. To the left and right of their car the city fell away in shambles; the sky grew wider and houses were of much less account than brick kilns or an occasional poplar. They reached their forlorn destination, an unpaved back alley with rose-colored walls that in some way seemed to reflect the garish sunset. The dead man had already been identified. He turned out to be Daniel Simon Azevedo, a man with a fair reputation in the old northern outskirts of town who had risen from teamster to electioneering thug and later degenerated into a thief and an informer. (The unusual manner of his death seemed to them fitting, for Azevedo was the last example of a generation of criminals who knew how to handle a knife but not a revolver.) The words chalked up on the wall were these:

The second letter of the Name has been uttered

The third murder took place on the night of February third. A little before one o'clock, the telephone rang in the office of Inspector Treviranus. With pointed secrecy, a man speaking in a guttural voice said his name was Ginzberg (or Ginsburg) and that he was ready—for a reasonable consideration—to shed light on the facts surrounding the double sacrifice of Azevedo and Yarmolinsky. A racket of whistles and tin horns drowned out the informer's voice. Then the line went dead. Without discounting the possibility of a practical joke (they were, after all, at the height of Carnival), Treviranus checked and found that he had been phoned from a sailors' tavern called Liverpool House on the Rue de Toulon—that arcaded waterfront street in which we find side by side the wax museum and the dairy bar, the brothel and the Bible seller. Treviranus called the owner back. The man (Black Finnegan by name, a reformed Irish criminal concerned about and almost weighed down by respectability) told him that the last person to have used the telephone was one of his roomers, a certain Gryphius, who had only minutes before gone out with some friends. At once Treviranus set out for Liverpool House. There the owner told him the following story:

Eight days earlier, Gryphius had taken a small room above the bar. He was a sharp-featured man with a misty gray beard, shabbily dressed in black. Finnegan (who used that room for a purpose Treviranus immediately guessed) had asked the roomer for a rent that was obviously steep, and Gryphius paid the stipulated sum on the spot. Hardly ever going out, he took lunch and supper in his room; in fact, his face was hardly known in the bar. That night he had come down to use the telephone in Finnegan's office. A coupé had drawn up outside. The coachman had stayed on his seat; some customers recalled that he wore the mask of a bear. Two harlequins got out of the carriage. They were very short men and nobody could help noticing that they were very drunk. Bleating their horns, they burst into Finnegan's office, throwing their arms around Gryphius, who seemed to know them but who did not warm to their company. The three exchanged a few words in Yiddish—he in a low, guttural voice, they in a piping falsetto—and they climbed the stairs up to his room. In a quarter of an hour they came down again, very happy. Gryphius, staggering, seemed as drunk as the others. He walked in the middle, tall and dizzy, between the two

masked harlequins. (One of the women in the bar remembered their costumes of red, green, and yellow loz-
enges.) Twice he stumbled; twice the harlequins held him
up. Then the trio climbed into the coupé and, heading for
the nearby docks (which enclosed a string of rectangular
bodies of water), were soon out of sight. Out front, from
the running board, the last harlequin had scrawled an obscene drawing and certain words on one of the market
slates hung from a pillar of the arcade.

Treviranus stepped outside for a look. Almost predict-
ably, the phrase read:

The last letter of the Name has been uttered

He next examined Gryphius-Ginzberg's tiny room. On
the floor was a star-shaped spatter of blood; in the corners, cigarette butts of a Hungarian brand; in the wardrobe, a book in Latin—a 1739 edition of Leusden's
Philologus Hebraeo-Graecus—with a number of annota-
tions written in by hand. Treviranus gave it an indignant
look and sent for Lönnrot. While the Inspector questioned
the contradictory witnesses to the possible kidnapping,
Lönnrot, not even bothering to take off his hat, began
reading. At four o'clock they left. In the twisted Rue de
Toulon, as they were stepping over last night's tangle of
streamers and confetti, Treviranus remarked, "And if tonight's events were a put-up job?"

Erik Lönnrot smiled and read to him with perfect gravity an underlined passage from the thirty-third chapter of
the *Philologus*: " '*Dies Judaeorum incipit a solis occasu
usque ad solis occasum diei sequentis.*' Meaning," he
added, " 'the Jewish day begins at sundown and ends the
following sundown.' "

The other man attempted a bit of irony. "Is that the
most valuable clue you've picked up tonight?" he said.

"No. Far more valuable is one of the words Ginzberg used to you on the phone."

The evening papers made a great deal of these recurrent disappearances. *La Croix de l'Epée* contrasted the present acts of violence with the admirable discipline and order observed by the last Congress of Hermits. Ernst Palast, in *The Martyr,* condemned "the unbearable pace of this unauthorized and stinting pogrom, which has required three months for the liquidation of three Jews." The *Jüdische Zeitung* rejected the ominous suggestion of an anti-Semitic plot, "despite the fact that many penetrating minds admit of no other solution to the threefold mystery." The leading gunman of the city's Southside, Dandy Red Scharlach, swore that in his part of town crimes of that sort would never happen, and he accused Inspector Franz Treviranus of criminal negligence.

On the night of March first, Inspector Treviranus received a great sealed envelope. Opening it, he found it contained a letter signed by one "Baruch Spinoza" and, evidently torn out of a Baedeker, a detailed plan of the city. The letter predicted that on the third of March there would not be a fourth crime because the paint and hardware store on the Westside, the Rue de Toulon tavern, and the Hôtel du Nord formed "the perfect sides of an equilateral and mystical triangle." In red ink the map demonstrated that the three sides of the figure were exactly the same length. Treviranus read this Euclidean reasoning with a certain weariness and sent the letter and map to Erik Lönnrot—the man, beyond dispute, most deserving of such cranky notions.

Lönnrot studied them. The three points were, in fact, equidistant. There was symmetry in time (December third, January third, February third); now there was symmetry in space as well. All at once he felt he was on the verge of solving the riddle. A pair of dividers and a compass completed his sudden intuition. He smiled, pronounced the word Tetragrammaton (of recent acquisition) and called the Inspector on the phone.

"Thanks for the equilateral triangle you sent me last night," he told him. "It has helped me unravel our mystery. Tomorrow, Friday, the murderers will be safely behind bars; we can rest quite easy."

"Then they aren't planning a fourth crime?"

"Precisely because they *are* planning a fourth crime we can rest quite easy."

Lönnrot hung up the receiver. An hour later, he was traveling on a car of the Southern Railways on his way to the deserted villa Triste-le-Roy. To the south of the city of my story flows a dark muddy river, polluted by the waste of tanneries and sewers. On the opposite bank is a factory suburb where, under the patronage of a notorious political boss, many gunmen thrive. Lönnrot smiled to himself, thinking that the best-known of them—Red Scharlach—would have given anything to know about this sudden excursion of his. Azevedo had been a henchman of Scharlach's. Lönnrot considered the remote possibility that the fourth victim might be Scharlach himself. Then he dismissed it. He had practically solved the puzzle; the mere circumstances—reality (names, arrests, faces, legal and criminal proceedings)—barely held his interest now. He wanted to get away, to relax after three months of desk work and of snail-pace investigation. He reflected that the solution of the killings lay in an anonymously sent triangle and in a dusty Greek word. The mystery seemed almost crystal clear. He felt ashamed for having spent close to a hundred days on it.

The train came to a stop at a deserted loading platform. Lönnrot got off. It was one of those forlorn evenings that seem as empty as dawn. The air off the darkening prairies was damp and cold. Lönnrot struck out across the fields.

He saw dogs, he saw a flatcar on a siding, he saw the line of the horizon, he saw a pale horse drinking stagnant water out of a ditch. Night was falling when he saw the rectangular mirador of the villa Triste-le-Roy, almost as tall as the surrounding black eucalyptus trees. He thought that only one more dawn and one more dusk (an ancient light in the east and another in the west) were all that separated him from the hour appointed by the seekers of the Name.

A rusted iron fence bounded the villa's irregular perimeter. The main gate was shut. Lönnrot, without much hope of getting in, walked completely around the place. Before the barred gate once again, he stuck a hand through the palings—almost mechanically—and found the bolt. The squeal of rusted iron surprised him. With clumsy obedience, the whole gate swung open.

Lönnrot moved forward among the eucalyptus trees, stepping on the layered generations of fallen leaves. Seen from up close, the house was a clutter of meaningless symmetries and almost insane repetitions: one icy Diana in a gloomy niche matched another Diana in a second niche; one balcony appeared to reflect another; double outer staircases crossed at each landing. A two-faced Hermes cast a monstrous shadow. Lönnrot made his way around the house as he had made his way around the grounds. He went over every detail; below the level of the terrace he noticed a narrow shutter.

He pushed it open. A few marble steps went down into a cellar. Lönnrot, who by now anticipated the architect's whims, guessed that in the opposite wall he would find a similar sets of steps. He did. Climbing them, he lifted his hands and raised a trapdoor.

A stain of light led him to a window. He opened it. A round yellow moon outlined two clogged fountains in the unkempt garden. Lönnrot explored the house. Through serving pantries and along corridors he came to identical courtyards and several times to the same courtyard. He climbed dusty stairways to circular anterooms, where he was multiplied to infinity in facing mirrors. He grew weary of opening or of peeping through windows that revealed, outside, the same desolate garden seen from various heights and various angles; and indoors he grew weary of the rooms of furniture, each draped in yellowing slipcovers, and the crystal chandeliers wrapped in tarlatan. A bedroom caught his attention—in it, a single flower in a porcelain vase. At a touch, the ancient petals crumbled to dust. On the third floor, the last floor, the house seemed endless and growing. The house is not so large, he thought. This dim light, the sameness, the mirrors, the many years, my unfamiliarity, the loneliness are what make it large.

By a winding staircase he reached the mirador. That evening's moon streamed in through the diamond-shaped panes; they were red, green, and yellow. He was stopped by an awesome, dizzying recollection.

Two short men, brutal and stocky, threw themselves on him and disarmed him; another, very tall, greeted him solemnly and told him, "You are very kind. You've saved us a night and a day."

It was Red Scharlach. The men bound Lönnrot's wrists. After some seconds, Lönnrot at last heard himself saying, "Scharlach, are you after the Secret Name?"

Scharlach remained standing, aloof. He had taken no part in the brief struggle and had barely held out his hand for Lönnrot's revolver. He spoke. Lönnrot heard in his voice the weariness of final triumph, a hatred the size of the universe, a sadness as great as that hatred.

"No," said Scharlach. "I'm after something more ephemeral, more frail. I'm after Erik Lönnrot. Three years ago, in a gambling dive on the Rue de Toulon, you yourself arrested my brother and got him put away. My men managed to get me into a coupé before the shooting was over, but I had a cop's bullet in my guts. Nine days and nine nights I went through hell, here in this deserted villa, racked with fever. The hateful two-faced Janus that looks on the sunsets and the dawns filled both my sleep and my wakefulness with its horror. I came to loathe my body, I came to feel that two eyes, two hands, two lungs, are as monstrous as two faces. An Irishman, trying to convert me to the faith of Jesus, kept repeating to me the saying of the *goyim*—All roads lead to Rome. At night, my fever fed on that metaphor. I felt the world was a maze from which escape was impossible since all roads, though they seemed to be leading north or south, were really leading to Rome, which at the same time was the square cell where my brother lay dying and also this villa, Triste-le-Roy. During those nights, I swore by the god who looks with two faces and by all the gods of fever and of mirrors that I would weave a maze around the man who sent my brother to prison. Well, I have woven it and it's tight. Its materials are a dead rabbi, a compass, an eighteenth-century sect, a Greek word, a dagger, and the diamond-shaped patterns on a paint-store wall."

Lönnrot was in a chair now, with the two short men at his side.

"The first term of the series came to me by pure chance," Scharlach went on. "With some associates of mine—among them Daniel Azevedo—I'd planned the theft of the Tetrarch's sapphires. Azevedo betrayed us. He got drunk on the money we advanced him and tried to pull the job a day earlier. But there in the hotel he got mixed up and around two in the morning blundered into Yarmolinsky's room. The rabbi, unable to sleep, had decided to do some writing. In all likelihood, he was preparing notes or a paper on the Name of God and had already typed out the words 'The first letter of the Name has been uttered.'

Azevedo warned him not to move. Yarmolinsky reached his hand toward the buzzer that would have wakened all the hotel staff; Azevedo struck him a single blow with his knife. It was probably a reflex action. Fifty years of violence had taught him that the easiest and surest way is to kill. Ten days later, I found out through the *Jüdische Zeitung* that you were looking for the key to Yarmolinsky's death in his writings. I read his *History of the Hasidic Sect.* I learned that the holy fear of uttering God's Name had given rise to the idea that that Name is secret and all-powerful. I learned that some of the Hasidim, in search of that secret Name, had gone as far as to commit human sacrifices. The minute I realized you were guessing that the Hasidim had sacrificed the rabbi, I did my best to justify that guess. Yarmolinsky died the night of December third. For the second 'sacrifice' I chose the night of January third. The rabbi had died on the Northside; for the second 'sacrifice' we wanted a spot on the Westside. Daniel Azevedo was the victim we needed. He deserved death—he was impulsive, a traitor. If he'd been picked up, it would have wiped out our whole plan. One of my men stabbed him; in order to link his corpse with the previous one, I scrawled on the diamonds of the paint-store wall 'The second letter of the Name has been uttered.' "

Scharlach looked his victim straight in the face, then continued. "The third 'crime' was staged on the third of February. It was, as Treviranus guessed, only a plant. Gryphius-Ginzberg-Ginsburg was me. I spent an interminable week (rigged up in a false beard) in that flea-ridden cubicle on the Rue de Toulon until my friends came to kidnap me. From the running board of the carriage, one of them wrote on the pillar, 'The last letter of the Name has been uttered.' That message suggested that the series of crimes was *threefold.* That was how the public understood it. I, however, threw in repeated clues so that you, Erik Lönnrot the reasoner, might puzzle out that the crime was *fourfold*. A murder in the north, others in the east and west, demanded a fourth murder in the south. The Tetragrammaton—the Name of God, JHVH—is made up of *four* letters; the harlequins and the symbol on the paint store also suggest *four* terms. I underlined a certain passage in Leusden's handbook. That passage makes it clear that the Jews reckoned the day from sunset to sunset; that passage makes it understood that the deaths occurred on the *fourth* of each month. I was the one who sent the triangle to Treviranus, knowing in advance that you would supply the missing point—the point that determines the perfect rhombus, the point that fixes the spot where death is expecting you. I planned the whole thing, Erik Lönnrot, so as to lure you to the loneliness of Triste-le-Roy."

Lönnrot avoided Scharlach's eyes. He looked off at the trees and the sky broken into dark diamonds of red, green, and yellow. He felt a chill and an impersonal, almost anonymous sadness. It was night now; from down in the abandoned garden came the unavailing cry of a bird. Lönnrot, for one last time, reflected on the problem of the patterned, intermittent deaths.

"In your maze there are three lines too many," he said at last. "I know of a Greek maze that is a single straight line. Along this line so many thinkers have lost their way that a mere detective may very well lose his way. Scharlach, when in another incarnation you hunt me down, stage (or commit) a murder at A, then a second murder at B, eight miles from A, then a third murder at C, four miles from A and B, halfway between the two. Lay in wait for me then at D, two miles from A and C, again halfway between them. Kill me at D, the way you are going to kill me here at Triste-le-Roy."

"The next time I kill you," said Scharlach, "I promise

you such a maze, which is made up of a single straight line and which is invisible and unending."

He moved back a few steps. Then, taking careful aim, he fired.

Translated by NORMAN THOMAS DI GIOVANNI

Alejo Carpentier (b. 1904) was born in Havana, of a French father and a Russian mother who had moved to Cuba two years earlier. He loved architecture but went into journalism, becoming editor of the magazine *Carteles* in 1924. In 1927 he was imprisoned for seven months for signing a manifesto against the dictator Machado. On release, he fled to Paris with the help of the poet Robert Desnos and lived there for eleven years. There he was friendly with the Surrealists, who opened his eyes to the splendors of his birthplace. For years he read everything he could find about Latin America, at the same time active in publishing, journalism, and musicology. After a brief visit in 1936, he returned to Cuba to live in 1939 and for years lived by doing radio programs he hated. In 1943 he met the actor Louis Jouvet, who took him on a trip to Haiti where Carpentier found the subject of his second novel, *El reino de este mundo* [1949, "The kingdom of this world"], about the black Haitian monarch Henri Christophe. (His first novel, published in 1931, was an unsuccessful portrait of Afro-Cuban culture.) His third novel, *Los pasos perdidos* (1953, *The Lost Steps*), established his reputation. Written while he was living in Venezuela, and based partly on a trip he took up the Orinoco River into uninhabited zones, it is the story of a musician who flees an empty life in modern civilization to travel into the primitive equatorial jungle, a trip ultimately through time to prehistoric America. The novel *El siglo de las luces* (1962, *Explosion in the Cathedral*) deals with the French Revolution viewed from the Caribbean. He is now working on a trilogy about the Cuban Revolution. A collection of his short works, *Guerra del tiempo* (1958, *War of Time*) includes the story which follows here, interesting as an exercise with time. One of the most important novelists of his generation, Carpentier has also played a major role as literary statesman, helping to bring Latin American writers together where once they wrote in cultural isolation.

Journey Back to the Source

I

"What d'you want, pop?"

Again and again came the question, from high up on the scaffolding. But the old man made no reply. He moved from one place to another, prying into corners and uttering a lengthy monologue of incomprehensible remarks. The tiles had already been taken down, and now covered the dead flower beds with their mosaic of baked clay. Overhead, blocks of masonry were being loosened with picks and sent rolling down wooden gutters in an avalanche of lime and plaster. And through the crenellations that were one by one indenting the walls, were appearing—denuded of their privacy—oval or square ceilings, cornices, garlands, dentils, astragals, and paper hanging from the walls like old skins being sloughed by a snake.

Witnessing the demolition, a Ceres with a broken nose and discolored peplum, her headdress of corn veined with black, stood in the back yard above her fountain of crumbling grotesques. Visited by shafts of sunlight piercing the shadows, the gray fish in the basin yawned in the warm weed-covered water, watching with round eyes the black silhouettes of the workmen against the brilliance of the sky as they diminished the centuries-old height of the house. The old man had sat down at the foot of the statue, resting his chin on his stick. He watched buckets filled with precious fragments ascending and descending. Muted sounds from the street could be heard, while overhead, against a basic rhythm of steel on stone, the pulleys screeched unpleasantly in chorus, like harsh-voiced birds.

The clock struck five. The cornices and entablatures were depopulated. Nothing was left behind but stepladders, ready for tomorrow's onslaught. The air grew cooler, now that it was disburdened of sweat, oaths, creaking ropes, axles crying out for the oil can, and the slapping of hands on greasy torsos. Dusk had settled earlier on the dismantled house. The shadows had enfolded it just at that moment when the now-fallen upper balustrade used to enrich the façade by capturing the sun's last beams. Ceres tightened her lips. For the first time the rooms would sleep unshuttered, gazing onto a landscape of rubble.

Contradicting their natural propensities, several capitals lay in the grass, their acanthus leaves asserting their vegetable status. A creeper stretched adventurous tendrils toward an Ionic scroll, attracted by its air of kinship. When night fell, the house was closer to the ground. Upstairs, the frame of a door still stood erect, slabs of darkness suspended from its dislocated hinges.

II

Then the old Negro, who had not stirred, began making strange movements with his stick, whirling it around above a graveyard of paving stones.

The white and black marble squares flew to the floors and covered them. Stones leaped up and unerringly filled the gaps in the walls. The nail-studded walnut doors fitted themselves into their frames, while the screws rapidly twisted back into the holes in the hinges. In the dead flower beds, the fragments of tile were lifted by the thrust of growing flowers and joined together, raising a sonorous whirlwind of clay, to fall like rain on the framework of the roof. The house grew, once more assuming its normal proportions, modestly clothed. Ceres became less gray. There were more fish in the fountain. And the gurgling water summoned forgotten begonias back to life.

The old man inserted a key into the lock of the front door and began to open the windows. His heels made a hollow sound. When he lighted the lamps, a yellow tremor ran over the oil paint of the family portraits, and people dressed in black talked softly in all the corridors, to the rhythm of spoons stirring cups of chocolate.

Don Marcial, Marqués de Capellanías, lay on his deathbed, his breast blazing with decorations, while four tapers with long beards of melted wax kept guard over him.

III

The candles lengthened slowly, gradually guttering less and less. When they had reached full size, the nun extinguished them and took away the light. The wicks whitened, throwing off red sparks. The house emptied itself of visitors and their carriages drove away in the darkness. Don Marcial fingered an invisible keyboard and opened his eyes.

The confused heaps of rafters gradually went back into place. Medicine bottles, tassels from brocades, the scapulary beside the bed, daguerreotypes, and iron palm leaves from the grill emerged from the mists. When the doctor shook his head with an expression of professional gloom, the invalid felt better. He slept for several hours and awoke under the black beetle-browed gaze of Father Anastasio. What had begun as a candid, detailed confession of his many sins grew gradually more reticent, painful, and full of evasions. After all, what right had the Carmelite to interfere in his life?

Suddenly Don Marcial found himself thrown into the middle of the room. Relieved of the pressure on his temples, he stood up with surprising agility. The naked woman who had been stretching herself on the brocade coverlet began to look for her petticoats and bodices, and soon afterward disappeared in a rustle of silk and a waft of perfume. In the closed carriage downstairs an envelope full of gold coins was lying on the brass-studded seat.

Don Marcial was not feeling well. When he straightened his cravat before the pier glass he saw that his face was congested. He went downstairs to his study where lawyers —attorneys and their clerks—were waiting for him to arrange for the sale of the house by auction. All his efforts had been in vain. His property would go to the highest bidder, to the rhythm of a hammer striking the table. He bowed, and they left him alone. He thought how mysterious were written words: those black threads weaving and unweaving, and covering large sheets of paper with a filigree of estimates; weaving and unweaving contracts, oaths, agreements, evidence, declarations, names, titles, dates, lands, trees, and stones; a tangled skein of threads, drawn from the inkpot to ensnare the legs of any man who took a path disapproved of by the Law; a noose around his neck to stifle free speech at its first dreaded sound. He had been betrayed by his signature; it had handed him over to the nets and labyrinths of documents. Thus constricted, the man of flesh and blood had become a man of paper.

It was dawn. The dining-room clock had just struck six in the evening.

IV

The months of mourning passed under the shadow of ever-increasing remorse. At first the idea of bringing a woman to his room had seemed quite reasonable. But little by little the desire excited by a new body gave way to increasing scruples, which ended as self-torment. One night, Don Marcial beat himself with a strap till the blood came, only to experience even intenser desire, though it was of short duration.

It was at this time that the Marquesa returned one afternoon from a drive along the banks of the Almendares. The manes of the horses harnessed to her carriage were damp with solely their own sweat. Yet they spent the rest of the day kicking the wooden walls of their stable as if maddened by the stillness of the low-hanging clouds.

At dusk, a jar full of water broke in the Marquesa's bathroom. Then the May rains came and overflowed the lake. And the old Negress who unhappily was a maroon and kept pigeons under her bed wandered through the patio, muttering to herself: "Never trust rivers, my girl; never trust anything green and flowing!" Not a day passed without water making its presence felt. But in the end that presence amounted to no more than a cup spilled over a Paris dress after the anniversary ball given by the Governor of the Colony.

Many relatives reappeared. Many friends came back

again. The chandeliers in the great drawing room glittered with brilliant lights. The cracks in the façade were closing up, one by one. The piano became a clavichord. The palm trees lost some of their rings. The creepers let go of the upper cornice. The dark circles around Ceres' eyes disappeared, and the capitals of the columns looked as if they had been freshly carved. Marcial was more ardent now, and often passed whole afternoons embracing the Marquesa. Crow's-feet, frowns, and double chins vanished, and flesh grew firm again. One day the smell of fresh paint filled the house.

V

Their embarrassment was real. Each night the leaves of the screens opened a little farther, and skirts fell to the floor in obscurer corners of the room, revealing yet more barriers of lace. At last the Marquesa blew out the lamps. Only Marcial's voice was heard in the darkness.

They left for the sugar plantation in a long procession of carriages—sorrel hindquarters, silver bits, and varnished leather gleamed in the sunshine. But among the pasqueflowers empurpling the arcades leading up to the house, they realized that they scarcely knew each other. Marcial gave permission for a performance of native dancers and drummers, by way of entertainment during those days impregnated with the smells of eau de cologne, of baths spiced with benzoin, of unloosened hair and sheets taken from closets and unfolded to let a bunch of vetiver drop onto the tiled floor. The steam of cane juice and the sound of the angelus mingled on the breeze. The vultures flew low, heralding a sparse shower, whose first large echoing drops were absorbed by tiles so dry that they gave off a diapason like copper.

After a dawn prolonged by an inexpert embrace, they

returned together to the city with their misunderstandings settled and the wound healed. The Marquesa changed her traveling dress for a wedding gown and the married pair went to church according to custom, to regain their freedom. Relations and friends received their presents back again, and they all set off for home with jingling brass and a display of splendid trappings. Marcial went on visiting María de las Mercedes for a while, until the day when the rings were taken to the goldsmiths to have their inscriptions removed. For Marcial, a new life was beginning. In the house with the high grilles, an Italian Venus was set up in place of Ceres, and the grotesques in the fountain were thrown into almost imperceptibly sharper relief because the lamps were still glowing when dawn colored the sky.

VI

One night, after drinking heavily and being sickened by the stale tobacco smoke left behind by his friends, Marcial had the strange sensation that all the clocks in the house where striking five, then half past four, then four, then half past three . . . It was as if he had become dimly aware of other possibilities. Just as, when exhausted by sleeplessness, one may believe that one could walk on the ceiling, with the floor for a ceiling and the furniture firmly fixed between the beams. It was only a fleeting impression, and did not leave the smallest trace on his mind, for he was not much given to meditation at the time.

And a splendid evening party was given in the music room on the day he achieved minority. He was delighted to know that his signature was no longer legally valid, and that worm-eaten registers and documents would now vanish from his world. He had reached the point at which courts of justice were no longer to be feared, because his bodily existence was ignored by the law. After getting tipsy on noble wines, the young people took down from the wall a guitar inlaid with mother-of-pearl, a psaltery, and a serpent. Someone wound up the clock that played the *ranz-des-vaches* and the "Ballad of the Scottish Lakes." Someone else blew on a hunting horn that had been lying curled in copper sleep on the crimson felt lining of the showcase, beside a transverse flute brought from Aranjuez. Marcial, who was boldly making love to Señora de Campoflorido, joined in the cacophony, and tried to pick out the tune of "Trípili-Trápala" on the piano, to a discordant accompaniment in the bass.

They all trooped upstairs to the attic, remembering that the liveries and clothes of the Capellanías family had been stored away under its peeling beams. On shelves frosted with camphor lay court dresses, an ambassador's sword, several padded military jackets, the vestment of a dignitary of the Church, and some long cassocks with damask buttons and damp stains among their folds. The dark shadows of the attic were variegated with the colors of amaranthine ribbons, yellow crinolines, faded tunics, and velvet flowers. A picaresque *chispero*'s costume and hair net trimmed with tassels, once made for a carnival masquerade, was greeted with applause. Señora de Campoflorido swathed her powdered shoulders in a shawl the color of a Creole's skin, once worn by a certain ancestress on an evening of important family decisions in hopes of reviving the sleeping ardor of some rich trustee of a convent of Clares.

As soon as they were dressed up, the young people went back to the music room. Marcial, who was wearing an alderman's hat, struck the floor three times with a stick and announced that they would begin with a waltz, a dance mothers thought terribly improper for young ladies because they had to allow themselves be taken round the waist, with a man's hand resting on the busks of the stays they had all had made according to the latest model in the *Jardin des Modes*. The doorways were blocked by maid-servants, stableboys, and waiters, who had come from remote outbuildings and stifling basements to enjoy the boisterous fun. Afterward they played blindman's buff and hide-and-seek. Hidden behind a Chinese screen with Señora de Campoflorido, Marcial planted a kiss on her neck, and received in return a scented handkerchief whose Brussels lace still retained the sweet warmth of her low-necked bodice.

And when the girls left in the fading light of dusk, to return to castles and towers silhouetted in dark gray against the sea, the young men went to the dance hall, where alluring *mulatas* in heavy bracelets were strutting about without ever losing their high-heeled shoes, even in the frenzy of the guaracha. And as it was carnival time, the members of the Arara Chapter Three Eyes Band were raising thunder on their drums behind the wall in a patio planted with pomegranate trees. Climbing onto tables and stools, Marcial and his friends applauded the gracefulness of a Negress with graying hair, who had recovered her beauty and almost become desirable as she danced, look-ing over her shoulder with an expression of proud disdain.

VII

The visits of Don Abundio, the family notary and executor, were more frequent now. He used to sit gravely down beside Marcial's bed, and let his acana-wood cane drop to the floor so as to wake him up in good time. Opening his eyes, Marcial saw an alpaca frock coat cov-ered with dandruff, its sleeves shiny from collecting se-curities and rents. All that was left in the end was an adequate pension, calculated to put a stop to all wild extravagance. It was at this time that Marcial wanted to enter the Royal Seminary of San Carlos.

After doing only moderately well in his examinations, he attended courses of lectures, but understood less and less of his master's explanations. The world of his ideas was gradually growing emptier. What had once been a general assembly of peplums, doublets, ruffs, and peri-wigs, of controversialists and debaters, now looked as lifeless as a museum of wax figures. Marcial contented himself with a scholastic analysis of the systems, and accepted everything he found in a book as the truth. The words "Lion," "Ostrich," "Whale," "Jaguar" were printed under the copper-plate engravings in his natural history book. Just as "Aristotle," "St. Thomas," "Bacon," and "Descartes" headed pages black with boring, close-printed accounts of different interpretations of the universe. Bit by bit, Marcial stopped trying to learn these things, and felt relieved of a heavy burden. His mind grew gay and lively, understanding things in a purely instinctive way. Why think about the prism, when the clear winter light brought out all the details in the fortresses guarding the port? An apple falling from a tree tempted one to bite it—that was all. A foot in a bathtub was merely a foot in a bathtub. The day he left the seminary he forgot all about his books. A gnomon was back in the category of goblins; a spectrum a synonym for a phantom; and an octandrian an animal armed with spines.

More than once he had hurried off with a troubled heart to visit the women who whispered behind blue doors under the town walls. The memory of one of them, who wore embroidered slippers and a sprig of sweet basil behind her ear, pursued him on hot evenings like the toothache. But one day his confessor's anger and threats reduced him to terrified tears. He threw himself for the last time between those infernal sheets, and then forever renounced his detours through unfrequented streets and that last-minute faintheartedness which sent him home in a rage, turning his back on a certain crack in the pavement —the signal, when he was walking with head bent, that he must turn and enter the perfumed threshold.

Now he was undergoing a spiritual crisis, peopled by religious images, paschal lambs, china doves, Virgins in heavenly blue cloaks, gold paper stars, the three Magi, angels with wings like swans, the Ass, the Ox, and a terrible St. Denis, who appeared to him in his dreams with a great space between his shoulders, walking hesitantly as if looking for something he had lost. When he blundered into the bed, Marcial would start awake and reach for his rosary of silver beads. The lampwicks, in their bowls of oil, cast a sad light on the holy images as their colors returned to them.

VIII

The furniture was growing taller. It was becoming more difficult for him to rest his arms on the dining table. The fronts of the cupboards with their carved cornices were getting broader. The Moors on the staircase stretched their torsos upward, bringing their torches closer to the banisters on the landing. Armchairs were deeper, and rocking chairs tended to fall over backward. It was no longer necessary to bend one's knees when lying at the bottom of the bath with its marble rings.

One morning when he was reading a licentious book, Marcial suddenly felt a desire to play with the lead soldiers lying asleep in their wooden boxes. He put the book back in its hiding place under the washbasin, and opened a drawer sealed with cobwebs. His schoolroom table was too small to hold such a large army. So Marcial sat on the

floor and set out his grenadiers in rows of eight. Next
came the officers on horseback, surrounding the color
sergeant; and behind, the artillery with their cannon, gun
sponges, and linstocks. Bringing up the rear were fifes and
tabors escorted by drummers. The mortars were fitted
with a spring, so that one could shoot glass marbles to a
distance of more than a yard.

Bang! . . . Bang! . . . Bang!

Down fell horses, down fell standard-bearers, down fell
drummers. Eligio the Negro had to call him three times
before he could be persuaded to go to wash his hands and
descend to the dining room.

After that day, Marcial made a habit of sitting on the
tiled floor. When he realized the advantages of this position, he was surprised that he had not thought of it before.
Grown-up people had a passion for velvet cushions, which
made them sweat too much. Some of them smelled like
a notary—like Don Abundio—because they had not discovered how cool it was to lie at full length on a marble
floor at all seasons of the year. Only from the floor could
all the angles and perspectives of a room be grasped properly. There were beautiful grains in the wood, mysterious
insect paths and shadowy corners that could not be seen
from a man's height. When it rained, Marcial hid himself
under the clavichord. Every clap of thunder made the
sound box vibrate, and set all the notes to singing. Shafts
of lightning fell from the sky, creating a vault of cascad-
ing arpeggios—the organ, the wind in the pines, and the
crickets' mandolin.

IX

That morning they locked him in his room. He heard
whispering all over the house, and the luncheon they
brought him was too delicious for a weekday. There were

six pastries from the confectioner's in the Alameda—whereas even on Sundays after Mass he was only allowed two. He amused himself by looking at the engravings in a travel book, until an increasing buzz of sound coming under the door made him look out between the blinds. Some men dressed all in black were arriving, bearing a brass-handled coffin. He was on the verge of tears, but at this moment Melchor the groom appeared in his room, his boots echoing on the floor and his teeth flashing in a smile. They began to play chess. Melchor was a knight. He was the king. Using the tiles on the floor as a chessboard, he moved from one square to the next, while Melchor had to jump one forward and two sideways, or vice versa. The game went on until after dusk, when the fire brigade went by.

When he got up, he went to kiss his father's hand as he lay ill in bed. The Marqués was feeling better, and talked to his son in his usual serious and edifying manner. His "Yes, Father's" and "No, Father's" were fitted between the beads of a rosary of questions, like the responses of an acolyte during Mass. Marcial respected the Marqués, but for reasons that no one could possibly have guessed. He respected him because he was tall, because when he went out to a ball his breast glittered with decorations; because he envied him the saber and gold braid he wore as an officer in the militia; because at Christmas time, on a bet, he had eaten a whole turkey stuffed with almonds and raisins; because he had once seized one of the *mulatas* who were sweeping out the rotunda and had carried her in his arms to his room—no doubt intending to whip her. Hidden behind a curtain, Marcial watched her come out soon afterward, in tears and with her dress unfastened, and he was pleased that she had been punished, as she was the one who always emptied the jam pots before putting them back in the cupboard.

His father was a terrible and magnanimous being, and it was his duty to love him more than anyone except God. To Marcial he was more godlike even than God because his gifts were tangible, everyday ones. But he preferred the God in heaven because he was less of a nuisance.

X

When the furniture had grown a little taller still, and Marcial knew better than anyone what was under the beds, cupboards, and cabinets, he had a great secret, which he kept to himself: life had no charms except when Melchor the groom was with him. Not God, nor his father, nor the golden bishop in the Corpus Christi procession was as important as Melchor.

Melchor had come from a very long distance away. He was descended from conquered princes. In his kingdom there were elephants, hippopotamuses, tigers, and giraffes, and men did not sit working, like Don Abundio in dark rooms full of papers. They lived by outdoing the animals in cunning. One of them had pulled the great crocodile out of the blue lake after first skewering him on a pike concealed inside the closely packed bodies of twelve roast geese. Melchor knew songs that were easy to learn because the words had no meaning and were constantly repeated. He stole sweetmeats from the kitchens; at night he used to escape through the stable door, and once he threw stones at the police before disappearing into the darkness of the Calle de la Amargura.

On wet days he used to put his boots to dry beside the kitchen stove. Marcial wished he had feet big enough to fill boots like those. His right-hand boot was called Calambín; the left one Calambán. This man who could tame unbroken horses by simply seizing their lips between two fingers, this fine gentleman in velvet and spurs who wore such tall hats, also understood about the coolness of marble floors in summer, and used to hide fruits or a cake, snatched from trays destined for the drawing room, behind the furniture. Marcial and Melchor shared a secret store of sweets and almonds, which they saluted with "*Urí, urí, urá*" and shouts of conspiratorial laughter. They had both explored the house from top to bottom, and were the only ones who knew that beneath the stables there was a small cellar full of Dutch bottles, or that in an unused loft over the maids' rooms was a broken glass case containing twelve dusty butterflies that were losing their wings.

XI

When Marcial got into the habit of breaking things, he forgot Melchor and made friends with the dogs. There were several in the house. The large one with stripes like a tiger; the basset trailing its teats on the ground; the greyhound that had grown too old to play; the poodle that was chased by the others at certain times and had to be shut up by the maids.

Marcial liked Canelo best because he carried off shoes from the bedrooms and dug up the rose trees in the patio. Always black with coal dust or covered with red earth, he devoured the dinners of all the other dogs, whined without cause, and hid stolen bones under the fountain. And now and again he would suck dry a new-laid egg and send the hen flying with a sharp blow from his muzzle. Everyone kicked Canelo. But when they took him away, Marcial made himself ill with grief. And the dog returned in triumph, wagging his tail, from somewhere beyond the poorhouse where he had been abandoned, and regained his place in the house, which the other dogs, for all their skill in hunting, or vigilance when keeping guard, could never fill.

Canelo and Marcial used to urinate side by side. Sometimes they chose the Persian carpet in the drawing room, spreading dark, cloud-like shapes over its pile. This usually cost them a thrashing. But thrashings were less painful than grown-up people realized. On the other hand, they gave a splendid excuse for setting up a concerted howling and arousing the pity of the neighbors. When the cross-eyed woman from the top flat called his father a "brute," Marcial looked at Canelo with smiling eyes. They shed a few more tears so as to be given a biscuit, and afterward all was forgotten. They both used to eat earth, roll on the ground, drink out of the goldfish basin, and take refuge in the scented shade under the sweet-basil bushes. During the hottest hours of the day quite a crowd filled the moist flower beds. There would be the gray goose with her pouch hanging between her bandy legs; the old rooster with his naked rump; the little lizard who kept saying "*Urí, Urá*" and shooting a pink ribbon out of his throat; the melancholy snake, born in a town where there were no females; and the mouse that blocked its hole with a turtle's egg. One day someone pointed out the dog to Marcial.

"Bow-wow," Marcial said.

He was talking his own language. He had attained the ultimate liberty. He was beginning to want to reach with his hands things that were out of reach.

XII

Hunger, thirst, heat, pain, cold. Hardly had Marcial reduced his field of perception to these essential realities when he renounced the light that accompanied them.

He did not know his own name. The unpleasantness of the christening over, he had no desire for smells, sounds, or even sights. His hands caressed delectable forms. He was a purely sensory and tactile being. The universe penetrated him through his pores. Then he shut his eyes—they saw nothing but nebulous giants—and entered a warm, damp body full of shadows: a dying body. Clothed in this body's substance, he slipped toward life.

But now time passed more quickly, rarefying the final hours. The minutes sounded like cards slipping from beneath a dealer's thumb.

Birds returned to their eggs in a whirlwind of feathers. Fish congealed into roe, leaving a snowfall of scales at the bottom of their pond. The palm trees folded their fronds and disappeared into the earth like shut fans. Stems were reabsorbing their leaves, and the earth reclaimed everything that was its own. Thunder rumbled through the arcades. Hairs began growing from antelope-skin gloves. Woolen blankets were unraveling and turning into the fleece of sheep in distant pastures. Cupboards, cabinets, beds, crucifixes, tables and blinds disappeared into the darkness in search of their ancient roots beneath the forest trees. Everything that had been fastened with nails was disintegrating. A brigantine, anchored no one knew where, sped back to Italy carrying the marble from the floors and fountain. Suits of armor, ironwork, keys, copper cooking pots, the horses' bits from the stables, were melting and forming a swelling river of metal running into the earth through roofless channels. Everything was undergoing metamorphosis and being restored to its original state. Clay returned to clay, leaving a desert where the house had once stood.

XIII

When the workmen came back at dawn to go on with the demolition of the house, they found their task completed. Someone had carried off the statue of Ceres and sold it to an antique dealer the previous evening. After complaining to their trade union, the men went and sat on the seats in the municipal park. Then one of them remembered some vague story about a Marquesa de Capellanías who had been drowned one evening in May among the arum lilies in the Almendares. But no one paid any attention to his story because the sun was traveling from east to west, and the hours growing on the right-hand side of the clock must be spun out by idleness—for they are the ones that inevitably lead to death.

Translated by FRANCES PARTRIDGE

Octavio Paz (b. 1914) was born in Mexico City. In 1937 he went to Spain for a congress of antifascist writers, and when the congress was over he remained to support the Republicans in the Spanish Civil War, although he didn't fight. Before returning to Mexico in 1938, he went to Paris, where Alejo Carpentier introduced him to surrealist Robert Desnos. Back in Mexico he was politically active, wrote a daily article on international politics for the workers' paper, *El Popular*, and helped to found two literary magazines, *Taller* (1938) and *El hijo pródigo* (1943). In 1944 he came to the U.S. on a Guggenheim Fellowship; in 1945 he returned to Paris where he developed a close friendship with André Breton and the Surrealists, whose influence on his work is evident in the following story. The Fifties were a period of intense literary activity; not only did he write many books of poetry and essays, but he helped with Carlos Fuentes' *Revista Mexicana de Literatura*. In 1962 he went to India as ambassador, remaining until 1968 when he resigned in protest against his government's use of violence against student demonstrators in Mexico City. He has taught at Cambridge, the University of Texas at Austin, and now at Harvard. He founded and edits *Plural*, an international monthly cultural journal in Mexico City. Of the many volumes of poetry and essays that he has written, some of those available in English are *Sun Stone*; *Selected Poems*; *Configurations*; and *Renga* (poetry); and (prose) *The Labyrinth of Solitude*; *¿Aguila o Sol? Eagle or Sun?*; *Claude Levi-Strauss*; *Alternating Current*; *Conjunctions and Disjunctions*; and *The Bow and the Lyre*. His poetry, largely erotic, reflects his theory of poetry as communication, a way of breaking through man's solitude and restoring totality of being. His prose displays a stunning range of interests and influences. He is a major interpreter of his country, but his synthetic vision takes in cultures East and West, past and present. Between Rubén Darío, for whom Oriental subjects were a desirably exotic element in poetry, and Paz, who lived six years in the Orient, the world has truly changed.

The Blue Bouquet

When I woke up I was soaked with sweat. The floor of my room had been freshly sprinkled and a warm vapor was rising from the red tiles. A moth flew around and around the naked bulb, dazzled by the light. I got out of the hammock and walked barefoot across the room, being careful not to step on a scorpion if one had come out of its hiding place to enjoy the coolness of the floor. I stood at the window for a few minutes, breathing in the air from the fields and listening to the vast, feminine breathing of the night. Then I walked over to the washstand, poured some water into the enamel basin, and moistened a towel. I rubbed my chest and legs with the damp cloth, dried myself a little, and got dressed, first making sure that no bugs had got into the seams of my clothes. I went leaping down the green-painted staircase and blundered into the hotelkeeper at the door. He was blind in one eye, a glum and reticent man, sitting there in a rush chair, smoking a cigarette, with his eyes half closed.

171

Now he peered at me with his good eye. "Where are you going, señor?" he asked in a hoarse voice.

"To take a walk. It's too hot to stay in my room."

"But everything's closed up by now. And we don't have any streetlights here. You'd better stay in."

I shrugged my shoulders, mumbled, "I'll be right back," and went out into the darkness. At first I couldn't see anything at all. I groped my way along the stone-paved street. I lit a cigarette. Suddenly the moon came out from behind a black cloud, lighting up a weather-beaten white wall. I stopped in my tracks, blinded by that whiteness. A faint breeze stirred the air and I could smell the fragrance of the tamarind trees. The night was murmurous with the sounds of leaves and insects. The crickets had bivouacked among the tall weeds. I raised my eyes: up there the stars were also camping out. I thought that the whole universe was a grand system of signals, a conversation among enormous beings. My own actions, the creak of a cricket, the blinking of a star, were merely pauses and syllables, odd fragments of that dialogue. I was only one syllable, of only one word. But what was that word? Who was uttering it? And to whom? I tossed my cigarette onto the sidewalk. It fell in a glowing arc, giving off sparks like a miniature comet.

I walked on, slowly, for a long while. I felt safe and free, because those great lips were pronouncing me so clearly, so joyously. The night was a garden of eyes.

Then when I was crossing a street I could tell that someone had come out of a doorway. I turned around but couldn't see anything. I began to walk faster. A moment later I could hear the scuff of huaraches on the warm stones. I didn't want to look back, even though I knew the shadow was catching up with me. I tried to run. I couldn't. Then I stopped short. And before I could defend myself

I felt the point of a knife against my back, and a soft voice said, "Don't move, señor, or you're dead."

Without turning my head I asked, "What do you want?"

"Your eyes, señor." His voice was strangely gentle, almost embarrassed.

"My eyes? What are you going to do with my eyes? Look, I've got a little money on me. Not much, but it's something. I'll give you everything I've got if you'll let me go. Don't kill me."

"You shouldn't be scared, señor. I'm not going to kill you. I just want your eyes."

"But what do you want them for?"

"It's my sweetheart's idea. She'd like to have a bouquet of blue eyes. There aren't many people around here that have them."

"Mine won't do you any good. They aren't blue, they're light brown."

"No, señor. Don't try to fool me. I know they're blue."

"But we're both Christians, hombre! You can't just gouge my eyes out. I'll give you everything I've got on me."

"Don't be so squeamish." His voice was harsh now. "Turn around."

I turned around. He was short and slight, with a palm sombrero half covering his face. He had a long machete in his right hand. It glittered in the moonlight.

"Hold a match to your face."

I lit a match and held it up in front of my face. The flame made me close my eyes and he pried up my lids with his fingers. He couldn't see well enough, so he stood on tiptoes and stared at me. The match burned my fingers and I threw it away. He was silent for a moment.

"Aren't you sure now? They aren't blue."

"You're very clever, señor," he said. "Light another match."

I lit another and held it close to my eyes. He tugged at my sleeve. "Kneel down."

I knelt. He grabbed my hair and bent my head back. Then he leaned over me, gazing intently, and the machete came closer and closer till it touched my eyelids. I shut my eyes.

"Open them up," he told me. "Wide."

I opened my eyes again. The match-flame singed my lashes.

Suddenly he let go. "No. They're not blue. Excuse me." And he disappeared.

I huddled against the wall with my hands over my face. Later I got up and ran through the deserted streets for almost an hour. When I finally stumbled into the plaza I saw the hotelkeeper still sitting at the door. I went in without speaking to him. The next day I got out of that village.

Translated by LYSANDER KEMP

Julio Cortázar (b. 1914) was born in Brussels, of Argentine parents. At the age of four he returned to Argentina, and grew up in Banfield, outside of Buenos Aires. His father left home when he was small, and his mother reared and educated him at some sacrifice; when he was twenty he gave up his university studies to teach high school in the country. There he began to write short stories. In 1946 his first story was published by Jorge Luis Borges. His stories have since been collected in this country in *The End of the Game and Other Stories, Cronopios and Famas,* and *All Fires the Fire.* In 1960 he published the novel, *Los premios (The Winners),* in which a group of strangers win a free cruise as a lottery prize but aren't allowed to be curious about their destination—they quickly divide into those who break rules and those who don't. *Rayuela (Hopscotch)* appeared in 1963, an anti-novel with interchangeable parts, which supports the theme of anarchy in a world where the order is absurd. In 1968 he published *62. Modelo para armar (62: A Model Kit),* based on a chapter in *Rayuela Libro de Manuel* ["The book of Manuel," 1975] is reminiscent of *Rayuela.* Cortázar has also written translations, poetry, essays, and literary criticism, some of which are collected in two miscellanies: *La vuelta al día en ochenta mundos* ["Around the day in eighty worlds," 1967] and *Ultimo Round* (1969). Two of his stories have been the bases for movies—Antonioni's *Blow-Up* and Godard's *Week-End.* He has made his home in Paris since 1951. In his short stories he applies a surrealistic fantasy to the normal, if not tedious situations of daily life, leading his characters determinedly, if briefly, toward a glimpse at the "cracks in reality." As J. M. Alonso wrote in the Winter '72 *Review,* whereas the narrator in a Borges story is always bookish and self-effacing, in Cortázar's works, the narrator's subjectivity becomes the subject of the story itself and his pain is part of its importance. For him, "invasion by the imaginary eventually turns out to be a subject with tragic implications" and the narrator mourns the loss of reality, although in the meantime the problems created by the invasion of unreality may appear to the reader as comical.

Letter to a Young Lady in Paris

Andrea, I didn't want to come live in your apartment in
the calle Suipacha. Not so much because of the bunnies,
but rather that it offends me to intrude on a compact order,
built even to the finest nets of air, networks that in your
environment conserve the music in the lavender, the heavy
fluff of the powder puff in the talcum, the play between
the violin and the viola in Ravel's quartet. It hurts me to
come into an ambience where someone who lives beautifully has arranged everything like a visible affirmation of
her soul, here the books (Spanish on one side, French and
English on the other), the large green cushions there, the
crystal ashtray that looks like a soap-bubble that's been cut
open on this exact spot on the little table, and always a
perfume, a sound, a sprouting of plants, a photograph
of the dead friend, the ritual of tea trays and sugar tongs
. . . Ah, dear Andrea, how difficult it is to stand counter
to, yet to accept with perfect submission of one's whole
being, the elaborate order that a woman establishes in her

own gracious flat. How much at fault one feels taking a small metal tray and putting it at the far end of the table, setting it there simply because one has brought one's English dictionaries and it's at this end, within easy reach of the hand, that they ought to be. To move that tray is the equivalent of an unexpected horrible crimson in the middle of one of Ozenfant's painterly cadences, as if suddenly the strings of all the double basses snapped at the same time with the same dreadful whiplash at the most hushed instant in a Mozart symphony. Moving that tray alters the play of relationships in the whole house, of each object with another, of each moment of their soul with the soul of the house and its absent inhabitant. And I cannot bring my fingers close to a book, hardly change a lamp's cone of light, open the piano bench, without a feeling of rivalry and offense swinging before my eyes like a flock of sparrows.

You know why I came to your house, to your peaceful living room scooped out of the noonday light. Everything looks so natural, as always when one does not know the truth. You've gone off to Paris, I am left with the apartment in the calle Suipacha, we draw up a simple and satisfactory plan convenient to us both until September brings you back again to Buenos Aires and I amble off to some other house where perhaps . . . But I'm not writing you for that reason, I was sending this letter to you because of the rabbits, it seems only fair to let you know; and because I like to write letters, and maybe too because it's raining.

I moved last Thursday in a haze overlaid by weariness, at five in the afternoon. I've closed so many suitcases in my life, I've passed so many hours preparing luggage that never mangages to get moved anyplace, that Thursday was a day full of shadows and straps, because when I look at valise straps it's as though I were seeing shadows, as though they were parts of a whip that flogs me in some indirect way, very subtly and horribly. But I packed the bags, let your maid know I was coming to move in. I was going up in the elevator and just between the first and second floors I felt that I was going to vomit up a little rabbit. I have never described this to you before, not so much, I don't think, from lack of truthfulness as that, just naturally, one is not going to explain to people at large that from time to time one vomits up a small rabbit. Always I have managed to be alone when it happens, guarding the fact much as we guard so many of our privy acts, evidences of our physical selves which happen to us in total privacy. Don't reproach me for it, Andrea, don't blame me. Once in a while it happens that I vomit up a bunny. It's no reason not to live in whatever house, it's no reason for one to blush and isolate oneself and to walk around keeping one's mouth shut.

When I feel that I'm going to bring up a rabbit, I put two fingers in my mouth like an open pincer, and I wait to feel the lukewarm fluff rise in my throat like the effervescence in a sal hepatica. It's all swift and clean, passes in the briefest instant. I remove the fingers from my mouth and in them, held fast by the ears, a small white rabbit. The bunny appears to be content, a perfectly normal bunny only very tiny, small as a chocolate rabbit, only it's white and very thoroughly a rabbit. I set it in the palm of my hand, I smooth the fluff, caressing it with two fingers; the bunny seems satisfied with having been born and waggles and pushes its muzzle against my skin, moving it with that quiet and tickling nibble of a rabbit's mouth against the skin of the hand. He's looking for something to eat, and then (I'm talking about when this happened at my house on the outskirts) I take him with me out to the balcony and set him down in the big flowerpot among the clover that I've grown there with this in mind. The bunny raises his ears as high as they can go, surrounds a tender clover leaf with a quick little wheeling motion of his snout, and I know that I can leave him there now and go on my way for a time, lead a life not very different from people who buy their rabbits at farmhouses.

Between the first and the second floors, then, Andrea, like an omen of what my life in your house was going to be, I realized that I was going to vomit a rabbit. At that point I was afraid (or was it surprise? No, perhaps fear of the same surprise) because, before leaving my house, only two days before, I'd vomited a bunny and so was safe for a month, five weeks, maybe six with a little luck. Now, look, I'd resolved the problem perfectly. I grew clover on the balcony of my other house, vomited a bunny, put it in with the clover and at the end of a month, when I suspected that any moment . . . then I made a present of the rabbit, already grown enough, to señora de Molina, who believed I had a hobby and was quiet about it. In another flowerpot tender and propitious clover was already growing, I awaited without concern the morning when the tickling sensation of fluff rising obstructed my throat, and the new little rabbit reiterated from that hour the life and habits of its predecessor. Habits, Andrea, are concrete forms of rhythm, are that portion of rhythm which helps to keep us alive. Vomiting bunnies wasn't so terrible once one had gotten into the unvarying cycle, into the method. You will want to know why all this work, why all that clover and señora de Molina. It would have been easier to kill the little thing right away and . . . Ah, you should vomit one up all by yourself, take it in two fingers, and set it in your opened hand, still attached to yourself by the act itself, by the indefinable aura of its proximity, barely now broken away. A month puts a lot of things at a distance; a month is size, long fur, long leaps, ferocious eyes, an absolute difference. Andrea, a month is a rabbit, it really makes a real rabbit; but in the maiden moment, the warm bustling fleece covering an inalienable presence . . . like a poem in its first minutes, "fruit of an Idumean night" as much one as oneself . . . and afterwards not so much one, so distant and isolated in its flat white world the size of a letter.

With all that, I decided to kill the rabbit almost as soon as it was born. I was going to live at your place for four months: four, perhaps with luck three—tablespoonsful of alcohol down its throat. (Do you know pity permits you to kill a small rabbit instantly by giving it a tablespoon of alcohol to drink? Its flesh tastes better afterward, they say, however, I . . . Three or four tablespoonsful of alcohol, then the bathroom or a package to put in the rubbish.)

Rising up past the third floor, the rabbit was moving in the palm of my hand. Sara was waiting upstairs to help me get the valises in . . . Could I explain that it was a whim? Something about passing a pet store? I wrapped the tiny creature in my handkerchief, put him into my overcoat pocket, leaving the overcoat unbuttoned so as not to squeeze him. He barely budged. His miniscule consciousness would be revealing important facts: that life is a movement upward with a final click, and is also a low ceiling, white and smelling of lavender, enveloping you in the bottom of a warm pit.

Sara saw nothing, she was too fascinated with the arduous problem of adjusting her sense of order to my valise-and-footlocker, my papers and my peevishness at her elaborate explanations in which the words "for example" occurred with distressing frequency. I could hardly get the bathroom door closed; to kill it now. A delicate area of heat surrounded the handkerchief, the little rabbit was extremely white and, I think, prettier than the others. He wasn't looking at me, he just hopped about and was being content, which was even worse than looking at me. I shut him in the empty medicine chest and went on unpacking, disoriented but not unhappy, not feeling guilty, not soaping up my hands to get off the feel of a final convulsion.

I realized that I could not kill him. But that same night I vomited a little black bunny. And two days later another white one. And on the fourth night a tiny grey one.

You must love the handsome wardrobe in your bedroom, with its great door that opens so generously, its empty shelves awaiting my clothes. Now I have them in there. Inside there. True, it seems impossible; not even Sara would believe it. That Sara did not suspect anything, was the result of my continuous preoccupation with a task that takes over my days and nights with the singleminded crash of the portcullis falling, and I go about hardened inside, calcined like that starfish you've put above the bathtub, and at every bath I take it seems all at once to swell with salt and whiplashes of sun and great rumbles of profundity.

They sleep during the day. There are ten of them. During the day they sleep. With the door closed, the wardrobe is a diurnal night for them alone, there they sleep out their night in a sedate obedience. When I leave for work I take the bedroom keys with me. Sara must think that I mistrust her honesty and looks at me doubtfully, every morning she looks as though she's about to say something to me, but in the end she remains silent and I am that much happier. (When she straightens up the bedroom between nine and ten, I make noise in the living room, put on a Benny Carter record which fills the whole apartment, and as Sara is a *saetas* and *pasodobles* fan, the wardrobe seems to be silent, and for the most part it is, because for the rabbits it's night still and repose is the order of the day.)

Their day begins an hour after supper when Sara brings in the tray with the delicate tinkling of the sugar tongs, wishes me good night—yes, she wishes me, Andrea, the most ironic thing is that she wishes me good night—shuts herself in her room, and promptly I'm by myself, alone with the closed-up wardrobe, alone with my obligation and my melancholy.

I let them out, they hop agilely to the party in the living room, sniffing briskly at the clover hidden in my pockets which makes ephemeral lacy patterns on the carpet which they alter, remove, finish up in a minute. They eat well, quietly and correctly; until that moment I have nothing to say, I just watch them from the sofa, a useless book in my hand—I who wanted to read all of Giraudoux, Andrea, and López's Argentine history that you keep on the lower shelf—and they eat up the clover.

There are ten. Almost all of them white. They lift their warm heads toward the lamps in the living room, the three motionless suns of their day; they love the light because their night has neither moon nor sun nor stars nor streetlamps. They gaze at their triple sun and are content. That's when they hop about on the carpet, into the chairs, ten tiny blotches shift like a moving constellation from one part to another, while I'd like to see them quiet, see them at my feet and being quiet—somewhat the dream of any god, Andrea, a dream the gods never see fulfilled—something quite different from wriggling in behind the portrait of Miguel de Unamuno, then off to the pale green urn, over into the dark hollow of the writing desk, always fewer than ten, always six or eight and I asking myself where the two are that are missing, and what if Sara should get up for some reason, and the presidency of Rivadavia which is what I want to read in López's history.

Andrea, I don't know how I stand up under it. You remember that I came to your place for some rest. It's not my fault if I vomit a bunny from time to time, if this moving changed me inside as well—not nominalism, it's not magic either, it's just that things cannot alter like that all at once, sometimes things reverse themselves brutally and when you expect the slap on the right cheek—. Like that, Andrea, or some other way, but always like that.

It's night while I'm writing you. It's three in the afternoon, but I'm writing you during their night. They sleep during the day. What a relief this office is! Filled with shouts, commands, Royal typewriters, vice presidents and mimeograph machines! What relief, what peace, what horror, Andrea! They're calling me to the telephone now. It was some friends upset about my monasterial nights, Luis inviting me out for a stroll or Jorge insisting—he's bought a ticket for me for this concert. I hardly dare to say no to them, I invent long and ineffectual stories about my poor health, I'm behind in the translations, any evasion possible. And when I get back home and am in the elevator—that stretch between the first and second floors—night after night, hopelessly, I formulate the vain hope that really it isn't true.

I'm doing the best I can to see that they don't break your things. They've nibbled away a little at the books on the lowest shelf, you'll find the backs repasted, which I did so that Sara wouldn't notice it. That lamp with the porcelain belly full of butterflies and old cowboys, do you like that very much? The crack where the piece was broken out barely shows, I spent a whole night doing it with a special cement that they sold me in an English shop—you know the English stores have the best cements—and now I sit beside it so that one of them can't reach it again with its paws (it's almost lovely to see how they like to stand on their hind legs, nostalgia for that so-distant humanity, perhaps an imitation of their god walking about and looking at them darkly; besides which, you will have observed

—when you were a baby, perhaps—that you can put a bunny in the corner against the wall like a punishment, and he'll stand there, paws against the wall and very quiet, for hours and hours).

At 5 A.M. (I slept a little stretched out on the green sofa, waking up at every velvety-soft dash, every slightest clink) I put them in the wardrobe and do the cleaning up. That way Sara always finds everything in order, although at times I've noticed a restrained astonishment, a stopping to look at some object, a slight discoloration in the carpet, and again the desire to ask me something, but then I'm whistling Franck's *Symphonic Variations* in a way that always prevents her. How can I tell you about it, Andrea, the minute mishaps of this soundless and vegetal dawn, half-asleep on what staggered path picking up butt-ends of clover, individual leaves, white hunks of fur, falling against the furniture, crazy from lack of sleep, and I'm behind in my Gide, Troyat I haven't gotten to translating, and my reply to a distant young lady who will be asking herself already if . . . why go on with all this, why go on with this letter I keep trying to write between telephone calls and interviews.

Andrea, dear Andrea, my consolation is that there are ten of them and no more. It's been fifteen days since I held the last bunny in the palm of my hand, since then nothing, only the ten of them with me, their diurnal night and growing, ugly already and getting long hair, adolescents now and full of urgent needs and crazy whims, leaping on top of the bust of Antinoös (it is Antinoös, isn't it, that boy who looks blindly?) or losing themselves in the living room where their movements make resounding thumps, so much so that I ought to chase them out of there for fear that Sara will hear them and appear before me in a fright and probably in her nightgown—it would have to be like that with Sara, she'd be in her nightgown—and then . . .

Only ten, think of that little happiness I have in the middle of it all, the growing calm with which, on my return home, I cut past the rigid ceilings of the first and second floors.

I was interrupted because I had to attend a committee meeting. I'm continuing the letter here at your house, Andrea, under the soundless grey light of another dawn. Is it really the next day, Andrea? A bit of white on the page will be all you'll have to represent the bridge, hardly a period on a page between yesterday's letter and today's. How tell you that in that interval everything has gone smash? Where you see that simple period I hear the circling belt of water break the dam in its fury, this side of the paper for me, this side of my letter to you I can't write with the same calm which I was sitting in when I had to put it aside to go to the committee meeting. Wrapped in their cube of night, sleeping without a worry in the world, eleven bunnies; perhaps even now, but no, not now— In the elevator then, or coming into the building; it's not important now where, if the when is now, if it can happen in any now of those that are left to me.

Enough now, I've written this because it's important to me to let you know that I was not all that responsible for the unavoidable and helpless destruction of your home. I'll leave this letter here for you, it would be indecent if the mailman should deliver it some fine clear morning in Paris. Last night I turned the books on the second shelf in the other direction; they were already reaching that high, standing up on their hind legs or jumping, they gnawed off the backs to sharpen their teeth—not that they were hungry, they had all the clover I had bought for them, I store it in the drawers of the writing desk. They tore the curtains, the coverings on the easy chairs, the edge of Augusto Torres' self-portrait, they got fluff all over the rug and besides they yipped, there's no word for it, they stood in a circle under the light of the lamp, in a circle as though they were adoring me, and suddenly they were yipping, they were crying like I never believed rabbits could cry.

I tried in vain to pick up all the hair that was ruining the rug, to smooth out the edges of the fabric they'd chewed on, to shut them up again in the wardrobe. Day is coming, maybe Sara's getting up early. It's almost queer, I'm not disturbed so much about Sara. It's almost queer, I'm not disturbed to see them gamboling about looking for something to play with. I'm not so much to blame, you'll see when you get here that I've repaired a lot of the things that were broken with the cement I bought in the English shop, I did what I could to keep from being a nuisance . . . As far as I'm concerned, going from ten to eleven is like an unbridgeable chasm. You understand: ten was fine, with a wardrobe, clover and hope, so many things could happen for the better. But not with eleven, because to say eleven is already to say twelve for sure, and Andrea, twelve would be thirteen. So now it's dawn and a cold solitude in which happiness ends, reminiscences, you and perhaps a good deal more. This balcony over the street is filled with dawn, the first sounds of the city waking. I don't think it will be difficult to pick up eleven small rabbits splattered over the pavement, perhaps they won't even be noticed, people will be too occupied with the other body, it would be more proper to remove it quickly before the early students pass through on their way to school.

Translated by PAUL BLACKBURN

João Guimarães Rosa (1908–1967) was born in Cordisburgo, in Minas Gerais, at the edge of Brazil's *sertão*, the vast highland expanse that covers a third of that big country. Reared on a farm, he studied medicine as a young man and practiced it during a local war. In 1934 he left medicine to enter the diplomatic service, serving in Hamburg, Colombia, and Paris, and as delegate to UNESCO, returning to Rio as Cabinet Chief in the Foreign Ministry until 1953. Then, in charge of the Department of Frontier Demarcation, he had frequent occasion to revisit his sources, the isolated backlands of the interior state of Minas Gerais, of which he writes. *Sagarana*, published in 1946 when he was 38, and under the same title here, was his first book, a collection of nine stories about life on the *sertão*, good storytelling in a more leisurely style than his later stories. In 1956 a collection of seven short novels was published (*Corpo de Baile*), the same year as his most famous book, the long novel *Grande Sertão: Veredas (The Devil to Pay in the Backlands)*, a monumental epic in which a bandit looks back on his life on the *sertão;* this is considered by many to be one of the finest novels in Latin America. In 1962 a volume of 21 very short stories was published as *Primeiras Estorias (The Third Bank of the River)*—the stories were more compressed, provided fewer details of life in the backland, and were more concerned with metaphysical themes, as in the title story reprinted below. *Tutameia: Terceiras Estorias* was published in 1967, three months before his death, and contained forty very short stories and some prefaces. *Estas Estorias*, containing nine short novels, came out posthumously in 1969. As time went by, Guimarães Rosa searched for greater economy and discipline in his story writing; at the time of his interview for *Into the Mainstream* he was writing two-page stories for a medical journal. Perhaps more than most writers, he suffers from translation. He was a brilliant linguist; and it is said he reinvented Portuguese as Joyce had earlier reinvented English.

The Third Bank of the River

Father was a reliable, law-abiding, practical man, and had been ever since he was a boy, as various people of good sense testified when I asked them about him. I don't remember that he seemed any crazier or even any moodier than anyone else we knew. He just didn't talk much. It was our mother who gave the orders and scolded us every day—my sister, my brother, and me. Then one day my father ordered a canoe for himself.

He took the matter very seriously. He had the canoe made to his specifications of fine *vinhático* wood; a small one, with a narrow board in the stern as though to leave only enough room for the oarsman. Every bit of it was hand-hewn of special strong wood carefully shaped, fit to last in the water for twenty or thirty years. Mother railed at the idea. How could a man who had never fiddled away his time on such tricks propose to go fishing and hunting now, at his time of life? Father said nothing. Our house was closer to the river then than it is now, less

189

than a quarter of a league away: there rolled the river, great, deep, and silent, always silent. It was so wide that you could hardly see the bank on the other side. I can never forget the day the canoe was ready.

Neither happy nor excited nor downcast, Father pulled his hat well down on his head and said one firm goodbye. He spoke not another word, took neither food nor other supplies, gave no parting advice. We thought Mother would have a fit, but she only blanched white, bit her lip, and said bitterly: "Go or stay; but if you go, don't you ever come back!" Father left his answer in suspense. He gave me a mild look and motioned me to go aside with him a few steps. I was afraid of Mother's anger, but I obeyed anyway, that time. The turn things had taken gave me the courage to ask: "Father, will you take me with you in that canoe?" But he just gave me a long look in return: gave me his blessing and motioned me to go back. I pretended to go, but instead turned off into a deep woodsy hollow to watch. Father stepped into the canoe, untied it, and began to paddle off. The canoe slipped away, a straight, even shadow like an alligator, slithery, long.

Our father never came back. He hadn't gone anywhere. He stuck to that stretch of the river, staying halfway across, always in the canoe, never to spring out of it, ever again. The strangeness of that truth was enough to dismay us all. What had never been before, was. Our relatives, the neighbors, and all our acquaintances met and took counsel together.

Mother, though, behaved very reasonably, with the result that everybody believed what no one wanted to put into words about our father: that he was mad. Only a few of them thought he might be keeping a vow, or—who could tell—maybe he was sick with some hideous disease like leprosy, and that was what had made him desert us

to live out another life, close to his family and yet far
enough away. The news spread by word of mouth, carried
by people like travelers and those who lived along the
banks of the river, who said of Father that he never
landed at spit or cove, by day or by night, but always
stuck to the river, lonely and outside human society.
Finally, Mother and our relatives realized that the provisions he had hidden in the canoe must be getting low and
thought that he would have to either land somewhere and
go away from us for good—that seemed the most likely—
or repent once and for all and come back home.

But they were wrong. I had made myself responsible
for stealing a bit of food for him every day, an idea that
had come to me the very first night, when the family had
lighted bonfires on the riverbank and in their glare
prayed and called out to Father. Every day from then on
I went back to the river with a lump of hard brown sugar,
some corn bread, or a bunch of bananas. Once, at the
end of an hour of waiting that had dragged on and on,
I caught sight of Father; he was way off, sitting in the
bottom of the canoe as if suspended in the mirror smooth-
ness of the river. He saw me, but he did not paddle over
or make any sign. I held up the things to eat and then
laid them in a hollowed-out rock in the river bluff, safe
from any animals who might nose around and where they
would be kept dry in rain or dew. Time after time, day
after day, I did the same thing. Much later I had a surprise: Mother knew about my mission but, saying nothing
and pretending she didn't, made it easier for me by
putting out leftovers where I was sure to find them.
Mother almost never showed what she was thinking.

Finally she sent for an uncle of ours, her brother, to
help with the farm and with money matters, and she got
a tutor for us children. She also arranged for the priest to
come in his vestments to the river edge to exorcise Father

and call upon him to desist from his sad obsession. Another time, she tried to scare Father by getting two soldiers to come. But none of it was any use. Father passed by at a distance, discernible only dimly through the river haze, going by in the canoe without ever letting anyone go close enough to touch him or even talk to him. The reporters who went out in a launch and tried to take his picture not long ago failed just like everybody else; Father crossed over to the other bank and steered the canoe into the thick swamp that goes on for miles, part reeds and part brush. Only he knew every hand's breadth of its blackness.

We just had to try to get used to it. But it was hard, and we never really managed. I'm judging by myself, of course. Whether I wanted to or not, my thoughts kept circling back and I found myself thinking of Father. The hard nub of it was that I couldn't begin to understand how he could hold out. Day and night, in bright sunshine or in rainstorms, in muggy heat or in the terrible cold spells in the middle of the year, without shelter or any protection but the old hat on his head, all through the weeks, and months, and years—he marked in no way the passing of his life. Father never landed, never put in at either shore or stopped at any part of the river islands or sandbars; and he never again stepped onto grass or solid earth. It was true that in order to catch a little sleep he may have tied up the canoe at some concealed islet-spit. But he never lighted a fire on shore, had no lamp or candle, never struck a match again. He did not more than taste food; even the morsels he took from what we left for him along the roots of the fig tree or in the hollow stone at the foot of the cliff could not have been enough to keep him alive. Wasn't he ever sick? And what constant strength he must have had in his arms to maintain himself and the canoe ready for the piling up of the floodwaters where danger rolls on the great current, sweeping the bodies of dead animals and tree trunks downstream—frightening, threatening, crashing into him. And he never spoke another word to a living soul. We never talked about him, either. We only thought of him. Father could never be forgotten; and if, for short periods of time, we pretended to ourselves that we had forgotten, it was only to find ourselves roused suddenly by his memory, startled by it again and again.

My sister married; but Mother would have no festivities. He came into our minds whenever we ate something especially tasty, and when we were wrapped up snugly at night we thought of those bare unsheltered nights of cold, heavy rain, and Father with only his hand and maybe a calabash to bail the storm water out of the canoe. Every so often someone who knew us would remark that I was getting to look more and more like my father. But I knew that now he must be bushy-haired and bearded, his nails long, his body cadaverous and gaunt, burnt black by the sun, hairy as a beast and almost as naked, even with the pieces of clothing we left for him at intervals.

He never felt the need to know anything about us; had he no family affection? But out of love, love and respect, whenever I was praised for something good I had done, I would say: "It was Father who taught me how to do it that way." It wasn't true, exactly, but it was a truthful kind of lie. If he didn't remember us any more and didn't want to know how we were, why didn't he go farther up the river or down it, away to landing places where he would never be found? Only he knew. When my sister had a baby boy, she got it into her head that she must show Father his grandson. All of us went and stood on the bluff. The day was fine and my sister was wearing the white dress she had worn at her wedding. She lifted the baby up in her arms and her husband held a parasol over the two of them. We called and we waited. Our father didn't come. My sister wept; we all cried and hugged one another as we stood there.

After that my sister moved far away with her husband, and my brother decided to go live in the city. Times changed, with the slow swiftness of time. Mother went away too in the end, to live with my sister because she was growing old. I stayed on here, the only one of the family who was left. I could never think of marriage. I stayed where I was, burdened down with all life's cumbrous baggage. I knew Father needed me, as he wandered up and down on the river in the wilderness, even though he never gave a reason for what he had done. When at last I made up my mind that I had to know and finally made a firm attempt to find out, people told me rumor had it that Father might have given some explanation to the man who made the canoe for him. But now the builder was dead; and no one really knew or could recollect any more except that there had been some silly talk in the beginning, when the river was first swollen by such endless torrents of rain that everyone was afraid the world was coming to an end; then they had said that Father might have received a warning, like Noah, and so prepared the canoe ahead of time. I could half-recall the story. I could not even blame my father. And a few first white hairs began to appear on my head.

I was a man whose words were all sorrowful. Why did I feel so guilty, so guilty? Was it because of my father, who made his absence felt always, and because of the river-river-river, the river—flowing forever? I was suffering the onset of old age—this life of mine only postponed the inevitable. I had bad spells, pains in the belly, dizziness, twinges of rheumatism. And he? Why, oh why must he do what he did? He must suffer terribly. Old as he was, was he not bound to weaken in vigor sooner or later and let the canoe overturn or, when the river rose,

let it drift unguided for hours downstream, until it finally
went over the brink of the loud rushing fall of the cata-
ract, with its wild boiling and death? My heart shrank. He
was out there, with none of my easy security. I was guilty
of I knew not what, filled with boundless sorrow in the
deepest part of me. If I only knew—if only things were
otherwise. And then, little by little, the idea came to me.

I could not even wait until next day. Was I crazy? No.
In our house, the word *crazy* was not spoken, had never
been spoken again in all those years; no one was condemned as crazy. Either no one is crazy, or everyone is.
I just went, taking along a sheet to wave with. I was very
much in my right mind. I waited. After a long time he
appeared; his indistinct bulk took form. He was there,
sitting in the stern. He was there, a shout away. I called
out several times. And I said the words which were making me say them, the sworn promise, the declaration. I
had to force my voice to say: "Father, you're getting old,
you've done your part. . . . You can come back now, you
don't have to stay any longer. . . . You come back, and
I'll do it, right now or whenever you want me to; it's what
we both want. I'll take your place in the canoe!" And as
I said it my heart beat to the rhythm of what was truest
and best in me.

He heard me. He got to his feet. He dipped the paddle
in the water, the bow pointed toward me; he had agreed.
And suddenly I shuddered deeply, because he had lifted
his arm and gestured a greeting—the first, after so many
years. And I could not. . . . Panic-stricken, my hair standing on end, I ran, I fled, I left the place behind me in a
mad headlong rush. For he seemed to be coming from
the hereafter. And I am pleading, pleading, pleading for
forgiveness.

I was struck by the solemn ice of fear, and I fell ill.
I knew that no one ever heard of him again. Can I be a

man, after having thus failed him? I am what never was
—the unspeakable. I know it is too late for salvation now,
but I am afraid to cut life short in the shallows of the
world. At least, when death comes to the body, let them
take me and put me in a wretched little canoe, and on the
water that flows forever past its unending banks, let me go
—down the river, away from the river, into the river—
the river.

Translated by BARBARA SHELBY

Juan José Arreola (b. 1918) was born in Ciudad Guzmán, Jalisco (Mexico), the fourth of fourteen children, and developed an early interest in writing and the theater. In the early 1940s he settled in Guadalajara where he wrote for several literary journals and met the actor Louis Jouvet, who took him to Paris. Returning to Mexico, he worked for a publishing house and then in the early 1950s founded his own, Los Presentes, which introduced Carlos Fuentes and has continued to encourage new writers. Three collections of his short stories. *Varia invención* [1949, "Various Inventions], *Confabulario* (1952) and *Punta de Plata* [1958, "Silvertip"], have been collected together with new pieces in the English volume, *Confabulario and Other Inventions* (1964); a fourth collection, which includes a one-act farce, was published in 1971. *La feria* (1963), a novel satirizing life in a small town in Jalisco, received the Villaurrutia prize. A master of fantasy and irony, Arreola directs his wit at those aspects of society which are increasingly outmoded and dehumanized, revealing human foibles with a keen sense of the absurd. He and his close friend Alfonso Reyes, one of Mexico's finest writers, specialized in a kind of story-essay which, with Arreola, became satirical. The following story is one of his most famous. It is interesting to compare his work—which includes satiric sketches and his famous "bestiaries"—with that of his friend Juan Rulfo, who was born in the same state, the same year, and who represents an altogether different direction in fiction writing.

I'm Telling You the Truth

Everybody who is interested in seeing the camel pass through the eye of the needle should inscribe his name on the list of patrons for the Niklaus Experiment.

Disassociated from a group of death-dealing scientists, the kind who manipulate uranium, cobalt, and hydrogen, Arpad Niklaus is guiding his present research toward a charitable and radically humanitarian end: the salvation of the souls of the rich.

He proposes a scientific plan to disintegrate a camel and make it pass in a stream of electrons through a needle's eye. A receiving apparatus (very similar to the television screen) will organize the electrons into atoms, the atoms into molecules, and the molecules into cells, immediately reconstructing the camel according to its original scheme. Niklaus has already managed to make a drop of heavy water change its position without touching it. He has also been able to evaluate, up to the point where the discretion of the material permits, the quantum energy discharged by a camel's hoof. It seems pointless here to burden the reader with that astronomical figure.

The only serious difficulty Professor Niklaus has run into is the lack of his own atomic plant. Such installations, extensive as cities, are incredibly expensive. But a special committee is already busy solving the problem by means of a world-wide subscription drive. The first contributions, still rather anemic, are serving to defray the cost of thousands of pamphlets, bonds, and explanatory prospectuses, as well as to assure Professor Niklaus the modest salary permitting him to continue with his calculations and theoretical investigations while the immense laboratories are being built.

At present, the committee can count only on the camel and the needle. As the societies for the prevention of cruelty to animals approve the project, which is inoffensive and even healthful for any camel (Niklaus speaks of a probable regeneration of all the cells), the country's zoos have offered a veritable caravan. New York City has not hesitated to risk its very famous white dromedary.

As for the needle, Arpad Niklaus is very proud of it and considers it the keystone of the experiment. It is not just any needle, but a marvelous object discovered by his assiduous talent. At first glance, it might be confused with a common ordinary needle. Mrs. Niklaus, displaying a fine sense of humor, takes pleasure in mending her husband's clothes with it. But its value is infinite. It is made from an extraordinary, as yet unclassified, metal, whose chemical formula, scarcely hinted at by Niklaus, seems to indicate that it involves a base composed exclusively of isotopes of nickel. This mysterious substance has made scientists ponder a great deal. There was even one who sustained the laughable hypothesis of a synthetic osmium or an abnormal molybdenum, or still another who dared to proclaim in public the words of an envious professor who was sure he had recognized Niklaus' metal in the form of tiny crystalline clusters encysted in dense masses of siderite. What is known with certainty is that Niklaus' needle can resist the friction of a stream of electrons flowing at ultrasonic speed.

In one of those explanations so pleasing to abstruse mathematicians, Professor Niklaus compares the camel in its transit to a spider's thread. He tells us that if we were to use that thread to weave a fabric, we would need all of sidereal space to stretch it out in, and that the visible and invisible stars would be caught in it like sprays of dew. The skein in question measures millions of light years, and Niklaus is offering to wind it up in about three-fifths of a second.

As can be seen, the project is completely viable, and, we might even say, overly scientific. It can already count on the sympathy and moral support (not officially confirmed yet) of the Interplanetary League, presided over in London by the eminent Olaf Stapledon.

In view of the natural expectation and anxiety that Niklaus' project has provoked everywhere, the committee is manifesting a special interest by calling the world powers' attention to it, so they will not let themselves be surprised by charlatans who are passing dead camels through subtle orifices. These individuals, who do not hesitate to call themselves scientists, are simply swindlers on the lookout for imprudent optimists. They proceed by an extremely vulgar method, dissolving the camel in sulphuric acid solutions each time lighter than the last. Then they distil the liquid through the needle's eye, using a steam clepsydra, believing that they have performed the miracle. As one can see, the experiment is useless, and there is no reason to finance it. The camel must be alive before and after the impossible transfer.

Instead of melting down tons of candle wax and spending money on indecipherable works of charity, persons interested in the eternal life who have more capital than they know what to do with should subsidize the disintegration of the camel, which is scientific, colorful, and, ultimately, lucrative. To speak of generosity in such a case is totally unnecessary. One must shut one's eyes and open one's purse generously, knowing full well that all expenses will be met pro rata. The reward for all the contributors will be the same; what is urgent is to hasten the date of payment as much as possible.

The total capital necessary cannot be known until the unpredictable end, and Professor Niklaus, in all honesty, refuses to work with a budget that is not fundamentally elastic. The subscribers should pay out their investment quotas patiently over the years. It is necessary to contract for thousands of technicians, managers, and workers. Regional and national subcommittees must be established. And the statute founding a school of successors for Professor Niklaus must not only be foreseen, but budgeted for in detail, since the experiment might reasonably extend over several generations. In this respect, it is not beside the point to indicate the ripe old age of the learned Niklaus.

Like all human plans, Experiment Niklaus offers two probable results: failure and success. Besides simplifying the problem of personal salvation, a success by Niklaus will convert the promoters of such a mystical experience into stockholders of a fabulous transport company. It will be very easy to develop the disintegration of human beings in a practical and economical way. The men of tomorrow will travel great distances in an instant and without danger, dissolved in electronic flashes.

But the possibility of a failure is even more attractive. If Arpad Niklaus is a maker of chimeras and is followed at his death by a whole line of imposters, his humanitarian work will only have increased in grandeur, like a geometric progression or the texture of a chicken bred by Carrel. Nothing will keep him from passing into history as the glorious innovator of the universal disintegration of capital. And the rich, impoverished en masse by the draining investments, will easily enter the kingdom of heaven by the narrow gate (the eye of the needle), though the camel may not pass through.

Translated by GEORGE B. SCHADE

Augusto Roa Bastos (b. 1917) was born in Asunción, Paraguay, the son of poor parents. He fought, as a teenager, in the Chaco War between Paraguay and Bolivia, and worked as a newspaperman and a filmscript writer, but he has been in political exile, living in Buenos Aires, since 1947. (Buenos Aires is the home of many political exiles now.) His most famous book is his prizewinning novel *Hijo de hombre* (1960, *Son of Man*) which portrays the struggle between the governing élite and the oppressed in Paraguay from the 1860s until after the Chaco War in the 1930s. Mixing past and future, he blends Indian myth and Christian legend with his special kind of "magic realism" to create a poetic image of an oppressed people whose potential has been tragically wasted. Among his short story collections are *El trueno entre las hojas* [1953, "Thunder among the leaves"], *El baldío* (1966, from which we have reprinted the title story), and *Madera quemada* [1967, "Burned wood"].

The Vacant Lot

Striped, swallowed up by darkness; they had no face. Nothing more than their vaguely human silhouettes, both bodies reabsorbed in their own shadows. Alike and so different nonetheless. One inert, traveling along the earth's surface with the passivity of innocence or the most absolute indifference. The other bent over, panting from the effort of dragging him through the brush and refuse. At times he would stop to catch his breath. Then he would begin again, arching his spine even more over his load. The smell from the stream's stagnant water must have been everywhere, now even more with the sweetish stench of the lot reeking of rust, animal feces, the pasty smell that comes from the threat of bad weather which the man would wave away from time to time, peeling it off his face. Slivers of glass or metal jostled around in the weeds, although most certainly neither of the two would hear this isochronal, ghostly little song. Nor the hushed sound of the city which seemed to vibrate there under the ground. Nor the one he was dragging along, perhaps only that soft, dull noise of the body as it bumped along the ground, the crackle of fragments of paper or the opaque thump of shoes against the tin cans and rubble. Sometimes the other's shoulder would get caught in the stiff branches or on a rock. He would then jerk him loose, muttering some enraged exclamation or at each strain making the pneumatic *ha* . . . of stevedores as they shoulder rebellious loads. It was obvious that his load was getting heavier. Not only because of the passive resistance that balked on him from time to time at the obstacles. But also because of his own fear perhaps, the repulsion or haste which would gradually eat up his strength, pushing him to finish up as soon as possible.

At first he dragged him along by the arms. If the night hadn't been so overcast, one could have seen the two linked pairs of hands, a negative of rescue in reverse. When the body caught on something again, he grabbed the two legs and, turning his back to him, he started towing, straining, digging in hard in the low places. The other man's head was knocking about gaily, as if delighted with the change. A car's lights taking a curve suddenly spread out a brightness which arrived in waves over the mounds of garbage, over the weeds, over the irregular land levels. The hauler lay down beside the other. For an instant, as if lightly sketched in, they had something of a face, one bluish, scared, the other covered with dust, watching them be impassive. Darkness immediately swallowed them up again.

He got up and kept on hauling a little farther, but by then they had reached a spot where the underbrush was higher. He arranged him as best he could, clothed him in garbage, dry branches, rubble. Unexpectedly he seemed to want to protect him from the smell that filled the vacant lot or from the rain which was about to fall. He stopped, wiped his arm across his dripping forehead, hawked, and angrily spat. At that moment he was startled by the wail of an infant. Weak and smothered, it rose up from the weed patch, as if the other had begun to complain by crying like a new baby from under the piles of garbage.

He was about to run away, but he stopped himself, stunned by the photoflash of lightning which also pulled the bridge's metallic hulk out from the darkness, showing him what a short distance he had traveled. He slumped his head, in defeat. He got down on his knees and sniffing around almost, headed toward the thin, strangled, insistent cry. Close to the heap was a whitish bulk. The man remained there for a long time, not knowing what to do. He got up to leave, took a few unsteady steps, but could go no farther. The wailing began to draw him back. He returned little by little, feeling his way along, breathing heavily. He knelt once more, still hesitating. Then he reached out his hand. The bundle's wrapping crackled. A small human form struggled there among the sheets of a newspaper. The man took it in his arms. His motion was clumsy and vaguely instinctive, the motion of someone who doesn't know what he's doing but nevertheless can't stop himself. He straightened up slowly, as if loathing such unexpected tender feelings which were like the most extreme helplessness, and taking off his jacket, he used it to clothe the damp, whimpering creature.

Picking up speed, almost running, he got away from the weed patch with its cry and disappeared into the darkness.

Translated by MARY JANE WILKIE

Hernando Téllez (1908–1966), the Colombian essayist and short story writer, was born in Bogotá. A learned writer, he worked for some of Colombia's most prominent magazines and newspapers, served as consul in Marseilles and as a senator in his own country. His literary reputation is based primarily on a collection of his short stories that appeared when he was over forty: *Cenizas para le viento y otras historias* [Ashes for the wind and other tales, 1950]. He was an essayist of some importance, writing on a variety of themes. In this country he is especially known for the following story, often anthologized, a gem of its type. Nothing happens, but tension mounts and with very few words we are made to feel the potential violence not only between these men but in the town.

Just Lather, That's All

He said nothing when he entered. I was passing the best of my razors back and forth on a strop. When I recognized him I started to tremble. But he didn't notice. Hoping to conceal my emotion, I continued sharpening the razor. I tested it on the meat of my thumb, and then held it up to the light.

At that moment he took off the bullet-studded belt that his gun holster dangled from. He hung it up on a wall hook and placed his military cap over it. Then he turned to me, loosening the knot of his tie, and said, "It's hot as hell. Give me a shave." He sat in the chair.

I estimated he had a four-day beard—the four days taken up by the latest expedition in search of our troops. His face seemed reddened, burned by the sun. Carefully, I began to prepare the soap. I cut off a few slices, dropped them into the cup, mixed in a bit of warm water, and began to stir with the brush. Immediately the foam began to rise.

"The other boys in the group should have this much beard, too," he remarked. I continued stirring the lather.

"But we did all right, you know. We got the main ones. We brought back some dead, and we got some others still alive. But pretty soon they'll all be dead."

"How many did you catch?" I asked.

"Fourteen. We had to go pretty deep into the woods to find them. But we'll get even. Not one of them comes out of this alive, not one."

He leaned back on the chair when he saw me with the lather-covered brush in my hand. I still had to put the sheet on him. No doubt about it, I was upset. I took a sheet out of a drawer and knotted it around his neck. He wouldn't stop talking. He probably thought I was in sympathy with his party.

"The town must have learned a lesson from what we did," he said.

"Yes," I replied, securing the knot at the base of his dark, sweaty neck.

"That was a fine show, eh?"

"Very good," I answered, turning back for the brush. The man closed his eyes with a gesture of fatigue and sat waiting for the cool caress of the soap. I had never had him so close to me. The day he ordered the whole town to file into the patio of the school to see the four rebels hanging there, I came face to face with him for an instant. But the sight of the mutilated bodies kept me from noticing the face of the man who had directed it all, the face I was now about to take into my hands.

It was not an unpleasant face, and the beard, which made him look a bit older than he was, didn't suit him badly at all. His name was Torres—Captain Torres. A man of imagination, because who else would have thought of hanging the naked rebels and then holding target practice on their bodies?

I began to apply the first layer of soap. With his eyes closed, he continued. "Without any effort I could go straight to sleep," he said, "but there's plenty to do this afternoon."

I stopped the lathering and asked with a feigned lack of interest, "A firing squad?"

"Something like that, but a little slower."

I got on with the job of lathering his beard. My hands started trembling again. The man could not possibly realize it, and this was in my favor. But I would have preferred that he hadn't come. It was likely that many of our faction had seen him enter. And an enemy under one's roof imposes certain conditions.

I would be obliged to shave that beard like any other one, carefully, gently, like that of any customer, taking pains to see that no single pore emitted a drop of blood. Being careful to see that the little tufts of hair did not lead the blade astray. Seeing that his skin ended up clean, soft, and healthy, so that passing the back of my hand over it I couldn't feel a hair. Yes, I was secretly a rebel, but I was also a conscientious barber, and proud of the precision required of my profession.

I took the razor, opened up the two protective arms, exposed the blade, and began the job—from one of the sideburns downward. The razor responded beautifully. His beard was inflexible and hard, not too long, but thick. Bit by bit the skin emerged. The razor rasped along, making its customary sound as fluffs of lather, mixed with bits of hair, gathered along the blade.

I paused a moment to clean it, then took up the strop again to sharpen the razor, because I'm a barber who does things properly. The man, who had kept his eyes closed, opened them now, removed one of his hands from under the sheet, felt the spot on his face where the soap had been cleared off, and said, "Come to the school today at six o'clock."

"The same thing as the other day?" I asked, horrified.

"It could be even better," he said.

"What do you plan to do?"

"I don't know yet. But we'll amuse ourselves." Once more he leaned back and closed his eyes. I approached with the razor poised.

"Do you plan to punish them all?" I ventured timidly.

"All."

The soap was drying on his face. I had to hurry. In the mirror I looked towards the street. It was the same as ever —the grocery store with two or three customers in it. Then I glanced at the clock—2:20 in the afternoon.

The razor continued on its downward stroke. Now from the other sideburn down. A thick, blue beard. He should have let it grow like some poets or priests do. It would suit him well. A lot of people wouldn't recognize him. Much to his benefit, I thought, as I attempted to cover the neck area smoothly.

There, surely, the razor had to be handled masterfully, since the hair, although softer, grew into little swirls. A curly beard. One of the tiny pores could open up and issue forth its pearl of blood, but a good barber prides himself on never allowing this to happen to a customer.

How many of us had he ordered shot? How many of us had he ordered mutilated? It was better not to think about it. Torres did not know that I was his enemy. He did not know it nor did the rest. It was a secret shared by very few, precisely so that I could inform the revolutionaries of what Torres was doing in the town and of what he was planning each time he undertook a rebel-hunting excursion.

So it was going to be very difficult to explain that I had him right in my hands and let him go peacefully— alive and shaved.

The beard was now almost completely gone. He seemed

younger, less burdened by years than when he had arrived. I suppose this always happens with men who visit barber shops. Under the stroke of my razor Torres was being rejuvenated—rejuvenated because I am a good barber, the best in the town, if I may say so.

How hot it is getting! Torres must be sweating as much as I. But he is a calm man, who is not even thinking about what he is going to do with the prisoners this afternoon. On the other hand I, with this razor in my hands—I stroking and restroking this skin, can't even think clearly.

Damn him for coming! I'm a revolutionary, not a murderer. And how easy it would be to kill him. And he deserves it. Does he? No! What the devil! No one deserves to have someone else make the sacrifice of becoming a murderer. What do you gain by it? Nothing. Others come along and still others, and the first ones kill the second ones, and they the next ones—and it goes on like this until everything is a sea of blood.

I could cut this throat just so—*zip, zip!* I wouldn't give him time to resist and since he has his eyes closed he wouldn't see the glistening blade or my glistening eyes. But I'm trembling like a real murderer. Out of his neck a gush of blood would spout onto the sheet, on the chair, on my hands, on the floor. I would have to close the door. And the blood would keep inching along the floor, warm, ineradicable, uncontainable, until it reached the street, like a little scarlet stream.

I'm sure that one solid stroke, one deep incision, would prevent any pain. He wouldn't suffer. But what would I do with the body? Where would I hide it? I would have to flee, leaving all I have behind, and take refuge far away. But they would follow until they found me. "Captain Torres' murderer. He slit his throat while he was shaving him—a coward."

And then on the other side. "The avenger of us all. A name to remember. He was the town barber. No one knew he was defending our cause."

Murderer or hero? My destiny depends on the edge of this blade. I can turn my hand a bit more, press a little harder on the razor, and sink it in. The skin would give way like silk, like rubber. There is nothing more tender than human skin and the blood is always there, ready to pour forth.

But I don't want to be a murderer. You came to me for a shave. And I perform my work honorably . . . I don't want blood on my hands. Just lather, that's all. You are an executioner and I am only a barber. Each person has his own place in the scheme of things.

Now his chin had been stroked clean and smooth. The man sat up and looked into the mirror. He rubbed his hands over his skin and felt it fresh, like new.

"Thanks," he said. He went to the hanger for his belt, pistol, and cap. I must have been very pale; my shirt felt soaked. Torres finished adjusting the buckle, straightened his pistol in the holster, and after automatically smoothing down his hair, he put on the cap. From his pants pocket he took out several coins to pay me for my services and then headed for the door.

In the doorway he paused for a moment and said, "They told me that you'd kill me. I came to find out. But killing isn't easy. You can take my word for it." And he turned and walked away.

Translated by DONALD A. YATES

Adolfo Bioy Casares (b. 1914), an Argentine, is probably best known as the long-time friend and collaborator of Jorge Luis Borges. In 1942 their detective story, "The Twelve Figures of the World," was published under the joint pseudonym of H. Bustos Domecq; this was the first of a lightly satirical series featuring don Isidro Parodi, a detective who puzzles out his cases from a prison cell. Subsequently they produced together a playful detective tale (*Un modelo para la muerte*, 1945), two gangster filmscripts, two fantasies (*Dos fantasías memorables*), and two collections of detective stories; they have also supervised a long series of detective novels for their Argentine publisher. With Bioy's wife, Silvina Ocampo, they edited an important collection of fantastic literature *Antología de la literatura fantástica* (1940). With both authors fiction (often fantasy) may serve as a vehicle for probing metaphysical questions and as Jean Franco has suggested they both see literature as a sort of "game which may shock the reader out of conventional attitudes." On his own, Bioy Casares has written many short stories and short novels. Some of those published in this country are *The Invention of Morel* (1940), about a machine that reproduces reality in space and time, involving the narrator in the dilemma of falling in love with a woman who exists on another level of reality altogether (a situation transformed by Robbe-Grillet into the film *Last Year at Marienbad*); *Sleep of the Heroes* (1954), in which a boy dreams an event which then occurs three years later, causing his death; and *Diary of the War of the Pig* (1969), in which the young men of Buenos Aires begin to kill the old, in effect killing the people they would eventually become. The story included here repeats another Bioy Casares theme, the failure of communication, with all its comic implications.

A Letter About Emilia

The other day in the editor's office, when I was waiting at the cashier's window for my latest check, you warned me that one of these days the public would begin to tire of Emilia, and I promised you some other women. Well, dear Mr. Grinberg, I was lying. Not deliberately, or because I was angry, but because I'm so inept when I act on impulse that if I'd tried to justify myself then and there I'd only have irritated you without convincing you. You said to me: "Emilia, with her blonde hair and her pixie face and her pear-shaped breasts, is a dish our readers have licked their chops over long enough. It's time you settled down to work, and I mean real work, not just one more version of the same sketch or the same water-color, I mean serious work." But the way I look at it, if you're to do serious work, your heart must be in it, you can't be like a schoolboy chained to his desk. I'll never stop wanting to draw Emilia. One look at her and I've no fear of repeating myself. For Emilia is a model with infinite possibilities, I'm forever discovering, in her face and her body, something new, something I've never caught and pinned down. I explore my model like a diver discovering forests, mountains and towers on the floor of the ocean; I bring back to your readers glimpses of a world of marvels. But you, Mr. Editor, you shake your head and you wave your hands and shout, "No!", and ask me to replace Emilia with an assortment of commonplace girls. "Just walk into a candy store," you tell me, "any day between five and seven, and take your pick. You have to stir your stumps, friend, get out of your rut." With the unerring instinct of a blind man, you sense that I am more interested in Emilia than I am in art.

It's curious, this is the second time I've heard the same words, or nearly the same. The first time was long ago. I was hanging some of my pictures for an exhibit entitled *Nine Young Painters* (it seems like a thousand years back), when one of my colleagues, who still continues to haunt the galleries and the art shows, murmured as though thinking aloud, "I'm beginning to believe you care more about women than about painting." And before the day was over you appeared yourself—probably that unerring instinct of yours was guiding you—and flung open doors for me by making that outrageous offer, which was a slap in the face for any painter, and which I accepted on the spot. (Though you were careful to say, "There's no rush. Never rush, is my motto, if you want a job done well.") I heaved a sigh of relief and gave up painting women the way artists look at them, as if they were so many still lives, to paint instead what the man in the street wants to see. It took me a while to realize that not only had I merely replaced one convention by another, but that I'd stepped down to an inferior level. But it was all right with me, because I had found my way. I had stopped trying to imitate the masters; at last I was my own man, relaxed and

spontaneous. You have to settle for being what you are;
it's a painful chore leading a double life. Though my old
friends, the New Painters, see you as a corrupter leading
me astray, involving me in slightly shady jobs, using money
and women as bait to lure me away from art, my own feeling, as I look back, is that you have been like a second
father to me. And it's because I think of you that way
that I'm writing you this letter.

How many women have come and gone through my
studio! Have you forgotten Irene, Mr. Grinberg? She was
tall and pale, with long, blonde braids, and when she posed
standing with her back to me, her feet made a marvelous
angle with the line of her body. You used to stare at her
like a famished wolf. And have you forgotten little Antoinette, with that famous suggestion of a squint which
you declared was her special fascination? When I think of
the lot of them I feel a kind of regret, but taking them
one by one, it's probably just as well for me that they're
far away.

You behaved like a real father, you gave me a piece
of your mind one day. "If you don't get your head screwed
on the right way, you'll get lost among all these women.
The Great Artist climbs up, raises himself above the
crowd; he finds the unique woman, and by sheer force of
repetition he imposes her image on us. Then the public
falls in love with the model and sets him up on a pedestal
—a pedestal where he's solid, where he's not going to be
knocked off with the flick of a finger."

You'd have thought there was a conspiracy to turn me
into the model of a dutiful son. Isaura, who scoffed at
the idea of wearing a coat—she was a strong young animal, she said—and was forever catching cold, fell really
ill. I couldn't reach Antoinette or Violeta. Saturna's telephone was out of order. I'd lost track of Irene. Concerned,
because by now it was Saturday and I had to turn in my

sketches by Monday, I crossed the street on my way to Chabuco Park for a little sunshine. I was going from the park proper to the section the pensioners call the Italian garden; on my left was a red gravel path, with symmetrical borders of lawn on either side, and at the end of it I caught sight of my friend Braulio; he was under the hood of his camera photographing a willowy blonde girl, dressed in green, seated on a marble bench beneath an arching branch of cypress. "It's straight out of Gaston Latouche," I thought to myself. As I was moving on, my mind turned from the composition to the model; it occurred to me that perhaps my problem was solved. I turned back. Braulio was fiddling with his plates, rather like a chef stirring and tasting his sauces. The girl was gone.

"Who is she?" I asked. "Will she be back?"

"She's got to come back, otherwise what am I to do with the pictures, eat them? No, friend, people don't act that way."

I explained the situation. "I need a model as soon as possible. Maybe you'd speak to the girl about it?"

"Count on me."

"Ask her if she'll come and talk it over. You know my address?"

"The street number doesn't matter. It's the house that looks like the figurehead of a ship."

Although my house, which stands on a corner, does not look like the figurehead of a ship, but like the prow itself, it was clear that Braulio placed it. Depending on my mood, I see it as a prow advancing triumphantly over the greenery of the park or as some barren peak poised over me with all the mass of its somber walls, in which a wretched little window is briefly flung open here or there.

I was boiling water for maté when the bell rang. I went to answer it: Emilia, the unique woman, the woman you clamored for and are now clamoring to be rid of, stepped inside my house.

"The photographer told me," she said. "I've never modelled before, but I'm ready for anything."

She began to laugh: it was one of her days for being in high spirits, even zany. I think I fell in love with her on the spot, though it's not impossible that the process actually took a whole week.

At the same time I was annoyed. "She's never modelled, she has no idea how much she'll earn; I shall have to tell her, and it's going to seem like very little."

Not wanting her to take me for an idiot—I'd said not a word for a good long minute—I explained my silence. "I'm thinking about something that can be settled later."

"What's that?"

"We can settle it later."

"I want to know at once. Don't ask me to wait, I never wait, I loathe uncertainty."

Curiosity lighted up her face and at the same time dimmed the intelligence of it. Emilia was astonishingly young.

"Well, I was thinking we'd have to agree on what I can pay you."

"Oh," she said, as though she'd hoped for something more interesting.

That afternoon we drank maté and worked. Mr. Grinberg, do you want to know my two guiding principles? Here they are: one, put first things first; two, everybody has to get to know himself. If I'm not to draw Emilia, maybe I'll give up drawing. With Emilia I'm content; the rest is secondary. Forgive me if I raise my voice a little, as though you were deaf, to make it clear that the rest takes in *all the rest*. Of course my relationship with Emilia is not so settled as I'd like it to be (or as she would: "A woman wants stability" is a phrase that's always on her lips). I comfort myself, or try to, with the thought that life itself is unstable, like a constantly changing light passing through us. I'm reminded of the people who lived next door, when I was a child. As soon as the heat set in, they would leave, loaded with suitcases, preceded by vans full of trunks, to spend the summer at Mar del Plata; anybody counting their luggage would assume they'd be gone till heaven knows when. And yet—even though time, in those days, crept by incredibly slowly—before you were used to the idea of their being away, there they were back again, with the suitcases, and the trunks, and the hired vans. As the Englishman with the black suit and the celluloid collar who preaches in the park keeps telling us, we build our tabernacles on shifting sands.

My life is calm and orderly. In the morning I work from the sketches I've made the day before, or draw from memory, until Tomasa comes in. Then, shopping-bag in arm, I go to the baker's, the butcher's, the grocer's. Would you believe me if I told you I enjoy the ritual of marketing, saying hello, passing the time of day with acquaintances— you might almost call them friends—whom I meet every day at the same hour, in the same places? By the time I get back the house has been cleaned and Tomasa is preparing lunch; I go on with my drawing. After lunch I go out to the park to enjoy the sunshine and shoot the breeze with the pensioners. Emilia gets depressed just looking at them, but my feeling is that if you're talking it's what people have to say that matters; even if I am a painter, I'm willing to overlook a person's appearance if his observations are to the point—or useful, like the one Arthur made yesterday. (Arthur is the man with eyes like fried eggs with the yolks running; I gather he used to be a horse-trainer in Rio de la Plata, although according to his own statement he was the chief elevator-man at Palacio Barolo.) "There you stand with your piece of charcoal, sweating and straining to catch the likeness of a girl, and I'll lay you seven to one she's quietly copying you, down to the tip of your little finger: the way you move, the way you speak, even the way your mind works. There's no end to it. A woman's a born mimic."

At five o'clock sharp I go home to wait for Emilia, who is invariably late. My happiness lasts for three hours (but there are many people who have less). At nine o'clock Emilia leaves, and we go our separate ways: twenty-one hours must go by—I look forward to them with apprehension and look back upon them, very often, with regret —in which Emilia moves through a hostile world. I know all about it, she's perfectly frank.

She doesn't go home at nine o'clock, she goes to the club. Honestly, Mr. Grinberg, it's beyond my comprehension how a refined, intelligent girl puts up with such people; my tolerance—my charity, I should say—has its limits. I don't go with her, I suffer what I must. At this stage of our relationship it's just about impossible for me to go to the club. In the beginning, Emilia herself asked me to go with her. I refused, to prove my superiority. Obviously if at this point I were to show up in one of the clubrooms, it would look like contemptible spying . . . Emilia goes because she has to go somewhere, but I assure you she has nothing in common with the people she meets there: a dull crew, not an artist in the lot, just run-of-the-mill. I can't ask her to stay home, home is too depressing. And why shouldn't it be, with her parents incessantly bickering, and a brother who can think of nothing but business, and a sister who's a schoolteacher unable to forgive anyone around her for the fact that she is ugly and virtuous? On the other hand, if Emilia stayed here, that would be asking for trouble. She has told me herself: "I'm not about to throw myself to the wolves. I will not have people talking about me." And I can understand her feelings.

You're wondering why I haven't married her. No out-sider would understand my hesitation, and he would be quick to draw unflattering conclusions. Marrying Irene, or Antoinette, or Violeta would have made no sense; and by the time Emilia came along I was a confirmed bachelor; I was prepared to love and to suffer, but not to change my habits. And afterwards—I don't know whether it was vanity or what else that prompted her—Emilia refused to consider it.

To understand Emilia you have to know the side of her which it's been hardest for me to accept. I mean her childishness. For instance last winter, when her nephew and niece—five-year old Norma and seven-year old Robert —were here from Tucuman on a visit, she was always mimicking the little girl, the faces she made, her tricks of speech. One afternoon, when we were drinking maté, she proposed that we should make believe we were Robert and Norma having their glass of milk. Don't scowl like that, Mr. Grinberg. A man in love will stoop to anything.

I start trembling when Emilia criticizes her friends in the club. Though I never contradict her, she will insist that Nogueira, for example—a fellow I've never even met— is as crude as they come; he held her too close while they were dancing; on the pretext of needing fresh air he whisked her out on to the balcony, where he kissed her; and ended by promising to telephone her "to work something out." Annoyed, I exclaimed, "But you must have en-couraged him!" This offends her, but, seeing me pale with anger, she is mollified; wasn't it a mistake, she asks, to tell me all this. A few days later, when another dance was announced, I asked her to promise that such an incident would not be repeated.

"I should never have told you!" she cried. "Besides, it was so long ago. It's as though I'd been a different person. I'd be incapable now, of doing such a thing."

In the face of such artless candor I'm defenseless. If I'm not thankful for her outburst of affection, I'm an ingrate; if I'm skeptical, I'm an insensitive brute, and I've ruined our marvellous understanding. Reactions of this kind— completely spontaneous—do not indicate anything ugly or perverse in her character, they are merely signs (and this is no novelty for me) of a purely feminine temperament. And so I try to push out of my mind that regrettable list which includes Viera, Centrone, Pasta (a down-at-the-heels actor), Ramponi, Grates, a Peruvian, an Armenian, and a few others.

But suddenly the nightmare is over. A miraculous change has come over Emilia. It's been six months now since she's spoken of any unpleasantness involving the friends she meets at the club. I've been extremely happy. I'd grown used to expecting—though with a sinking heart—the in- evitable incidents, faithfully confessed the next day, and invariably forgiven. Because actually they were not very serious, they did not upset our way of life; they sprang from regrettable weaknesses which Emilia hated in herself; all her lapses could be attributed to the effects of alcohol, or simply to her extreme childishness (and her complete candor made her all the more vulnerable). Can you under- stand what it means to have the feeling—and presently the conviction—that the nightmare which has haunted you is ended at last?

As I said, lately I've been very happy. Only the other night I was thinking that I was not used to the idea of having life, or Emilia, deal so kindly with me, that normally I should expect to find a crack somewhere, a crack through which I would catch sight of some frightful truth. Yet, contrary to all my experience, each day seemed to confirm the fact that I had been unbelievably lucky. It wasn't merely that the infidelities at the club had ended: it was hearing Emilia say: "I'm going to stay longer tonight. Anyway, the people who gossip are too late to undo the follies we've committed, and the people who don't won't make up for the ones we haven't."

She must love me very deeply, I thought, to make a decision so opposed to the convictions of a lifetime. When a woman loves him like that, a man has no cause to envy anyone.

It was daybreak when I left her on her doorstep. Walking back home I recited poetry, and suddenly I experienced the exaltation of someone discovering—or dreaming of discovering—a miracle: in the hardness of the paving stones beneath my feet, in the unreal light flooding the street, I seemed to find a symbol of man's mysterious good luck. Not only have you got Emilia, I told myself, like a man counting the trophies he has won, you're an intelligent fellow too. Oh, yes, Mr. Grinberg, I've known my hours of triumph.

The next day, on the telephone, Emilia explained that "to keep the savages quiet," she would not come that afternoon. And since then she stays, every other day, until dawn, and the days between she doesn't come at all.

If I had the least grain of common sense—if I'd just keep to the facts instead of letting my imagination run riot —I'd be a happy man. In the long run, what does the change amount to? True, there are days when I don't see her at all, but there are others when I'm with her for twelve hours, instead of the three I had before; I used to see her twenty-one hours out of the week, and now it's thirty-six at the very least.

And so I can count my blessings, especially when I forget that when two people are in love, if one of them is going to influence the other it usually happens at the very start. But when years have gone by, why the devil should there suddenly be an influence? Why has Emilia given up going to the club? Why no relapses, why no more nocturnal escapades? Is it because of me? Terrified, like a sick man wondering in the middle of the night whether his illness may be incurable, I ask myself whether some other man has not found his way into Emilia's life.

Let me tell you, Mr. Grinberg, what happened at our last anniversary. There's a special date, right in the middle of the dog days, which Emilia and I always celebrate with a little dinner. I pick up a corn-fed pullet at the market in Las Violetas, I take pains to find the Chilean champagne that Emilia prefers; her contribution consists of almonds and other tidbits, whose chief merit lies in the fact that she has chosen them. I was afraid this year that there might be complications, because that same night there was to be a benefit at the club, with dancing and a lottery. The results of the drawing would be announced at midnight; and the grand prize, which Emilia had set her heart on, was a manila shawl.

"If I win the shawl, I'll put it on top of the piano," she declared, laughing, because she knows a shawl on the piano is the height of bad taste, and knows too that her personality is strong enough to carry it off, to give this little corner of the room the charm of a bygone day or another way of life. "And I'll set Mabel on top of the shawl." Mabel is a rag doll that she still plays with.

I think I know Emilia. Over the years I've had ample evidence of her impatience and her curiosity, and I refused to deceive myself about the way this anniversary celebration would end. Emilia arrived earlier than usual, weighed down with parcels: grapes, almonds, a bottle of catsup, even an avocado. It was so hot that I opened the window all the way; Emilia says she can't breathe with the windows closed. Shortly before midnight a man in some house nearby began to sing *The Barber of Seville* in a rich, thrilling voice. The open window bothered me, not only on account of these hearty *Figaro-ci, Figaro-la*'s hammering away deep inside my skull, but because I could feel a slight draught which was certain to give me a cold; but I didn't dare close the window, because Emilia is a fresh air fiend, even in midwinter she has me living with everything wide open. You can imagine my surprise, Mr. Grinberg, when I heard her ask:

"You won't suffocate if I shut the window?"

I stared at her, not knowing whether to thank her for a kindness or to treat it as a joke. "The roles are reversed," I said. "Are we playing now that I'm you and you're me?"

She did not hear, because at this moment the clock on the mantel began to strike twelve. She went out to the kitchen for the champagne, which was chilling on ice. There was something strange about the way she walked. When she came back with the bottle and the glasses, I watched again, and discovered what it was that had struck me: there was something masculine about her walk. I had the distinct impression that Emilia was imitating me.

It occurred to me suddenly that her early arrival, and now this hurry to fetch the champagne and the glasses concealed her intention to leave as soon as possible. She's casting about now, I thought, for some appropriate formula. "Well," she'll begin, and after a pause she'll go on, in an innocent voice, "Why don't we run over to the club, I'll just dash in to see if I've won the drawing, and be with you again in five minutes." But experience has taught me that a woman at a dance is capable of anything. I could see myself waiting for hours on the corner of the street, and foresaw that I'd have dismal memories of this night.

I've spoken of Emilia's impatience, but my own is no less. To have my doubts at an end, I was ready to anticipate the decision I dreaded, ready even to provoke it. I ought to be generous, I told myself; if Emilia wanted something I should gratify her wish, whatever it cost me.

"Shall we go to the club," I asked, "to see if you won the shawl?"

Her answer left me dumbfounded. "What a crazy idea! Whatever for? To find out tonight that I didn't win? Tomorrow will do just as well."

In every lover there's a streak of the fool, of the suicide. I persisted. "But Emilia, can you survive till tomorrow, not knowing?"

"What I believe is, you have to live with uncertainty, build on it, settle in it. The long and short of it is, there's nothing in life you can count on."

I stared at her blankly. A gray hair in her head would not have struck me as any more spurious than these words on her lips; and yet I must admit she sounded perfectly natural.

All of a sudden she lay back, staring into space with wide, fixed eyes; a smile hovered about her lips, a smile I did not recognize—arrogant, obscene, with a hint of ferocity in it. I don't know what there was about that smile that went against my grain. I mumbled something or other to rouse her out of her daydreaming. Can you guess how she shut me up?

"Please be quiet, Emilia, can't you see I'm trying to think?"

Yes, I know, there are women who, out of vanity or affectation, will address themselves aloud by their own name. But Emilia was speaking to *me*.

Was an ideal being fulfilled in Emilia, the ideal all lovers dream about, of becoming one with the beloved? Did she truly believe that she was I and I was she? Why had it taken me so long, I wondered, to realize it had been my luck to find the perfect pattern of a loving woman? Trembling with gratitude, I stretched out my hand. But hers did not respond to the pressure of mine; it was as if Emilia had gone off, leaving her hand behind. Suddenly I remembered what she had said only a few minutes ago: "What I believe is, you have to live with uncertainty, build on it, settle on it. The long and short of it is, there's nothing in life you can count on."

Those aren't her words, I thought, or mine either. Like a flash it came to me: there are impatient people (like Emilia, like me) and there are others who control their impatience—some of them are colorful characters, like the Englishman who preaches in Chabuco Park. You yourself, Mr. Grinberg, didn't you say to me one time, "There's no rush. Never rush, is my motto, if you want a job done well." All this doesn't mean that my rival is you, or the Englishman in the park, there are lots of people who might say something like that. But what it does mean is that not only is there another man in Emilia's life, but that Emilia, when she's with me, is imitating this other man; when she kisses me, she pictures him kissing her, and when I kiss her, she pictures herself kissing him.

I was too upset to conceal my chagrin; I don't know whether Emilia remarked it. For a week I avoided seeing her. It was no life at all. When she came back, it seemed as though she was giving me to understand, though not in so many words, that *he* existed. Probably, with that childishness and that simplicity that are so much a part of her, she was playing at being that other man. It must look as if I've fallen pretty low, my position must seem ridiculous. But isn't there always something a bit ridiculous about love? Is this woman really so wonderful? Is it understandable that this man should be dying for love of her? And why should the love that is returned be nobler than the love that is disinterested and without hope? You may think, possibly, that I am the most unfortunate of men. I only know that without Emilia I should be no less unfortunate. You'll say that possessing her this way is not possessing her at all. But is there actually any other way of possessing anyone? People live together, parents and children, husband and wife, but don't they know that communication is only an illusion, that in the last analysis each of us is locked up in his own secret? All I ask is that her rival will not treat her too well, because then she would leave me, and that he will not treat her too harshly, because then, imitating him, she'll give me a rough time. Lately we've been through a stormy period, but luckily it's over now.

Translated by GREGORY WOODRUFF

María Luisa Bombal (b. 1910) was born in Viña del Mar, Chile. She studied at the Sorbonne, doing a thesis on Próspero Mérimée, and returned to Chile to write for the theater. In Buenos Aires, the literary magazine *Sur,* under the direction of Victoria Ocampo, published her first stories, psychological in emphasis, in a mood halfway between reality and a dream world. Her first novella, *La última niebla* (1935), was the story of a woman who, frustrated in her marriage and unable to sleep, goes for a walk, meets a stranger, and for one night knows real love. The lover (of whom she has dreamed) appears again years later in a coach, but she can't find him in the mist, and she finally has to accept that she imagined him. In her second novella, *La amortajada* (1938, *The Shrouded Woman*), a woman lying in her coffin, mourned by her family, has a chance to recall the intense loves and hates in her life and to realize (too late) the consequences. In 1944 Ms. Bombal married a banker and went to live in New York; with his help she rewrote, in an expanded, English version, her first novella as *The House of Mist,* a version in which the lover turns out to be the husband. The author lives now in Buenos Aires. The story that follows was included in the second Latin American edition of *La última niebla* in 1941 and is one of the best-known of the few works penned by this creator of magical realism. It is as precisely structured as a poem.

The Tree

The pianist sits down, coughs affectedly and concentrates for a moment. The cluster of lights illuminating the hall slowly diminishes to a soft, warm glow, as a musical phrase begins to rise in the silence, and to develop, clear, restrained and judiciously capricious.

"Mozart, perhaps," thinks Brigida. As usual, she has forgotten to ask for the program. "Mozart, perhaps, or Scarlatti." She knew so little music! And it wasn't because she had no ear for it, or interest. As a child it was she who had demanded piano lessons; no one needed to force them on her, as with her sisters. Her sisters, however, played correctly now and read music at sight, while she. . . . She had given up her studies the year she began them. The reason for her inconsistency was as simple as it was shameful; she had never succeeded in learning the key of F; never. "I don't understand; my memory only reaches to the key of G." How indignant her father was! "I'd give anyone this job of being a man alone with several daughters

233

to bring up! Poor Carmen! She surely must have suffered
because of Brigida. This child is retarded."

Brigida was the youngest of six girls, all different in
character. When the father finally reached his sixth daughter, he was so perplexed and tired out by the first five that
he preferred to simplify matters my declaring her retarded.
"I'm not going to struggle any longer, it's useless. Let her
be. If she won't study, all right. If she likes to spend time
in the kitchen listening to ghost stories, that's up to her.
If she likes dolls at sixteen, let her play with them." And
Brigida had kept her dolls and remained completely
ignorant.

How pleasant it is to be ignorant! Not to know exactly
who Mozart was, to ignore his origin, his influence, the
details of his technique! To just let him lead one by the
hand, as now.

And, indeed, Mozart is leading her. He leads her across
a bridge suspended over a crystalline stream which runs in
a bed of rosy sand. She is dressed in white, with a lace
parasol—intricate and fine as a spider web—open over her
shoulder.

"You look younger every day, Brigida. I met your husband yesterday, your ex-husband, I mean. His hair is all
white."

But she doesn't answer, she doesn't stop, she continues
to cross the bridge which Mozart has improvised for her
to the garden of her youthful years when she was eighteen:
tall fountains in which the water sings; her chestnut braids,
which when undone reach her ankles, her golden complexion, her dark eyes opened wide and as if questioning;
a small mouth with full lips, a sweet smile and the slender-
est and most graceful body in the world. What was she
thinking about as she sat on the edge of the fountain?
Nothing. "She is as stupid as she is pretty," they said. But
it never mattered to her that she was stupid, or awkward

at dances. One by one, her sisters were asked to marry. No one proposed to her.

Mozart! Now he offers her a staircase of blue marble which she descends, between a double row of lilies of ice. And now he opens for her a gate of thick iron bars with gilded points so that she can throw herself on the neck of Luis, her father's close friend. Ever since she was a very small child, when they all abandoned her, she would run to Luis. He would pick her up and she would put her arms around his neck, laughing with little warbling sounds, and shower him with kisses like a downpour of rain, haphazardly, upon his eyes, forehead and hair, already grey (had he ever been young?).

"You are a garland," Luis would say to her. "You are like a garland of birds."

That is why she married him. Because, with that solemn and taciturn man, she didn't feel guilty of being as she was: silly, playful and lazy. Yes; now that so many years have passed she understands that she did not marry Luis for love; nevertheless, she doesn't quite understand why, why she went away one day, suddenly. . . .

But at this point Mozart takes her nervously by the hand, and dragging her along at a pace which becomes more urgent by the second, compels her to cross the garden in the opposite direction, to recross the bridge at a run, almost in headlong flight. And after having deprived her of the parasol and the transparent skirt, he closes the door of her past with a chord at once gentle and firm, and leaves her in a concert hall, dressed in black, mechanically applauding while the artificial lights are turned up.

Once more the half-shadow, and once more the foreboding silence.

And now Beethoven's music begins to surge under a spring moon. How far the sea has withdrawn! Brigida walks across the beach towards the sea now recoiled in the distance, shimmering and calm, but then, the sea swells, slowly grows, comes to meet her, envelops her, and with gentle waves, gradually pushes her, pushes her until it makes her rest her cheek upon the body of a man. And then it recedes, leaving her forgotten upon Luis' breast.

"You don't have a heart, you don't have a heart," she used to say to Luis. Her husband's heart beat so deep inside that she could rarely hear it, and then only in an unexpected way. "You are never with me when you are beside me," she protested in the bedroom when he ritually opened the evening papers before going to sleep. "Why did you marry me?"

"Because you have the eyes of a frightened little doe," he answered, and kissed her. And she, suddenly happy, proudly received upon her shoulder the weight of his grey head. Oh, his shiny, silver hair!

"Luis, you have never told me exactly what color your hair was when you were a boy, and you have never told me either what your mother said when you began to get grey at fifteen. What did she say? Did she laugh? Did she cry? And were you proud or ashamed? And at school, your friends, what did they say? Tell me, Luis, tell me . . ."

"Tomorrow I'll tell you. I'm sleepy, Brigida. I'm very tired. Turn off the light."

Unconsciously he moved away from her to fall asleep, and she unconsciously pursued her husband's shoulder all night long, sought his breath. She tried to live beneath his breath, like a plant shut up and thirsty which stretches out its branches in search of a more favorable climate.

In the morning, when the maid opened the blinds, Luis was no longer at her side. He had got up cautiously and had left without saying good morning to her for fear of his "garland of birds," who insisted on vehemently holding him back by the shoulders. "Five minutes, just five minutes. Your office won't disappear because you stay five minutes longer with me, Luis."

Her awakenings. Ah, how sad her awakenings! But—it was strange—scarcely did she step into her dressing room than her sadness vanished, as if by magic.

Waves toss and break very far away, murmuring like a sea of leaves. Is it Beethoven? No.

It is the tree close to the window of the dressing room. It was enough for her to enter to feel a wonderfully pleasant sensation circulating within her. How hot it always was in the bedroom, in the mornings! And what a harsh light! Here, on the other hand, in the dressing room, even one's eyes were rested, refreshed. The drab cretonnes, the tree that cast shadows on the walls like rippling, cold water, the mirrors that reflected the foliage and receded into an infinite, green forest. How pleasant that room was! It seemed like a world submerged in an aquarium. How that huge gum tree chattered! All the birds of the neighborhood came to take shelter in it. It was the only tree on that narrow, sloping street which dropped down directly to the river from one corner of the city.

"I'm busy. I can't accompany you . . . I have a lot to do, I won't make it for lunch . . . Hello, yes, I'm at the Club. An engagement. Have your dinner and go to bed . . . No. I don't know. You better not wait for me, Brigida."

"If I only had some girl friends!," she sighed. But everybody was bored with her. If she only would try to be a little less stupid! But how to gain at one stroke so much lost ground? To be intelligent you should begin from childhood, shouldn't you?

Her sisters, however, were taken everywhere by their husbands, but Luis—why shouldn't she confess it to herself?—was ashamed of her, of her ignorance, her timidity and even her eighteen years. Had he not asked her to say that she was at least twenty-one, as if her extreme youth were a secret defect?

And at night, how tired he always was when he went to bed! He never listened to everything she said. He did smile at her, with a smile which she knew was mechanical. He showered her with caresses from which he was absent. Why do you suppose he had married her? To keep up a habit, perhaps to strengthen the friendly relationship with her father. Perhaps life consisted, for men, of a series of ingrained habits. If one should be broken, probably confusion, failure would result.

And then they would begin to wander through the streets of the city, to sit on the benches of the public squares, each day more poorly dressed and with longer beards. Luis' life, therefore, consisted in filling every minute of the day with some activity. Why hadn't she understood it before! Her father was right when he declared her backward.

"I should like to see it snow some time, Luis."

"This summer I'll take you to Europe, and since it is winter there, you will be able to see it snow."

"I know it is winter in Europe when it is summer here. I'm not that ignorant!"

Sometimes, as if to awaken him to the emotion of real love, she would throw herself upon her husband and cover him with kisses, weeping, calling him Luis, Luis, Luis . . .

"What? What's the matter with you? What do you want?"

"Nothing."

"Why do you call me that way then?"

"No reason, just to call you. I like to call you." And he would smile, taking kindly to that new game.

Summer arrived, her first summer since she was married. New duties kept Luis from offering her the promised trip.

"Brigida, the heat is going to be terrible this summer in Buenos Aires. Why don't you go to the farm with your father?"

"Alone?"

"I would go to see you every week on week-ends."

She had sat down on the bed, ready to insult him. But she sought in vain for cutting words to shout at him. She didn't know anything, anything at all. Not even how to insult.

"What's the matter with you? What are you thinking about, Brigida?"

For the first time Luis had retraced his steps and bent over her, uneasy, letting the hour of arrival at his office pass by.

"I'm sleepy . . ." Brigida had replied childishly, while she hid her face in the pillows.

For the first time he had called her from the Club at lunch time. But she had refused to go to the telephone, furiously wielding that weapon she had found without thinking: silence.

That same evening she ate opposite her husband without raising her eyes, all her nerves taut.

"Are you still angry, Brigida?"

But she did not break the silence.

"You certainly know that I love you, my garland. But I can't be with you all the time. I'm a very busy man. One reaches my age a slave to a thousand duties."

". . ."

"Do you want to go out tonight?"

". . ."

"You don't want to? Patience. Tell me, did Roberto call from Montevideo?"

". . ."

"What a pretty dress! Is it new?"

". . ."

"Is it new, Brigida? Answer, answer me . . ."

But she did not break the silence this time either. And immediately the unexpected, the astonishing, the absurd happened. Luis gets up from his chair, throws the napkin violently on the table and leaves the house, slamming doors behind him.

She had got up in her turn, stunned, trembling with indignation at such injustice. "And I, and I," she murmured confused; "I who for almost a year . . . when for the first time I allow myself one reproach . . . Oh, I'm going away, I'm going away this very night! I shall never set foot in this house again . . ." And she furiously opened the closets of her dressing room, crazily threw the clothes on the floor.

It was then that someone rapped with his knuckles on the window panes.

She had run, she knew not how or with what unaccustomed courage, to the window. She had opened it. It was the tree, the gum tree which a great gust of wind was shaking, which was hitting the glass with its branches, which summoned her from outside as if she should see it writhing like an impetuous black flame beneath the fiery sky of that summer evening.

A heavy shower would soon beat against its cold leaves. How delightful! All night long she could hear the rain pattering, trickling through the leaves of the gum tree as if along the ducts of a thousand imaginary gutters. All night long she would hear the old trunk of the gum tree creak and groan, telling her of the storm, while she snuggled up very close to Luis, voluntarily shivering between the sheets of the big bed.

Handfuls of pearls that rain abundantly upon a silver roof. Chopin. *Études* by Frédéric Chopin.

How many weeks did she wake up suddenly, very early, when she scarcely perceived that her husband, now also stubbornly silent, had slipped out of bed?

The dressing room: the window wide open, an odor of river and pasture floating in that kindly room, and the mirrors veiled by a halo of mist.

Chopin and the rain that slips through the leaves of the gum tree with the noise of a hidden waterfall that seems to drench even the roses of the cretonnes, become intermingled in her agitated nostalgia.

What does one do in the summertime when it rains so much? Stay in one's room the whole day feigning convalescence or sadness? Luis had entered timidly one afternoon. He had sat down very stiffly. There was a silence.

"Brigida, then it is true? You no longer love me?"

She had become happy all of a sudden, stupidly. She might have cried out: "No, no; I love you, Luis; I love you," if he had given her time, if he had not added, almost immediately, with his habitual calm:

"In any case, I don't think it is wise for us to separate, Brigida. It is necessary to think it over a great deal."

Her impulses subsided as abruptly as they had arisen. Why become excited uselessly! Luis loved her with tenderness and moderation; if some time he should come to hate her he would hate her justly and prudently. And that was life. She approached the window, rested her forehead against the icy glass. There was the gum tree calmly receiving the rain that struck it, softly and steadily. The room stood still in the shadow, orderly and quiet. Everything seemed to come to a stop, eternal and very noble. That was life. And there was a certain greatness in accepting it as it was, mediocre, as something definitive, irremediable. And from the depths of things there seemed to issue and to rise, a melody of grave, slow words to which she stood listening: "Always." "Never" . . . And thus the hour, the days and the years go by. Always! Never! Life, life!

On regaining her bearings she realized that her husband had slipped out of the room. Always! Never! . . .

And the rain, secretly and constantly, continued to murmur in the music of Chopin.

Summer tore the leaves from its burning calendar. Luminous and blinding pages fell like golden swords, pages of an unwholesome humidity like the breath of the swamps; pages of brief and violent storm, and pages of hot wind, of the wind that brings the "carnation of the air" and hangs it in the immense gum tree.

Children used to play hide-and-seek among the enormous twisted roots that raised the paving stones of the sidewalk, and the tree was filled with laughter and whispering. Then she appeared at the window and clapped her hands; the children dispersed, frightened, without noticing the smile of a girl who also wanted to take part in the game.

Alone, she would lean for a long time on her elbows at the window watching the trembling of the foliage—some breeze always blew along that street which ran straight to the river—and it was like sinking one's gaze in shifting water or in the restless fire of a hearth. One could spend one's idle hours this way, devoid of all thought, in a stupor of well-being.

Scarcely did the room begin to fill with the haze of twilight when she lit the first lamp, and the first lamp shone in the mirrors, multiplied like a firefly wishing to hurry the night.

And night after night she dozed next to her husband, suffering at intervals. But when her pain increased to the point of wounding her like a knife thrust, when she was beset by too urgent a desire to awaken Luis in order to hit him or caress him, she slipped away on tiptoe to the dress-

ing room and opened the window. The room instantly
filled with discreet sounds and presences, with mysterious
footfalls, the fluttering of wings, the subtle crackling of
vegetation, the soft chirping of a cricket hidden under the
bark of the gum tree submerged in the stars of a hot
summer night.

Her fever passed as her bare feet gradually became
chilled on the matting. She did not know why it was so
easy for her to suffer in that room.

Chopin's melancholy linked one *Etude* after another,
linked one melancholy after another, imperturbably.

And autumn came. The dry leaves whirled about for
a moment before rolling upon the grass of the narrow
garden, upon the sidewalk of the sloping street. The leaves
gave way and fell . . . The top of the gum tree remained
green, but underneath, the tree turned red, darkened like
the worn-out lining of a sumptuous evening cape. And the
room now seemed to be submerged in a goblet of dull gold.

Lying upon the divan, she patiently waited for suppertime, for the improbable arrival of Luis. She had resumed
speaking to him, she had become his wife again without
enthusiasm and without anger. She no longer loved him.
But she no longer suffered. On the contrary, an unexpected
feeling of plenitude, of placidity had taken hold of her.
Now no one or nothing could hurt her. It may be that
true happiness lies in the conviction that one has ir-
remediably lost happiness. Then we begin to move through
life without hope or fear, capable of finally enjoying all the
small pleasures, which are the most lasting.

A terrible din, then a flash of light throws her backwards, trembling all over.

Is it the intermission? No. It is the gum tree, she
knows it.

They had felled it with a single stroke of the axe. She
could not hear the work that began very early in the

morning. "The roots were raising the paving stones of the
sidewalk and then, naturally, the neighbors' committee . . ."

Bewildered, she has lifted her hands to her eyes. When
she recovers her sight she stands up and looks around her.
What is she looking at? The hall suddenly lighted, the
people who are dispersing? No. She has remained imprisoned in the web of her past, she cannot leave the
dressing room. Her dressing room invaded by a white,
terrifying light. It was as if they had ripped off the roof;
a hard light came in everywhere, seeped through her
pores, burned her with cold. And she saw everything in
the light of that cold light; Luis, his wrinkled face, his
hands crossed by coarse, discolored veins, and the cretonnes with gaudy colors. Frightened, she has run to the
window. The window now opens directly on a narrow
street, so narrow that her room almost strikes the front
of an imposing skyscraper. On the ground floor, show
windows and more show windows, full of bottles. On the
street corner, a row of automobiles lined up in front of
a service station painted red. Some boys in shirt sleeves
are kicking a ball in the middle of the street.

And all that ugliness had entered her mirrors. Now in
her mirrors there were nickel-plated balconies and shabby
clothes-lines and canary cages.

They had taken away her privacy, her secret; she found
herself naked in the middle of the street, naked beside an
old husband who turned his back on her in bed, who had
given her no children. She does not understand how until
then she had not wanted to have children, how she had
come to submit to the idea that she was going to live without children all her life. She does not understand how she
could endure for a year Luis' laughter, that over-cheerful
laughter, that false laughter of a man who has become
skilled in laughter because it is necessary to laugh on certain occasions.

A lie! Her resignation and her serenity were a lie; she wanted love, yes, love; and trips and madness, and love, love ...

"But, Brigida, why are you going? Why did you stay?," Luis had asked.

Now she would have known how to answer him:

"The tree, Luis, the tree! They have cut down the gum tree."

Translated by ROSALIE TORRES-RIOSECO

Juan Rulfo (b. 1918) was born in the southern part of Jalisco, Mexico, a hot, desolate region brought vividly to life in the chapter on Rulfo in *Into the Mainstream*. Rulfo lost his father at the age of seven in the revolt of the Cristeros which took place in the late 1920s; his mother died six years later. From a Guadalajara boarding school he went to an orphanage and then at 15 to Mexico City to study, supporting himself with odd jobs. For ten years with the Immigration Department, he helped to process refugees of Nazi Germany; in 1945 he switched to publicity work with B. F. Goodrich, then work on an irrigation program near Veracruz, and then work on films and television. Since 1962 he has worked for the Instituto Indigenista in Mexico City, a group devoted to Indians. In 1940 he wrote his first novel, which he later destroyed. His first short story was published in 1942 and in 1953 the collection *El llano en llamas (The Burning Plain and Other Stories)*, from which the following story was taken. He then wrote his only published novel, *Pedro Páramo*, which appeared in 1955. *Pedro Páramo* is the story of a young man's journey to find and know his father; he arrives to find his father dead and the town his father tyrannized, a ghost town. Reconstructing his father's life in an effort to discover his own identity, the son uncovers a picture of small-town despotism that has ruined the town. Rulfo writes of the land and the people of southern Jalisco, a dying land from which most of the people have fled, while those who remain are haunted by the past, resigned, and embittered. Here, says Rulfo, "the dead carry more weight than the living." In the story included here, Rulfo's restraint is perfectly matched to the stark landscape he evokes, the characters in this case haunted not only by the dead but by their guilt.

Talpa

Natalia threw herself into her mother's arms, crying on and on with a quiet sobbing. She'd bottled it up for many days, until we got back to Zenzontla today and she saw her mother and began feeling like she needed consolation.

But during those days when we had so many difficult things to do—when we had to bury Tanilo in a grave at Talpa without anyone to help us, when she and I, just the two of us alone, joined forces and began to dig the grave, pulling out the clods of earth with our hands, hurrying to hide Tanilo in the grave so he wouldn't keep on scaring people with his smell so full of death—then she didn't cry.

Not afterward either, on the way back, when we were traveling at night without getting any rest, groping our way as if asleep and trudging along the steps that seemed like blows on Tanilo's grave. At that time Natalia seemed to have hardened and steeled her heart so she wouldn't feel it boiling inside her. Not a single tear did she shed.

She came here, near her mother, to cry, just to upset her, so she'd know she was suffering, upsetting all the rest of us besides. I felt that weeping of hers inside me too as if she was wringing out the cloth of our sins.

Because what happened is that Natalia and I killed Tanilo Santos between the two of us. We got him to go with us to Talpa so he'd die. And he died. We knew he couldn't stand all that traveling; but just the same, we pushed him along between us, thinking we'd finished him off forever. That's what we did.

The idea of going to Talpa came from my brother Tanilo. It was his idea before anyone else's. For years he'd been asking us to take him. For years. From the day when he woke up with some purple blisters scattered about on his arms and legs. And later on the blisters became wounds that didn't bleed—just a yellow gummy thing like thick distilled water came out of them. From that time I remember very well he told us how afraid he was that there was no cure for him any more. That's why he wanted to go see the Virgin of Talpa, so she'd cure him with her look. Although he knew Talpa was far away and we'd have to walk a lot under the sun in the daytime and in the cold March nights, he wanted to go anyway. The blessed Virgin would give him the cure to get rid of that stuff that never dried up. She knew how to do that, by washing them, making everything fresh and new like a recently rained-on field. Once he was there before Her, his troubles would be over; nothing would hurt him then or hurt him ever again. That's what he thought.

And that's what Natalia and I latched on to so we could take him. I had to go with Tanilo because he was my brother. Natalia would have to go too, of course, because she was his wife. She had to help him, taking him by the arm, bearing his weight on her shoulders on the trip there and perhaps on the way back, while he dragged along on his hope.

I already knew what Natalia was feeling inside. I knew something about her. I knew, for example, that her round legs, firm and hot like stones in the noonday sun, had been alone for a long time. I knew that. We'd been together many times, but always Tanilo's shadow separated us; we felt that his scabby hands got between us and took Natalia away so she'd go on taking care of him. And that's the way it'd be as long as he was alive.

I know now that Natalia is sorry for what happened. And I am too; but that won't save us from feeling guilty or give us any peace ever again. It won't make us feel any better to know that Tanilo would've died anyway because his time was coming, and that it hadn't done any good to go to Talpa, so far away, for it's almost sure he would've died just as well here as there, maybe a little afterward, because of all he suffered on the road, and the blood he lost besides, and the anger and everything—all those things together were what killed him off quicker. What's bad about it is that Natalia and I pushed him when he didn't want to go on anymore, when he felt it was useless to go on and he asked us to take him back. We jerked him up from the ground so he'd keep on walking, telling him we couldn't go back now.

"Talpa is closer now than Zenzontla." That's what we told him. But Talpa was still far away then, many days away.

We wanted him to die. It's no exaggeration to say that's what we wanted before we left Zenzontla and each night that we spent on the road to Talpa. It's something we can't understand now, but it was what we wanted. I remember very well.

I remember those nights very well. First we had some light from a wood fire. Afterward we'd let the fire die down, then Natalia and I would search out the shadows to hide from the light of the sky, taking shelter in the loneliness of the countryside, away from Tanilo's eyes, and we disappeared into the night. And that loneliness pushed us toward each other, thrusting Natalia's body into my arms, giving her a release. She felt as if she was resting; she forgot many things and then she'd go to sleep with her body feeling a great relief.

It always happened that the ground on which we slept was hot. And Natalia's flesh, the flesh of my brother Tanilo's wife, immediately became hot with the heat of the earth. Then those two heats burned together and made one wake up from one's dreams. Then my hands groped for her; they ran over her red-hot body, first lightly, but then they tightened on her as if they wanted to squeeze her blood out. This happened again and again, night after night, until dawn came and the cold wind put out the fire of our bodies. That's what Natalia and I did along the roadside to Talpa when we took Tanilo so the Virgin would relieve his suffering.

Now it's all over. Even from the pain of living Tanilo found relief. He won't talk any more about how hard it was for him to keep on living, with his body poisoned like it was, full of rotting water inside that came out in each crack of his legs or arms. Wounds this big, that opened up slow, real slow, and then let out bubbles of stinking air that had us all scared.

But now that he's dead things are different. Now Natalia weeps for him, maybe so he'll see, from where he is, how full of remorse her soul is. She says she's seen Tanilo's face these last days. It was the only part of him that she cared about—Tanilo's face, always wet with the sweat which the effort to bear his pain left him in. She felt it approaching her mouth, hiding in her hair, begging her, in a voice she could scarcely hear, to help him. She says he told her that he was finally cured, that he no longer had any pain. "Now I can be with you, Natalia. Help me to be with you," she says he said to her.

We'd just left Talpa, just left him buried there deep down in that ditch we dug to bury him.

Since then Natalia has forgotten about me. I know how her eyes used to shine like pools lit up by the moon. But suddenly they faded, that look of hers was wiped away as if it'd been stamped into the earth. And she didn't seem to see anything any more. All that existed for her was her Tanilo, whom she'd taken care of while he was alive and had buried when his time came to die.

It took us twenty days to get to the main road to Talpa. Up to then the three of us had been alone. At that point people coming from all over began to join us, people like us who turned onto that wide road, like the current of a river, making us fall behind, pushed from all sides as if we were tied to them by threads of dust. Because from the ground a white dust rose up with the swarm of people like corn fuzz that swirled up high and then came down again; all the feet scuffling against it made it rise again, so that dust was above and below us all the time. And above this land was the empty sky, without any clouds, just the dust, and the dust didn't give any shade.

We had to wait until nighttime to rest from the sun and that white light from the road.

Then the days began to get longer. We'd left Zenzontla about the middle of February, and now that we were in the first part of March it got light very early. We hardly got our eyes closed at night when the sun woke us up

again, the same sun that'd gone down just a little while
ago.

I'd never felt life so slow and violent as when we were
trudging along with so many people, just like we were a
swarm of worms all balled together under the sun, wriggling through the cloud of dust that closed us all in on
the same path and had us corralled. Our eyes followed
the dust cloud and struck the dust as if stumbling against
something they could not pass through. And the sky was
always gray, like a heavy gray spot crushing us all from
above. Only at times, when we crossed a river, did the
dust clear up a bit. We'd plunge our feverish and blackened heads into the green water, and for a moment a blue
smoke, like the steam that comes out of your mouth when
it's cold, would come from all of us. But a little while
afterward we'd disappear again, mixed in with the dust,
sheltering each other from the sun, from that heat of the
sun we all had to endure.

Eventually night will come. That's what we thought
about. Night will come and we'll get some rest. Now we
have to get through the day, get through it somehow to
escape from the heat and the sun. Then we'll stop—afterward. What we've got to do now is keep plugging right
along behind so many others just like us and in front of
many others. That's what we have to do. We'll really
only rest well when we're dead.

That's what Natalia and I thought about, and maybe
Tanilo too, when we were walking along the main road to
Talpa among the procession, wanting to be the first to
reach the Virgin, before she ran out of miracles.

But Tanilo began to get worse. The time came when
he didn't want to go any farther. The flesh on his feet
had burst open and begun to bleed. We took care of him
until he got better. But, he'd decided not to go any farther.

"I'll sit here for a day or two and then I'll go back to Zenzontla." That's what he said to us.

But Natalia and I didn't want him to. Something inside us wouldn't let us feel any pity for Tanilo. We wanted to get to Talpa with him, for at that point he still had life left in him. That's why Natalia encouraged him while she rubbed his feet with alcohol so the swelling would go down. She told him that only the Virgin of Talpa would cure him. She was the only one who could make him well forever. She and no one else. There were lots of other Virgins, but none like the Virgin of Talpa. That's what Natalia told him.

Then Tanilo began to cry, and his tears made streaks down his sweaty face, and he cursed himself for having been bad. Natalia wiped away the streaky tears with her shawl, and between us we lifted him off the ground so he'd walk on a little further before night fell.

So, dragging him along was how we got to Talpa with him.

The last few days we started getting tired too. Natalia and I felt that our bodies were being bent double. It was as if something was holding us and placing a heavy load on top of us. Tanilo fell down more often and we had to pick him up and sometimes carry him on our backs. Maybe that's why we felt the way we did, with our bodies slack and with no desire to keep on walking. But the people who were going along by us made us walk faster.

At night that frantic world calmed down. Scattered everywhere the bonfires shone, and around the fire the pilgrims said their rosaries, with their arms crossed, gazing toward the sky in the direction of Talpa. And you could hear how the wind picked up and carried that noise, mixing it together until it was all one roaring sound. A little bit afterward everything would get quiet. About midnight you could hear someone singing far away. Then you closed your eyes and waited for the dawn to come without getting any sleep.

We entered Talpa singing the hymn praising Our Lord.
We'd left around the middle of February and we got to Talpa the last days of March, when a lot of people were already on their way back. All because Tanilo took it into his head to do penance. As soon as he saw himself surrounded by men wearing cactus leaves hanging down like scapularies, he decided to do something like that too. He tied his feet together with his shirt sleeves so his steps became more desperate. Then he wanted to wear a crown of thorns. A little later he bandaged his eyes, and still later, during the last part of the way, he knelt on the ground and shuffled along on his knees with his hands crossed behind him; so that thing that was my brother Tanilo Santos reached Talpa, that thing so covered with plasters and dried streaks of blood that it left in the air a sour smell like a dead animal when he passed by.

When we least expected it we saw him there among the dancers. We hardly realized it and there he was with a long rattle in his hand, stomping hard on the ground with his bare bruised feet. He seemed to be in a fury, as if he was shaking out all the anger he'd been carrying inside him for such a long time, or making a last effort to try to live a little longer.

Maybe when he saw the dances he remembered going every year to Tolimán during the novena of Our Lord and dancing all night long until his bones limbered up without getting tired. Maybe that's what he remembered and he wanted to get back the strength he used to have.

Natalia and I saw him like that for a moment. Right afterward we saw him raise his arms and slump to the ground with the rattle still sounding in his bloodspecked

hands. We dragged him out so he wouldn't be tromped
on by the dancers, away from the fury of those feet that
slipped on stones and leaped about stomping the earth
without knowing that something had fallen among them.

Holding him up between us as if he was crippled, we
went into the church with him. Natalia had him kneel down
next to her before that little golden figure of the Virgin
of Talpa. And Tanilo started to pray and let a huge tear
fall, from way down inside him, snuffing out the candle
Natalia had placed in his hands. But he didn't realize this;
the light from so many lit candles kept him from realizing
what was happening right there. He went on praying with
his candle snuffed out. Shouting his prayers so he could
hear himself praying.

But it didn't do him any good. He died just the same.

". . . from our hearts filled with pain we all send her
the same plea. Many laments mixed with hope. Her tenderness is not deaf to laments nor tears, for She suffers
with us. She knows how to take away that stain and to
leave the heart soft and pure to receive her mercy and
charity. Our Virgin, our mother, who wants to know nothing of our sins, who blames herself for our sins, who
wanted to bear us in her arms so life wouldn't hurt us, is
right here by us, relieving our tiredness and the sicknesses
of our souls and our bodies filled with thorns, wounded
and supplicant. She knows that each day our faith is
greater because it is made up of sacrifices . . ."

That's what the priest said from up in the pulpit. And
after he quit talking the people started praying all at once
with a noise just like a lot of wasps frightened by smoke.

But Tanilo no longer heard what the priest was saying.
He'd become still, with his head resting on his knees. And
when Natalia moved him so he'd get up he was already
dead.

Outside you could hear the noise of the dancing, the

drums and the hornpipes, the ringing of bells. That's when I got sad. To see so many living things, to see the Virgin there, right in front of us with a smile on her face, and to see Tanilo on the other hand as if he was in the way. It made me sad.

But we took him there so he'd die, and that's what I can't forget.

Now the two of us are in Zenzontla. We've come back without him. And Natalia's mother hasn't asked me anything, what I did with my brother Tanilo, or anything. Natalia started crying on her shoulder and poured out the whole story to her.

I'm beginning to feel as if we hadn't reached any place; that we're only here in passing, just to rest, and that then we'll keep on traveling. I don't know where to, but we'll have to go on, because here we're very close to our guilt and the memory of Tanilo.

Maybe until we begin to be afraid of each other. Not saying anything to each other since we left Talpa may mean that. Maybe Tanilo's body is too close to us, the way it was stretched out on the rolled petate, filled inside and out with a swarm of blue flies that buzzed like a big snore coming from his mouth, that mouth we couldn't shut in spite of everything we did and that seemed to want to go on breathing without finding any breath. That Tanilo, who didn't feel pain any more but who looked like he was still in pain with his hands and feet twisted and his eyes wide open like he was looking at his own death. And here and there all his wounds dripping a yellow water, full of that smell that spread everywhere and that you could taste in your mouth, like it was a thick and bitter honey melting into your blood with each mouthful of air you took.

I guess that's what we remember here most often—that

Tanilo we buried in the Talpa graveyard, that Tanilo Natalia and I threw earth and stones on so the wild animals wouldn't come dig him up.

Translated by GEORGE D. SCHADE

Carlos Fuentes (b. 1929) was born in Mexico City. The son of a diplomat, he was well-educated in various North and South American capitals. When he left law school in 1955, his literary career was launched. In 1954 Juan José Arreola, who had just founded a publishing house called Los Presentes, published his first volume of short stories, *Los días enmascarados*. His first novel, *La región más transparente* ["Where the air is clear," 1958], portrayed a group of climbers from different parts of society who make their fortunes after the Mexican Revolution. The experimental style was frankly derivative of such writers as Faulkner and Dos Passos. His second novel, *Las buenas conciencias*, (1959, *The Good Conscience*), also deals with post-revolutionary Mexico and the ways in which the idealistic young betray their ideals in rising to the top. In 1962 two of his works were published: *Aura*, a novella in which identity is part of the plot and theme; and *La muerte de Artemio Cruz (The Death of Artemio Cruz)*, probably his most famous novel, which through the device of flashbacks from the deathbed of a *caudillo* recalls his idealism during the Revolution and an early love affair, which contrast sharply with the loveless marriage and cynical ruthlessness that characterized his life as he rose to power. In 1964 Fuentes published a second collection of stories, *Cantar de ciegos* ["Tales of the blind"] from which the following story was taken, and in 1967 the novel *Zona Sagrada* (included as *Holy Place* in the anthology *Triple Cross*), a travesty of the Telemachus myth which takes on the theme of transvestism. The 1967 novel *Cambio de piel (Change of Skin)* presents the events of one day in the lives of four people. *Cumpleaños* [1969, "Birthday"] was a short novel. Fuentes is one of the few Latin American writers who lives from his writing; his works are internationally popular, he has sold film rights to some, and he has written a number of filmscripts himself. A world traveler who generates an aura of glamour, he nevertheless shares with many Mexican writers (especially in his early works) the national preoccupation with Mexican identity and the role of the Mexican past in contemporary life.

The Doll Queen

I

I went because that card—such a strange card—reminded me of her existence. I found it in a forgotten book whose pages had revived the ghost associated with the childish calligraphy. For the first time in a long time I was rearranging my books. I met surprise after surprise since some, placed on the highest shelves, had not been read for a long time. So long a time that the edges of the leaves were grainy, and a mixture of gold dust and greyish scale fell onto my open palm, reminiscent of the lacquer covering certain bodies glimpsed first in dreams and later in the deceptive reality of the first ballet performance to which we're taken. It was a book from my childhood—perhaps from that of many children—that related a series of more or less truculent exemplary tales which had the virtue of precipitating us upon our elders' knees to ask them, over and over again: Why? Children who are ungrateful to their parents; maidens kidnapped by flashy horsemen and returned home in shame—as well as those who willingly abandon hearth and home; old men who in exchange for an overdue mortgage demand the hand of the sweetest and most long-suffering daughter of the threatened family. . . . Why? I do not recall their answers. I only know that from among the stained pages fell, fluttering, a white card in Amilamia's atrocious hand: *Amilamia wil not forget her good frend—com see me here lik I draw it.*

And on the other side was that map of a path starting from an X that indicated, doubtlessly, the park bench where I, an adolescent rebelling against prescribed and tedious education, forgot my classroom schedule in order to spend several hours reading books which if not actually written by me, seemed to be: who could doubt that only from *my* imagination could spring all those corsairs, those couriers of the tzar, all those boys slightly younger than I who rowed all day up and down the great American rivers on a raft. Clutching the arm of the park bench as if it were the frame of a magical saddle, at first I didn't hear the sound of the light steps and of the little girl who would stop behind me after running down the graveled garden path. It was Amilamia, and I don't know how long the child would have kept me silent company if her mischievous spirit, one afternoon, had not chosen to tickle my ear with down from a dandelion she blew towards me, her lips puffed out and her brow furrowed in a frown.

She asked my name and after considering it very seriously, she told me hers with a smile while if not candid, was not too rehearsed. Quickly I realized that Amilamia had discovered, if discovered is the word, a form of expression midway between the ingenuousness of her years and the forms of adult mimicry that well-brought-up children have to know, particularly those for the solemn moments of introduction and of leavetaking. Amilamia's seriousness, apparently, was a gift of nature, whereas her moments of spontaneity, by contrast, seemed artificial. I like to remember her, afternoon after afternoon, in a succession of snapshots that in their totality sum up the complete Amilamia. And it never ceases to surprise me that I cannot think of her as she really was, or remember how she actually moved, light, questioning, constantly looking around her. I must remember her fixed forever in time, as in a photograph album. Amilamia in the distance, a point on the spot where the hill began to descend from a lake of clover towards the flat meadow where I, sitting on the bench, used to read: a point of fluctuating shadow and sunshine and a hand that waved to me from high on the hill. Amilamia frozen in her flight down the hill, her white skirt billowing, the flowered panties gathered around her thighs with elastic, her mouth open and eyes half-closed against the streaming air, the child crying with pleasure. Amilamia sitting beneath the eucalyptus trees, pretending to cry so that I would go over to her. Amilamia lying on her stomach with a flower in her hand: the petals of a flower which I discovered later didn't grow in this garden, but somewhere else, perhaps in the garden of Amilamia's house, since the single pocket of her blue-checked apron was often filled with those white blossoms. Amilamia watching me read, holding with both hands to the bars of the green bench, asking questions with her grey eyes: I recall that she never asked me what I was reading, as if she could divine in my eyes the images born of the pages. Amilamia laughing with pleasure when I lifted her by the waist and whirled her around my head; she seemed to discover a new perspective on the world in that slow flight. Amilamia turning her back to me and waving goodbye, her arm held high, the fingers waving excitedly. And Amilamia in the thousand postures she

affected around my bench, hanging upside down, her
bloomers billowing; sitting on the gravel with her legs
crossed and her chin resting on her fist; lying on the grass
baring her belly-button to the sun; weaving tree branches,
drawing animals in the mud with a twig, licking the bars
of the bench, hiding beneath the seat, silently breaking
off the loose bark from the ancient treetrunks, staring at
the horizon beyond the hill, humming with her eyes closed,
imitating the voices of birds, dogs, cats, hens, and horses.
All for me, and nevertheless, nothing. It was her way of
being with me, all these things I remember, but at the
same time her manner of being alone in the park. Yes,
perhaps my memory of her is fragmentary because reading alternated with the contemplation of the chubby-
cheeked child with smooth hair changing in the reflection
of the light: now wheat-colored, now burnt chestnut. And
it is only today that I think how Amilamia in that moment
established the other point of support for my life, the one
that created the tension between my own irresolute childhood and the open world, the promised land that was beginning to be mine through my reading.

Not then. Then I dreamed about the women in my
books, about the quintessential female—the word disturbed me—who assumed the disguise of the Queen in
order to buy the necklace secretly, about the imagined
beings of mythology—half recognizable, half white-
breasted, damp-bellied salamanders—who awaited mon-
archs in their beds. And thus, imperceptibly, I moved
from indifference towards my childish companion to an
acceptance of the child's gracefulness and seriousness
and from there to an unexpected rejection of a presence
that became useless to me. She irritated me, finally. I who
was fourteen was irritated by that child of seven who was
not yet memory or nostalgia, but rather the past and its
reality. I had let myself be dragged along by weakness.

We had run together, holding hands, across the meadow.
Together we had shaken the pines and picked up the cones
that Amilamia guarded jealously in her apron pocket.
Together we had constructed paper boats and followed
them, happy and gay, to the edge of the drain. And that
afternoon amidst shouts of glee, when we tumbled together
down the hill and rolled to a stop at its foot, Amilamia was
on my chest, her hair between my lips; but when I felt
her panting breath in my ear and her little arms sticky
from sweets around my neck, I angrily pushed away her
arms and let her fall. Amilamia cried, rubbing her
wounded elbow and knee, and I returned to my bench.
Then Amilamia went away and the following day she returned, handed me the paper without a word, and disappeared, humming, into the woods. I hesitated whether
to tear up the card or keep it in the pages of the book:
Afternoons on the Farm. Even my reading had become
childish because of Amilamia. She did not return to the
park. After a few days I left for my vacation and when I
returned it was to the duties of my first year of prep school.
I never saw her again.

II

And now, almost rejecting the image that is unaccustomed without being fantastic, but is all the more painful
for being so real, I return to that forgotten park and
stopping before the grove of pines and eucalyptus I recognize the smallness of the bosky enclosure that my memory
has insisted on drawing with an amplitude that allowed
sufficient space for the vast swell of my imagination. After
all, Strogoff and Huckleberry, Milday de Winter and
Geneviève de Brabante were born, lived and died here: in
a little garden surrounded by mossy iron railings, sparsely
planted with old, neglected trees, barely adorned by a

concrete bench painted to look like wood that forces me to believe that my beautiful wrought-iron green-painted bench never existed, or else was a part of my orderly, retrospective delirium. And the hill. . . . How could I believe the promontory that Amilamia climbed and descended during her daily coming and going, that steep slope we rolled down together, was *this*. A barely elevated patch of dark stubble with no more heights and depths than those my memory had created.

Com see me here lik I draw it. So I would have to cross the garden, leave the woods behind, descend the hill in three loping steps, cut through that narrow grove of chestnuts—it was here, surely, where the child gathered the white petals—open the squeaking park gate and suddenly recall . . . know . . . find oneself in the street, realize that every afternoon of one's adolescence, as if by a miracle, he had succeeded in suspending the beat of the surrounding city, annulling that flood-tide of whistles, bells, voices, sobs, engines, radios, imprecations. Which was the true magnet, the silent garden or the feverish city?

I wait for the light to change and cross to the other sidewalk, my eyes never leaving the red iris detaining the traffic. I consult Amilamia's paper. After all, that rudimentary map is the true magnet of the moment I am living, and just thinking about it startles me. I was obliged, after the lost afternoons of my fourteenth year, to follow the channels of discipline; now I find myself, at twenty-nine, duly certified with a diploma, owner of an office, assured of a moderate income, a bachelor still, with no family to maintain, slightly bored with sleeping with secretaries, scarcely excited by an occasional outing to the country or to the beach, feeling the lack of a central attraction such as those once afforded me by my books, my park, and Amilamia. I walk down the street of this gray, low-buildinged suburb. The one-story houses with their doorways scaling paint succeed each other monotonously. Faint neighborhood sounds barely interrupt the general uniformity: the squeal of a knife-sharpener here, the hammering of a shoe-repairman there. The children of the neighborhood are playing in the dead-end streets. The music of an organ-grinder reaches my ears, mingled with the voices of children's rounds. I stop a moment to watch them with the sensation, also fleeting, that Amilamia must be among these groups of children, immodestly exhibiting her flowered panties, hanging by her knees from some balcony, still fond of acrobatic excesses, her apron pocket filled with white petals. I smile, and for the first time I am able to imagine the young lady of twenty-two who, even if she still lives at this address, will laugh at my memories, or who perhaps will have forgotten the afternoons spent in the garden.

The house is identical to all the rest. The heavy entry door, two grilled windows with closed shutters. A one-story house, topped by a false neo-classic balustrade that probably conceals the practicalities of the flat-roofed *azotea*: clothes hanging on lines, tubs of water, servant's quarters, a chicken coop. Before I ring the bell, I want to free myself of any illusion. Amilamia no longer lives here. Why would she stay fifteen years in the same house? Besides, in spite of her precocious independence and aloneness, she seemed like a well-brought-up, well-behaved child, and this neighborhood is no longer elegant; Amilamia's parents, without doubt, have moved. But perhaps the new renters will know where.

I press the bell and wait. I ring again. Here is another contingency: no one is home. And will I feel the need again to look for my childhood friend? No. Because it will not be possible a second time to open a book from my adolescence and accidentally find Amilamia's card. I would return to my routine, I would forget the moment whose importance lay in its fleeting surprise.

I ring once more. I press my ear to the door and am surprised: I can hear a harsh and irregular breathing on the other side; the sound of labored breathing, accompanied by the disagreeable odor of stale tobacco, filters through the cracks in the hall.

"Good afternoon. Could you tell me. . . ?"

As soon as he hears my voice, the person moves away with heavy and unsure steps. I press the bell again, shouting this time:

"Hey! Open up! What's the matter? Don't you hear me?"

No response. I continue ringing the bell, without result. I move back from the door, still staring at the small cracks, as if distance might give me perspective, or even penetration. With all my attention fixed on that damned door, I cross the street, walking backwards; a piercing scream, followed by a prolonged and ferocious blast of a whistle, saves me in time; dazed, I seek the person whose voice has just saved me. I see only the automobile moving down the street and I hang onto a lamp post, a hold that more than security offers me a point of support during the sudden rush of icy blood to my burning, sweaty skin. I look towards the house that had been, that was, that must be, Amilamia's. There, behind the balustrade, as I had known there would be, fluttering clothes are drying. I don't know what else is hanging there—skirts, pyjamas, blouses—I don't know. All I can see is that starched little blue-checked apron, clamped by clothespins to the long cord that swings between an iron bar and a nail in the white wall of the *azotea*.

III

In the Bureau of Records they have told me that the property is in the name of a Señor R. Valdivia, who rents the house. To whom? That they don't know. Who is Valdivia? He has declared himself a businessman. Where does he live? Who are *you?* the young lady asked me with haughty curiosity. I haven't been able to present a calm and sure appearance. Sleep has not relieved my nervous fatigue. Valdivia. As I leave the Bureau the sun offends me. I associate the repugnance provoked by the hazy sun sifting through the clouds—therefore all the more intense—with the desire to return to the damp, shadowy park. No. It is only the desire to know whether Amilamia lives in that house and why they refuse to let me enter. But the first thing I must do is reject the absurd idea that kept me awake all night. Having seen the apron drying on the flat roof, the one where she kept the flowers, and so believing that in that house lived a seven-year-old girl that I had known fourteen or fifteen years before. . . . She must have a little girl! Yes. Amilamia, at twenty-two, is the mother of a girl who dressed the same, looked the same, repeated the same games, and—who knows— perhaps even went to the same park. And deep in thought I again arrived at the door of the house. I ring the bell and await the whistling breathing on the other side of the door. I am mistaken. The door is opened by a woman who can't be more than about fifty. But wrapped in a shawl, dressed in black and in black low-heeled shoes, with no make-up and her salt and pepper hair pulled into a knot, she seems to have abandoned all illusion or pretext of youth; she is observing me with eyes so indifferent they seem almost cruel.

"You want something?"

"Señor Valdivia sent me." I cough and run my hand over my hair. I should have picked up my briefcase at the office. I realize that without it I cannot play my role very well.

"Valdivia?" the woman asks without alarm, without interest.

"Yes. The owner of this house."

One thing is clear. The woman will reveal nothing in her face. She looks at me, calmly.

"Oh, yes. The owner of the house."

"May I come in?"

I think that in bad comedies the traveling salesman sticks a foot in the door so they can't close the door in his face. I do the same, but the woman steps back and with a gesture of her hand invites me to come into what must have been a garage. On one side there is a glass-paned door, its paint faded. I walk towards the door over the yellow tiles of the entryway and ask again, turning towards the woman who follows me with tiny steps:

"This way?"

I notice for the first time that in her white hands she is carrying a chapelet which she toys with ceaselessly. I haven't seen one of those old-fashioned rosaries since my childhood and I want to comment on it, but the brusque and decisive manner with which the woman opens the door precludes any gratuitous conversation. We enter a long narrow room. The woman hastens to open the shutters. But because of four large perennial plants growing in porcelain and crusted glass pots the room remains in shadow. The only other objects in the room are an old high-backed cane-trimmed sofa and a rocking chair. But it is neither the plants nor the sparcity of the furniture that draws my attention.

The woman invites me to sit on the sofa before she

sits in the rocking chair. Beside me, on the cane arm of the sofa, there is an open magazine.

"Señor Valdivia sends his apologies for not having come in person."

The woman rocks, unblinkingly. I peer at the comic book out of the corner of my eye.

"He sends his greetings and. . . ."

I stop, awaiting a reaction from the woman. She continues to rock. The magazine is covered with red-penciled scribbling.

". . . and asks me to inform you that he must disturb you for a few days. . . ."

My eyes search rapidly.

". . . A new evaluation of the house must be made for the tax lists. It seems it hasn't been done for. . . . You have been living here since. . . ?"

Yes. That is a stubby lipstick lying under the chair. If the woman smiles, it is only with the slow-moving hands caressing the chapelet; I sense, for an instant, a swift flash of ridicule that does not quite disturb her features. She still does not answer.

". . . for at least fifteen years, isn't that true?"

She does not agree. She does not disagree. And on the pale thin lips there is not the least sign of lipstick. . . .

". . . you, your husband, and. . . ?"

She stares at me, never changing expression, almost daring me to continue. We sit a moment in silence, she playing with the rosary, I leaning forwards, my hands on my knees. I rise.

"Well, then, I'll be back this afternoon with the papers. . . ."

The woman nods while, in silence, she picks up the lipstick and the comic book and hides them in the folds of her shawl.

IV

The scene has not changed. This afternoon, while I am writing down false figures in my notebook and feigning interest in establishing the quality of the dulled floor-boards and the length of the living room, the woman rocks, as the three decades of the chapelet whisper through her fingers. I sigh as I finish the supposed inventory of the living room and I ask her for permission to go to the other rooms in the house. The woman rises, bracing her long black-clad arms on the seat of the rocking chair and adjusting the shawl on her narrow bony shoulders.

She opens the opaque glass door and we enter a dining room with very little more furniture. But the table with the aluminum legs and the four nickel and plastic chairs lack even the slight hint of distinction of the living room furniture. Another window with wrought-iron grill and closed shutters must at times illuminate this bare-walled dining room, bare of either shelves or bureau. The only object on the table is a plastic fruit dish with a cluster of black grapes, two peaches, and a buzzing corona of flies. The woman, her arms crossed, her face expressionless, stops behind me. I take the risk of breaking the order of things: it is evident that these rooms will not tell me anything that I really want to know.

"Couldn't we go up to the roof?" I ask. "I believe that is the best way of measuring the total area."

The woman's eyes light up as she looks at me, or perhaps it is only the contrast with the penumbra of the dining room.

"What for?" she says finally. "Señor . . . Valdivia . . . knows the dimensions very well."

And those pauses, one before and one after the owner's name, are the first indications that something is at last perturbing the woman and forcing her, in defense, to resort to a certain irony.

"I don't know." I make an effort to smile. "Perhaps I prefer to go from top to bottom and not . . ." my false smile drains away, ". . . from bottom to top."

"You will go the way I show you," the woman says, her arms crossed across her chest, the silver cross hanging against her dark belly.

Before smiling weakly, I force myself to think how, in this shadow, my gestures are useless, not even symbolic. I open the notebook with a crunch of the cardboard cover and continue making my notes with the greatest possible speed, never glancing up, the numbers and estimates of this task whose fiction—the light flush in my cheeks and the perceptible dryness of my tongue tell me—is deceiving no one. And after filling the graph paper with absurd signs, with square roots and algebraic formulas, I ask myself what is preventing me from getting to the point, from asking about Amilamia and getting out of here with a satisfactory answer. Nothing. And nevertheless, I am sure that even if I obtained a response, the truth does not lie along this road. My slim and silent companion is a person I wouldn't look twice at in the street, but in this almost uninhabited house with the coarse furniture, she ceases to be an anonymous face in the crowd and is converted into a stock character of mystery. Such is the paradox, and if memories of Amilamia have once again awakened my appetite for the imaginary, I shall follow the rules of the game, I shall exhaust all the appearances, and I shall not rest until I find the answer—perhaps simple and clear, immediate and evident—that lies beyond the unexpected veils the señora of the rosary places in my path. Do I bestow a more-than-justified strangeness upon my reluctant Amphitryon? If that is so, I shall only take more pleasure in the labyrinths of my own invention. And

the flies are still buzzing around the fruit dish, occasionally
pausing on the damaged end of the peach, a nibbled bite
—I lean closer using the pretext of my notes—where little
teeth have left their mark in the velvety skin and ochre
flesh of the fruit. I do not look towards the señora. I
pretend I am taking notes. The fruit seems to be bitten
but not touched. I crouch down to see it better, rest my
hands upon the table, moving my lips closer as if I wished
to repeat the act of biting without touching. I look down
and I see another sign close to my feet: the track of two
tires that seem to be bicycle tires, the print of two rubber
tires that come as far as the edge of the table and then
lead away, growing fainter, the length of the room, towards
the señora. . . .

I close my notebook.

"Let us continue, señora."

As I turn towards her, I find her standing with her
hands resting on the back of a chair. Seated before her,
coughing the smoke of his black cigarette, is a man with
heavy shoulders and hidden eyes: these eyes, hardly visible
behind swollen wrinkled lids as thick and droopy as the neck
of an ancient turtle, seem nevertheless to follow my every
movement. The half-shaven cheeks, criss-crossed by a
thousand gray furrows, hang from protruding cheekbones,
and his greenish hands are folded beneath his arms. He is
wearing a coarse blue shirt, and his rumpled hair is so
curly it looks like the bottom of a barnacle-covered ship.
He does not move, and the true sign of his existence is
that difficult whistling breathing (as if every breath must
breach a flood-gate of phlegm, irritation, and abuse) that
I had already heard through the chinks of the entry hall.

Ridiculously, he murmurs: "Good afternoon. . . ." and
I am disposed to forget everything: the mystery, Amilamia,
the assessment, the bicycle tracks. The apparition of this
asthmatic old bear justifies a prompt retreat. I repeat "Good

afternoon," this time with an inflection of farewell. The turtle's mask dissolves into an atrocious smile: every pore of that flesh seems fabricated of brittle rubber, of painted, peeling oilcloth. The arm reaches out and detains me.

"Valdivia died four years ago," says the man in a distant, choking voice that issues from his belly instead of his larynx: a weak, high-pitched voice.

Held by that strong, almost painful, claw, I tell myself it is useless to pretend. But the wax and rubber faces observing me say nothing and for that reason I am able, in spite of everything, to pretend one last time, to pretend that I am speaking to myself when I say:

"Amilamia. . . ."

Yes; no one will have to pretend any longer. The fist that clutches my arm affirms its strength for only an instant, immediately its grip loosens, then it falls, weak and trembling, before rising to take the waxen hand touching the shoulder: the señora, perplexed for the first time, looks at me with the eyes of a violated bird and sobs with a dry moan that does not disturb the rigid astonishment of her features. Suddenly the ogres of my imagination are two solitary, abandoned, wounded old people, scarcely able to console themselves in the shuddering clasp of hands that fills me with shame. My fantasy has brought me to this stark dining room to violate the intimacy and the secret of two human beings exiled from life by something I no longer have the right to share. I have never despised myself more. Never have words failed me in such a clumsy way. Any gesture of mine would be in vain: shall I approach them, shall I touch them, shall I caress the woman's head, shall I ask them to excuse my intrusion? I return the notebook to my jacket pocket. I toss into oblivion all the clues in my detective story: the comic book, the lipstick, the nibbled fruit, the bicycle tracks, the blue-checked apron. . . . I decide to leave this house in silence. The old man, from behind those thick eyelids, must have noticed me. The high breathy voice says:

"Did you know her?"

That past, so natural they must use it every day, finally destroys my illusions. There is the answer. Did you know her? How many years? How many years must the world have lived without Amilamia, assassinated first by my forgetfulness, and revived, scarcely yesterday, by a sad impotent memory? When did those serious gray eyes cease to be astonished by the delight of an always solitary garden? When did those lips cease to pout or press together thinly in that ceremonious seriousness with which, I now realize, Amilamia must have discovered and consecrated the objects and events of life that, she knew perhaps intuitively, was fleeting?

"Yes, we played together in the park. A long time ago."

"How old was she?" says the old man, his voice even more muffled.

"She must have been about seven. No, older than seven."

The woman's voice rises, along with the arms that seem to implore:

"What was she like, señor? Tell us what she was like, please."

I close my eyes. "Amilamia is my memory, too. I can only compare her to the things that she touched, that she brought, that she discovered in the park. Yes. Now I see her, coming down the hill. No. It isn't true that it was a barely elevated patch of stubble. It was a hill, with grass, and Amilamia's coming and going had traced a path, and she waved to me from the top before she started down, accompanied by the music, yes, the music I saw, the painting I smelled, the tastes I heard, the odors I touched . . . my hallucination. . . ." Do they hear me? "She came, waving, dressed in white, in a blue-checked apron . . . the one you have hanging on the *azotea*. . . ."

They take my arms and still I do not open my eyes.

"What was she like, señor?"

"Her eyes were gray and the color of her hair changed in the reflection of the sun and the shadow of the trees. . . ."

They lead me gently, the two of them; I hear the man's labored breathing, the cross on the rosary hitting against the woman's body.

"Tell us, please. . . ."

"The air brought tears to her eyes when she ran; when she reached my bench her cheeks were silvered with happy tears. . . ."

I do not open my eyes. Now we are going upstairs. Two, five, eight, nine, twelve steps. Four hands guide my body.

"What was she like, what was she like?"

"She sat beneath the eucalyptus and wove garlands from the branches and pretended to cry so I would quit my reading and go over to her. . . ."

Hinges creak. The odor overpowers everything else: it routs the other senses, it takes its seat like a yellow Mogol upon the throne of my hallucination; heavy as a coffin, insinuating as the slither of draped silk, ornamented as a Turkish sceptre, opaque as a deep, lost vein of ore, brilliant as a dead star. The hands no longer hold me. More than the sobbing, it is the trembling of the old people that envelops me. Slowly, I open my eyes: first through the dizzying liquid of my cornea then through the web of my eyelashes, the room suffocated in that enormous battle of perfumes is disclosed, effluvia and frosty, almost flesh-like petals; the presence of the flowers is so strong here they seem to take on the quality of living flesh—the sweetness of the jasmine, the nausea of the lilies, the tomb of the tuberose, the temple of the gardenia. Illuminated through the incandescent wax lips of heavy sputtering candles, the small windowless bedroom with its aura of wax and

humid flowers assaults the very center of my plexus, and
from there, only there at the solar center of life, am I able
to revive and to perceive beyond the candles, among the
scattered flowers, the accumulation of used toys: the
colored hoops and wrinkled balloons, cherries dried to
transparency, wooden horses with scraggly manes, the
scooter, blind and hairless dolls, bears spilling their saw-
dust, punctured oil-cloth ducks, moth-eaten dogs, wornout
jumping ropes, glass jars of dried candy, wornout shoes,
the tricycle (three wheels? no, two, and not like a bicycle
—two *parallel* wheels below), little woolen and leather
shoes; and, facing me, within reach of my hand, the small
coffin raised on paper flower-decorated blue boxes, flowers
of life this time, carnations and sunflowers, poppies and
tulips, but like the others, the ones of death, all part of a
potion brewed by the atmosphere of this funeral hot-house
in which reposes, inside the silvered coffin, between the
black silk sheets, upon the pillow of white satin, that motionless and serene face framed in lace, highlighted with
rose-colored tints, eyebrows traced by the lightest trace of
pencil, closed lids, real eyelashes, thick, that cast a tenuous
shadow on cheeks as healthy as those of the days in the
park. Serious red lips, set almost in the angry pout that
Amilamia feigned so I would come to play. Hands joined
over the breast. A chapelet, identical to the mother's,
strangling that cardboard neck. Small white shroud on the
clean, pre-pubescent, docile body.

The old people, sobbing, have knelt.

I reach out my hand and run my fingers over the porcelain face of my friend. I feel the coldness of those painted
features, of the doll-queen who presides over the pomp of
this royal chamber of death. Porcelain, cardboard, and
cotton. *Amilamia will not forget her good friend—com
see me here lik I draw it.*

I withdraw my fingers from the false cadaver. Traces of my finger prints remain where I touched the skin of the doll.

And nausea crawls in my stomach where the candle smoke and the sweet stench of the lilies in the enclosed room have settled. I turn my back on Amilamia's sepulchre. The woman's hand touches my arm. Her wildly staring eyes do not correspond with the quiet, steady voice.

"Don't come back, señor. If you truly loved her, don't come back again."

I touch the hand of Amilamia's mother. I see through nauseous eyes the old man's head buried between his knees, and I go out of the room to the stairway, to the living room, to the patio, to the street.

V

If not a year, nine or ten months have passed. The memory of that idolatry no longer frightens me. I have forgotten the odor of the flowers and the image of the petrified doll. The real Amilamia has returned to my memory and I have felt, if not content, sane again: the park, the living child, my hours of adolescent reading, have triumphed over the spectres of a sick cult. The image of life is the more powerful. I tell myself that I shall live forever with my real Amilamia, the conqueror of the caricature of death. And one day I dare look again at that notebook with graph paper where I wrote the information of the false assessment. And from its pages, once again, falls Amilamia's card with its terrible childish scrawl and its map for getting from the park to her house. I smile as I pick it up. I bite one of the edges, thinking that in spite of everything, the poor old people would accept this gift.

Whistling, I put on my jacket and knot my tie. Why not visit them and offer them this paper with the child's own writing?

I am running as I approach the one-story house. Rain is beginning to fall in large isolated drops that bring from the earth with magical immediacy an odor of damp benediction that seems to stir the humus and precipitate the fermentation of everything living with its roots in the dust.

I ring the bell. The shower increases and I become insistent. A shrill voice shouts: "I'm going!" and I wait for the figure of the mother with her eternal rosary to open the door for me. I turn up the collar of my jacket. My clothes, my body, too, smell different in the rain. The door opens:

"What do you want? How wonderful you've come!"

The misshapen girl sitting in the wheelchair lays one hand on the doorknob and smiles at me with an indecipherably wry grin. The hump on her chest converts the dress into a curtain over her body, a piece of white cloth that nonetheless lends an air of coquetry to the blue-checked apron. The little woman extracts a pack of cigarettes from her apron pocket and rapidly lights a cigarette, staining the end with orange-painted lips. The smoke causes the beautiful gray eyes to squint. She arranges the coppery, wheat-colored, permanently waved hair: She stares at me all the time with a desolate, inquisitive, and hopeful—but at the same time fearful—expression.

"No, Carlos. Go away. Don't come back."

And from the house, at the same moment, I hear the high breathy breathing of the old man, coming closer and closer.

"Where are you? Don't you know you're not supposed to answer the door? Go back! Devil's spawn! Do I have to beat you again?"

And the water from the rain trickles down my forehead, over my cheeks, and into my mouth, and the little frightened hands drop the comic book onto the damp stones.

Translated by MARGARET S. PEDEN

Gabriel García Márquez (b. 1928) was born in Aracataca, on the Caribbean coast of Colombia, the son of a telegraph operator. As a small child he lived with his grandparents near a banana *finca* called Macondo. He studied law, first at the National University of Colombia in Bogotá, where he wrote his first story, and then in Cartagena, where he also worked for a newspaper. In 1950 he moved to Barranquilla, where he formed a new circle of friends who exposed him to a wide range of literature. Giving up his law studies, he began "Leaf Storm," which the publishing house Losada rejected with the advice that the author "take up another line of work." (The information here is from the Summer 1973 special García Márquez issue of *Books Abroad*.) For the next few years he worked for various newspapers and a press agency in Latin America, Europe, and New York City. During this time he wrote *El coronel no tiene quien le escriba* (1961) and most of the stories from *Los funerales de la Mamá Grande* (1962, both volumes translated as *No One Writes to the Colonel and Other Stories*). In 1961 he went to Mexico to write filmscripts, one of which he worked on with Carlos Fuentes. In 1965 the idea for his novel, *Cien años de soledad* (*One Hundred Years of Solitude*), came to him on a car trip from Mexico City to Acapulco; he shut himself up for eighteen months and wrote it. It was published in Buenos Aires in 1967 and in 1970 in this country, an immediate bestseller winning literary prizes all over the world. In both the stories and the novel he has created the fictional world of Macondo, the backwater town in which dotty characters survive civil wars and banana barons and natural calamities with aplomb but who see a cake of ice as an act of magic.

Balthazar's Marvelous Afternoon

The cage was finished. Balthazar hung it under the eave, from force of habit, and when he finished lunch everyone was already saying that it was the most beautiful cage in the world. So many people came to see it that a crowd formed in front of the house, and Balthazar had to take it down and close the shop.

"You have to shave," Ursula, his wife, told him. "You look like a Capuchin."

"It's bad to shave after lunch," said Balthazar.

He had two weeks' growth, short, hard, and bristly hair like the mane of a mule, and the general expression of a frightened boy. But it was a false expression. In February he was thirty; he had been living with Ursula for four years, without marrying her and without having children, and life had given him many reasons to be on guard but none to be frightened. He did not even know that for some people the cage he had just made was the most beautiful one in the world. For him, accustomed to making cages since childhood, it had been hardly any more difficult than the others.

"Then rest for a while," said the woman. "With that beard you can't show yourself anywhere."

While he was resting, he had to get out of his hammock several times to show the cage to the neighbors. Ursula had paid little attention to it until then. She was annoyed because her husband had neglected the work of his carpenter's shop to devote himself entirely to the cage, and for two weeks had slept poorly, turning over and muttering incoherencies, and he hadn't thought of shaving. But her annoyance dissolved in the face of the finished cage. When Balthazar woke up from his nap, she had ironed his pants and a shirt; she had put them on a chair near the hammock and had carried the cage to the dining table. She regarded it in silence.

"How much will you charge?" she asked.

"I don't know," Balthazar answered. "I'm going to ask for thirty pesos to see if they'll give me twenty."

"Ask for fifty," said Ursula. "You've lost a lot of sleep in these two weeks. Furthermore, it's rather large. I think it's the biggest cage I've ever seen in my life."

Balthazar began to shave.

"Do you think they'll give me fifty pesos?"

"That's nothing for Mr. Chepe Montiel, and the cage is worth it," said Ursula. "You should ask for sixty."

The house lay in the stifling shadow. It was the first week of April and the heat seemed less bearable because of the chirping of the cicadas. When he finished dressing, Balthazar opened the door to the patio to cool off the house, and a group of children entered the dining room.

The news had spread. Dr. Octavio Giraldo, an old physician, happy with life but tired of his profession, thought about Balthazar's cage while he was eating lunch with his invalid wife. On the inside terrace, where they put the table on hot days, there were many flowerpots and two cages with canaries. His wife liked birds, and she liked them so much that she hated cats because they could eat them up. Thinking about her, Dr. Giraldo went to see a patient that afternoon, and when he returned he went by Balthazar's house to inspect the cage.

There were a lot of people in the dining room. The cage was on display on the table: with its enormous dome of wire, three stories inside, with passageways and compartments especially for eating and sleeping and swings in the space set aside for the birds' recreation, it seemed like a small-scale model of a gigantic ice factory. The doctor inspected it carefully, without touching it, thinking that in effect the cage was better than its reputation, and much more beautiful than any he had ever dreamed of for his wife.

"This is a flight of the imagination," he said. He sought out Balthazar among the group of people and, fixing his maternal eyes on him, added, "You would have been an extraordinary architect."

Balthazar blushed.

"Thank you," he said.

"It's true," said the doctor. He was smoothly and delicately fat, like a woman who had been beautiful in her youth, and he had delicate hands. His voice seemed like that of a priest speaking Latin. "You wouldn't even need to put birds in it," he said, making the cage turn in front of the audience's eyes as if he were auctioning it off. "It would be enough to hang it in the trees so it could sing by itself." He put it back on the table, thought a moment, looking at the cage, and said:

"Fine, then I'll take it."

"It's sold," said Ursula.

"It belongs to the son of Mr. Chepe Montiel," said Balthazar. "He ordered it specially."

The doctor adopted a respectful attitude.

"Did he give you the design?"

"No," said Balthazar. "He said he wanted a large cage, like this one, for a pair of troupials."

The doctor looked at the cage.

"But this isn't for troupials."

"Of course it is, Doctor," said Balthazar, approaching the table. The children surrounded him. "The measurements are carefully calculated," he said, pointing to the different compartments with his forefinger. Then he struck the dome with his knuckles, and the cage filled with resonant chords.

"It's the strongest wire you can find, and each joint is soldered outside and in," he said.

"It's even big enough for a parrot," interrupted one of the children.

"That it is," said Balthazar.

The doctor turned his head.

"Fine, but he didn't give you the design," he said. "He gave you no exact specifications, aside from making it a cage big enough for troupials. Isn't that right?"

"That's right," said Balthazar.

"Then there's no problem," said the doctor. "One thing is a cage big enough for troupials, and another is this cage. There's no proof that this one is the one you were asked to make."

"It's this very one," said Balthazar, confused. "That's why I made it."

The doctor made an impatient gesture.

"You could make another one," said Ursula, looking at her husband. And then, to the doctor: "You're not in any hurry."

"I promised it to my wife for this afternoon," said the doctor.

"I'm very sorry, Doctor," said Balthazar, "but I can't sell you something that's sold already."

The doctor shrugged his shoulders. Drying the sweat from his neck with a handkerchief, he contemplated the cage silently with the fixed, unfocused gaze of one who looks at a ship which is sailing away.

"How much did they pay you for it?"

Balthazar sought out Ursula's eyes without replying.

"Sixty pesos," she said.

The doctor kept looking at the cage. "It's very pretty." He sighed. "Extremely pretty." Then, moving toward the door, he began to fan himself energetically, smiling, and the trace of that episode disappeared forever from his memory.

"Montiel is very rich," he said.

In truth, José Montiel was not as rich as he seemed, but he would have been capable of doing anything to become so. A few blocks from there, in a house crammed with equipment, where no one had ever smelled a smell that couldn't be sold, he remained indifferent to the news of the cage. His wife, tortured by an obsession with death, closed the doors and windows after lunch and lay for two hours with her eyes opened to the shadow of the room, while José Montiel took his siesta. The clamor of many voices surprised her there. Then she opened the door to the living room and found a crowd in front of the house, and Balthazar with the cage in the middle of the crowd, dressed in white, freshly shaved, with that expression of decorous candor with which the poor approach the houses of the wealthy.

"What a marvelous thing!" José Montiel's wife exclaimed, with a radiant expression, leading Balthazar inside. "I've never seen anything like it in my life," she said, and added, annoyed by the crowd which piled up at the door:

"But bring it inside before they turn the living room into a grandstand."

Balthazar was no stranger to José Montiel's house. On different occasions, because of his skill and forthright way of dealing, he had been called in to do minor carpentry jobs. But he never felt at ease among the rich. He used to think about them, about their ugly and argumentative wives, about their tremendous surgical operations, and he always experienced a feeling of pity. When he entered their houses, he couldn't move without dragging his feet.

"Is Pepe home?" he asked.

He had put the cage on the dining-room table.

"He's at school," said José Montiel's wife. "But he shouldn't be long," and she added, "Montiel is taking a bath."

In reality, José Montiel had not had time to bathe. He was giving himself an urgent alcohol rub, in order to come out and see what was going on. He was such a cautious man that he slept without an electric fan so he could watch over the noises of the house while he slept.

"Adelaide!" he shouted. "What's going on?"

"Come and see what a marvelous thing!" his wife shouted.

José Montiel, obese and hairy, his towel draped around his neck, appeared at the bedroom window.

"What is that?"

"Pepe's cage," said Balthazar.

His wife looked at him perplexedly.

"Whose?"

"Pepe's," replied Balthazar. And then, turning toward José Montiel, "Pepe ordered it."

Nothing happened at that instant, but Balthazar felt as

if someone had just opened the bathroom door on him. José Montiel came out of the bedroom in his underwear.

"Pepe!" he shouted.

"He's not back," whispered his wife, motionless.

Pepe appeared in the doorway. He was about twelve, and had the same curved eyelashes and was as quietly pathetic as his mother.

"Come here," José Montiel said to him. "Did you order this?"

The child lowered his head. Grabbing him by the hair, José Montiel forced Pepe to look him in the eye.

"Answer me."

The child bit his lip without replying.

"Montiel," whispered his wife.

José Montiel let the child go and turned toward Balthazar in a fury. "I'm very sorry, Balthazar," he said. "But you should have consulted me before going on. Only to you would it occur to contract with a minor." As he spoke, his face recovered its serenity. He lifted the cage without looking at it and gave it to Balthazar.

"Take it away at once, and try to sell it to whomever you can," he said. "Above all, I beg you not to argue with me." He patted him on the back and explained, "The doctor has forbidden me to get angry."

The child had remained motionless, without blinking, until Balthazar looked at him uncertainly with the cage in his hand. Then he emitted a guttural sound, like a dog's growl, and threw himself on the floor screaming.

José Montiel looked at him, unmoved, while the mother tried to pacify him. "Don't even pick him up," he said. "Let him break his head on the floor, and then put salt and lemon on it so he can rage to his heart's content." The child was shrieking tearlessly while his mother held him by the wrists.

"Leave him alone," José Montiel insisted.

Balthazar observed the child as he would have observed the death throes of a rabid animal. It was almost four o'clock. At that hour, at his house, Ursula was singing a very old song and cutting slices of onion.

"Pepe," said Balthazar.

He approached the child, smiling, and held the cage out to him. The child jumped up, embraced the cage which was almost as big as he was, and stood looking at Balthazar through the wirework without knowing what to say. He hadn't shed one tear.

"Balthazar," said José Montiel softly. "I told you already to take it away."

"Give it back," the woman ordered the child.

"Keep it," said Balthazar. And then, to José Montiel: "After all, that's what I made it for."

José Montiel followed him into the living room.

"Don't be foolish, Balthazar," he was saying, blocking his path. "Take your piece of furniture home and don't be silly. I have no intention of paying you a cent."

"It doesn't matter," said Balthazar. "I made it expressly as a gift for Pepe. I didn't expect to charge anything for it."

As Balthazar made his way through the spectators who were blocking the door, José Montiel was shouting in the middle of the living room. He was very pale and his eyes were beginning to get red.

"Idiot!" he was shouting. "Take your trinket out of here. The last thing we need is for some nobody to give orders in my house. Son of a bitch!"

In the pool hall, Balthazar was received with an ovation. Until that moment, he thought that he had made a better cage than ever before, that he'd had to give it to the son of José Montiel so he wouldn't keep crying, and that none of these things was particularly important. But then he realized that all of this had a certain importance for many people, and he felt a little excited.

"So they gave you fifty pesos for the cage."

"Sixty," said Balthazar.

"Score one for you," someone said. "You're the only one who has managed to get such a pile of money out of Mr. Chepe Montiel. We have to celebrate."

They bought him a beer, and Balthazar responded with a round for everybody. Since it was the first time he had ever been out drinking, by dusk he was completely drunk, and he was talking about a fabulous project of a thousand cages, at sixty pesos each, and then a million cages, till he had sixty million pesos. "We have to make a lot of things to sell to the rich before they die," he was saying, blind drunk. "All of them are sick, and they're going to die. They're so screwed up they can't even get angry any more." For two hours he was paying for the jukebox, which played without interruption. Everybody toasted Balthazar's health, good luck, and fortune, and the death of the rich, but at mealtime they left him alone in the pool hall.

Ursula had waited for him until eight, with a dish of fried meat covered with slices of onion. Someone told her that her husband was in the pool hall, delirious with happiness, buying beers for everyone, but she didn't believe it, because Balthazar had never got drunk. When she went to bed, almost at midnight, Balthazar was in a lighted room where there were little tables, each with four chairs, and an outdoor dance floor, where the plovers were walking around. His face was smeared with rouge, and since he couldn't take one more step, he thought he wanted to lie down with two women in the same bed. He had spent so much that he had had to leave his watch in pawn, with the promise to pay the next day. A moment later, spread-eagled in the street, he realized that his shoes were being taken off, but he didn't want to abandon the happiest dream of his life. The women who passed on their way to five-o'clock Mass didn't dare look at him, thinking he was dead.

Translated by J. S. BERNSTEIN

eagled in the street, he realized that his shoes wer...
taken off, but he didn't want to abandon the...
dream of his life. The women who passed on th...

José Donoso (b. 1924) was born in Santiago, Chile, the son of a doctor. In his early twenties he spent a year on the pampas in Argentina, then finished school and entered the University of Chile. In 1949 he went to Princeton on a scholarship. In 1955 he published his first book of short stories, and in 1957, living with a fisherman's family in Isla Negra, finished his first novel, *Coronación (Coronation)*. It was published in the U.S. by Knopf in 1963, the year he began writing his masterpiece *El odsano pájoro de la noche (The Obscene Bird of Night)*. In 1965 he wrote *El lugar sin límites (Hell Has No Limits)* at the home of Carlos Fuentes in Mexico and then finished *Esta Domingo (This Sunday)*. He taught at the Writers Workshop in Iowa City from 1965 to 1967, then moved to Spain to finish *Obscene Bird*, a project made more difficult by a recurring ulcer that precipitated a bout of madness. *Obscene Bird* was published in 1970. In 1971 he moved to Calaceite, Teruel. The Fall 1973 *Review* focuses on Donoso and especially *Obscene Bird*, as a "giant thalidomine novel filled with grotesques . . . a delirious, non-stop flight of the imagination." In his earlier, more straight-forward novels he had focused on the relationship of the aristocracy and the servant class, "two faces of the same being," but progressively his concept of the double faces of identity became more complex. In *El lugar sin límites (Hell Has No Limits)* (included in the collection *Triple Cross*), the main character is a transvestite in whom both sexes coexist. In *The Obscene Bird of Night*, a complex novel, the characters are fragmented and difficult to identify or distinguish from one another, channeled through the consciousness of the narrator, a deaf-mute, who helps to carry the Donoso theme that in everyone exists the possibility of being both beautiful and monstrous. The more traditional story we are reprinting here carries another Donoso theme: the individual's need to escape a role imposed on him by society.

Paseo

1

This happened when I was very young, when my father and Aunt Mathilda, his maiden sister, and my uncles Gustav and Armand were still living. Now they are all dead. Or I should say, I prefer to think they are all dead: it is too late now for the questions they did not ask when the moment was right, because events seemed to freeze all of them into silence. Later they were able to construct a wall of forgetfulness or indifference to shut out everything, so that they would not have to harass themselves with impotent conjecture. But then, it may not have been that way at all. My imagination and my memory may be deceiving me. After all, I was only a child then, with whom they did not have to share the anguish of their inquiries, if they made any, nor the result of their discussions.

What was I to think? At times I used to hear them closeted in the library, speaking softly, slowly, as was their custom. But the massive door screened the meaning of their words, permitting me to hear only the grave and measured counterpoint of their voices. What was it they were saying? I used to hope that, inside there, abandoning the coldness which isolated each of them, they were at last speaking of what was truly important. But I had so little faith in this that, while I hung around the walls of the vestibule near the library door, my mind became filled with the certainty that they had chosen to forget, that they were meeting only to discuss, as always, some case in jurisprudence relating to their specialty in maritime law. Now I think that perhaps they were right in wanting to blot out everything. For why should one live with the terror of having to acknowledge that the streets of a city can swallow up a human being, leaving him without life and without death, suspended as it were, in a dimension more dangerous than any dimension with a name?

One day, months after, I came upon my father watching the street from the balcony of the drawing-room on the second floor. The sky was close, dense, and the humid air weighed down the large, limp leaves of the ailanthus trees. I drew near my father, eager for an answer that would contain some explanation:

"What are you doing here, Papa?" I murmured.

When he answered, something closed over the despair on his face, like the blow of a shutter closing on a shameful scene.

"Don't you see? I'm smoking . . ." he replied.

And he lit a cigarette.

It wasn't true. I knew why he was peering up and down the street, his eyes darkened, lifting his hand from time to time to stroke his smooth chestnut whiskers: it was in hope of seeing them reappear, returning under the trees of the sidewalk, the white bitch trotting at heel.

Little by little I began to realize that not only my father

but all of them, hiding from one another and without confessing even to themselves what they were doing, haunted the windows of the house. If someone happened to look up from the sidewalk he would surely have seen the shadow of one or another of them posted beside a curtain, or faces aged with grief spying out from behind the window panes.

In those days the street was paved with quebracho wood, and under the ailanthus trees a clangorous streetcar used to pass from time to time. The last time I was there neither the wooden pavements nor the streetcars existed any longer. But our house was still standing, narrow and vertical like a little book pressed between the bulky volumes of new buildings, with shops on the ground level and a crude sign advertising knitted undershirts covering the balconies of the second floor.

When we lived there all the houses were tall and slender like our own. The block was always happy with the games of children playing in the patches of sunshine on the sidewalks, and with the gossip of the servant girls on their way back from shopping. But our house was not happy. I say it that way, "it was not happy" instead of "it was sad," because that is exactly what I mean to say. The word "sad" would be wrong because it has too definite a connotation, a weight and a dimension of its own. What took place in our house was exactly the opposite: an absence, a lack, which because it was unacknowledged was irremediable, something that if it weighed, weighed by not existing.

My mother died when I was only four years old, so the presence of a woman was deemed necessary for my care. As Aunt Mathilda was the only woman in the family and she lived with my uncles Armand and Gustav, the three of them came to live at our house, which was spacious and empty.

Aunt Mathilda discharged her duties towards me with that propriety which was characteristic of everything she did. I did not doubt that she loved me, but I could never feel it as a palpable experience uniting us. There was something rigid in her affections, as there was in those of the men of the family. With them, love existed confined inside each individual, never breaking its boundaries to express itself and bring them together. For them to show affection was to discharge their duties to each other perfectly, and above all not to inconvenience, never to inconvenience. Perhaps to express love in any other way was unnecessary for them now, since they had so long a history together, had shared so long a past. Perhaps the tenderness they felt in the past had been expressed to the point of satiation and found itself stylized now in the form of certain actions, useful symbols which did not require further elucidation. Respect was the only form of contact left between those four isolated individuals who walked the corridors of the house which, like a book, showed only its narrow spine to the street.

I, naturally, had no history in common with Aunt Mathilda. How could I, if I was no more than a child then, who could not understand the gloomy motivations of his elders? I wished that their confined feeling might overflow and express itself in a fit of rage, for example, or with some bit of foolery. But she could not guess this desire of mine because her attention was not focused on me: I was a person peripheral to her life, never central. And I was not central because the entire center of her being was filled up with my father and my uncles. Aunt Mathilda was born the only woman, an ugly woman moreover, in a family of handsome men, and on realizing that for her marriage was unlikely, she dedicated herself to looking out for the comfort of those three men, by keeping house for them, by taking care of their clothes and providing their favorite dishes. She did these things without the least servility, proud of her role because she did not question her brothers' excellence. Furthermore, like all women, she possessed in the highest degree the faith that physical well-being is, if not principal, certainly primary, and that to be neither hungry nor cold nor uncomfortable is the basis for whatever else is good. Not that these defects caused her grief, but rather they made her impatient, and when she saw affliction about her she took immediate steps to remedy what, without doubt, were errors in a world that should be, that had to be, perfect. On another plane, she was intolerant of shirts which were not stupendously well-ironed, of meat that was not of the finest quality, of the humidity that owing to someone's carelessness had crept into the cigar-box.

After dinner, following what must have been an ancient ritual in the family, Aunt Mathilda went upstairs to the bedrooms, and in each of her brothers' rooms she prepared the beds for sleeping, parting the sheets with her bony hands. She spread a shawl at the foot of the bed for that one, who was subject to chills, and placed a feather pillow at the head of this one, for he usually read before going to sleep. Then, leaving the lamps lighted beside those enormous beds, she came downstairs to the billiard room to join the men for coffee and for a few rounds, before, as if bewitched by her, they retired to fill the empty effigies of the pajamas she had arranged so carefully upon the white, half-opened sheets.

But Aunt Mathilda never opened my bed. Each night, when I went up to my room, my heart thumped in the hope of finding my bed opened with the recognizable dexterity of her hands. But I had to adjust myself to the less pure style of the servant girl who was charged with doing it. Aunt Mathilda never granted me that mark of importance because I was not her brother. And not to be

"one of my brothers" seemed to her a misfortune of
which many people were victims, almost all in fact, including me, who after all was only the son of one of
them.

Sometimes Aunt Mathilda asked me to visit her in her
room where she sat sewing by the tall window, and she
would talk to me. I listened attentively. She spoke to me
about her brothers' integrity as lawyers in the intricate
field of maritime law, and she extended to me her enthusiasm for their wealth and reputation, which I would carry
forward. She described the embargo on a shipment of
oranges, told of certain damages caused by miserable tug-
boats manned by drunkards, of the disastrous effects that
arose from the demurrage of a ship sailing under an
exotic flag. But when she talked to me of ships her words
did not evoke the hoarse sounds of ships' sirens that I
heard in the distance on summer nights when, kept awake
by the heat, I climbed to the attic, and from an open
window watched the far-off floating lights, and those
blocks of darkness surrounding the city that lay forever
out of reach for me because my life was, and would ever
be, ordered perfectly. I realize now that Aunt Mathilda
did not hint at this magic because she did not know of it.
It had no place in her life, as it had no place in the life
of anyone destined to die with dignity in order afterwards
to be installed in a comfortable heaven, a heaven identical
to our house. Mute, I listened to her words, my gaze fastened on the white thread that, as she stretched it against
her black blouse, seemed to capture all of the light from
the window. I exulted at the world of security that her
words projected for me, that magnificent straight road
which leads to a death that is not dreaded since it is exactly
like this life, without anything fortuitous or unexpected.
Because death was not terrible. Death was the final incision, clean and definitive, nothing more. Hell existed, of

course, but not for us. It was rather for chastising the other inhabitants of the city and those anonymous seamen who caused the damages that, when the cases were concluded, filled the family coffers.

Aunt Mathilda was so removed from the idea of fear that, since I now know that love and fear go hand in hand, I am tempted to think that in those days she did not love anyone. But I may be mistaken. In her rigid way she may have been attached to her brothers by a kind of love. At night, after supper, they gathered in the billiard room for a few games. I used to go in with them. Standing outside that circle of imprisoned affections, I watched for a sign that would show me the ties between them did exist, and did, in fact, bind. It is strange that my memory does not bring back anything but shades of indeterminate grays in remembering the house, but when I evoke that hour, the strident green of the table, the red and white of the balls and the little cube of blue chalk become inflamed in my memory, illumined by the low lamp whose shade banished everything else into dusk. In one of the family's many rituals, the voice of Aunt Mathilda rescued each of the brothers by turn from the darkness, so that they might make their plays.

"Now, Gustav . . ."

And when he leaned over the green table, cue in hand, Uncle Gustav's face was lit up, brittle as paper, its nobility contradicted by his eyes, which were too small and spaced too close together. Finished playing, he returned to the shadow, where he lit a cigar whose smoke rose lazily until it was dissolved in the gloom of the ceiling. Then his sister said:

"All right, Armand . . ."

And the soft, timid face of Uncle Armand, with his large, sky-blue eyes concealed by gold-rimmed glasses, bent down underneath the light. His game was generally

bad because he was "the baby" as Aunt Mathilda sometimes referred to him. After the comments aroused by
his play he took refuge behind his newspaper and Aunt
Mathilda said:

"Pedro, your turn . . ."

I held my breath when I saw him lean over to play,
held it even more tightly when I saw him succumb to his
sister's command. I prayed, as he got up, that he would
rebel against the order established by his sister's voice.
I could not see that this order was in itself a kind of re-
bellion, constructed by them as a protection against chaos,
so that they might not be touched by what can be neither
explained nor resolved. My father, then, leaned over the
green cloth, his practiced eye gauging the exact distance
and positions of the billiards. He made his play, and
making it, he exhaled in such a way that his moustache
stirred about his half-opened mouth. Then he handed me
his cue so I might chalk it with the blue cube. With this
minimal role that he assigned to me, he let me touch the
circle that united him with the others, without letting me
take part in it more than tangentially.

Now it was Aunt Mathilda's turn. She was the best
player. When I saw her face, composed as if from the defects of her brothers' faces, coming out of the shadow, I
knew that she was going to win. And yet . . . had I not
seen her small eyes light up that face so like a brutally
clenched fist, when by chance one of them succeeded in
beating her? That spark appeared because, although she
might have wished it, she would never have permitted
herself to let any of them win. That would be to introduce
the mysterious element of love into a game that ought not
to include it, because affection should remain in its place,
without trespassing on the strict reality of a carom shot.

2

I never did like dogs. One may have frightened me when I was very young, I don't know, but they have always displeased me. As there were no dogs at home and I went out very little, few occasions presented themselves to make me uncomfortable. For my aunt and uncles and for my father, dogs, like all the rest of the animal kingdom, did not exist. Cows, of course, supplied the cream for the dessert that was served in a silver dish on Sundays. Then there were the birds that chirped quite agreeably at twilight in the branches of the elm tree, the only inhabitant of the small garden at the rear of the house. But animals for them existed only in the proportion in which they contributed to the pleasure of human beings. Which is to say that dogs, lazy as city dogs are, could not even dent their imagination with a possibility of their existence.

Sometimes, on Sunday, Aunt Mathilda and I used to go to mass early to take communion. It was rare that I succeeded in concentrating on the sacrament, because the idea that she was watching me without looking generally occupied the first plane of my conscious mind. Even when her eyes were directed to the altar, or her head bowed before the Blessed Sacrament, my every movement drew her attention to it. And on leaving the church she told me with sly reproach that it was without doubt a flea trapped in the pews that prevented me from meditating, as she had suggested, that death is the good foreseen end, and from praying that it might not be painful, since that was the purpose of masses, novenas and communions.

This was such a morning. A fine drizzle was threatening to turn into a storm, and the quebracho pavements extended their shiny fans, notched with streetcar rails, from sidewalk to sidewalk. As I was cold and in a hurry to get home I stepped up the pace beside Aunt Mathilda, who was holding her black mushroom of an umbrella above our heads. There were not many people in the street since it was so early. A dark-complexioned gentleman saluted us without lifting his hat, because of the rain. My aunt was in the process of telling me how surprised she was that someone of mixed blood had bowed to her with so little show of attention, when suddenly, near where we were walking, a streetcar applied its brakes with a screech, making her interrupt her monologue. The conductor looked out through his window:

"Stupid dog!" he shouted.

We stopped to watch.

A small white bitch escaped from between the wheels of the streetcar and, limping painfully, with her tail between her legs, took refuge in a doorway as the streetcar moved on again.

"These dogs," protested Aunt Mathilda. "It's beyond me how they are allowed to go around like that."

Continuing our way we passed by the bitch huddled in the corner of a doorway. It was small and white, with legs which were too short for its size and an ugly pointed snout that proclaimed an entire genealogy of misalliances: the sum of unevenly matched breeds which for generations had been scouring the city, searching for food in the garbage cans and among the refuse of the port. She was drenched, weak, trembling with cold or fever. When we passed in front of her I noticed that my aunt looked at the bitch, and the bitch's eyes returned her gaze.

We continued on our way home. Several steps further I was on the point of forgetting the dog when my aunt surprised me by abruptly turning around and crying out:

"Psst! Go away . . .!"

She had turned in such absolute certainty of finding the bitch following us that I trembled with the mute question which arose from my surprise: How did she know? She couldn't have heard her, since she was following us at an appreciable distance. But she did not doubt it. Perhaps the look that had passed between them of which I saw only the mechanics—the bitch's head raised slightly toward Aunt Mathilda, Aunt Mathilda's slightly inclined toward the bitch—contained some secret commitment? I do not know. In any case, turning to drive away the dog, her peremptory "psst" had the sound of something like a last effort to repel an encroaching destiny. It is possible that I am saying all this in the light of things that happened later, that my imagination is embellishing with significance what was only trivial. However, I can say with certainty that in that moment I felt a strangeness, almost a fear of my aunt's sudden loss of dignity in condescending to turn around and confer rank on a sick and filthy bitch.

We arrived home. We went up the stairs and the bitch stayed down below, looking up at us from the torrential rain that had just been unleashed. We went inside, and the delectable process of breakfast following communion removed the white bitch from my mind. I have never felt our house so protective as that morning, never rejoiced so much in the security derived from those old walls that marked off my world.

In one of my wanderings in and out of the empty sitting-rooms, I pulled back the curtain of a window to see if the rain promised to let up. The storm continued. And, sitting at the foot of the stairs still scrutinizing the house, I saw the white bitch. I dropped the curtain so that I might not see her there, soaked through and looking like one spellbound. Then, from the dark outer rim of the room, Aunt Mathilda's low voice surprised me. Bent over to strike a match to the kindling wood already arranged in the fireplace, she asked:

"Is it still there?"

"What?"

I knew what.

"The white bitch . . ."

I answered yes, that it was.

3

It must have been the last storm of the winter, because I remember quite clearly that the following days opened up and the nights began to grow warmer.

The white bitch stayed posted on our doorstep scrutinizing our windows. In the mornings, when I left for school, I tried to shoo her away, but barely had I boarded the bus when I would see her reappear around the corner or from behind the mailbox. The servant girls also tried to frighten her away, but their attempts were as fruitless as mine, because the bitch never failed to return.

Once, we were all saying good-night at the foot of the stairs before going up to bed. Uncle Gustav had just turned off the lights, all except the one on the stairway, so that the large space of the vestibule had become peopled with the shadowy bodies of furniture. Aunt Mathilda, who was entreating Uncle Armand to open the window of his room so a little air could come in, suddenly stopped speaking, leaving her sentence unfinished, and the movements of all of us, who had started to go up, halted.

"What is the matter?" asked Father, stepping down one stair.

"Go on up," murmured Aunt Mathilda, turning around and gazing into the shadow of the vestibule.

But we did not go up.

The silence of the room was filled with the secret voice of each object: a grain of dirt trickling down between the wallpaper and the wall, the creaking of polished woods, the quivering of some loose crystal. Someone, in addition to ourselves, was where we were. A small white form came out of the darkness near the service door. The bitch crossed the vestibule, limping slowly in the direction of Aunt Mathilda, and without even looking at her, threw herself down at her feet.

It was as though the immobility of the dog enabled us to move again. My father came down two stairs. Uncle Gustav turned on the light. Uncle Armand went upstairs and shut himself in his room.

"What is this?" asked my father.

Aunt Mathilda remained still.

"How could she have come in?" she asked aloud.

Her question seemed to acknowledge the heroism implicit in having either jumped walls in that lamentable condition, or come into the basement through a broken pane of glass, or fooled the servants' vigilance by creeping through a casually opened door.

"Mathilda, call one of the girls to take her away," said my father, and went upstairs followed by Uncle Gustav.

We were left alone looking at the bitch. She called a servant, telling the girl to give her something to eat and the next day to call a veterinarian.

"Is she going to stay in the house?" I asked.

"How can she walk in the street like that?" murmured Aunt Mathilda. "She has to get better so we can throw her out. And she'd better get well soon because I don't want animals in the house."

Then she added:

"Go upstairs to bed."

She followed the girl who was carrying the dog out.

I sensed that ancient drive of Aunt Mathilda's to have everything go well about her, that energy and dexterity which made her sovereign of immediate things. Is it possible that she was so secure within her limitations, that for her the only necessity was to overcome imperfections, errors not of intention or motive, but of condition? If so, the white bitch was going to get well. She would see to it because the animal had entered the radius of her power. The veterinarian would bandage the broken leg under her watchful eye, and protected by rubber gloves and an apron, she herself would take charge of cleaning the bitch's pustules with disinfectant that would make her howl. But Aunt Mathilda would remain deaf to those howls, sure that whatever she was doing was for the best.

And so it was. The bitch stayed in the house. Not that I saw her, but I could feel the presence of any stranger there, even though confined to the lower reaches of the basement. Once or twice I saw Aunt Mathilda with the rubber gloves on her hands, carrying a vial full of red liquid. I found a plate with scraps of food in a passage of the basement where I went to look for the bicycle I had just been given. Weakly, buffered by walls and floors, at times the suspicion of a bark reached my ears.

One afternoon I went down to the kitchen. The bitch came in, painted like a clown with red disinfectant. The servants threw her out without paying her any mind. But I saw that she was not hobbling any longer, that her tail, limp before, was curled up like a feather, leaving her shameless bottom in plain view.

That afternoon I asked Aunt Mathilda:

"When are you going to throw her out?"

"Who?" she asked.

She knew perfectly well.

"The white bitch."

"She's not well yet," she replied.

Later I thought of insisting, of telling her that surely there was nothing now to prevent her from climbing the garbage cans in search of food. I didn't do it because I believe it was the same night that Aunt Mathilda, after losing the first round of billiards, decided that she did not feel like playing another. Her brothers went on playing, and she, ensconced in the leather sofa, made a mistake in calling their names. There was a moment of confusion. Then the thread of order was quickly picked up again by the men, who knew how to ignore an accident if it was not favorable to them. But I had already seen.

It was as if Aunt Mathilda were not there at all. She was breathing at my side as she always did. The deep, silencing carpet yielded under her feet as usual and her tranquilly crossed hands weighed on her skirt. How is it possible to feel with the certainty I felt then the absence of a person whose heart is somewhere else? The following nights were equally troubled by the invisible slur of her absence. She seemed to have lost all interest in the game, and left off calling her brothers by their names. They appeared not to notice it. But they must have, because their games became shorter and I noticed an infinitesimal increase in the deference with which they treated her.

One night, as we were going out of the dining-room, the bitch appeared in the doorway and joined the family group. The men paused before they went into the library so that their sister might lead the way to the billiard room, followed this time by the white bitch. They made no comment, as if they had not seen her, beginning their game as they did every night.

The bitch sat down at Aunt Mathilda's feet. She was very quiet. Her lively eyes examined the room and followed the players' strategies as if all of that amused her greatly. She was fat now and had a shiny coat. Her whole body, from her quivering snout to her tail ready to waggle, was full of an abundant capacity for fun. How long had she stayed in the house? A month? Perhaps more. But in that month Aunt Mathilda had forced her to get well, caring for her not with displays of affection, but with those hands of hers which could not refrain from mending what was broken. The leg was well. She had disinfected, fed and bathed her, and now the white bitch was whole.

In one of his plays Uncle Armand let the cube of blue chalk fall to the floor. Immediately, obeying an instinct that seemed to surge up from her picaresque past, the bitch ran towards the chalk and snatched it with her mouth away from Uncle Armand, who had bent over to pick it up. Then followed something surprising: Aunt Mathilda, as if suddenly unwound, burst into a peal of laughter that agitated her whole body. We remained frozen. On hearing her laugh, the bitch dropped the chalk, ran towards her with her tail waggling aloft, and jumped up onto her lap. Aunt Mathilda's laugh relented, but Uncle Armand left the room. Uncle Gustav and my father went on with the game: now it was more important than ever not to see, not to see anything at all, not to comment, not to consider oneself alluded to by these events.

I did not find Aunt Mathilda's laugh amusing, because I may have felt the dark thing that had stirred it up. The bitch grew calm sitting on her lap. The cracking noises of the balls when they hit seemed to conduct Aunt Mathilda's hand first from its place on the edge of the sofa, to her skirt, and then to the curved back of the sleeping animal. On seeing that expressionless hand reposing there, I noticed that the tension which had kept my aunt's features clenched before, relented, and that a certain peace was now softening her face. I could not resist. I drew closer to her on the sofa, as if to a newly kindled fire. I hoped that she would reach out to me with a look or include me with a smile. But she did not.

4

When I arrived from school in the afternoon, I used to
go directly to the back of the house and, mounting my
bicycle, take turn after turn around the narrow garden,
circling the pair of cast-iron benches and the elm tree.
Behind the wall, the chestnut trees were beginning to
display their light spring down, but the seasons did not
interest me for I had too many serious things to think
about. And since I knew that no one came down into the
garden until the suffocation of midsummer made it imperative, it seemed to be the best place for meditating
about what was going on inside the house.

One might have said that nothing was going on. But
how could I remain calm in the face of the entwining
relationship which had sprung up between my aunt and
the white bitch? It was as if Aunt Mathilda, after having
resigned herself to an odd life of service and duty, had
found at last her equal. And as women-friends do, they
carried on a life full of niceties and pleasing refinements.
They ate bonbons that came in boxes wrapped frivolously
with ribbons. My aunt arranged tangerines, pineapples
and grapes in tall crystal bowls, while the bitch watched
her as if on the point of criticizing her taste or offering a
suggestion.

Often when I passed the door of her room, I heard a
peal of laughter like the one which had overturned the
order of her former life that night. Or I heard her engage
in a dialogue with an interlocutor whose voice I did not
hear. It was a new life. The bitch, the guilty one, slept
in a hamper near her bed, an elegant, feminine hamper,
ridiculous to my way of thinking, and followed her everywhere except into the dining-room. Entrance there was
forbidden her, but waiting for her friend to come out

again, she followed her to the billiard room and sat at her side on the sofa or on her lap, exchanging with her from time to time complicitory glances.

How was it possible, I used to ask myself? Why had she waited until now to go beyond herself and establish a dialogue? At times she appeared insecure about the bitch, fearful that, in the same way she had arrived one fine day, she might also go, leaving her with all this new abundance weighing on her hands. Or did she still fear for her health? These ideas, which now seem so clear, floated blurred in my imagination while I listened to the gravel of the path crunching under the wheels of my bicycle. What was not blurred, however, was my vehement desire to become gravely ill, to see if I might also succeed in harvesting some kind of relationship. Because the bitch's illness had been the cause of everything. If it had not been for that, my aunt might have never joined in league with her. But I had a constitution of iron, and furthermore, it was clear that Aunt Mathilda's heart did not have room for more than one love at a time.

My father and my uncles did not seem to notice any change. The bitch was very quiet, and abandoning her street ways, seemed to acquire manners more worthy of Aunt Mathilda. But still, she had somehow preserved all the sauciness of a female of the streets. It was clear that the hardships of her life had not been able to cloud either her good humor or her taste for adventure which, I felt, lay dangerously dormant inside her. For the men of the house it proved easier to accept her than to throw her out, since this would have forced them to revise their canons of security.

One night, when the pitcher of lemonade had already made its appearance on the console-table of the library, cooling that corner of the shadow, and the windows had

been thrown open to the air, my father halted abruptly
at the doorway of the billiard room:

"What is that?" he exclaimed, looking at the floor.

The three men stopped in consternation to look at a
small, round pool on the waxed floor.

"Mathilda!" called Uncle Gustav.

She went to look and then reddened with shame. The
bitch had taken refuge under the billiard table in the
adjoining room. Walking over to the table my father saw
her there, and changing direction sharply, he left the room,
followed by his brothers.

Aunt Mathilda went upstairs. The bitch followed her. I
stayed in the library with a glass of lemonade in my hand,
and looked out at the summer sky, listening to some far-
off siren from the sea, and to the murmur of the city
stretched out under the stars. Soon I heard Aunt Mathilda
coming down. She appeared with her hat on and with her
keys chinking in her hand.

"Go up and go to bed," she said. "I'm going to take
her for a walk on the street so that she can do her
business."

Then she added something strange:

"It's such a lovely night."

And she went out.

From that night on, instead of going up after dinner
to open her brothers' beds, she went to her room, put her
hat tightly on her head and came downstairs again, chinking her keys. She went out with the bitch without ex-
plaining anything to anyone. And my uncles and my father
and I stayed behind in the billiard room, and later we sat
on the benches of the garden, with all the murmuring of
the elm tree and the clearness of the sky weighing down
on us. These nocturnal walks of Aunt Mathilda's were
never spoken of by her brothers. They never showed any

awareness of the change that had occurred inside our house.

In the beginning Aunt Mathilda was gone at the most for twenty minutes or half an hour, returning to take whatever refreshment there was and to exchange some trivial commentary. Later, her sorties were inexplicably prolonged. We began to realize, or I did at least, that she was no longer a woman taking her dog out for hygienic reasons: outside there, in the streets of the city, something was drawing her. When waiting, my father furtively eyed his pocket watch, and if the delay was very great Uncle Gustav went up to the second floor pretending he had forgotten something there, to spy for her from the balcony. But still they did not speak. Once, when Aunt Mathilda stayed out too long, my father paced back and forth along the path that wound between the hydrangeas. Uncle Gustav threw away a cigar which he could not light to his satisfaction, then another, crushing it with the heel of his shoe. Uncle Armand spilt a cup of coffee. I watched them, hoping that at long last they would explode, that they would finally say something to fill the minutes that were passing by one after another, getting longer and longer and longer without the presence of Aunt Mathilda. It was twelve-thirty when she arrived.

"Why are you all waiting up for me?" she asked smiling.

She was holding her hat in her hand, and her hair, ordinarily so well-groomed, was mussed. I saw that a streak of mud was soiling her shoes.

"What happened to you?" asked Uncle Armand.

"Nothing," came her reply, and with it she shut off any right of her brothers to meddle in those unknown hours that were now her life. I say they were her life because, during the minutes she stayed with us before going up to her room with the bitch, I perceived an

animation in her eyes, an excited restlessness like that in
the eyes of the animal: it was as though they had been
washed in scenes to which even our imagination lacked
access. Those two were accomplices. The night protected
them. They belonged to the murmuring sound of the city,
to the sirens of the ships which, crossing the dark or illumined streets, the houses and factories and parks,
reached my ears.

Her walks with the bitch continued for some time. Now
we said good-night immediately after dinner, and each one
went up to shut himself in his room, my father, Uncle
Gustav, Uncle Armand and I. But no one went to sleep
before she came in, late, sometimes terribly late, when
the light of the dawn was already striking the top of our
elm. Only after hearing her close the door of her bedroom
did the pacing with which my father measured his room
cease, or was the window in one of his brothers' rooms
finally closed to exclude that fragment of the night which
was no longer dangerous.

Once I heard her come up very late, and as I thought
I heard her singing softly, I opened my door and peeked
out. When she passed my room, with the white bitch
nestled in her arms, her face seemed to me surprisingly
young and unblemished, even though it was dirty, and I
saw a rip in her skirt. I went to bed terrified, knowing
this was the end.

I was not mistaken. Because one night, shortly after,
Aunt Mathilda took the dog out for a walk after dinner,
and did not return.

We stayed awake all night, each one in his room, and
she did not come back. No one said anything the next
day. They went—I presume—to their office, and I went
to school. She wasn't home when we came back and we
sat silently at our meal that night. I wonder if they found
out something definite that very first day. But I think not,

because we all, without seeming to, haunted the windows of the house, peering into the street.

"Your aunt went on a trip," the cook answered me when I finally dared to ask, if only her.

But I knew it was not true.

Life continued in the house just as if Aunt Mathilda were still living there. It is true that they used to gather in the library for hours and hours, and closeted there they may have planned ways of retrieving her out of that night which had swallowed her. Several times a visitor came who was clearly not of our world, a plain-clothes-man perhaps, or the head of a stevedore's union come to pick up indemnification for some accident. Sometimes their voices rose a little, sometimes there was a deadened quiet, sometimes their voices became hard, sharp, as they fenced with the voice I did not know. But the library door was too thick, too heavy for me to hear what they were saying.

Translated by LORRAINE O'GRADY FREEMAN

Clarice Lispector (b. 1925) was born of Russian parents in Tchetchelnik, in the Ukraine. They moved to Brazil when she was two months old and she grew up as a child in Recife, moving to Rio when she was twelve to continue her studies. She began writing in her teens and was especially interested in the fiction of Katherine Mansfield, Virginia Woolf, and Rosamund Lehmann. While she was an undergraduate at the National Faculty of Law, she began writing journalistic pieces. In 1944, the year she was graduated and married a fellow law student, she published her first novel, *Perto do Coração Selvagem* ["Close to the Savage Heart"]. She was then eighteen. Her husband's career as a diplomat took them abroad for long periods; from 1945 to 1949 she lived in Europe and from 1952 until 1960 in the United States. She has published six novels, four short story collections, and some children's books, although only two of her works are available in English: *The Apple in the Dark,* a novel, and *Family Ties,* the excellent collection from which the following story is taken. She has been greatly influenced by existential writers, but as Alexandrino E. Severino writes in *Studies in Short Fiction* she is part of a group of contemporary Brazilian writers—which includes João Guimarães Rosa—who, living in an "opaque, fragmented, chaotic world, a world without God or apparent ultimate purpose . . . endeavor, nevertheless, to arrest a moment of truth. Having no preconceived ideals—out of place in the modern world's context—these writers attempt to find in the most insignificant events of their daily lives a private vision of endurable truth wrested from the wasteland of their day-to-day existence."

The Imitation of the Rose

Before Armando came home from work the house would have to be tidied and Laura herself ready in her brown dress so that she could attend her husband while he dressed, and then they would leave at their leisure, arm in arm as in former times. How long was it since they had last done that?

But now that she was "well" again, they would take the bus, she looking like a wife, watching out of the bus window, her arm in his: and later they would dine with Carlota and João, sitting back intimately in their chairs. How long was it since she had seen Armando sit back with intimacy and converse with another man? A man at peace was one who, oblivious of his wife's presence, could converse with another man about the latest news in the headlines. Meantime, she would talk to Carlota about women's things, submissive to the authoritarian and practical goodness of Carlota, receiving once more her friend's attention and vague disdain, her natural abruptness, instead of that perplexed affection full of curiosity—watching Armando, finally oblivious of his own wife. And she herself, finally returning to play an insignificant role with gratitude. Like a cat which, having spent the night out of doors, as if nothing had happened, had unexpectedly found a saucer of milk waiting. People fortunately helped to make her feel that she was "well" again. Without watching her, they actively helped her to forget, they themselves feigning forgetfulness as if they had read the same directions on the same medicine bottle. Or, perhaps, they had really forgotten. How long was it since she last saw Armando sit back with abandon, oblivious of her presence? And she herself?

Interrupting her efforts to tidy up the dressing table, Laura gazed at herself in the mirror. And she herself? How long had it been? Her face had a domestic charm, her hair pinned behind her large pale ears. Her brown eyes and brown hair, her soft dark skin, all lent to that face, no longer so very young, the unassuming expression of a woman. Perhaps someone might have seen in that ever so tiny hint of surprise in the depths of her eyes, perhaps someone might have seen in that ever so tiny hint of sorrow the lack of children which she never had?

With her punctilious liking for organization—that same inclination which had made her as a school-girl copy out her class notes in perfect writing without ever understanding them—to tidy up the house before the maid had her afternoon off so that, once Maria went out, she would have nothing more to do except (1) calmly get dressed; (2) wait for Armando once she was ready; (3) what was the third thing? Ah yes. That was exactly what she would do. She would wear her brown dress with the cream lace collar. Having already had her bath. Even during her time at the Sacred Heart Convent she had always been tidy and clean, with an obsession for personal hygiene and a certain horror of disorder. A fact which never caused Carlota, who was already a little odd even as a school girl, to admire her. The reactions of the two women had always been different. Carlota, ambitious and laughing heartily; Laura, a little slow, and virtually always taking care to be slow. Carlota, seeing danger in nothing; and Laura ever cautious. When they had given her *The Imitation of Christ* to read, with the zeal of a donkey she had read the book without understanding it, but may God forgive her, she had felt that anyone who imitated Christ would be lost—lost in the light, but dangerously lost. Christ was the worst temptation. And Carlota, who had not even attempted to read it, had lied to the Sister, saying that she had finished it.

That was decided. She would wear her brown dress with the cream collar made of real lace.

But when she saw the time, she remembered with alarm, causing her to raise her hand to her breast, that she had forgotten to drink her glass of milk.

She made straight for the kitchen and, as if she had guiltily betrayed Armando and their devoted friends through her neglect, standing by the refrigerator she took the first sips with anxious pauses, concentrating upon each sip with faith as if she were compensating everyone and showing her repentance.

If the doctor had said, "Take milk between your meals, and avoid an empty stomach because that causes anxiety," then, even without the threat of anxiety, she took her milk without further discussion, sip by sip, day by day—she never failed, obeying blindly with a touch of zeal, so that she might not perceive in herself the slightest disbelief. The embarrassing thing was that the doctor appeared to contradict himself, for while giving precise instructions that she chose to follow with the zeal of a convert, he had also said, "Relax! Take things easy; don't force yourself to succeed—completely forget what has happened and everything will return to normal." And he had given her a pat on the back that had pleased her and made her blush with pleasure.

But in her humble opinion, the one command seemed to cancel out the other, as if they were asking her to eat flour and whistle at the same time. In order to fuse both commands into one, she had invented a solution: that glass of milk which had finished up by gaining a secret power, which almost embodied with every sip the taste of a word and renewed that firm pat on the back, that glass of milk she carried into the sitting room where she sat "with great naturalness," feigning a lack of interest, "not forcing herself"—and thereby cleverly complying with the second order. It doesn't matter if I get fat, she thought, beauty has never been the most important thing.

She sat down on the couch as if she were a guest in her own home, which, so recently regained, tidy and impersonal, recalled the peace of a stranger's house. A feeling that gave her great satisfaction: the opposite of Carlota who had made of her home something similar to herself. Laura experienced such pleasure in making something impersonal of her home; in a certain way perfect, because impersonal.

Oh, how good it was to be back, to be truly back, she smiled with satisfaction. Holding the almost empty glass, she closed her eyes with a pleasurable weariness. She had ironed Armando's shirts, she had prepared methodical lists for the following day, she had calculated in detail what she had spent at the market that morning; she had not paused, in fact, for a single minute. Oh, how good it was to be tired again!

If some perfect creature were to descend from the planet Mars and discover that people on the Earth were tired and growing old, he would feel pity and dismay. Without ever understanding what was good about being people, about feeling tired and failing daily; only the initiated would understand this nuance of depravity and refinement of life.

And she had returned at last from the perfection of the planet Mars. She, who had never had any ambitions except to be a wife to some man, gratefully returned to find her share of what is daily fallible. With her eyes closed she sighed gratefully. How long was it since she had felt tired? But now every day she felt almost exhausted. She had ironed, for example, Armando's shirts; she had always enjoyed ironing and, modesty aside, she pressed clothes to perfection. And afterward she felt exhausted as a sort of compensation. No longer to feel that alert lack of fatigue. No longer to feel that point—empty, aroused, and hideously exhilarating within oneself. No longer to feel that terrible independence. No longer that monstrous and simple facility of not sleeping—neither by day nor by night —which in her discretion had suddenly made her superhuman by comparison with her tired and perplexed husband. Armando, with that offensive breath which he developed when he was silently preoccupied, stirring in her a poignant compassion, yes, even within her alert perfection, her feeling and love . . . she, superhuman and tranquil in her bright isolation, and he—when he had come to visit her timidly bringing apples and grapes that the nurse, with a shrug of her shoulders, used to eat— he visiting her ceremoniously like a lover with heavy breath and fixed smile, forcing himself in his heroism to try to understand . . . he who had received her from a father and a clergyman, and who did not know what to do with this girl from Tijuca, who unexpectedly, like a tranquil boat spreading its sails over the waters, had become superhuman.

But now it was over. All over. Oh, it had been a mere weakness: temperament was the worst temptation. But later she had recovered so completely that she had even started once more to exercise care not to plague others with her former obsession for detail. She could well remember her companions at the convent saying to her, "That's the thousandth time you've counted that!" She remembered them with an uneasy smile.

She had recovered completely: now she was tired every day, every day her face sagged as the afternoon wore on, and the night then assumed its old finality and became more than just a perfect starry night. And everything completed itself harmoniously. And, as for the whole world, each day fatigued her; as for the whole world, human and perishable. No longer did she feel that perfection or youth. No longer that thing which one day had clearly spread like a cancer . . . her soul.

She opened her eyes heavy with sleep, feeling the consoling solidity of the glass in her hand, but closed them again with a comfortable smile of fatigue, bathing herself like a *nouveau riche* in all his wealth, in this familiar and slightly nauseating water. Yes, slightly nauseating: what did it matter?. For if she, too, was a little nauseating, she was fully aware of it. But her husband didn't think so and then what did it matter, for happily she did not live in surroundings which demanded that she should be more clever and interesting, she was even free of school which so embarrassingly had demanded that she should be alert. What did it matter? In exhaustion—she had ironed Armando's shirts without mentioning that she had been to the market in the morning and had spent some time there with that delight she took in making things yield—in exhaustion she found a refuge, that discreet and obscure place from where, with so much constraint toward herself and others, she had once departed. But as she was saying, fortunately she had returned.

And if she searched with greater faith and love she would find within her exhaustion that even better place, which would be sleep. She sighed with pleasure, for one moment of mischievous malice tempted to go against that warm breath she exhaled, already inducing sleep . . . for one moment tempted to doze off. "Just for a moment, only one tiny moment!" she pleaded with herself, pleased at being so tired, she pleaded persuasively, as one pleads with a man, a facet of her behavior that had always delighted Armando. But she did not really have time to sleep now, not even to take a nap, she thought smugly and with false modesty. She was such a busy person! She had always envied those who could say "I couldn't find the time," and now once more she was such a busy person.

They were going to dinner at Carlota's house, and everything had to be organized and ready, it was her first dinner out since her return and she did not wish to arrive late, she had to be ready. "Well, I've already said this a thousand times," she thought with embarrassment. It would be sufficient to say it only once. "I did not wish to arrive late." For this was a sufficient reason: if she had never been able to bear without enormous vexation giving trouble to anyone, now more than ever, she should not. No, no, there was not the slightest doubt: she had no time to sleep. What she must do, stirring herself with familiarity in that intimate wealth of routine—and it hurt her that Carlota should despise her liking for routine—what she must do was (1) wait until the maid was ready; (2) give her the money so that she could bring the meat in the morning, top round of beef; how could she explain that the difficulty of finding good meat was, for her, really an interesting topic of conversation, but if Carlota were to find out, she would despise her; (3) to begin washing and dressing herself carefully, surrendering, without reservations to the pleasure of making the most of the time at her disposal. Her brown dress matched her eyes, and her collar in cream lace gave her an almost childlike appearance, like some child from the past. And, back in the nocturnal peace of Tijuca, no longer that dazzling light of ebullient nurses, their hair carefully set, going out to enjoy themselves after having tossed her like a helpless chicken into the void of insulin—back to the nocturnal peace of Tijuca, restored to her real life.

She would go out arm in arm with Armando, walking slowly to the bus stop with those low thick hips which her girdle parceled into one, transforming her into a striking woman. But when she awkwardly explained to Armando that this resulted from ovarian insufficiency, Armando, who liked his wife's hips, would saucily retort, "What good would it do me to be married to a ballerina?" That was how he responded. No one would have suspected it, but at times Armando could be extremely devious. From time to time they repeated the same phrases. She explained that it was on account of ovarian insufficiency. Then he would retort, "What good would it do me to be married to a ballerina?" At times he was shameless and no one would have suspected it.

Carlota would have been horrified if she were to know that they, too, had an intimate life and shared things she could not discuss, but nevertheless she regretted not being able to discuss them. Carlota certainly thought that she was only neat and ordinary and a little boring; but if she were obliged to take care in order not to annoy the others with details, with Armando she let herself go at times and became boring. Not that this mattered because, although he pretended to listen, he did not absorb everything she told him. Nor did she take offense, because she understood perfectly well that her conversation rather bored other people, but it was nice to be able to tell him that she had been able to find good meat, even if Armando shook his head and did not listen. She and the maid conversed a great deal, in fact more so she than the maid, and she was careful not to bother the maid, who at times suppressed her impatience and became somewhat rude—the fault was really hers because she did not always command respect.

But, as she was saying . . . her arm in his, she short and he tall and thin, though he was healthy, thank God, and she was chestnut-haired. Chestnut-haired as she obscurely felt a wife ought to be. To have black or blonde hair was an exaggeration, which, in her desire to make the right choice, she had never wanted. Then, as for green eyes, it seemed to her that if she had green eyes it would be as if she had not told her husband everything. Not that Carlota had given cause for any scandal, although Laura, were she given the opportunity, would hotly defend her, but the opportunity had never arisen. She, Laura, was obliged reluctantly to agree that her friend had a strange and amusing manner of treating her husband, not because "they treated each other as equals," since this was now common enough, but you know what I mean to say. And Carlota was even a little different, even she had remarked on this once to Armando and Armando had agreed without attaching much importance to the fact. But, as she was saying, in brown with the lace collar . . . her reverie filled her with the same pleasure she experienced when tidying out drawers, and she even found herself disarranging them in order to tidy them up again.

She opened her eyes and, as if it were the room that had taken a nap and not she, the room seemed refurbished and refreshed with its chairs brushed and its curtains, which had shrunk in the last washing, looking like trousers that are too short and the wearer looking comically at his own legs. Oh! how good it was to see everything tidy again and free of dust, everything cleaned by her own capable hands, and so silent and with a vase of flowers as in a waiting room. She had always found waiting rooms pleasing, so respectful and impersonal. How satisfying life together was, for her who had at last returned from extravagance. Even a vase of flowers. She looked at it.

"Ah! how lovely they are," her heart exclaimed suddenly, a bit childish. They were small wild roses which she had bought that morning at the market, partly because the man had insisted so much, partly out of daring. She had arranged them in a vase that very morning, while drinking her sacred glass of milk at ten o'clock.

But in the light of this room the roses stood in all their complete and tranquil beauty. "I have never seen such lovely roses," she thought enquiringly. And, as if she had not just been thinking precisely this, vaguely aware that she had been thinking precisely this, and quickly dismissing her embarrassment upon recognizing herself as being a little tedious, she thought in a newer phase of surprise, "Really, I have never seen such pretty roses." She looked at them attentively. But her attention could not be sustained for very long as simple attention, and soon transformed itself into soothing pleasure, and she was no longer able to analyze the roses and felt obliged to interrupt herself with the same exclamation of submissive enquiry. "How lovely they are!"

They were a bouquet of perfect roses, several on the same stem. At some moment they had climbed with quick eagerness over each other but then, their game over, they had become tranquilly immobilized. They were quite perfect roses in their minuteness, not quite open, and their pink hue was almost white. "They seem almost artificial," she uttered in surprise. They might give the impression of being white if they were completely open, but with the center petals curled in a bud, their color was concentrated and, as in the lobe of an ear, one could sense the redness circulate inside them. "How lovely they are," thought Laura, surprised. But without knowing why, she felt somewhat restrained and a little perplexed. Oh, nothing serious, it was only that such extreme beauty disturbed her.

She heard the maid's footsteps on the brick floor of the kitchen, and from the hollow sound she realized that she was wearing high heels and that she must be ready to leave. Then Laura had an idea which was in some way highly original: why not ask Maria to call at Carlota's house and leave the roses as a present?

And also because that extreme beauty disturbed her. Disturbed her? It was a risk. Oh! no, why a risk? It merely disturbed her; they were a warning. Oh! no, why a warning? Maria would deliver the roses to Carlota.

"Dona Laura sent them," Maria would say. She smiled thoughtfully: Carlota would be puzzled that Laura, being able to bring the roses personally, since she wanted to present them to her, should send them before dinner with the maid. Not to mention that she would find it amusing to receive the roses . . . and would think it "refined."

"These things aren't necessary between us, Laura!" the other would say with that frankness of hers which was somewhat tactless, and Laura would exclaim in a subdued cry of rapture, "Oh, no! no! It is not because of the invitation to dinner! It is because the roses are so lovely that I felt the impulse to give them to you!"

Yes, if at the time the opportunity arose and she had the courage, that was exactly what she would say. What exactly would she say? It was important not to forget. She would say, "Oh, no! no! It is not because of the invitation to dinner! It is because the roses are so lovely that I felt the impulse to give them to you!"

And Carlota would be surprised at the delicacy of Laura's sentiments—no one would imagine that Laura, too, had her ideas. In this imaginary and pleasurable scene which made her smile devoutly, she addressed herself as "Laura," as if speaking to a third person. A third person full of that gentle, rustling, pleasant, and tranquil faith, Laura, the one with the real lace collar, dressed discreetly, the wife of Armando, an Armando, after all, who no longer needed to force himself to pay attention to all of her conversation about the maid and the meat . . . who no longer needed to think about his wife, like a man who is happy, like a man who is not married to a ballerina.

"I couldn't help sending you the roses," Laura would say, this third person so, but so. . . . And to give the roses was almost as nice as the roses themselves.

And she would even be rid of them.

And what exactly would happen next? Ah yes; as she was saying, Carlota, surprised at Laura who was neither intelligent nor good but who had her secret feelings. And Armando? Armando would look at her with a look of real surprise—for it was essential to remember that he must not know the maid had taken the roses in the afternoon! Armando would look with kindness upon the impulses of his little wife and that night they would sleep together.

And she would have forgotten the roses and their beauty. No, she suddenly thought, vaguely warned. It was necessary to take care with that alarmed look in others. It was necessary never to cause them alarm, especially with everything being so fresh in their minds. And, above all, to spare everyone the least anxiety or doubt. And that the attention of others should no longer be necessary—

no longer this horrible feeling of their watching her in silence, and her in their presence. No more impulses.

But at the same time she saw the empty glass in her hand and she also thought, " 'He' said that I should not force myself to succeed, that I should not think of adopting attitudes merely to show that I am."

"Maria," she called, upon hearing the maid's footsteps once more. And when Maria appeared she asked with a note of rashness and defiance, "Would you call at Dona Carlota's house and leave these roses for her? Just say that Dona Laura sent them. Just say it like that. Dona Laura. . . ."

"Yes, I know," the maid interrupted her patiently.

Laura went to search for an old sheet of tissue paper. Then she carefully lifted the roses from the vase, so lovely and tranquil, with their delicate and mortal thorns. She wanted to make a really artistic bouquet: and at the same time she would be rid of them. And she would be able to dress and resume her day. When she had arranged the moist blooms in a bouquet, she held the flowers away from her and examined them at a distance, slanting her head and half-closing her eyes for an impartial and severe judgment.

And when she looked at them, she saw the roses. And then, irresistibly gentle, she insinuated to herself, "Don't give the roses away, they are so lovely."

A second later, still very gentle, her thought suddenly became slightly more intense, almost tempting, "Don't give them away, they are yours." Laura became a little frightened: because things were never hers.

But these roses were. Rosy, small, and perfect: they were hers. She looked at them, incredulous: they were beautiful and they were hers. If she could think further ahead, she would think: hers as nothing before now had ever been.

And she could even keep them because that initial uneasiness had passed which had caused her vaguely to avoid looking at the roses too much.

"Why give them away then? They are so lovely and you are giving them away? So when you find something nice, you just go and give it away? Well, if they were hers," she insinuated persuasively to herself, without finding any other argument beyond the previous one which, when repeated, seemed to her to be ever more convincing and straightforward.

"They would not last long—why give them away then, so long as they were alive?" The pleasure of possessing them did not represent any great risk, she pretended to herself, because, whether she liked it or not, shortly she would be forced to deprive herself of them and then she would no longer think about them, because by then they would have withered.

"They would not last long; why give them away then?" The fact that they would not last long seemed to free her from the guilt of keeping them, in the obscure logic of the woman who sins. Well, one could see that they would not last long (it would be sudden, without danger). And it was not even, she argued in a final and victorious rejection of guilt, she herself who had wanted to buy them; the flower seller had insisted so much and she always became so intimidated when they argued with her. . . . It was not she who had wanted to buy them . . . she was not to blame in the slightest. She looked at them in rapture, thoughtful and profound.

"And, honestly, I never saw such perfection in all my life."

All right, but she had already spoken to Maria and there would be no way of turning back. Was it too late then? She became frightened upon seeing the tiny roses that waited impassively in her own hand. If she wanted, it would not be too late. . . . She could say to Maria, "Oh Maria, I have decided to take the roses myself when I go to dinner this evening!" And of course she would not take them. . . . And Maria need never know. And, before changing, she would sit on the couch for a moment, just for a moment, to contemplate them. To contemplate that tranquil impassivity of the roses. Yes, because having already done the deed, it would be better to profit from it . . . she would not be foolish enough to take the blame without the profit. That was exactly what she would do.

But with the roses unwrapped in her hand she waited. She did not arrange them in the vase, nor did she call Maria. She knew why. Because she must give them away. Oh, she knew why.

And also because something nice was either for giving or receiving, not only for possessing. And above all, never for one *to be*. Above all, one should never *be* a lovely thing. A lovely thing lacked the gesture of giving. One should never keep a lovely thing, as if it were guarded within the perfect silence of one's heart. (Although, if she were not to give the roses, would anyone ever find out? It was horribly easy and within one's reach to keep them, for who would find out? And they would be hers, and things would stay as they were and the matter would be forgotten . . .)

"Well then? Well then?" she mused, vaguely disturbed.

Well, no. What she must do was to wrap them up and send them, without any pleasure now; to parcel them up and, disappointed, send them; and, terrified, be rid of them. Also, because a person had to be coherent, one's thoughts had to be consistent: if, spontaneously, she had decided to relinquish them to Carlota, she should stand by that decision and give them away. For no one changed their mind from one minute to another.

But anyone can repent, she suddenly rebelled. For if it was only the minute I took hold of the roses that I noticed how lovely they were, for the first time, actually, as I held them, I noticed how lovely they were. Or a little before that? (And they were really hers.) And even the doctor himself had patted her on the back and said, "Don't force yourself into pretending that you are well, because you *are* well!" And then that hearty pat on the back. So she was not obliged, therefore, to be consistent, she didn't have to prove anything to anyone, and she would keep the roses. (And in all sincerity—in all sincerity they were hers.)

"Are they ready?" Maria asked.

"Yes," said Laura, surprised.

She looked at them, so mute in her hand. Impersonal in their extreme beauty. In their extreme and perfect tranquillity as roses. That final instance: the flower. That final perfection; its luminous tranquillity.

Like someone depraved, she watched with vague longing the tempting perfection of the roses . . . with her mouth a little dry, she watched them.

Until, slowly, austerely, she wrapped the stems and thorns in the tissue paper. She was so absorbed that only upon holding out the bouquet she had prepared did she notice that Maria was no longer in the room—and she remained alone with her heroic sacrifice.

Vacantly, sorrowfully, she watched them, distant as they were at the end of her outstretched arm—and her mouth became even dryer, parched by that envy and desire.

"But they are mine," she said with enormous timidity.

When Maria returned and took hold of the bouquet, for one tiny moment of greed Laura drew back her hand, keeping the roses to herself for one more second—they are so lovely and they are mine—the first lovely thing and mine! And it was the flower seller who had insisted. . . . I did not go looking for them! It was destiny that had decreed! Oh, only this once! Only this once and I swear never more! (She could at least take one rose for herself, no more than this! One rose for herself. And only she would know and then never more; oh, she promised herself that never more would she allow herself to be tempted by perfection, never more.)

And the next moment, without any transition, without any obstacle, the roses were in the maid's hand, they were no longer hers, like a letter already in the post! One can no longer recover or obliterate statements! There is no point in shouting, "That was not what I wanted to say!" Her hands were now empty but her heart, obstinate and resentful, was still saying, "You can catch Maria on the stairs, you know perfectly well that you can, and take the roses from her hand and steal them—because to take them now would be to steal them." To steal what was hers? For this was what a person without any feeling for others would do: he would steal what was his by right! Have pity, dear God. You can get them back, she insisted, enraged. And then the front door slammed.

Slowly, she sat down calmly on the couch. Without leaning back. Only to rest. No, she was no longer angry, not even a little. But that tiny wounded spot in the depths of her eyes was larger and thoughtful. She looked at the vase.

"Where are my roses?" she said then very quietly.

And she missed the roses. They had left an empty space inside her. Remove an object from a clean table and by the cleaner patch which remains one sees that there has been dust all around it. The roses had left a patch without dust and without sleep inside her. In her heart, that one rose, which at least she could have taken for herself without prejudicing anyone in the world, was gone. Like something missing. Indeed, like some great loss. An absence that flooded into her like a light. And also around the mark left by the roses the dust was disappearing. The center of fatigue opened itself into a circle that grew larger. As if she had not ironed a single shirt for Armando. And in the clearing they had left, one missed those roses.

"Where are my roses?" she moaned without pain, smoothing the pleats of her skirt.

Like lemon juice dripping into dark tea and the dark tea becoming completely clear, her exhaustion gradually became clearer. Without, however, any tiredness. Just as the firefly alights. Since she was no longer tired, she was on the point of getting up to dress. It was time to start getting ready.

With parched lips, she tried for an instant to imitate the roses deep down inside herself. It was not even difficult.

It was just as well that she did not feel tired. In this way she would go out to dinner feeling more refreshed. Why not wear her cameo brooch on her cream-colored collar? The one the Major had brought back from the war in Italy. It would add a final touch to her neckline. When she was ready she would hear the noise of Armando's key in the door. She must get dressed. But it was still early. With the rush-hour traffic, he would be late in arriving. It was still afternoon. An extremely beautiful afternoon. But, in fact, it was no longer afternoon. It was evening. From the street there arose the first sounds of darkness and the first lights.

Moreover, the key penetrated with familiarity the keyhole.

Armando would open the door. He would press the light switch. And suddenly in the frame of the doorway that face would appear, betraying an expectancy he tried to conceal but could not restrain. Then his breathless suspense would finally transform itself into a smile of utter relief. That embarrassed smile of relief which he would never suspect her of noticing. That relief which, probably with a pat on the back, they had advised her poor husband to conceal. But which had been, for this woman whose heart was filled with guilt, her daily recompense for having restored to her husband the possibility of happiness and peace, sanctified at the hands of an austere priest who only permitted submissive happiness to humans and not the imitation of Christ.

The key turned in the lock, that dark, expectant face entered, and a powerful light flooded the room.

And in the doorway, Armando himself stopped short with that breathless expression as if he had run for miles in order to arrive in time. She was about to smile. So that she might dispel the anxious expectancy on his face, which always came mixed with the childish victory of having arrived in time to find his boring, good-hearted, and diligent wife. She was about to smile so that once more he might know that there would no longer be any danger in his arriving too late. She was about to smile in order to teach him gently to confide in her. It had been useless to advise them never to touch on the subject: they did not speak about it but they had created a language of facial expressions whereby fear and confidence were communicated, and question and answer were silently telegraphed. She was about to smile. She was taking her time, but meant to smile.

Calmly and sweetly she said, "It came back, Armando. It came back."

As if he would never understand, he averted his smiling, distrusting face. His main task for the moment was to try and control his breathless gasps after running up the stairs, now that, triumphantly, he had arrived in time, now that she was there to smile at him. As if he would never understand.

"What came back?" he finally asked her in an expressionless tone.

But while he was seeking never to understand, the man's face, ever more full of suspense, had already understood without a single feature having altered. His main task was to gain time and to concentrate upon controlling his breath. Which suddenly was no longer difficult. For unexpectedly he noticed to his horror that the room and the woman were calm and showing no signs of haste. Still more suspicious, like someone about to end up howling with laughter upon observing something absurd, he meantime insisted upon keeping his face averted, from where he spied her cautiously, almost her enemy. And from where he already began to feel unable to restrain himself, from seeing her seated with her hands folded on her lap, with the serenity of the firefly that is alight.

In her innocent, chestnut gaze, the embarrassed vanity of not having been able to resist.

"What came back?" he asked suddenly with severity.

"I couldn't help myself," she said and her final compassion for this man was in her voice, one last appeal for pardon which already came mingled with the arrogance of an almost perfect solitude.

"I couldn't prevent it," she repeated, surrendering to him with relief the compassion which she with some effort had been able to contain until he arrived.

"It was on account of the roses," she said modestly.

As if a photograph were about to capture that moment, he still maintained the same disinterested expression, as if the photographer had asked him only for his face and not his soul. He opened his mouth and involuntarily his face took on for an instant an expression of comic detachment which he had used to conceal his annoyance when he had asked his boss for an increase in salary. The next moment, he averted his eyes, mortified by his wife's shamelessness as she sat there unburdened and serene.

But suddenly the tension fell. His shoulders dropped, the features of his face relaxed and a great heaviness settled over him. Aged and strange, he watched her.

She was seated wearing her little housedress. He knew that she had done everything possible not to become luminous and remote. With fear and respect he watched her. Aged, tired, and strange. But he did not even have a word to offer. From the open door he saw his wife sitting upright on the couch, once more alert and tranquil as if on a train. A train that had already departed.

Translated by GIOVANNI PONTIERO

René Marqués (b. 1919) was born into a peasant family in Arecibo, Puerto Rico. He was an agricultural engineer but his interest in writing took him to the Central University of Madrid to study literature. He returned to Puerto Rico to found the society Pro Arte, and collaborated on the prestigious literary review *Asomante,* where he published his first play. Then, on a Rockefeller Foundation grant, he studied drama at Columbia University in New York from 1949 to 1950. In 1954 he was made director of the Teatro Experimental del Ateneo Puertorriqueño, and also received a Guggenheim grant that allowed him to finish his novel *La víspera del hombre* [1959, "The eve of man"], in which the author articulates the most debated question in his country today: whether Puerto Rico should be independent or should accept U.S. domination. In the play *La muerte no entrará en palacio* [1957, "Death will not enter the palace"], this theme is presented in terms of the conflict of the generations. One of his finest stories, translated as "There's a Body Reclining on the Stern" (collected in the anthology *Doors and Mirrors*) is the moving portrait of a tragically doomed man dominated by an acquisitive wife; on a deeper level it symbolizes the emasculation of one culture by another. His concern with the struggle for both national and personal identity is also apparent in *La carreta* (1952, *The Oxcart*) a play dramatizing the dilemma of the Puerto Rican peasant who emigrates to New York and then goes home again, but is unable to readjust to his old way of life. Marqués is preoccupied by the inherent conflict of Spanish traditions and U.S. materialism.

Although René Marqués is probably better-known as a playwright, with many plays to his credit, he is also one of Puerto Rico's outstanding short story writers. There have been several collections of his plays and short stories.

Island of Manhattan

"Cordelia of the waves,
Bitter Cordelia."
   —Gabriela Mistral

Juanita raised the collar of her wool jacket and took a deep breath. She would never get used to this subterranean life. Every time she came out of the subway station, she felt an irrepressible relief.

She stood in the middle of the sidewalk, stepping aside to avoid the avalanche of people. Even so, a huge man brutally pushed against her.

"Animal," she whispered.

The man stopped in his tracks, looked at her and said, almost smiling, "Take it easy, spik." Then, as she walked away quickly, he began to follow her.

She didn't know if it were the insult or the mocking smile that made her shake with anger.

"Yankee! Brute!" she shouted. But the man did not even look back this time.

Juanita looked at her watch. Twenty-five to ten. She had time. She absentmindedly wound her watch and thought about the five payments she still owed on it. She straightened her shoulders and began to walk towards Madison.

She was walking slowly, as if she were strolling around the little plaza in Lares. She laughed to herself at the beauty of it. The memory of Lares seemed a dream. Or was this the total dream!

The important thing was that she was not in a hurry. For the first time in four years she was not in a hurry. Twenty-five minutes in which to walk three blocks. She stopped next to an overflowing garbage can to straighten her stockings. She pulled the garter down and snapped it over the stocking. She noticed that there was a run.

"Damn it! And a new pair!"

At that moment she heard a whistle. She quickly lowered her skirt and looked up to see a young man leaning against the railing. She looked him up and down.

"You have a long way to go before you can whistle like a man," she mocked.

The youngster turned tomato-red, but was Don Juan enough to say, "With you I could learn in a day."

She laughed loudly, nervously, and walked on. To learn in one day. Without knowing why, she stopped laughing. No. Perhaps not in one day. But one learns quickly. A year in Rio Piedras, two in San Juan, four in New York. Yes, above all, these years. How far I've come! The farm in San Isidro where the old man was a tenant farmer. The humid shade of the guamas. The little plaza. The moldy vestments of the big-bellied priest. The white candle of the first communion.

She felt a sweet sadness, tranquil, without anxiety or

bitterness. The candle of her first communion. The white candle that today she wasn't going to have. Perhaps if she had shared that thought with someone she would not have laughed so loudly just then. No, there would be no white candle, nor lights, nor flowers. Nor a big-bellied priest.

"Goddammit! That bag is mine. You spik! Let it go! You dirty Portorican!"

"I made that bag myself, coño. It's mine, you half of a man, you Yankee!"

The two little boys wrestled furiously on the sidewalk, saw that the small, dark one with kinky hair was winning.

She smiled. "Take advantage of this, jibarito! There blocking her way. She was tempted to intervene, but she won't be many times when you'll be on top!" she shouted as she walked past.

"At ten in front of Joe's Bar," Nico had said. To meet him or not—she had given a lot of thought to this. Nico knew everything about her life—the year at the University, her work in radio, the shame in New York. Yes, above all, that. Still he kept insisting. Jenny felt confused.

"Why do you call yourself Nick instead of Nico?"

"Because I'm a foreman. This way everyone respects me."

"Wouldn't they respect you if they called you Nico?"

"Don't ask too many questions, baby. . . ." And he laughed showing shining teeth against his dark complexion.

How could he speak seriously of marriage? This thought unsettled her. She experienced a rare feeling of sin, of being immoral and yet accepting a moral solution.

"Do you know what I am, Nico?"

"Sure, you are my Jenny."

"I'm a prostitute."

"You are my Jenny."

And to her it didn't seem natural that a man—a real man—would accept the situation like that.

"You don't seem Puerto Rican."

"I'm an American citizen."

"You're from Quebradillas."

"But still an American citizen."

She was also an American citizen, but there was a huge abyss between her American citizenship and her Puerto Rican heritage.

"Nico, sometimes I believe I could understand an American better than I understand you."

"But, baby, you don't have to understand anything. The only thing you have to do is love me."

Did I love him ever? Yes, that had to be love. I had never loved anyone like that before, except that Lareño from San Isidro, barefoot and pale. It had been such a long time ago.

She probably began to love Nico during her only year at the University. He was in his second year of Industrial Arts and she, with a scholarship and the dream of a rural school, was in her freshman year. It was through Nico that she had gotten involved in the strike at the University.

"Man and woman, side by side, must protest against injustice," he had said.

When they were both expelled for protesting, she fully understood what Nico had meant. The street of Rio Piedras had seemed wide and frank with its real immediacy.

And she remembered clearly the university carrillon behind her repeating the sonorous melody—"London Bridge is falling down, falling down. . . ."

But it was not the English bridge that was falling in her life, but the dream of a rural school near San Isidro.

A beer bottle fell on the sidewalk breaking into a

thousand pieces. Juanita jumped back surprised. From the window came the voice of a woman—shrill, strident, hysterical, like an uncontainable torrent.

"And if you like to drink beer, go to the bar! I am fed up with cleaning up your vomit! Do you hear me? Fed up! What I have here is not a house, but a pigpen! We live like pigs! And as if it weren't enough, you come here with your drunken vomit! When I get a few pennies together, I'm going back to Puerto Rico. And I'm taking the children with me!"

The voice of the man—thick, hoarse, stuttering sadly.

"But, Negra, don't be like this. If we can find something better? . . ."

"You can look for something, but don't count on me." And Juanita heard a door slam, furiously, and with finality.

She kicked the pieces of glass with her foot, looked again at the vacant window and straightening her shoulders, walked on.

Yes, Nico was a winner. In seven years he had conquered the city. Already he was a foreman. And he called himself Nick and spoke English. Juanita admired that capacity for adjusting. But she was suspicious. She had a peasant fear of that extraordinary ability to submit to New York. "It isn't natural," she thought.

"You've changed so much, Nico," she had told him.

"Nonsense, I am the same." And he had affirmed this with a long kiss.

Was he the same? Or was she the one who had changed? Six years was a long time. And she remembered his voice burning with indignation when they had been expelled from the University.

"I'm going to New York. Here on the island there is no feeling for justice."

With Nico's departure, she found herself lost and

she almost returned to Lares. But an awakening instinct to fight back kept her in San Juan. She kept herself alive selling hog dogs and Coca-Colas until she got the job at the radio station. It all began with her reciting a poem by Llorens on an amateur program. The rest just happened, like rain falling from heaven. She began acting in soap operas.

Her acting in radio programs didn't carry her to stardom, but those obscure roles of perverse women gave her room and board and the cotton dresses she made herself. She owed this opportunity to Nico too. It was he who had insisted on correcting her country accent. By the time Nico had left for the states, she was able to tighten her teeth to let out sibilant "eses." And she had also learned not to pronounce "i" for "e." Nico's lessons had prepared her for radio. She began to receive fan letters, one of them even from Lares.

Now, in the cold air of the city, she could laugh at the soap operas in San Juan. But at that time, no. Justice always triumphed in the scripts. And the unjust were justly punished. Nevertheless, her position was precarious. When a villainess died, she no longer had a job. And although her honor wanted the death of the villainess, her stomach wanted to prolong the life of that despicable being.

Then came the strike and its clamor of confused voices. "Our rights. . . . Justice. . . . The law. . . . Our rights. . . . Justice. . . . The owner. . . . Justice. . . . The owner. . . . Justice. . . . the worker. . . ."

And thinking of Nico, she went on strike. Another time, on strike!

She wrote him in New York, sure that he would approve of her decision. But the letter was returned. The great city had swallowed him up.

The day when she fainted, carrying a picket sign in front of the radio station, the strike ended. It was the fourth month of abstinence, of almost fasting. The fourth month of picket lines, of insults from scabs. And she raised a prayer to heaven for returning "our daily bread." But she soon found out that "our daily bread" doesn't always come from heaven.

The strike had been a success. Justice had triumphed, said some. But others, the owners of the station, didn't say anything. The owners of the station smiled, kindly patronizing smiles. And the scabs replaced the ex-strikers.

Juanita remembered how on another occasion the street had appeared wide and frank in its immediacy. And how as she had left the station, the amplifiers in the vestibule repeated the melody, "Enjoy yourself. It's later than you think."

Late? If it were too late to enjoy yourself, it was not too late to escape.

And so the noise of the plane's motors united the group of immigrants in a huge uncertainty of space—of the earth they seemed to leave behind and gain again.

At that moment the noise of a passing bus brought her back to reality. She was at Madison. She walked one block to the right and stopped to cross the street. Joe's Bar was on the other side. She saw a crowd of people exactly in the spot where she was to meet Nico. What was happening? Were the Irish police at it again or was it only an accident? The green light changed and she crossed the Avenue rapidly. Then she noticed the flags and the speakers' platform. It was another meeting. Meetings were boring to her. But there was no way to avoid it. Had Nico arrived yet? She looked around for him. No, he wasn't there. Well, she would have to wait. She stood in front of the bar where there were fewer people. She opened her purse and took out a mirror to touch up her lipstick.

At the beginning the English words didn't mean anything to her. She was thinking in Spanish, which made her deaf to the foreign language. Still, little by little, her brain began to perceive the English words. Later, the fiery speech began to make itself intelligible to her. She put away her lipstick, closed her purse and looked toward the rostrum.

A man was speaking about eight black men condemned to death for having tried to rape a blonde woman. Juanita at the beginning believed that she had heard it incorrectly. No, no, it was not possible. But the man went on repeating it and repeating it. Nevertheless, the whole idea of this stuck in her craw. To kill eight men for having *tried* to rape a woman? My God . . . Eight lives! And only for trying! What would have happened to the eight black men had they actually destroyed that delicate virginal tissue? Well, they could not do more to them after killing them. No, but they could do something before. Perhaps they could tear their flesh piece by piece with great red-hot tongs, like the print in the sacristy of the church in Lares. But no, the man was saying that they were only going to be hanged.

She tried to imagine the eight hanging by ropes, hanging from the branch of a tamarind tree. Would it be from a tree that they would hang them? "No, it isn't natural," she said.

And she thought of her own virginity. It was the day of her visit to the Insular Office in New York. The woman who was filling out the forms had stopped her suddenly and had looked fixedly at her.

"You were a striker at the University?"

Surprised, she had nodded her head.

"And a striker at the radio station in Puerto Rico?" She felt the need to talk, to explain something. But she didn't know what to say. Again, she just nodded her head. The woman got up and disappeared behind a green glass door marked Private. Juanita began to look at the posters announcing educational films. "A Voice in the Mountain," read one. She thought of how abandoned her own voice sounded in this mountain of steel and armored cement.

Then the woman returned and, sitting down, continued her work filling out forms.

"Sign here," she said, handing her the fountain pen.

Juanita signed and sat there waiting.

"That is all," said the other.

"They will get in touch with me if there is something?" she asked tentatively.

"Of course," said the woman.

But she left the office with the certainty that it was all useless, that they would not help her find work here. She didn't know why she had this certainty. She didn't know if the questions about the strike were personal questions of the employer or something official which could hurt her. She didn't know anything. But she felt a terrible and total hopelessness. She began to think that this was the end.

For that reason, she was almost thankful for the impertinence of the blond man in the street. She needed the company of someone, the warmth of another voice. She needed the presence of another human being to whom she could communicate the feeling that she was alive, that she did exist. So she let herself be led. They went to Palisades Park. He was reasonably attentive to her. He made her play the Wheel of Fortune and she won a canary. A canary that didn't sing, but was alive. A canary living locked up in his cage.

They returned late to Manhattan. And they drank whiskey. It was the first time she had drunk whiskey. But she didn't make a big fuss about it. She drank it slowly with the same resignation with which she would have taken a laxative. Her hopelessness was drowning in a dense cloud. Then suddenly she found herself in a narrow and bad-smelling little room. The canary slept in his cage. And the man undressed her with hot, impatient hands. She wanted to fight, but she felt weak. The panic and the horror, more than the whiskey, had paralyzed her.

Hours later, she found herself on a dark street, leaning against a brick wall with the stabbing cold of the morning sneaking in through the tears in her dress. And when she raised her hand to her mouth to choke a sob, she discovered the bill in her clenched fist.

They didn't hang anyone then. The police were not aware that there was one less virgin around. Only Doña Casilda, the Cuban in Harlem, knew it, she who performed the abortion. The rest had been easy, too easy.

And suddenly Juanita began to feel a tremendous burning in her blood. It was like a blaze which rose and rose. And the word *Justice* in the mouth of the speaker began to take on a special meaning. And the word *Injustice* too. She thought of the white, blonde woman. She thought of the eight black men too. And she understood. She understood with clarity the language and almost with horror the ideas. Her hard, peasant guts had finally perceived something monstrous.

And that perception warmed her soul. And shook her conscience. Virgin of Carmen! Was it possible?

She forgot the platform and the meeting. She didn't see the people surrounding her. She saw instead herself as if projected on a screen. And she saw the blonde and the eight men. And now she heard the words of the speaker in a different way. It was almost as if she had not heard them. As if those words were conceived in her brain and spoken by another. She was not able to say if it was what she was thinking now in English or what the other man was saying in Spanish.

But there was no longer any language barrier. For that matter, when the speaker was asking in English that justice be done for the eight men, she shouted in Spanish, "Yes, we are going to do it!" But she could have sworn that she had said it in English.

On hearing the shout in Spanish, many faces turned towards her . . . smiling, hostile, impassive. But Juanita didn't see the faces. She knew that they were there, but she didn't see them. She only saw the piece of paper that began to circulate from the platform among the crowd. She saw the paper appear and disappear from hand to hand, the distance between it and her gradually decreasing.

Suddenly she felt two strong hands on her shoulders. "What the hell are you doing here?"

She recognized the voice, but wasn't surprised nor did she have any interest in turning around. The paper continued within her eyeshot. Did she have a pencil in her purse? She opened her purse and looked for it . . . only a lipstick.

"Do you have a pencil?" she asked, half turning her head.

"Come on," she heard Nico say. Later his voice became urgent, almost hopeless. "Come on. Let's get out of here." And she felt that he was trying to drag her outside the circle of spectators.

Juanita brusquely shook his hands off her shoulders. "Leave me alone," she said. And once free, she was face to face with him. She saw that he was pale and in anguish. His face was soaked with perspiration in spite of the cool air of the Avenue.

"What has happened to you?" she asked.

He looked again at the people surrounding him. He came near her again and whispered in a tone of supplication that she had never known before, "Let's get away from here, for the love of God! Come on!"

He said this in Spanish. And what was strange, in a Spanish with a Puerto Rican accent, free from the North American accent that he had acquired in his six years in the city. Seeing that she just looked at him saying nothing, he tried to pretend anguish, smiling.

"Remember, today we get married."

"Married?" Yes, that was right. Today they were getting married.

After six years they had found each other in New York.

"You see what I am now," she had said then with a brutal frankness to hide her shame.

But he wasn't ashamed. Nico was a conqueror. She believed that they had found each other too late. But he, no. Nick was a man of the city. And she had conquered his scruples. She had fastened herself to this man who had been her only inspiration when she had arrived in Rio Piedras saying "Lari" and swallowing her "eses."

Marry? Yes, Nico was there. And today they were getting married. But it wasn't haste for the wedding that she now saw in him. It was something that she didn't understand.

"I'm not leaving yet. Wait for me." And she turned from him.

The paper with the petition for a new trial for the black men was coming nearer. She felt his body behind her, the hands compulsively grabbing her two arms, his breath burning in her right ear.

"Please, you don't understand. This is dangerous."

"Dangerous?" She was bothered by the pressure of Nico's hands on her arms.

"Don't hold me so tight," she said.

His voice continued in Spanish, more urgently, more brokenly.

"Are you crazy? Look at that flag. We'll find ourselves in the police files. Come on, come on, I tell you."

She looked towards the platform and she finally understood. The breeze had begun to softly unfurl one of the two flags, withered and quiet until that instant, the same instant in which the petition reached her hands. And the voice of the man in her ears, like a deaf shout. "Let it go! Pass it on, so they don't see you with it!"

But the voice didn't strike her consciousness. What did a flag matter to her? What mattered in this instance was justice. And justice was that piece of paper which was in her hands for the first time in her life. For that reason, his voice sounded strange, remote, indifferent.

A woman offered her a stump of a pencil. She took it and looked at the blunt point. She almost simultaneously felt that they were going to snatch the paper from her hands.

She turned around and looked at Nico grabbing the paper away from her convulsively. She saw his disjointed features, his pale lips, his forehead perspiring and contracted. She lowered her eyes to look at the paper crumpled in his hands and raised her eyes again to look at the livid face. In that short time she discovered the strange trembling in her body.

She had the impression that she wasn't looking at a human being. And she discovered what she hadn't discovered moments before. Nico's fear. An almost animal fear, an infra-human fear coming through his eyes, through his soul, through his pores. And she understood. For the second time that morning she had understood with a painful clarity. She understood Nico also, almost suddenly. She saw how much humanity he had had to give up to become foreman. She understood the price of his triumph in the city. And she understood his fear. But the understanding disgusted her. She felt such a violent loathing that it almost brought on a contraction in her stomach.

And again Juanita began to feel a tremendous warmth in her blood. It was like a blaze that rose and rose. She had to exert an extraordinary strength to contain the fire that burned at her lips. Remembering him and lowering her voice she was able to condense to a brief threat all the tumult of her feelings. "Give me that paper or I'll tear your face to shreds."

Also to him this Juanita was different from his sweet "Jenny." If the new dread of the threat hadn't added up to all his fears, he would have felt deceived. But only horror reigned in him now.

"If you sign that, I'll never marry you."

She wanted to laugh, but she controlled herself. She took the paper and pressing her made-up face close to his livid one, she almost spat out the words, "If I were a decent woman, I could afford the luxury of saying, 'I would rather become a whore than marry you!' "

She began to laugh finally and, seeing his expression, she added in a voice that was almost a shout, "But as I am what I am, I can only say to you, 'Coward! I don't ever want to see you again!' "

And she turned her back on him. She held the paper against her purse and signed it with the blunt pencil. In that instant a little band next to the platform began to play a tune she had never heard before. She handed the paper and pencil on to a black man and began to make her way through the crowd. Only when she came to the corner of 114th Street did she stop. The street opened wide and frank in its real immediacy. She raised the collar of her wool jacket and breathed deeply.

The fresh air gave her a rare sensation of joy this time.

She felt that the justice that would free the eight condemned men had given her back her own freedom. And she began to walk down the street. A clock in a drugstore told her it was twelve o'clock. Seeing the two clock hands together, she instinctively made the sign of the cross, as if here in the city the angelus of the church of Lares was ringing.

Translated by FAYE EDWARDS *and* GLADYS ORTIZ

Juan Carlos Onetti (b. 1909) was reared in Montevideo, Uruguay, but he moved to Buenos Aires when he was about twenty and drifted into journalism. He returned to Uruguay in 1954, took over the paper *Acción,* and then accepted a library post at the Institute of Art and Letters. In 1974 he became something of a *cause célèbre* (sharing headlines with Solzhenitsyn in Latin America) when he was arrested by Uruguay's anti-intellectual right-wing government for having participated in a jury that awarded first prize to a short story declared obscene and subversive by the government. But unlike Solzhenitsyn, Onetti has not been known for political dissent. For most of his life his writings have been commercial failures about failed lives. In the Sixties, critical recognition began to come, Mario Vargas Llosa claiming that Onetti's *El pozo* [1939, "The pit"] marked the beginning of the new novel in Latin America. For Onetti as for his characters, subjective reality has been the isolation, loneliness, and disillusionment of modern man. Luis Harss and Barbara Dohmann, in their chapter on Onetti, say that his character typically "suffers from advancing age, an obsessive fear of death, a hopeless longing to rescue his wasted life, and a compulsive need to retreat through time to recuperate that moment of truth presumably buried somewhere in the lost blitheness of childhood." Each character feels a need to break the pattern of his life, to escape the loneliness and routine. In his first novel, *El pozo,* the narrator is a forty-year-old man writing a memoir of his life. In *El astillero* (1961, published here as *The Shipyard*) a middle-aged man runs an empty shipyard. In *La Vida Breve* (1950, to be published here as *The Short Life*), the colorless narrator conjures up new personalities ("short lives") for himself, which turn out to be mere extensions of his former self. In this novel Onetti introduces the mythical town of Santa María, which was to become his "Yoknapatawpha County." Onetti has written five novels, six short novels, and two books of short stories. The following story from *Un sueño realizado* ["A dream come true"] illustrates Onetti's theme of naïve youth turning into middle-aged conformity and disillusion.

354

Welcome, Bob

For H. A. T.

One thing is sure, he will be older each day, farther from
the time when they called him Bob, with blond hair
hanging down on his forehead, with his smile and shining
eyes; from the time when he entered the living room
quietly, mumbling a greeting or bringing his hand up toward his ear, and went to sit under the lamp over by the
piano, with a book or simply without speaking, apart, his
mind far away, looking at us for an hour with an expressionless face, shifting his fingers from time to time to
manipulate his cigarette and brush the ashes from the lapel
of his light suit.

Equally far—now that they call him Robert and he gets
drunk on anything, shielding his mouth with a dirty hand
when he coughs—from the Bob who drank beer, never
more than two glasses during the longest of evenings, a
pile of ten-piece coins on his table in the club's bar to
spend in the juke box. Almost always alone, listening to

jazz, his face dreamy, happy and pale, hardly moving his head in greeting when I passed, following me with his eyes as long as I stayed, as long as it was possible for me to endure his blue stare tirelessly resting on me, keeping up without effort an intense contempt and the slightest trace of mockery. And sometimes with some other young fellow, Saturdays, someone as maddeningly young as he, with whom he talked about solos, horns and choruses and of the tremendous city Bob was going to build on the coast when he was an architect. Seeing me pass, he would break off to offer me his curt hello and not take his eyes off my face from then on, slipping inaudible words and smiles out the side of his mouth toward his companion who always ended up staring at me and silently duplicating his contempt and mockery.

Sometimes I felt strong and tried to return his stare: I leaned my face on one hand and puffed smoke out over my glass, staring at him without batting an eyelash, without dropping the attention on my face, which I felt must be kept cold, a bit gloomy. At that time Bob looked very much like Inez. Looking at him across the bar-lounge of the club, I could see something of her in his face and maybe some evenings I looked at him as I looked at her. But I almost always preferred to forget Bob's eyes and sat with my back to him and looked at the mouths of those speaking at my table, sometimes silent and sad so he would know that in me there was something besides the thing for which he judged me harshly, something close to him. Other times I drank a little to encourage myself and thought: "Bobby boy, go tell it to sis," while I fondled the hands of the girls at my table or reeled out a long cynical theory about anything, just so they would laugh and Bob hear it.

But those days, no matter what I did, neither Bob's attitude nor his facial expression showed any signs of change. I'm simply telling what follows as proof that he took notice of my little comedies in the bar. One evening I was waiting for Inez next to the piano in the living room of their home, when he came in. He had on a raincoat buttoned up to the collar, his hands in his pockets. He nodded a greeting, immediately began looking around him and walked farther into the room as if he had wiped me out with his rapid nod. I watched him move about near the table, on the rug, walking on it with his beige rubber-soled shoes. He touched a flower with one finger, sat down on the edge of the table and started smoking, with his eyes on the vase of flowers, his calm profile turned toward me, slightly inclined, relaxed and thoughtful. I pressed a grave key imprudently with my left hand—I stood leaning on the piano—and then found myself forced to repeat the sound every three seconds, staring at him all the while.

I felt nothing but hatred and humiliating respect for him and kept on pushing in the key, pounding it with a cowardly fierceness into the silence of the house, until suddenly I found myself situated outside, observing the scene as if I were at the top of the stairs or in the doorway, conscious of him, Bob, silent and absent there beside the string of smoke that rose trembling from his cigarette; conscious of myself, tall and stiff, rather pathetic, a bit ridiculous in the semi-gloom, striking the grave key with my index finger every three seconds exactly. It occurred to me then that I wasn't beating that sound into the piano merely out of foolish bravado but was actually sending him a call. The deep note my finger stubbornly gave life to on the rim of each last vibration was the only word of supplication, finally discovered, with which I could ask his implacable youth for tolerance and understanding. He continued motionless until Inez slammed the bedroom door upstairs before coming down to join me. Then Bob straightened up and walked lazily to the other end of the piano, placed an elbow on it, gazed at me for a minute and said with a handsome smile: "Is tonight a milk or a whisky night? Impetus toward salvation or dive into the abyss?"

I couldn't give him an answer, I couldn't smash his face. I stopped playing the note and slowly drew my hand back from the piano. Inez was halfway down the stairs when he told me, moving away: "Well, it could be that you're just improvising."

The duel lasted three or four months and I couldn't quit going to the club evenings—I remember off hand a tennis championship match was taking place at the time—because, whenever I didn't show up around there for awhile, Bob met my return with increased contempt and irony in his eyes and settled more comfortably into his seat with a smug grin.

When the time came that I saw no other solution but to marry Inez as soon as possible, Bob and his tactic changed. I don't know how he guessed my need to marry his sister and how I embraced that need with all the strength left in me. My passion for that need had dissolved the past and all ties with the present. I paid no attention to Bob then; but, shortly after, I couldn't help noticing how he had changed around that time and sometimes I stopped at some corner and stood cursing him through my teeth, realizing that his face no longer mocked but weighed me with gravity and intense interest, as one weighs danger or a complicated job, or evaluates an obstacle and measures it with everything in him. But I no longer gave him serious thought and even came to believe that an understanding of what was deep in me was beginning to appear in his stony, staring features, an understanding of a clean something back in my past that the deep-felt need of marrying Inez had cleared from under the years and experiences to bring me closer to him.

Then I saw he was waiting for the right evening; but I

saw it at the last moment—that evening when Bob arrived
and came to sit at the table where I was alone and dismissed the waiter with a signal. I waited a little, watching
him: he was so much like her when he moved his eyebrows
or when he spoke and the tip of his nose flattened out a
bit. "You're not going to marry Inez," he said after awhile.
I looked at him, smiled, and stopped looking at him. "No,
you're not going to marry her because a thing like that can
be prevented if there's someone really determined not to
let it happen." I smiled some more and said, "A few years
back that would have made me want to marry Inez even
more. Now it doesn't affect things one way or the other.
But I'm ready to listen, if you care to explain. . . ." He
drew up his head and kept on watching me in silence.
Perhaps he had his words on the tip of his tongue and was
only waiting for me to complete mine in order to say his.
"If you'd care to explain why you don't want me to marry
her," I said slowly and leaned back against the wall. I saw
at once that I had never suspected how deeply and re-
solutely he hated me. His face was pale, the smile on it
partly held and squeezed back by his lips and his teeth.

"It would really have to be split up into chapters," he
said, "it wouldn't end this evening. But it can be reduced
to two or three words. You're not going to marry her
because you're old and she is young. I don't know if
you're thirty or forty, it makes no difference. But you're
a finished man, that is you're washed up, like all men your
age when they're not extraordinary." He drew on his
cigarette which had gone out, looked into the street and
back at me. My head rested against the wall and I went on
waiting. "Naturally you have reasons to believe there's
something extraordinary about you. To believe you've
saved a lot of things from shipwreck. But that's not true."
I started smoking, profile toward him. He disturbed me,
but I didn't believe him. He stirred up a warm hatred in

me but I was sure that nothing would make me lose faith in myself now that I had discovered the need of marrying Inez. No. We were at the same table and I was as clean and young as he. "You could be wrong," I said. "Would you mind mentioning anything washed up about me. . . ." "No, no," he said quickly, "I'm not that childish. I'm not going to be pulled into that little game. You're an egoist. You're sensual in a dirty way. You're tied up with rotten things and it's these things that drag you down. You're going nowhere, you don't really want to. That's it, nothing more. You're old and she is young. I shouldn't even think about her in front of you. And you dare think of . . ." I couldn't push his face in that time either, so I just made up my mind to ignore him, went to the juke box, picked nothing special and dropped in the coin. I went back to my seat slowly and listened. The music wasn't very loud; someone was singing softly between long pauses. Beside me, Bob was saying that not even he, anyone like him, was worthy of looking into Inez's eyes. Poor kid, I thought admiringly. He went on, saying that the most repulsive thing about what he called old age, what determined decomposition or perhaps was the symbol of decomposition was to think in concepts, to put women into the word woman, shoving them in without caring that they might mold themselves to the concept formed by a second-rate experience. But, he was also saying, the word experience wasn't exact either. There were no experiences any more, nothing but habits and repetitions, wilted names to go on tagging things with and half make them up. He said that, more or less. And I was wondering whether he would drop dead or find the way to kill me right then and there, had I told him the images he was stirring inside me when he said that not even he deserved to touch Inez with the tip of his finger, poor kid, or kiss the hem of her garments, her footprints or things like that. After a pause, the music had stopped and the machine put out its lights, increasing the silence. Bob said: "Nothing else," and went off with his usual sure step, neither fast nor slow.

If Inez's face appeared to me in Bob's features that evening, if at any moment the fraternal likeness made good use of the trick of some particular trait to offer me Inez in Bob, that was really the last time I saw the girl. True I was with her again two evenings later for the usual date and one noon, at an appointment forced by my desperation, in vain, knowing beforehand that all resort to words and presence would be useless, that all my importunate pleas would die out in an astonishing manner, as if they had never dissolved into the enormous blue air of the plaza, under the peaceful green foliage halfway through the good season.

The small, fleeting parts of Inez's face Bob had revealed to me that evening, although directed against me, joining his aggression, also had the enthusiasm and candor of the girl. But how could I speak to Inez, reach her, convince her through the sudden apathetic woman of the last two meetings. How could I recognize or even evoke her, looking at the woman with long rigid body in the armchair in her home and on the bench in the plaza, maintaining the same unyielding rigidity at the two different times and places; the woman with tensed neck, eyes straight before her, mouth lifeless, hands firmly settled in her lap. I looked at her and it was "No." I knew all the air surrounding her was "No."

I never learned what anecdote had been selected by Bob for what happened; in any case, I am certain he didn't lie, that nothing, not even Inez, could make him lie then. I never saw Inez or her empty, hardened form again. I learned that she married and no longer lives in Buenos Aires. Then, in the middle of hatred and suffering, I liked to imagine Bob imagining the things I had done and selecting the right one or the aggregate of things that could kill me in Inez and kill her in me.

For nearly a year now I have been seeing Bob almost daily, in the same café, surrounded by the same people. When they introduced us—they call him Robert now—, I understood that the past is without time and that in it yesterday gets mixed up with a day ten years ago. Worn traces of Inez still showed on his face and a movement of Bob's mouth succeeded in making me see the longish body of the girl again, her unhurried, easy step, and in making the same changeless blue eyes look at me again from under a loose hair-do laced and held in place by a red ribbon. Absent and lost for good, she could be preserved alive and intact, definitely unmistakable, one and the same with what was essential in her. But it was a tough job digging into the face, the words and the gestures of Robert to find Bob and be able to hate him. The afternoon of the first meeting I waited hours for him to be left by himself or go out so that I might speak to him or hit him. Still and silent, sometimes spying on his face or evoking Inez in the brilliant windows of the café, I cunningly composed insulting phrases and found the patient tone in which I would deliver them and I picked the spot on his body on which to strike the first blow. But he left at nightfall together with three friends and I resolved to wait, as he had waited years back for the right night when I should be alone.

When I saw him again, when we began this second friendship which I hope will never come to an end, I left off thinking of any form of attack. It was decided that I would never again speak to him of Inez or the past and that I would keep it all alive in me silently. This is exactly what I do almost every afternoon in the presence of Robert and the familiar faces in the café. My hatred will be preserved warm and fresh as long as I can continue seeing and listening to Robert. No one knows of my revenge but I live it, joyful and furious, from one day to the next. I speak to him, smile, smoke, drink coffee. Thinking all the while of Bob, his purity, his faith, the boldness of his past dreams. Thinking of the Bob who loved music, the Bob who planned to ennoble the life of men by building a city of blinding beauty for five million inhabitants, along the river's coast; the Bob who could never lie, the Bob who declared the war of the young against the old ones, Bob the owner of the future and the world. Thinking in detail, with satisfaction, of all this in front of the man called Robert with fingers soiled by tobacco, who leads a grotesque life, working in any stinking office, married to a fleshy woman whom he refers to as "my wife"; the man who spends these long Sundays sunk into his seat in the café, going through the newspapers and laying bets with the bookies over the phone.

No one has ever loved a woman as passionately as I love his ruin, the hopeless manner in which he has sunk into the filthy life of men. No one was ever so enraptured as I am before his sudden false enthusiasms, the unconvincing projects a destroyed and distant Bob sometimes dictates to him, only to help him measure exactly how foul he has become forever.

I don't know if I ever welcomed Inez in the past with such joy and love as I daily welcome Bob into the shadowy and stinking world of adults. He is still a recent arrival and every so often he suffers his crisis of nostalgia. I've seen him teary and drunk, damning himself and vowing his imminent return to the days of Bob. I can assure you that then my heart flows over and becomes sensitive and affectionate as a mother's. Deep inside, I know he will never leave, because he has no place to go; but I grow gentle and patient and try to go along with him. Like the handful of native earth or those photographs of streets and monuments or the songs that immigrants like to bring along with them, I build up plans for him, beliefs and different tomorrows that have the light and taste of the country of youth from which he came some time ago. And he accepts; he always protests so that I'll redouble my promises, but he ends up saying yes, he ends up forcing a smile, believing that some day he must return to Bob's world and hours and he feels at peace in the middle of his thirty years, moving about without disgust or uneasiness among the powerful corpses of old ambitions, the repulsive forms of dreams gradually wasted under the indifferent, constant pressure of so many thousands of inevitable feet.

Translated by HARDIE ST. MARTIN

Mario Benedetti (b. 1920) was born in Montevideo, Uruguay, and he writes especially of life in Montevideo, and, by extension, of cities everywhere. Novelist, short-story writer, poet, essayist, literary critic, playwright, and publisher, he has written for journals in Uruguay, Argentina, and Mexico. Over and over in his stories he captures the problems of the city dweller, trapped in an impersonal world, building a shell to protect himself from authentic feelings. As Jean Franco stated in *The Modern Culture of Latin America,* many of Uruguay's problems stem from its high level of literacy and large middle class. "Modern Uruguay is a country of clerks and civil servants, and the hazards that face them are not those of violence and oppression but of smugness and the excessive concern for security." Thus Benedetti's stories and novels are often set among office workers and members of the middle class, and in many, "the characters' low-key lives take on a tragic tinge simply because they are caught in the trap of routine." Besides many novels and collections of short stories, Benedetti has written a full-length study of twentieth-century Uruguayan literature. He lives now in Buenos Aires. The following story is from his 1959 collection, *Montevideanos.*

Gloria's Saturday

Even before I was fully awake, I heard the rain falling. My first thought was that it must be a quarter past six and I was due at the office, but I'd left my rubber-soled shoes at my mother's and so I'd have to line the other ones, the every-day pair, with newspaper, because it bugs me to feel the dampness seeping in and chilling my feet and ankles. Then I thought, it's Sunday, I can stay and snuggle beween the sheets for a while. It always gives me a childish kick to know I can look forward to a holiday. To feel time's at my disposal, as though it were free, instead of having to race two blocks, five mornings out of the week, to be able to punch the time-clock. To feel I can be serious for once, and think about things that matter: life, death, soccer, the war. During the week I've no time. When I reach the office there are fifty or sixty items to attend to: I have to enter them in the ledger, stamp them "posted as of current date," and initial the stamp in green ink. By noon I'm about half-way through, and I run four blocks to grab a place on the bus platform. If I don't run the four blocks I'm stuck and have to walk, and I get sick to my stomach if I have to walk too close to the streetcars. It doesn't make me sick, actually, it makes me afraid, hideously afraid.

That doesn't mean I think about death much, just that it disgusts me to picture myself lying with my skull bashed in or my guts spilling out, surrounded by a couple of hundred passers-by, all wrapped up in their own affairs, but still curious enough to stand on tiptoe for a good look, and be able to tell all about it next day over dessert after the family dinner. A family dinner like the one I polish off in twenty-five minutes, all alone, because Gloria has gone off to her shop a half-hour earlier, leaving everything ready for me over a low flame on the oil-stove: I've only to wash my hands, gulp down the soup, the veal chop, the omelet and the stewed fruit, glance at the paper, and make a second dash for the bus. When I get to the office, around two o'clock, I enter the twenty or thirty transactions that are still pending; and about five, notepad in hand, I hurry to answer the vice-president's buzzer, so that he can dictate the half-dozen letters that have to go out, and which it's up to me to deliver, translated into English or German, before seven.

Twice a week Gloria is waiting for me when I come out, so we can enjoy ourselves a bit, and we go to a movie where she cries her eyes out, while I maul my hat or chew on the program. The other nights she goes to visit her mother, and I do accounts for two bakeries, whose owners —two of them come from Galicia and one from Mallorca —do all right for themselves by using rotten eggs in their cakes, and still better by running furnished tenements in the most crowded section of the south side of town. So that by the time I get home she's sound asleep, or—when we come home together—we have supper and fall into bed right afterwards, like tired animals. There are precious few nights that we've enough energy left over for the conjugal rites, and so, without even reading a book or exchanging what Gloria calls a bit of chit-chat about the arguments between my fellow-workers or her boss's bullying (he himself says he has a heart of gold, but the girls in the shop call it a heart of stone), without sometimes, even saying goodnight, we fall asleep with the lights on, because she wanted to read the crime pages and I wanted to look at the sports section.

Chit-chat is saved up for Saturdays like this one. (Because actually it was a Saturday, the tag-end of a Saturday afternoon nap.) I get up at three-thirty and make the tea and bring it back to bed; and then she wakes up and reviews the week's events and looks through my socks and catches up with her mending; then, at a quarter to five, she gets up to listen to the program of dance music. But there wouldn't have been any chit-chat this Saturday, because the night before, after the movie, I'd gone over-board singing the praises of Margaret Sullavan, and Gloria, without a moment's hesitation, started in pinching me, and when I wouldn't budge she got back at me with something much worse, really underhanded, about this terrific guy in the shop, and that's cheating, of course, because Margaret Sullavan is just a picture on a screen, and this creep at the shop is flesh and blood. The upshot of this nonsense was that we went to bed without speaking and then lay in the dark for a half-hour, each of us waiting for the other to make the first move to patch up the quarrel. I shouldn't have minded making the first move, I've done it plenty of times, but in the midst of this sham hatred sleep overcame us, and peace was postponed till today, saved for the blank space of this Saturday afternoon.

And so when I saw it was raining I thought, so much the better, the bad weather would automatically bring us closer: we weren't going to be such idiots as to sulk in silence through a rainy Saturday afternoon, in a two-room apartment where privacy simply doesn't exist and you just have to live face to face. She moaned a little when she woke up, but I thought nothing of it. She always moans when she wakes up.

But when she was fully awake and I got a good look at her, I saw she was really ill and in pain, you could tell by the circles around her eyes. Forgetting that we weren't speaking, I asked what was the matter. She had a pain in her side. It hurt badly, and she was scared.

I said I'd go call the doctor, and she said yes, call her right away. She was trying to smile but, looking at her sunken eyes, I was of two minds whether to stay with her or go make the telephone call. Then I thought that if I didn't go she'd be even more frightened, and I went downstairs and called the doctor.

The guy who answered said she was out. I don't know why it occurred to me that he might be lying, and I said that wasn't true, I'd seen her going in. Then he asked me to hold on a second, and after five minutes he came back to the telephone with some fishy story about how I was in luck, she'd come in this very moment. I said well, isn't that just dandy, had him take down the address, said it was urgent.

When I got back Gloria was being nauseated, and the pain was much worse. I didn't know what to do. I put a hot-water bottle on her, and then an ice-pack. Nothing seemed to soothe her, and I gave her an aspirin. At six o'clock the doctor still hadn't come, and I was in no state to buck anyone up. I told three or four stories, trying to sound cheerful, but it made me mad to see the face she pulled when she tried to smile, because I could tell she didn't want to dishearten me. I took a glass of milk, nothing more, because my stomach was tied up in knots. At half-past six the doctor came, finally. An enormous cow of a woman, too big for our tiny apartment. She produced a couple of titters that were meant to be encouraging, and then set about kneading Gloria's belly, digging her nails in and then suddenly letting go. Gloria bit her lips, saying yes, it hurt there, and in that place a bit more even, and farther on worse still. It kept on hurting worse and worse.

The cow went on, digging her nails in and then letting go. When she stood up there was fright in her eyes too, and she asked for alcohol to disinfect herself. Out in the hallway she told me it was peritonitis, they'd have to operate at once. I told her we belonged to a health plan, and she promised to have a word with the surgeon.

I went down in the elevator with her and telephoned the taxi stand and Gloria's mother. I had to walk back up, someone on the fifth floor had left the elevator door open. Gloria was twisted up into a ball, and though her eyes were dry I could tell she had been crying. I helped her put on my overcoat and scarf, and it brought back memories of a Sunday when she'd worn some country clothes and a pair of my pants, and how we'd laughed at the way her behind stuck out, the thoroughly unmasculine outline of her hips.

But now, wearing my clothes, she was only a travesty of that afternoon, and we had to move fast, not stopping to think. As we were leaving, her mother arrived; poor darling, she said, for heaven's sake, wrap yourself up. Then Gloria seemed to realize she'd have to be strong, and made up her mind to put up a front. In the taxi she joked a couple of times about how the shop would be forced to give her leave of absence and how I'd have no socks for Monday, and, seeing her mother weeping buckets, she said do you think this is some episode out of a soap opera? I knew the pain was getting worse every minute, and she knew I knew, and huddled closer against me.

By the time we got to the hospital, all she could do was moan. They left us in a little waiting-room, and after a while the surgeon came. Tall, with a kindly, absent-minded expression, wearing a coat that was unbuttoned and none too clean. He asked us to step outside and closed the door. Gloria's mother sat down in a low chair, crying harder and harder. I stared out at the street: it had stopped raining. I didn't even have the comfort of a smoke. Even back in high school, I was the only one out of thirty-eight who had never even tried a cigarette. That was when I first met Gloria: she wore her dark hair in braids and couldn't get through geography. There were two ways to get closer to Gloria: either I could teach her geography myself, or we could study it together. I took the second way, and of course we both flunked.

Then the doctor came out and asked was I the brother or the husband. The husband, I told him, and he gave a wheezing kind of cough. "It's not peritonitis," he said, "the doctor's an ass." "Oh?" "It's something else. We'll know better in the morning." In the morning. That is: "We'll know better if she gets through the night. If we operate now, she's done for. It's serious all right, but if she gets through the day I think she'll pull through." I thanked him —I've no idea what for—and he added: "It's against regulations, but you can stay with her tonight."

First a nurse came along with my overcoat and scarf. Then Gloria passed by, on a stretcher, with her eyes closed, unconscious.

At eight o'clock I was able to go into the little private room where they'd put her. It had a table and a chair, in addition to the bed. I sat down straddling the seat of the chair, with my elbows resting on the back. My eyelids smarted, as though I'd been straining my eyes, forcing

them to stay wide open. I couldn't leave off staring at her.
The sheet was no whiter than her pallid face, and her forehead was glittering and waxen. It was a joy to listen to her
breathing, even like this, with her eyes closed. I pretended
she wasn't speaking to me because I had a crush on
Margaret Sullavan, that I wasn't speaking to her because
she had a yen for that guy in the shop. But deep down I
knew the truth, and I felt as though I were dangling in mid-
air, as though this forced insomnia was something pitiful
and unreal demanded of me by this momentary tension,
a tension that at any minute might come to an end.

As each eternity passed a clock ticked somewhere far
off, and only an hour had gone by. Once I stood up, went
out to the corridor, and paced back and forth a few times.
A fellow came up to me, chewing on a cigarette, his mouth
twisted in a joyful grin. "So you're waiting too?" Yes, I
said, I was waiting too. "It's the first," he went on, "she
seems to be having a hard time." Then I could feel myself
going limp, and I went back to the room and sat down
again, astride the chair. I began to count the floor tiles,
playing superstitious games, trying to kid myself. I looked
at the tiles and made a rough guess at how many there
were in each row, and told myself if it was an odd number
she'd pull through. And it was an odd number. And she
would pull through if the clock chimed before I had
counted to ten. And the clock chimed when I was counting
five or six. Suddenly I caught myself thinking, "If she gets
through today. . . ." and panic gripped me. I had to assure
the future, visualize it at all cost. I had to build a future
if I was to snatch her away from this death that was growing up all around her. And I started planning: that when
vacation time came, we'd go to Floresta, that next Sunday
—because this future I was scheming had to be just around
the corner—we'd have dinner with my brother and his
wife, and we'd all laugh about what a scare my mother-in-

law had had, that I would make a public statement announcing that I had formally broken with Margaret Sullavan, that Gloria and I would have a child, two children, four, and each time I would settle down to wait impatiently in the corridor.

Then a nurse came in and sent me outside while she gave Gloria an injection. Then I came back in and went on to outline that facile, transparent future. But she shook her head and muttered something or other. That was all. And then there was nothing but Gloria fighting for life, only the two of us and the threat of death, only me hanging on, watching her nostrils flutter as they continued, thank Christ, to open and close, only this tiny room, and the clock ticking.

Then I took out my notepad and started to write this, so that I could read it to her when we were back home again, read it to myself when we were back home again. Back home. How good that sounded. But at the same time it sounded far away, as far away as the first woman when you're eleven years old, or rheumatism when you're twenty, or death itself only yesterday. Suddenly my mind started wandering: I thought about today's game, had it been called off on account of rain, about the English umpire who would be appearing in the stadium for the first time, the entries I'll be making in the ledger tomorrow. But then the sight of her filled me up again, with her glittering, waxen forehead, her parched lips twitching with fever, and I felt utterly lost, a stranger in this Saturday which was to have been mine.

Half-past eleven now. I thought of God, of my old hope that perhaps he really did exist. Out of strict honesty, I refused to pray. You pray only to something you really believe in. And I couldn't believe in Him really. All I have is the hope that He exists. Then I realized that I was not praying only to see if my honesty might touch Him per-

haps. And then I prayed. A savage prayer, full of qualms,
a prayer meant to crush, to leave no doubt that I would not
and could not worship Him, a prayer like a mailed fist.
I listened to this silent prayer as I stammered it out, but
all I could really hear was her breathing, hard and labored.
Another eternity, and twelve o'clock struck. If she gets
through today. And she'd done it. The day was behind
her at last, and she was still breathing. The two of us kept
on breathing, and I fell asleep. I had no dreams.

Someone shook my arm; it was ten past four. She was
not there. Then the surgeon came in and asked the nurse,
had she told me yet. Yes, I yelled—though it wasn't true—
and he was a son-of-a-bitch, worse than the doctor even,
because he'd said if she got through today, and then after
all . . . I yelled, I think in my frenzy I even spit at him, and
he looked at me with his kindly, hatefully understanding
face, and I knew I was wrong, that it was all my fault,
for going to sleep, for letting her go without one single last
look, without the future I had schemed for her, without
my insulting, punished prayer.

Then I asked them where I could see her. Some dull
curiosity drove me to watch her as she slipped away, taking
with her my children, my holidays, and all the spiritless
fondness I felt for God.

Translated by GREGORY WOODRUFF

Pedro Juan Soto (b. 1928) was born in Puerto Rico. He moved to New York when he was eighteen and went to college, supporting himself in part as mail carrier, movie usher, busboy, and reporter for a Spanish-language newspaper. When he graduated, he was drafted into the U.S. Army, part of the first generation of Puerto Ricans thus to experience the full impact of U.S. domination (in 1916, U.S. citizenship was imposed on all Puerto Ricans). Both he and René Marqués, who is also represented in this volume, were part of the generation of young authors who revolutionized the short story in Puerto Rico and whose themes reflected their awareness of U.S. dominance and the often-difficult adjustment of the Puerto Ricans to U.S. culture. It was during the group's early years that the island's independence movement began. Pedro Juan Soto's first published stories centered around Puerto Ricans in New York, where he lived for ten years, and became part of his first collection, *Spiks* (1956), in which, as Victoria Ortiz says, he has "transferred to paper the essence of Puerto Rican life in the hostile atmosphere of New York City." The following story is from the English edition of *Spiks*. His best-known novel, *Usmail* (a play on "U.S. Mail"), is about the brutality with which Puerto Ricans are treated on a small island off Puerto Rico which has been taken over as a U.S. naval base. Of his other novels, *Ardiente suelo, fría estación (Hot Land, Cold Season)* has been published here. He has also written for the theater.

The Innocents

*climb to the sun on that cloud with the pigeons without
horses without women and not smell when they burn the
tin cans in the lot without people to make fun of me*

From the window, wearing the suit made and sold to fit
the man he was not, he saw the pigeons hovering under the
eaves across the way.

or with doors and windows always open to have wings

He began to flap his hands and make noises like the
pigeons when he heard the voice behind him.

"Baby, baby."

The shriveled woman was seated at the table (under it
was the flimsy suitcase fastened with rope, its only key),
watching him with intense eyes, sunk in her chair like a
hungry and abandoned cat.

"Pan," he said.

Giving it a light nudge away from the table, the woman
pushed the chair out and went to the cupboard. She got the
piece of bread that was lying exposed on the boxes of rice

377

and took it to the man, who was still gesticulating and mouthing sounds.

to be a pigeon

"Don' make noise, Pipe."

He crumbled the piece of bread on the window sill without paying attention to her.

"Don' make noise, baby."

The men playing dominoes under the store awning were looking up.

He stopped moving his tongue.

without people to make fun of me

"A pasiar a la plaza," he said.

"Yes. Hortensia's comin to take you for a walk."

"A la plaza."

"No, not to the plaza. They took it away. It flew away."

He pouted. He listened again to the fluttering of the pigeons.

"No, it wasn' the pigeons," she said. "It was the Evil One, the Devil."

"Ah."

"You have to pray to Papá Dios to bring back the plaza."

"Papá Dios," he said, looking outside. "Trai la plaza y el río . . ."

"No, no, Don' open yer mouth," she said. "Kneel down an talk to Papá Dios without openin yer mouth."

He knelt in front of the window, joined his hands and looked out over the roofs.

want to be a pigeon

She looked out below, at the idleness of the men on a Saturday morning and the briskness of the women hurrying to and from the market.

Slowly, sorrowfully, but erect, as if balancing a bundle on her head, she walked toward the room where her daughter, in front of the mirror, was taking the pins out of her hair and piling them on the bureau top.

"Don' take him today, Hortensia."

The younger woman glanced at her out of the corner of her eye.

"Don' start that again, mama. Nothin ain gonna happen to him. They'll take good care of him and it don' cost us nothin."

As it was freed from the pins, her hair fell over her ears in a pile of tight curls.

"But I know how to take care of him. He's my boy. Who knows better than me?"

Hortensia studied the slight and slender figure in the mirror.

"Yer old, mama."

A fleshless hand appeared in the mirror.

"I ain dead yet. I can still take care of him."

"It ain that."

The curls were still tight, despite her attempts to loosen them with the comb.

"Pipe's innocent," said the mother, her words water for a sea of grief. "He's a baby."

Hortensia put the comb down. She took a pencil from the open bag on the dresser and began to blacken her scanty brows.

"You can't cure that," she said to the mirror. "You know it. Tha's why the best thing is . . ."

"In Puerto Rico this wouldn' of happened."

"In PR it was different," said Hortensia over her shoulder. "People knew him. He could go out because people knew him. But in New York people don' care and you don' even know yer neighbors. Life's tough. Its years an years I been sewin and sewin an I ain even married yet."

Looking for the lipstick, she saw her mother's face crumble in the mirror.

"But that ain the reason either. They can take better care of him there."

"Tha's what you say," said the mother.

Hortensia tossed the makeup and comb into her bag and closed it. She turned: flimsy blouse, gleaming lips, blackened eyebrows, tight curls.

"After a year here, we deserve somethin better."

"It ain his fault what happens to us."

"But its gonna be if he stays here. Jus look."

She darted at her mother, taking her arm and pushing up the short sleeve. On the loose upper arm was a purple blotch.

"He raised his hand to you already, an me in the factory I aint easy thinkin what could be happenin with you an him. An with this already . . ."

"He didn' mean it," said the mother, pulling her sleeve down and looking at the floor as she twisted her arm so that Hortensia would let go.

"He didn' mean it, with one hand on yer throat? If I hadn' of grabbed that bottle, God only knows. We ain gotta man aroun to stand up to him, an I'm turnin into a wreck an yer scared of him."

"He's a baby," said the mother in her docile voice, drawing into her body like a snail.

Hortensia half closed her eyes.

"Don' start with that again. I'm young an I got my life in fron of me an he ain. Yer tired too an if he wasn' here you could live better fer the years you got left an you know it but you don' dare say it cause yer scared its wrong but I say it for you *yer tired* an tha's why you signed those papers cause you know that in that place they take better care of him an then you can sit an watch the people go by in the street an when you want you can get up an go out an walk aroun like them but you'd rather think its a crime an that *I'm* the criminal so you can be a martyred mother an *you bein a martyred mother* can't deny that but you gotta think of yerself an me. Cause if that horse threw him when he was ten . . ."

The mother left the room quickly, as if pushed, as if the room itself blew her out, while Hortensia was saying: ". . . an the other twenny years he lived like that, sense-less . . ."

She turned to watch her leave, without following, leaning on the dresser where she now felt her fists hammering out a beat for her near scream.

". . . we lived them with him."

In the mirror she caught sight of the hysterical carnival mask that was her face.

and there's no roosters and there's no dogs and there's no bells and there's no river wind and there's no movie buzzer and the sun doesn't come in here and I don't like

"Enough," said the mother, bending over to brush the crumbs off the sill. The throng of kids hit and chased a rubber ball down the street.

and the cold sleeps sits walks here inside and I don't like it

"Enough, baby, enough. Say Amen."

"Amen."

She helped him get up and put his hat in his hand, seeing that Hortensia, serious and red-eyed, was coming toward them.

"Les go, Pipe. Give mama a kiss."

She put her bag on the table and bent down to pick up the suitcase. The mother threw herself on his neck—her hands like pliers—and kissed the burned hazelnut of a face, smoothing her fingers over the skin she had shaved that morning.

"Les go," said Hortensia, carrying bag and suitcase.

He wriggled out of his mother's arms and walked to the door, swinging the hand which carried the hat.

"Baby, put on yer hat," said the mother, and she blinked so that he would not see her tears.

Turning, he raised it and left it on top of his vaselined hair, so small it looked like a toy, as if it wanted to compensate for the waste of material in the suit.

"No, leave it here," said Hortensia.

Pipe pouted. The mother fixed her eyes on Hortensia and her chin trembled.

"Okay," said Hortensia, "carry it in yer hand."

He walked again to the door and his mother followed, hunching over a bit now and holding back the arms that wanted to stretch out toward him.

Hortensia stopped her.

"Mama, they're gonna take care of him."

"I don' want them to beat . . ."

"No. There's doctors. An you . . . every other week. I'll take you."

They both made an effort to keep their voices steady.

"Go lie down, mama."

"Tell him to stay there . . . not to make noise an to eat everythin."

"Yeah."

Hortensia opened the door and looked out to see if Pipe had stayed on the landing. He was amusing himself by spitting over the bannister and watching the saliva.

"I'll be home early, mama."

The mother stood next to the chair that was already superfluous, trying to see him through the body which blocked the entrance.

"Lie down, mama."

The mother did not answer. With her hands joined in front of her, she was rigid until her chest and her shoulders shook convulsively and the delicate and gulping sobbing began.

Hortensia pulled the door shut and went hurriedly downstairs with Pipe. Facing the immense clarity of a June midday, she longed for hurricanes and eclipses and snowfalls.

Translated by VICTORIA ORTIZ

Guillermo Cabrera Infante (b. 1929) was born in
Gibara, on the north coast of Cuba. When he was seven, his
parents were arrested as Communists and spent several months
in prison. In 1941 they moved to Havana. When he was
eighteen he wrote a story mimicking *El señor presidente* and,
to his surprise, it was published. In 1952 he was jailed for
publishing a story containing English four-letter words, so for
a while he wrote under a pen name. In the late 1950s he wrote
most of the stories that were gathered later in *Así en la paz
como en la guerra* ["In peace as in war], and he founded the
literary supplement *Lunes de Revo'ución*. In 1961, as editor of
Lunes, he organized a protest against the censorship of a film
called *P.M.,* and the magazine was banned; thus began his
quarrel with the Cuban Revolution which had forced out the
dictator Batista in 1959. He began writing *Ella cantaba boleros*
(the banned film was about a black bolero singer) which later
became *Tres tristes tigres.* The next year he was sent to Brussels as cultural attaché. In 1963 his short story collection was
published in Europe and the next year *TTT* (as he calls it)
received the coveted Bibliotèca Breve award. In 1965, returning
to Cuba for his mother's funeral, he felt harassed and became
a permanent exile. In 1970, living in London, he began work
on the filmscript for Malcolm Lowry's *Under the Volcano.* His
novel, *TTT,* was translated in "closelaboration" with Suzanne
Jill Levine and published in this country in 1972 as *Three
Trapped Tigers.* David Gallagher writes that while *TTT* func-
tions on one level as a documentary of pre-revolutionary
Havana night life, it also "offers a very complex vision of
friendship . . . the same yearning for intimate, sensitive communication that was suppressed in the novels of Vargas Llosa
by the characters' need to adopt a tough, *macho* posture is
suppressed in *TTT* by the characters' need to be witty." The
story that follows is often anthologized, but this translation
from *Review 73* is by the author himself.

Nest, Door, Neighbors

An odd old couple—Americans residing in Havana circa 1957—lived next door then. They were a very small and extremely quiet pair whom we never met socially. Though we shared with them the same terrace—actually a long and narrow balcony constantly aspiring to the condition of terrace—divided by a low concrete partition, I don't think I ever said hello to them. In fact, I don't recall meeting either of them even once in the communal corridor and they rarely came out onto the terrace—except to warm themselves in the sun on the two or three days in winter when it's cold in Cuba. On these rare occasions they always kept themselves to themselves and so did we.

I remember they had a green awning over their side of the terrace. I *remember*! It is as if Damocles said he remembered there was some sort of sword hanging over him. Remember, hell! To remember you have first to forget—and how could I ever forget?

Long before the event I'm going to tell you about, the Americans' godawful awning became my wife's pet obsession.

—As they never lower it—she used to say,—the awning's always rolled up—which is a good gag line as (unconscious) gag lines go. But then she had to follow her tag line (or her tagmeme) with trying tirades against awnings, waste, Americans, wasted Americans awnings, the English language, onions, *awnings,* awnings and awnings.

—That awning might as well not be up there at all— she habitually concluded.—It's all such a waste!

One evening I was sitting comfortably in a canvas chair on the terrace, my head in a book, when my wife came to tell me that two sparrows had made a nest in the crookedly folded awning. **Hay un nido de gorriones en el toldo,** she told me, speaking in that language which is Spanish when it is written but becomes Cuban when read.

—That sparrow over there—she said (pointing) though I've often wondered if she actually said **gorrión,** sparrow, or **gorrón,** Cuban for lazy bum—, it stays inside all the time while the other one has to go out to find straws.

—An ideal arrangement—I commented.

—How come?

—**Es el macho.** The one flying around is the female.

—How do you know?—she asked suspiciously.

—Because she's duller.

—**Caramba!**—she said and glared at me but didn't say anything else. Oh well, *those* were the days. . . !

Snugly tucked in the pocket of the awning the fat little cock-sparrow was curiously but unconcernedly watching its smaller, drabber mate trying to get into the fold with its beak full of dried grass.

I suggested that we—meaning she—ought to tell the people next door, least they pull the awning down and the eggs fall out and smash. My wife looked at me as if I were a rare breed: **el hombre tierno.** The original tender-hearted man.

—They might have hatched by then—she added maternally,—and they would fall out and crash before they could fly. Such a waste of lives!

—Naturally—I said absentmindedly, about to go back to my book.

—You speak English, why don't you go and tell them? The connection between my English and their awning was a faulty one, so I said **Algun día,** which can be translated from suave, vague Spanish into rough but still imprecise English as—someday.

It was as if I had said next century. Her face changed and she said sourly but softly:

—Then you should go do it today.

—I can't go now my love. I have to finish this book. Her former admiration died as admirations die generally —with their boos on.

—So it's more important to finish a book than to save the lives of those poor little birds?—she said **sadly.** Even more so, as you don't know how sad **pobres pajaritos** sounds, unless of course you read it aloud in the evening.

—But darling, they haven't even *finished* building their nest!

—And you have to wait till you see the poor little dead creatures smashed flat on the ground before you go and tell them? Is that it?

—But—

—No es así?

—Look dear, I have to write a paper on the living dead languages for—a dead-bird look from her. She's won.—

All right, all right! I'll go as soon as I've finished this page
See?—showing page.—It's the smallest one in the book

> staggering; in most cases a translator has no choice but to
> duplicate as nearly as possible the cognitive content of
> the original, sacrificing the pun as such, or to render a
> pun in the second—the second?—language, not departing
> any further than necessary from the cognitive meaning of
> the utterance as a whale. An example often cited to show
> boat problem and triumphant compromise is a translation
> into French of the two-line gag: "Is life worth living?"
> "It depends on the liver!" The French reply to *"La vie,
> vaut-elle la peine?"* (an "idiomatic" dead ringer for "Is
> life worth living?") is "Question de *foie*," where foie is
> the name of the organ we call liver, though the pun lies
> in its homonymy with *foi* ("faith").

> **(Vale la vida la pena? Eso depende del pene.**
> *Where* **pena** *is the Spanish dead ringer for "worth" and
> also a synonym of "sorrow," but looks exactly like the
> feminine gender of* **pene,** *the organ we call penis, a live
> ringer.)*

> But since a *Hamlet* or a *Faust* or an *Iliad* or a *Don
> Quixote* no less than a facile witticism depends for its
> effect on the selection and arrangement of its parts, down
> to the smallest LINGUISTIC OVERTONES 139

But when I got up to go she had already changed her
mind.

—Look, leave it till tomorrow. It's rather late now and
anyhow they've never lowered the awning before, have
they?

—Right you are!—I said. If you think you are, I
thought.—Tomorrow it is. I'll go and tell them when I
come from school.

—Good—she said.—But don't make tomorrow **mañana,**
I stared at her, then I returned to my book.

detail, every choice made by a translator is crucial to the meaning of the whale *whole! whole!* He must constantly choose among synonyms, and often chance the word order within the sentence because of the structural difference between two languages. He may have to deicide whether to clarify, in the translation, an expression that is ambiguous in the original, or whether to substitute a different metaphorical reference for one that would convey the intended meaning to readers of the *target?* language. He may have to supply for slang or tobba— *taboo* diction in the original, some informal phrasing that will sound natural to the readers of the translation— though not necessarily with the exact flavor or naturalness that the original carries to its readers

His decision may have to begin even with the title
UN NIDO DE GORRIONES EN UN TOLDO

Next day when I got back from work I decided to go and tell the old couple about the nest. It was a little after five in the evening. The building where I live (eternal edifice! I still live there on the page, though the building itself and its surroundings have since 1965 disappeared forever) is a big block of flats made of stucco and erected around a patio with a tall thin areca palm standing stiff above an undergrowth of crotons, cacti and amapolas.

As a brazen breeze made the evening fresh, I felt more like taking my time. It was the beginning of spring and the setting sun was a rosy spout and everything—including the aloof areca—was soaking pink. (Even my pen was dipped in pink and I was about to write that the stucco looked like a meringue shell when I, the writer, hurried him, the character, indoors.)

But the door next-door was its stolid, solid mahogany self.

After ringing the bell twice a blonde girl came to the door. How old was she? Wearing as she was a loose red and yellow striped gown, a bright yellow ribbon tied at the waist, sandals on her feet, gorgeous golden hair falling long and wavy across the pleasant dome of an unwrinkled forehead, I wondered if she was yet sixteen. She was not beautiful but had the All-American girl's naive appeal, freckles and all. She nervously twirled one long end of her cordon belt and for a moment it became a yellow baton.

But I never pictured her as a majorette. Then I thought she looked like a vintage Doris Day. Today I'd rather say she was a young version of Lee Remick, Carol Lynley in her prime, Tuesday Weld *avant l'image*. In eight words—she didn't look at all like a maid. Thelma Ritter could be a maid in my ideal cast but not Doris Day—and the au-pair girl had yet to come.

—Están los de la casa?

—Sorry—un-Doris-Day-like, tight-lipped shy smile—No Spanish.

No Spanish spoken here and my English was as broken then as it is baroque now.

—The old ones, are they at home?—I asked her and I knew González-González was a ventriloquist who was using me as his dummy.

—You mean grandpa and granny?—she said.—No, they've gone out. Won't be back till suppertime.

But it wasn't only I who had a ventriloquist hidden somewhere. Her voice didn't seem to belong either to her or to the Doris Day image. As a matter of fact it became Thelma Ritter better. She spoke rapidly, swallowing her final words and I could barely catch them—**captar** being the exact verb.

—Well . . . it's about their sparrows . . . they have a net—*nest*.

Did she chuckle or merely gasp?

—That's news to me! Didn't know my grandparents bred sparrows.

Well, I hadn't thought her capable of teasing me or of cracking jokes. But then you can't call *that* a joke, even if she meant it as one. When I realized she *was* kidding me, I began to be flustered, and decided to tell her all about the next, nest and the awning to extricate myself and then take leave. I told her, as best I could, how concerned *I* was that they shouldn't destroy the nest unwittingly. I found that unconsciously or not I had left my wife out of the story completely. I did not even mention that I lived next door.

She smiled more graciously than shyly, seemed to reflect mildly on my story for a moment, shook her head in mock-blonde disbelief and then said:

—Won't you come in, please? I'd like you to show me where the nest is. I'll surely tell my grandparents about the sparrows when they come back.

I went in. The apartment was less luxuriously furnished than I had imagined. (I have this habit of always imagining better homes than other people actually live in.) The kitchen was arranged differently and the living-room looked bigger —probably because it had less furniture. But it was very much like our apartment, though instead of Cuban Kitsch it was decorated American Atrocious—with some redundant rugs scattered around for warm comfort.

When we went out—she straight ahead, I hesitantly—through a bedroom onto the terrace, the sun was dabbing, dubbing night purple on the *façade* of the neighboring buildings. The French blinds over the doorway to our balcony were down. Looking blindly at the shuttered doors I remembered it was Friday—the day of my wife's French lesson.

In the awning, the sparrows seemed busy finishing their nest before sunset—or rather before summer. Sootier than ever, one of them was bringing back a long curved Pascalian **palito** that refused to get through such a small opening. The bird fluttered, tried to hold its claws on the selvage and pushed at the reluctant reed, which bent still further but definitely did not want to go into the untidy nest. Something was wrong somewhere and the bird was puzzled but couldn't tell why.

The very moment I recognized as the *male* the toiling, troubled sparrow struggling with the stubborn straw, the female put her tiny head out of the entrance as if trying to get out—just when her husband was trying to get in. Naturally, she found her exit blocked by the unusually industrious male. But she tried, tried and tried again to leave the nest as the male did all he could to get in. (She's tried, he's tired.) In the end the male grew bored with the strenuous job and let go of the straw. Next the sparrow dove into the nest and darted out again—or was it the female this time, finally being able to come out? Whichever it was, it flew swiftly away to disappear among the distant trees.

—That's cute—said the girl and immediately corrected herself:—or stupid. Or both!

Then she giggled and then she laughed. She had a frank or freak laugh which scarcely stirred her body further. It was like a laughing voice—or laughter *parlando*.

It was beginning to get chilly. The tropical breeze was becoming a persistent norther cooling the terrace and the evening. The sun, a rosy wreck, had already sunk in the deep blue sea. We went back in.

—Won't you sit down?

I accepted her invitation a bit too eagerly and sat down on a stool backed against the window-frame. She was already going into the living room but, having half-seen me already sitting there, she smiled in profile and turned back from the doorway into the bedroom. She sat on the bed—the only other piece of furniture in the room. I realized my *faux pas* only when she tried to dismiss it so graciously. (Her sitting down on the bed reminds me of the story about the king and his peasant guest who drank the lemon water from the wash-bowl, and how the king soothed the court's *Schadenfreude* by drinking the concoction himself with gusto, having added a dash of sugar to invent lemonade.) But I dared neither laugh off nor repair my uncool, uncouth error. That was my first mistake. My second one was that I did what almost all curteous and timid people do these days—shy- then-Freudian. Namely, to lay another egg.

—Hwat is jour name—I asked her in my implacable accent.

She smiled again and for a moment I had the impression she was thinking of something other than her name.

—Jill. And yours?

—**Silvestre.**

—That's a pretty name.

I must have shaken my head in disapproval. I hated my name.

—I mean I like it—she said.—I don't think I should ever be able to pronounce it though. But I like it the way you say it.

—Of course you can pronounce it.

(Positive teaching—I am a teacher but I don't teach languages—I teach language.)

—No, I couldn't.

—Try. You only have to say all the e's alike, like in better.

(What did I tell you?)

—I never could.

—Try just once.

—I'll never be able to, believe me.

—Try.

She tried. She did her best to pronounce this hideous

name of mine but said something that sounded rather
like—

—No, not silver tray. I am not a tray and definitely not
made of silver, as you can see—almost turning around—
for yourself.

I was about to coin a counterfeit on my being brass not
Silver Latin—but it was not necessary. She was already
laughing again. I didn't mind her laugh so much now that
we were both laughing.

—You see. I'll never manage it. But I like the way you
say it. Say it again.

—Silvestre.

—Say it.

—Silvestre.

—Say it.

—Silvestre.

—Go on. Sayitsayit*say*it!

She threw herself back on the bed, laughing. (I liked
her laugh less than boringly repeating over and over my
name, a senseless repetition that acted on me like speech
therapy—my name is now a dumb appendix I've learned
to live with ever since. And yet to this very day and hour
I find myself disliking her laugh intensely whenever I hear
it in my memory.) Laughing, I could see her bare crooked
teeth with a wire brace to straighten them. I think her
laugh needed a brace too.

When she stopped laughing some two days later she lay
back, her face to the ceiling. Her gown had risen a lot
above her knees and I could almost see where her thighs
began or ended.

—Journeym is—

That was me trying to avoid the silence with a void
voice.

—. . . nice all so.

I shut up my merciless mouth.

Then she spoke, very slowly at the start.

—There's nothing nice about me.

She almost sniggered.

—Not even my name.

She pursed her lips.

—Not my name especially. It's stupid or cute or both and it doesn't suit me at all. At all! It's not nice. I'm not nice, nothing is nice around me—she embraced the room, Havana, the world with her vertical arms.—Nothing is nice, nothing's nice! Nothingsnice!

The fresh silence lasted longer then the last but I filled it up with my worries. I knew that if she said another word it would be something outlandish. But it would be worse if I said something first—I would certainly lay yet another egg.

She sat up again. She was serious, deadly so. She remained silent and for a moment I thought that she would utter the next word and it would be a four-letter word. Would I understand it?

(I knew then almost all the English swear-words used by men but not even one foul word used by women. I was convinced that there should be in English a different set of four-letter words strictly for feminine use, as happens in Spanish. But then again most swear-words in English become something else when translated into Spanish. For instance, the word hell could be literally rendered as **infierno**, which is not a particularly strong term—a **terno** —in Spain and even less in Cuba, perhaps because we are closer to it. Furthermore, our hell has never enjoyed the prestige of taboo its English counterpart had in films and elsewhere. On the other hand, the Spanish idiomatic dead ringer for hell is **carajo**—which exactly means prick in at least two of the meanings of the word in English. I must confess that this subject was as confusing linguistically to me in the past as it was humanly perplexing to have this girl in front of me in the present.)

In the present that had by now become a pretense—it was all a false predicament because she just looked at me and I noticed that her eyes were not angry. The anger, if there was any, lay only in her twisted mouth—and that could be the force of gravity or even her wire brace's fault—I don't know, I'm no dentist. But, though her eyes were not angry, there was something odd about her pupils, an awkward movement or perhaps some strange fixedness —I don't know, I'm no optician, either. Though I can safely say that the effect was uncanny.

—I must live.

That was my voice—or rather, my accent.

—*What?*

—I have to go now.

—Oh, I see. You mean *leave.*

—Jess.

Did she smile? At least her words died in her distending lips smiling vertically at the ceiling.

—Don't go yet.

I was concerned about her grandparents—or my wife —suddenly coming in.

—I most too.

Yes, she was smiling, then she was sneakingly snickering, then she stood up suddenly, and deftly untied the plaited cloth cord. Her dress became loose and I noticed that it was one of those convertible gowns that change shape with a belt.

—I love your accent. Don't ever lose it.

I never did lose my accent but she was ever loosing her gown. That kind of dress was all the rage at the time and for some unfathomable, albeit shallow, reason I found it stunningly sexy. Until then my mind had reasons which my eyes knew nothing of—from that moment on, my eyes could have their reasons too. Her dress fell over more loose until it went down to her feet. She kicked the shapeless gown away with the technique of habit. (There is plenty of opportunities here for word-play, puns and wisecracks— she was kicking the habit, see?—but I didn't care for them at that time, as I was concentrated on watching her dress and her undressing.) The airborne garment flew across the room to crash against a wall and it fell in a heap to the floor. From where I was it looked to me like a dead dress.

She was standing there, naked except for the black lingerie. She was barefoot to boot. I could see she had strong legs, (pink) feet firmly planted in the (motley) Moorish mosaic. For the first time I stopped wondering how old she was.

—I like your hair too—she said.

Was she going to tell me not to lose it either?

—I've always liked very black hair.

I said precisely nothing.

—I like black. Black night, black hair, black—

Undergarments? Forests? People?

—. . . boards.

She came over to me and ran her hand through my hair. Abruptly she stooped to kiss me. Her kiss was harsh and I could feel the brace pressing against my lips—then against my teeth, then against my gums, then against my tongue. I looked at her eyes. I was wrong, they were not odd but longing. Mine were probably squinting.

I took her firmly by the waist with one arm and caressed her thighs, her back, her lingeried, lingering breasts.

Then I tried to undo her black bra.

—Don't! Please don't! *Please!*

She spoke into my mouth, her words soothing my bruised lips with her placating plosives, her everlasting liquids, her sinuous sibilants. There was no annoyance in her voice, only rigidness—then, without pausing for breath, she went on kissing me. *Kissing kissing kissing kissing kissing kissing kissing* I couldn't think of relatives nor of birds *kissing her*.

Then we stopped kissing—she stopped kissing me to straighten herself up. But she stood facing me—her navel looking vacantly at me like a blind Cyclops.

I tasted blood in my mouth. But before I could discover whether she had cut into my lips or not—searching for blood on my lips with the tip of my finger, inspecting my probing forefinger—I felt a stinging blow on my face and my head went hot all over. She had slapped me three or four times before I knew what was hitting me. Both my cheeks were burning red and a tear started from my right eye. (Or was it from my left eye?)

—That's what it is, isn't it?—she shouted.

She left the room in a twitching rage. The last I saw of her were her legs. She's got legs like a ball player, I thought.

I remained on the stool, uncertain whether to get up or to stay on or vanish. I thought of nothing. No, I was thinking about my sitting on the stool all the time, like a concert pianist. Playing by boxed ear.

I heard sobs and tried to locate where they came from—someone was crying in the next room—or perhaps in the apartment next door. I got up and as I didn't dare to go out onto the terrace I went into the living-room—where I found Jill collapsed across the table, her head in her arms, her shoulders quivering. I was sorry for her and forgot the strip and the teasing and the slap-sting. Did I forget it all because I truly felt sorry for her or because I expected more kisses and perhaps something extra? Or was I merely slaphappy?

When I touched one of her bare shoulders she stopped trembling.

—Leave me alone—she said. Her ventriloquist wasn't Ritter but Garbo.

—Please don't cry.

From the table rose a sound between a stifled sob and a guffaw.

—What makes *you* think I was crying?

She lifted her head and released such a guttural laugh that it sounded almost like a belch.

—Did you think *I* was crying? Why, that's the funniest thing I've heard today. And I've heard some funny things today, believe me!

(I did not know then what she meant but now I'm inclined to think she alluded to my accent.)

She got up and put her face close to mine so that I could see she wasn't crying. She was not crying but she squinted.

—Me? Crying?

She laughed nastily.

—Jerk!

She moved towards the door and put her hand on the knob. But instead of opening the door she rested her head against the top panel. Now she really was crying, she was really crying, she was crying. She was just crying quietly softly sweetly but all the same I was afraid that the whole neighborhood would hear through the thick-panelled solid mahogany Spanish-American door.

—You fool! Fool fool fool!—she muttered to the door. Then I felt she obviously didn't mean me, and I wondered whom she meant as I went over to her and put my hand on her head. (Her hair looked soft and silky but it wasn't. It didn't need a shampoo but it surely needed something—I don't know what, I'm no hair stylist.) She stopped crying but did not look at me again. She turned the knob and opened the door. I tried to close it but she resisted it. I insisted. She persisted. I desisted.

She pulled the door gently, firmly open.

—Will I ever see you again?—was my silly question.
She gave me a brave girl look. No more tears. She shook
her hair—probably as she tried hard not to give me a silly
answer.

—They're sending me back home tomorrow morning.

—I see.

I did not see. I understand now what she meant but
then I thought she had to start packing in a hurry when she
added—

—He's packed me off today.

She opened the door wide and I went out. I gave her a
long last look and saw that there would eventually be more
tears. But not even her good-by look was meant for me.
It was then that I noticed that her underwear needed mending.

—Good-by, Jill.

—By, Silver Try.

Two or three days later I was reading a different book
on the same subject—or maybe just the opposite—anyway,
I had tried to forget it all and noticed that it was easier
trying to forget than trying to remember—though perhaps
remembering was a lot easier than forgetting—well, what
the hell!, I thought, ¡ que carajo!, after all I'm no psychologist—I'm only a fool who's probably a week older
and not any wiser for that—but when the heavy door
closed darkly on me *yesterday*—I stood for a while facing
it, staring back at its black, blind stare—I noticed that
there was a white speck on it—a square spot—a blank
blemish—it was a card with a name—or rather two—on
it: Mr. & Mrs. Clemmons—and I tried to ring again immediately after she closed the door this morning, not because
I wanted to see her again but to convince myself that the
thing—whatever it was—had not happened, that I had
imagined it all just as I was about to ring for the first time
—which is *just now*—which in fact I didn't—or which

indeed I did—but no one came to the door—no one
would come because there was nobody there—it all actually
came from a quotation in Hawthorne on the noiseless steps
of things that almost happen—that the house, Havana, the
world, was as empty as the apartment, which was uninhabited or inhabited possibly by Miss Havisham's ghost—
in a minute—that it all came from Poe, from James—or
perhaps from within myself—nothing—nice or not nice
—*nothing* has happened!—she like an event, has not occurred—or as *She* she was invented: a figurine of speech and
the story a filum of my imagination Jill never existed. My
name was never Silvestre. She wasn't she. I, Latin *ni tal*
I. It was all untrue.

—Silvestre?

It was my wife's voice speaking from behind me. I could
only see her hand (grabbing the doorframe) with half an
eye. She was poised vaguely somewhere on the threshold
of my consciousness. Extreme of.

—What horrible people!

—Yes dear?

—Qué gente horrible pero qué, qué gente!

—People? What people dear?

—*Our next-door neighbors,* that's who! They're horrible!

On the last exclamation mark I raised my face from
the book and looked at the twin terrace. (From abstract
written language to the concrete balcony.) One of the old
people, the woman (at first I thought it was the man),
was lowering the awning and the chirping sparrows were
fluttering around the rapidly distending canvas.

—That old couple! !Esos viejos! They're lowering their
awning!

—So I see my love.

Two little eggs had fallen on the floor but a third one
had just broken against the edge of the divider, making a
yellow liquid viscous obscene stain on the bright brown

brick. The old woman seemed as astonished as the bird and as my wife—and twice as helpless as she ran inside, trembling, calling in a voice—as we say in Spanish—soft but altered:—Walter! Walter!

The two sparrows went on chirping distressedly (or gaily) and fluttering wildly (or methodically or even ritually) around the broken eggs. The garrulous female alighted beside the formless mess and pecked it and ate from the coloidal yolk a little. Then she lifted a damp straw and flew up to where the nest had been. Then she tried to find the nest but there was only a void. Then she dove onto the canvas and scrabbled on the faded cloth, skidding on the once green awning in her quest for her nest. She seemed more bewildered or birdbrained than ever and the straw fell from her oblique beak. Both she and the male sparrow flew away when the old lady returned with the old man. I couldn't see his face nor his demeanour, for my wife—indignation let loose—intruded. However, I think I saw an air-mail envelope in the old man's hands.

My wife went to the end of our balcony and glared at our neighbors futilely, blindly but invisibly challenging the distraught old couple—obviously oblivious of her. Then she came over to the narrator, venting her fury on him and his totally innocent book in a compact single indictment in the form of a question:

—Soyoudidntellthemaboutitafterall?

Then I looked at my wife that is no longer my wife as I look now at her word-sentence and I see myself saying nothing on my behalf. Not even that oft-repeated four-letter Spanish word. **Nada.** My defence was my diffidence.

But today, many years and a few translations later, I often wonder what that Jill did. What did *she*—not "surely" but exactly—tell her grandparents about the sparrows, about their present, *past*, nest and future lives now destroyed, about our finally common awning?

Norberto Fuentes (b. 1943) was born in Havana, Cuba. After studying art, he turned to journalism, and it was as a newspaperman that he witnessed the operations of the Cuban Revolutionary Army against counterrevolutionary bandits in the Escambray Mountains in the early 1960s. The stories collected under the title *Los Condenados de Condado* ["The condemned of Condado"], based on those experiences, were awarded the Casa de las Américas prize in 1968. At present, Fuentes works as a journalist in Havana and promises more stories and perhaps a novel in the near future. The stories in *Los Condenados de Condado*, from which the following story was taken, achieve a curiously cumulative effect that one rarely finds in a short story collection. And several of the stories remind us, in case we need reminding, that during a revolution there are often occasions to smile.

Honor Cleaned

The old worker dared to say to him:

"It's a little late. Listen to the roosters. They're saying how late it is. Why don't you go home a while and rest that young head a bit? Everything can be fixed up. Follow an old man's advice. Why don't you go home?"

"Nothing doing!" shouted the militiaman seated on the stool beside the table where he put his submachine gun and the belt with the canister of eight magazines. He had the stool leaning against the wall. His shirt was crumpled and outside his pants. Sleep weighed his eyelids.

I said nothing doing. No one will sleep in this house until my man's honor is cleaned. And well cleaned. Till it shines.

The old man repeated once again what he had been saying since noon: but how can we clean it? Look at how late it is.

"You're pretty foxy too, old man. Shut up now. You ask me how to clean my honor. I still haven't figured that out.

And nevertheless, something inside me tells me that my revenge must be long and terrible. It can't be any other way. It's clear that you weren't in that barracks today. You say we should fix these things up tomorrow. Honor can't wait," he declared firmly, and immediately he pressed his temples in order to squeeze some idea out of his brain.

"Ay, I can't think of anything that will be revenge." Florentina, seated between her parents like a chastened schoolchild, had lost the vigor of her rudder-like hips, and now her lank black hair fell listless over her shoulders and her skin seemed to fuse into one piece with her clothing. That one piece was a crushed, damp handkerchief.

"You, don't cry no more snot out of those eyes," the militiaman ordered, ending with a "two-timing bitch!"

"That I won't allow," the mother who had seemed to be sleeping jumped up.

"Oh no?" asked the militiaman, and he took the sub-machine gun from the table. "Let's see if you won't."

"My God, don't do that," said the mother.

And he went on speaking:

"Won't allow? Who asked you to give birth to a two-timing bitch?"

A long sob issued from Florentina's soul.

Finally the militiaman started to cry as well and he took a piece of paper from his pocket. It was a lined sheet, torn from a school notebook, where Florentina had written in large and scattered letters. Did you see this, old man? Did you take a good look?

"Yes, my son. I haven't seen anything else since noon. When you arrived."

"But did you read what it says carefully? Look here. The candies you sent me were delicious. You read that? And here, here, look here. If you have any dirty clothes send them to me so I can wash them. You see?" And now he was crying with real vehemence, undoing the knot in his throat that had formed when the company instructor had called him.

"Hey, Ramón Palomo!" shouted the instructor from the barracks' door.

"Listen, Ramón Palomo, you know this Florentina López, who lives near your brother's place?"

"Sure, comrade instructor, she's my girlfriend, my official fiancée whose hand was asked for just as it should be."

And the instructor said to him:

"Well, be careful with those girl friends who write to bandits," and he let fall a sheet of notebook paper, neatly written on and folded with tremendous care.

The letter remained on the wooden floor, partly unfolded. In the barracks there was the same silence as when God had not yet thought to make the sky and the earth.

"From where?" Ramón Palomo's voice trembled.

"From that Rosalío Valdés you hunted yesterday when he tried to break through the lines."

The instructor said then: Well, hurry up for exercises. And he gave a half turn, leaving the entrance free.

Ramón Palomo untied his laces and took off his boots. In the barracks they continued not speaking. Ramón Palomo lay down on his cot. The militiamen began leaving the barracks and on reaching the door they took the trouble to walk around the letter.

They all left.

Then Ramón Palomo approached the door.

The next day, at nine in the morning, Florentina's father walked from his house to a yucca field he was preparing. When he returned in the afternoon, Ramón Palomo was still sleeping with his head on the table and the submachine gun on his knees. The old man brought his own pillow. A soft pillow. And he put it under Ramón Palomo's head. Ramón Palomo didn't wake up. Florentina's mother decided to put the submachine gun away in the wardrobe, just in case it went off by itself.

Ramón Palomo opened his eyes at nine that night and had a plate of porridge which they offered and served him. He asked for his weapon and left without saying good-bye.

Florentina, who had locked herself in her room since morning, did not go out again for many days. As time went by and for almost a year, whenever Florentina went into town people talked about her behind her back.

REMITTANCE

Document found in the knapsack of a bandit killed in battle this 11th of May, 1963:

Mr. Rosalío Valdés, Pray God and the Virgin Mary that as these lines reach your hands you find yourself enjoying good health. Sir, this is in answer to your adorable letter and at the same time to tell you not to think of me any more and I am sorry I can't make you happy. I know you are in love with me but you should realize that I am engaged and I cannot accept your holy love although I know that you deserve it you are so good. How can I leave one engagement for another and think how difficult it is for me. I took a liking to you and nothing more. You know that there cannot be any desire. I am sorry to the bottom of my heart that you have gone to all this trouble, but I can't be any other way. Ah, if I weren't engaged it would be very different. I will always have good feelings about you, but no desire. Don't write to me again and I am sorry to say it but I see no other solution. I enjoy seeing your writing. You can write as a friend, but not with desire. I won't write anymore because I'm afraid they'll see me. With that, I, who hope that God will always accompany and help you, say good-bye. With that, receive an affectionate greeting from

Florentina López

P.S. Thanks for the delicious candies that you sent me. If

you have any dirty clothes, send them to me with the boys, so I can wash them, with that,

Florentina López

Translated by VICTORIA ORTIZ

Mario Vargas Llosa (b. 1936) was born in Arequipa, Peru and spent his childhood in Cochabamba (Bolivia) with his divorced mother and doting grandparents. In 1945 the family moved back to Peru, first to the provincial town of Piura which figures in his novel *The Green House,* and then to Lima in 1946, where his parents reunited. In 1950, at the age of 14, he was sent for two years as a boarder to the Leoncio Prado, a quasimilitary boarding school. In 1958 he published *Los jefes,* a collection of six early short stories about adolescents. (In 1958 he visited France and in 1959—when he received a doctorate from the University of Madrid—he returned to live there for many years.) His first novel, *La ciudad y los perros* [1962, as *The Time of the Hero*], was about a quasimilitary school in which boys learned a sordid combination of bullying and perversion. In Spain it received the important Biblioteca Breve prize. His second novel, *La Casa Verde* (1966, *The Green House*) was the first novel to receive Latin America's prestigious new Rómulo Gallegos prize. The green house is a brothel in Piura, paralleled ironically by the mission nuns in the jungle who kidnap Aguaruna Indian girls, teach them Christianity, and then turn them out fit only to be servants or prostitutes in towns like Piura. In *Conversación en la Catedral* (1969, *Conversation in the Cathedral*), Vargas Llosa continues with the theme of giving in to prevailing social pressures. It is perhaps the most difficult novel of a writer who demands more than the usual effort from his readers. The novella *Los cachorros* (1967) focuses on the activities of upper-class adolescents in the Lima suburbs. In 1972 he also published a study of García Márquez. David Gallagher suggests that, in Vargas Llosa's work, *machismo,* or the assertion of masculinity, is each boy's passport to group acceptance, which is but an early form of conformity that in their elders "must contain the appearance of unimpeachable respectability at all costs and against the most pressing ethical considerations."

410

Sunday

He held his breath for a moment, dug his nails into the palms of his hands, and said in a rush: "I'm in love with you." He saw her blush suddenly, as if someone had slapped her cheeks, which were of a glowing paleness and very soft. Terrified, he felt confusion mounting in him and turning his tongue to stone. He wanted to run away, to be done with it. In the silent winter morning had come this inner weakness that always disheartened him in decisive moments. A few minutes before, in the animated, smiling crowd that circulated through Central Park in Miraflores, Miguel was still repeating to himself: "Now. When I get to Pardo Avenue. I'll risk it. Oh, Rubén, if you only knew how much I hate you!" Still earlier, in church, while he sought out Flora with his eyes, he discovered her at the foot of a column and, elbowing his way through without excusing himself to the ladies he pushed, managed to get close to her and greet her in a low voice. He stubbornly told himself again, as he did that morning sprawled on his bed, watching for the appearance of dawn: "There's nothing else to do. I have to do it today. In the morning. You'll pay for it, Rubén." The night before, he had cried for the first time in many years when he learned of the cheap trap they were preparing for him. People kept going into the Park, and Pardo Avenue was deserted. They walked along the mall, under the fig trees with their tall dense tops. "I'll have to hurry," Miguel thought. "If I don't, I'm out of luck." He looked around out of the corner of his eye: there was nobody, he could try it. Slowly he put out his left hand to touch hers; the contact showed him what was happening. He begged for a miracle to happen, for that humiliation to cease. "What'll I say to her?" he thought. "What'll I tell her?" She had just withdrawn her hand, and he felt he was dismissed, ridiculous. All the radiant phrases that he had feverishly prepared the night before were dissolved like bubbles of foam.

"Flora," he stammered, "I've waited a long time for this moment. Ever since I met you, I've thought only of you. I'm in love for the first time, believe me. I've never known a girl like you."

Once more a compact white blot on his brain, emptiness. He could no longer increase the pressure: his skin yielded like rubber, and his nails were digging into the bone. Nevertheless, he went on talking, with some difficulty, at long intervals, overcoming his shameful stammering, trying to describe a total, unreflecting passion, until he discovered with relief that they were coming to the first oval on Pardo Avenue, and then he fell silent. Between the second and third fig trees beyond the oval stood Flora's house. They stopped, looked at each other. Flora was still excited, and her confusion had filled her eyes with a damp brilliance. Miguel told himself desolately that she had never seemed so beautiful to him: a blue ribbon held her hair, and he could see the beginning of her neck and her ears, two question marks, tiny and perfect.

"Look, Miguel," Flora said. Her voice was soft, full of music, assured. "I can't give you an answer now. But Mama doesn't want me to go with boys until I finish school."

"Every mama says the same thing, Flora," Miguel persisted. "How's she going to find out? We can see each other whenever you say, even if it's only on Sundays."

"I'll give you an answer now, but I must think about it first," Flora said, lowering her eyes. After a few moments she added, "Forgive me, but I have to go now. It's getting late."

Miguel felt a profound lassitude, something that spread all through his body and softened it.

"You're not angry with me, are you, Flora?" he asked humbly.

"Don't be silly," she replied vivaciously. "I'm not angry."

"I'll wait as long as you like," Miguel said. "But we'll go on seeing each other, won't we? We're going to the movies this afternoon, aren't we?"

"I can't this afternoon," she said gently. "Martha asked me over to her house."

A warm, violent looseness in his guts came flooding over him, and he felt wounded, ashamed, in the face of that answer which he had expected and which now seemed like a cruelty to him. What Melanés had murmured grimly in his ear on Saturday afternoon was true. Martha would leave them alone; that was her usual tactic. Afterward, Rubén would tell those Sharpies—his gang—how he and his sister had planned the circumstances, the time, and the place. Martha would have claimed the right to spy from behind the curtain as payment for her services. Anger suddenly made his hands perspire.

"Don't be like that, Flora. Let's go to the matinee as we planned. I won't mention this to you, I promise."

"I can't go, really," Flora replied. "I have to go to Martha's. She came to my house yesterday to invite me. But I'm going with her to Salazar Park later."

Not even in these last words did he see any hope. For some time afterward he contemplated the spot where her fragile little figure in blue had disappeared under the majestic arch of the fig trees on the avenue. He could compete with a simple adversary, not with Rubén. He remembered the names of the girls Martha invited one Sunday afternoon. He could no longer do anything; he was defeated. Then once more arose the image that saved him every time he suffered a frustration: from a distant background of clouds swollen by black smoke, he was marching at the head of a company of cadets from the Naval School toward a grandstand erected in the park. Important men in formal dress, top hats in hand, and ladies with sparkling jewels were applauding him. Massed on the walks, a crowd in which the faces of his friends and enemies stood out was observing him in astonishment, murmuring his name. Dressed in blue, a roomy cape billowing behind him, Miguel marched ahead, looking at the horizon. With his sword raised, its tip described a semicircle in the air. There in the center of the grandstand was Flora, smiling. On one corner he discovered Rubén, ragged and ashamed. He confined himself to throwing him a brief contemptuous glance. He went marching on, disappeared among the victors.

Like breath on a mirror when one rubs it, the image disappeared. He stood in the doorway of his house. He hated everybody; everybody hated him. He entered and went directly up to his room. He threw himself face-down on the bed. In the warm darkness between his eyes and eyelids the girl's face appeared—"I love you, Flora," he

said in a loud voice—and then Rubén, with his insolent
jaw and his hostile smile. They stood beside each other,
came closer; Rubén's eyes twisted round to look mockingly
at him, while his mouth moved toward Flora.

He leaped out of bed. The wardrobe mirror showed him
a livid face and rings under his eyes. "He shan't see you,"
he decided. "He won't do that to me. I won't let him
pull that dirty trick on me."

Pardo Avenue was still empty. Quickening his pace,
without stopping, he walked toward the crossing at Grau
Avenue; there he hesitated. He felt cold: he had forgotten
his jacket in his room, and his one shirt was not enough
to protect him from the wind that came in from the sea
and was caught in the thick branches of the fig trees in a
soft rustling. His dreaded image of Flora and Rubén together gave him strength, and he went on walking. From
the door of the neighborhood bar next to the Montecarlo
theater he saw them at their usual table, in possession of
the nook formed by the back and left-hand walls. Francisco, Melanés, Tobías, and the Scholar discovered him
and, after a moment's surprise, turned toward Rubén, their
faces malicious, excited. He recovered his self-possession
immediately. He certainly knew how to behave in front
of men.

"Hello," he said to them, approaching. "What's new?"

"Sit down." The Scholar held out a chair for him. "What
miracle's brought you here?"

"You haven't been here for ages," Francisco remarked.

"I wanted to see you," Miguel said cordially. "I already
knew you were here. What's so surprising about that? Or
aren't I a Sharpie any more?"

He sat down between Melanés and Tobías. Rubén sat
across from him.

"Cuncho!" called the Scholar. "Bring another glass. And
it had better be clean."

Cuncho brought the glass, and the Scholar filled it with beer. Miguel said, "To the Sharpies!" and drank.

"You almost drank the glass too," Francisco observed. "How violent you are!"

"I bet you went to one-o'clock mass," said Mélanes, one eyelid creased in satisfaction, as always when he was thinking up some mischief. "Or did you?"

"I did," Miguel said imperturbably. "But only to see a young lady, that's all."

He looked at Rubén with challenging eyes, but the latter did not take the hint. He was drumming with his fingers on the table, the tip of his tongue between his teeth, whistling "The Popof Girl" by Pérez Prado.

"Well!" Melanés applauded. "Well, Don Juan. Tell us, which girl?"

"That's a secret."

"There aren't any secrets among Sharpies," Tobías reminded him. "Have you forgotten already? Come on, who was she?"

"What do you care?" Miguel asked.

"A good deal," Tobías said. "I have to know who you go with so as to know who you are."

"In the meantime, drink up," Melanés told Miguel. "One to zero."

"Why should I guess who she is?" Francisco asked. "Why not you?"

"I already know," Tobías said.

"Me too," said Melanés. He turned to Rubén with innocent eyes and voice. "And you, brother-in-law, can you guess who she is?"

"No," Rubén answered coldly. "Nor do I care."

"I have a little fire in my stomach," the Scholar remarked. "Isn't anyone going to order a beer?"

Melanés passed a pathetic finger across his throat.

"I have no money, darling," he said, in English.

"I'll buy a bottle," Tobías announced with a solemn gesture. "Let's see who follows me. We have to put out this kid's fire."

"Cuncho, take down half a dozen *Cristales*," Miguel ordered.

There were shouts of joy, exclamations.

"You're a real Sharpie," Francisco agreed.

"A dirty, lousy one," added Melanés. "Yes, sir, a real dude-type Sharpie."

Cuncho brought the beers. They drank. They listened to Melanés tell sexy stories—crude, extravagant, exciting—and a loud argument about football started between Tobías and Francisco. The Scholar recounted an anecdote. He was coming from Lima to Miraflores on a bus. The other passengers got off at Arequipa Avenue. "At the top of Javier Prado, that big blubber of a Tomasso got on, that six-foot albino who's still in grade school, lives around the Ravine—you know him now? Pretending great interest in the automobile, he began asking the driver questions, leaning over the front seat while he quietly scraped the upholstery on the back with a knife.

"He did it because I was there," the Scholar went on. "He wanted to show off."

"He's mentally deficient," Francisco remarked. "You do those things when you're ten years old. At his age it's not funny."

"What happened afterward is funny." The Scholar laughed. " 'Look, driver, don't you see this big blubber's ruining your car?' "

" 'What?' " the driver exclaimed, braking suddenly. His ears red, his eyes frightened, Tomasso was struggling with the door.

"With his knife," added the Scholar. "Imagine how fast he left the seat.

"The fat kid managed to get out at last. He began to run

along Arequipa Avenue. The driver ran after him shouting, 'Grab that wretch!' "

"Did he catch him?" Melanés asked.

"I don't know. I disappeared. I stole the ignition key for a keepsake. I've got it here."

He took a little silver-plated key from his pocket and tossed it on the table. The bottles were empty. Rubén looked at his watch and got to his feet.

"I'm going," he said. "I'll be seeing you."

"Don't go," Miguel said. "I'm rich today. I'm inviting you all to lunch."

A whirlwind of slaps fell on him; the Sharpies were thanking him confusedly, flattering him.

"I can't," Rubén said. "I have to go."

"Go and don't come back, my fine friend," Tobías remarked. "And greet Martha for me."

"We'll think about you a lot, brother-in-law," Melanés said.

"No!" Miguel exclaimed. "I'm inviting everybody or nobody. If Rubén leaves, that's that."

"You heard him, Sharpie Rubén," Francisco said. "You'll have to stay."

"You have to stay," said Melanés. "You have no choice."

"I'm leaving," Rubén said.

"It just so happens you're drunk," Miguel remarked. "You're leaving because you're afraid of making a fool of yourself in front of us, that's what's the matter."

"How many times have I carried *you* home half-dead?" Rubén demanded. "How many times have I helped you climb up the grating so your father wouldn't catch you? I can hold ten times more'n you can."

"You used to be able to," Miguel said. "Now it's harder to. You want to find out?"

"Gladly," Rubén replied. "Shall we meet tonight, right here?"

"No. Now." Miguel turned to the others, extending his arms. "I'm making a challenge, Sharpies."

Happily he proved that the ancient formula had kept its power intact. In the midst of the noisy enthusiasm he had provoked, he saw Rubén sit down, pale.

"Cuncho!" Tobías shouted. "The menu. And two large beers. A Sharpie has just given a challenge."

They ordered steaks and a dozen beers. Tobías put out three bottles for each competitor and the rest for the others. They ate, scarcely speaking. Miguel drank after each mouthful and tried to show some animation, but the fear of not sufficiently holding his own grew as the beer deposited its acid taste in his mouth. When they finished the six bottles, it was some time before Cuncho took away their plates.

"You order," Miguel told Rubén.

"Three more apiece."

After the first glass of the new round, Miguel felt his ears ringing; his head was a slow roulette wheel; everything was going round.

"I have to pee," he said. "I'm going to the bathroom."

The Sharpies laughed.

"Are you giving up?" Rubén asked.

"I'm going to pee," Miguel shouted. "If you want, have 'em bring more."

In the bathroom he vomited. Then he carefully washed his face, trying to erase every tell-tale sign. His watch showed four-thirty. In spite of his dark discomfort he felt happy. Rubén could do nothing now. He went back to the others.

"Your health," said Rubén, raising his glass.

He's furious, Miguel thought. But I've annoyed him now.

"You smell like a corpse," Melanés observed. "Somebody's died around here."

"I just got here," Miguel asserted, trying to conquer his nausea and dizziness.

"Your health!" Rubén repeated.

When they had finished the last beer, his stomach felt like lead, and the voices of the others reached his ears as a confused mixture of sounds. A hand suddenly appeared under his eyes; it was white, with long fingers; it took him by the chin, made him raise his head. Rubén's face had grown larger. He looked funny, so disheveled and angry.

"D'you give up, snotty?"

Miguel got up suddenly and pushed Rubén aside, but before the fight could develop, the Scholar intervened.

"Sharpies don't fight, ever," he said, forcing them to sit down. "They're both drunk. It's all over. Let's vote."

Melanés, Francisco, and Tobías unwillingly agreed to concede that it was a tie.

"I'd already won," Rubén said. "This fella can't even talk. Look at him."

Miguel's eyes were actually glassy, his mouth was open, and a trickle of saliva dripped from his tongue.

"Shut up," the Scholar ordered. "You're no champion, let's say, at drinking beer."

"You're no beer-drinking champion," Melanés said for emphasis. "You're only a swimming champion, the holy terror of the pools."

"You'd better not say anything," Rubén retorted. "Don't you see envy's gnawing at you?"

"Long live the Esther Williams of Miraflores!" said Melanés.

"A tremendous old fella, and he doesn't even know how to swim," Rubén said. "Don't you want me to give you a few lessons?"

"We know how already, you big wonder," said the Scholar. "You won a swimming championship. All the girls 're dying for you. You're a little old champion."

"This one here's no champion of anything," Miguel remarked with difficulty. "He's pure affectation."

"You're dying," Rubén retorted. "Shall I take you home, little girl?"

"I'm not drunk," Miguel assured him. "You're pure affectation."

"You're all cut up because I'm going to fall for Flora," Rubén said. "You're dying of jealousy. You think I don't catch on to these things?"

"Pure affectation," Miguel said. "You won because your father's president of the Federation. Everybody knows he cheated, he disqualified Rabbit Villarán, and you only won because of that."

"At least I can swim better 'n you," Rubén said. "You don't even know how to race the waves."

"You don't swim any better 'n anybody else," Miguel retorted. "Anybody can leave *you* behind."

"Anybody," Melanés put in. "Even Miguel, who's an old mother."

"Permit me to laugh."

"We'll permit you," said Tobías. "That's all we needed."

"You're better 'n me because it's winter," Rubén went on. "If it weren't, I'd challenge you to go to the beach, to see if you're so exceptional in the water."

"You won the championship because of your father," Miguel said. "You're pure affectation. When you want t' swim with me, just le' me know, informally. At the beach, at the Terraces, wherever y' like."

"At the beach," Rubén said. "Right now."

"You're pure affectation," said Miguel.

Rubén's face suddenly lighted up, and his eyes, in addition to being filled with rancor, turned arrogant.

"I'll bet you to see who reaches the surf first," he said.

"Pure affectation," Miguel repeated.

"If you win," Rubén said, "I promise you I won't go after Flora. And if I win, you can take your music somewhere else."

"What did you think?" stammered Miguel. "Damn it, what'd you think?"

"Sharpies," Rubén said, extending his arms, "I'm making a challenge."

"Miguel's in no shape now," said the Scholar. "Why not just draw straws for Flora?"

"And why're *you* butting in?" Miguel asked. "I accept. "Le's go t' the beach."

"You're crazy," Francisco remarked. "I'm not going down to the beach in this cold. Make some other bet."

"He's accepted," said Rubén. "Let's go."

"When a Sharpie makes a challenge, everybody puts his tongue in his pocket," Melanés remarked. "Let's go to the beach. And if they don't dare go in the water, we'll throw them in ourselves."

"They're both drunk," the Scholar persisted. "The challenge isn't valid."

"Shut up, Scholar," Miguel bellowed. "I'm a big boy now, I don' need you t' take care of me."

"Well," said the Scholar, shrugging his shoulders, "just suit yourself."

They went out. Outside a quiet gray atmosphere awaited them. Miguel breathed deeply; he felt better. Francisco, Melanés, and Rubén walked ahead, Miguel and the Scholar behind. On Grau Avenue there were pedestrians, the majority of them servant girls wearing bright dresses, on their day off. Ashen-gray men with thick straight hair were walking about, looking covetously at them; the girls laughed, showing their gold teeth. The Sharpies paid no attention to them. They went on with long strides, and excitement was building in them little by little.

"You feel better now?" the Scholar asked.

"Yes," Miguel answered. "The air's done me good."

At the corner of Pardo Avenue they turned. They marched spread out like a squad, all in line, under the fig trees on the mall, over paving stones upraised here and there by the enormous tree roots that occasionally burst through the surface like hooks. Going down along Diagonal Avenue, they passed two girls. Rubén bowed ceremoniously.

"Hello, Rubén," they chanted in duet.

Tobías mocked them in a high-pitched voice.

"Hello, Prince Rubén."

Diagonal Avenue ends in a little ravine which forks off: on one side the Malecón winds along, paved and shining; on the other, there is a slope that follows the hill and leads to the sea. They call it "the slope to the baths"; its paving is similar and shines from the passage of automobile tires and the bathers' feet of many summers past.

"Let's warm up, champions," Melanés shouted, starting to run. The others imitated him.

They ran against the wind and the thin mist that rose from the beach, gripped in an emotional whirlwind. The air penetrated their lungs through their ears, mouths, and noses, and a sensation of relief and sobriety spread through their bodies as the slope steepened, and in a moment their feet were now obeying only a mysterious force that came from the deepest part of the earth. Their arms like propellers, a breath of salt on their tongues, the Sharpies ran down the incline at top speed, as far as the circular platform suspended above the bathhouse. The sea vanished some fifty yards from the bank in a thick cloud that seemed about to dash against the cliffs, the tall dark rocks fronting all along the bay.

"Let's go back," Francisco said. "I'm cold."

At the edge of the platform there is a fence discolored here and there by moss. An opening indicates the beginning of the nearly vertical lower steps leading down to the beach. From there, at their feet, the Sharpies contemplated a narrow ribbon of clear water and the unaccustomed surface of foamy waves.

"I'm leaving if this guy'll give up," Rubén said.

"Who's talking about giving up?" retorted Miguel. "What'd you think?"

Rubén went down the steps three at a time, unbuttoning his shirt.

"Rubén!" shouted the Scholar. "Are you crazy? Come back!"

But Miguel and the others went down too, and the Scholar followed them.

In summer, from the veranda of the long narrow building nestled against the hill where the bathers' rooms are located, as far as the curved edge of the sea, there was a slope with gray stones where people would bask in the sun. The little beach swarmed with animation from morning till night. Now water filled the slope, and there were no bright-colored shadows, no elastic girls with sunburned bodies. No children's melodramatic cries resounded when a wave managed to splash them before it ebbed, dragging noisy stones and pebbles. They could not even see the edge of the beach, for the tide came in as far as the space bounded by the shaded columns that supported the building and, as the undertow went out, they could scarcely see the wooden steps and concrete supports that were ornamented with barnacles and algae.

"You can't see the breakers," Rubén said. "How'll we do it?"

They stood in the gallery on the left, in the women's section. Their faces were serious.

"Wait till tomorrow," the Scholar urged. "By noon it'll be clear. That way we'll be able to check on you."

"Since we've gone this far, let 'em do it now," said Melanés. "They can check on each other."

"Sounds all right to me," Rubén said. "How 'bout you?"

"Me too," Miguel agreed.

When they had undressed, Tobías joked about the blue veins that ran up Miguel's smooth belly. They went down the stairs. The wooden steps, continually lapped by the water for some months, were slippery and very smooth. Grasping the iron handrail in order not to fall, Miguel felt a tremor rising from the soles of his feet to his head. He was thinking that the fog and cold favored him in one way; his success now depended not on his skill, but chiefly on his resistance, and Rubén's skin was also purple, marked with millions of goose-pimples. One step below, Rubén's well-proportioned body was bent: he was waiting tensely for the end of the undertow and the arrival of the next wave, which came quietly, gracefully, thrusting forward its border of foam. When the wave crest was a couple of yards from the stairway, Rubén dived in, his arms lance-stiff, his hair disheveled by the force of his dive. His body cleaved the air cleanly and dropped in without bending. Without lowering his head or flexing his legs, he rebounded in the foam, almost sank, and immediately slipped into it, taking advantage of the tide. His arms appeared and disappeared in a frantic bubbling, and his feet began tracing a fast, cautious wake. Miguel in turn went down another stairway and waited for the next wave. He knew that the bottom was shallow there, that he must dive in like a board, hard and rigid, without moving a muscle, or he would strike against the rocks. He closed his eyes and dove, and he did not hit bottom, but his body was flailed from forehead to knees, and a very sharp stinging sensation arose while he struggled with all his strength to recover the warmth in his limbs that the water had suddenly taken out of them. He was on that unfamiliar section of the sea at Miraflores near the bank, where eddies and opposing currents are encountered, and last summer was so long ago that Miguel had forgotten how to get across them easily. He did not remember that he must relax his body and let go, let himself be carried along drifting submissively, swing his arms only when a wave rises and he is on the crest, on that liquid sheet that escorts the foam and floats on the currents. He did not remember that it is important to bear patiently and with a certain malice that first contact with a sea, exasperated by the bank, that pulls at his limbs and blows water in his mouth and eyes; to offer no resistance, to be a cork, to limit himself to gulping air each time a wave rolls in, to submerge himself—barely, if it breaks far off and comes in gently, or to the very bottom if it breaks nearby—to grasp some stone and wait alertly for the subdued thunder of its passage in order to emerge in just one stroke and continue advancing, furtively, with his hands, until he encounters a new obstacle and then to relax, not fighting against the eddies, to revolve freely in their slow, slow spiral and escape suddenly with a single stroke at the opportune moment. Then a calm surface unexpectedly appears, stirred by harmless combers; the water is clear, smooth, and in some places hidden stones are visible below its surface.

After crossing the choppy area Miguel stopped, exhausted, and gulped air. He saw Rubén nearby, looking at him. His hair fell in bangs over his face. His teeth were clenched.

"Shall we?"

"Let's go."

After swimming for a few minutes Miguel felt the cold that had momentarily vanished coming over him again, and he speeded up his strokes because it was in his legs,

especially in his calves, that the water had a greater effect,
first making them insensitive, then stiffening them. He was
swimming with his face in the water, and each time his
right arm rose out of it, he turned his head to expel air
and breathe in another supply, at which he submerged his
face and chin once more, just barely, so as not to hinder
his own progress but, on the contrary, to split the water
like a prow and make his forward movement easier. With
each stroke he glanced at Rubén swimming smoothly,
effortlessly on the surface, not splashing now, with the
delicacy and ease of a seagull gliding. Miguel tried to forget
Rubén and the sea and the breakers, which must still be
far off, for the water was clear and calm, and they were
swimming only through newly risen surf. He wanted to
remember nothing but Flora's face and the down on her
arms that sparkled on sunny days like a little forest of
golden threads. But he could not prevent another image
from succeeding to that of the girl—the image of a
mountain of raging water, not necessarily these breakers
(to which he had come once two summers ago and whose
waves were intensified with greenish-black foam, because
in that spot, more or less, the stones ended and the mud
began that the waves brought up to the surface and deposited among nests of seaweed and stagnant water,
staining the sea), but rather in a real ocean stirred by
inner cataclysms in which were thrown up unusual waves
that could have swamped an entire ship and upset it
with astonishing rapidity, hurling passengers, lifeboats,
masts, sails, sailors, porthole covers, and flags into the air.

He stopped swimming; his body sank until it was vertical; he raised his head and saw Rubén, who was getting
farther away. He thought of calling to him on some pretext, of saying to him, "Why don't we rest a minute?"
But he did not. All the cold in his body seemed to be
concentrated in his calves; his muscles felt cramped,

his skin taut; his heart was pounding. He thrust feverishly
with his feet. He was in the center of a circle of dark water,
walled in by the mist. He tried to make out the beach, or
at least the shadow of the cliffs, but that dark mist dissolving at his passage was not transparent. He saw only a
narrow surface, blackish-green, and a layer of clouds low
over the water. Then he felt afraid. The recollection of the
beer he had drunk assailed him, and he thought, "I expect
it's sapped my strength." At once his arms and legs seemed
to disappear. He decided to go back, but after a few strokes
in the direction of the beach, he turned and swam as
quickly as he could. "I won't go in to the bank alone," he
told himself. "It's better to stay close to Rubén. If I get
too tired, I'll tell him, 'You beat me, but let's go back.'"
Now he was swimming without any style, his head raised,
beating the water with stiff arms, his eyes fastened on the
imperturbable body ahead of him.

His agitation and the effort took the numbness out of
his legs; his body regained a little warmth; the distance
that separated him from Rubén had decreased, and that
calmed him. Shortly afterward he caught up with him,
stretched out his arm and caught one of his feet. The other
stopped at once. Rubén's eyes were very red, and his
mouth hung open.

"I think we've got off course," Miguel said. "It seems
to me we're swimming parallel to the beach."

His teeth were chattering, but his voice was steady.
Rubén looked in all directions. Miguel watched him
tensely.

"I don't see the beach now," Rubén said.

"I haven't seen it for a long time," Miguel said. "There's
a lot of mist."

"We're not off course," Rubén went on. "Look. You
can see the foam now."

As a matter of fact, some combers were coming toward

them edged with a border of foam that dissolved and
suddenly reappeared. They looked at each other in silence.

"We're close to the breakers now, then," Miguel said at
last.

"Yes. We swam fast."

"I've never seen so much mist."

"Aren't you pretty tired?" Rubén asked.

"Me? You're crazy. Let's go on."

Immediately he regretted his words, but it was already
too late. Rubén had said, "Okay, let's go on."

He managed to count twenty strokes before telling himself that he could not go on. He was making almost no
headway; his right leg was half-paralyzed by the cold;
his arms felt awkward and heavy. Panting, he shouted,
"Rubén!" The latter went on swimming. "Rubén, *Rubén!*"
He turned and began swimming—splashing desperately,
rather—toward the beach, and suddenly he was praying to
God to save him. He would be good in the future, would
obey his parents, would not miss mass on Sunday. Then
he remembered having confessed to the Sharpies, "I go
to church only to see a young lady," and he felt a knife-
sharp conviction: God was going to punish him, to drown
him in those turbid waters that he was frantically beating,
waters below which an awful death, and afterward hell
perhaps, were waiting for him. Then in his anxiety there
arose, like an echo, a certain phrase Father Alberto once
pronounced in religion class about the divine goodness
that knows no limits, and while he flailed at the sea with
his arms—his legs dangled like crossed sounding leads—
moving his lips, he begged God to be good to him who was
so young, and he swore he would go to the seminary if he
were saved. But a moment later he corrected himself,
shocked, and promised that instead of becoming a priest
he would make sacrifices and do other penances, would
give to charity, and there he perceived that vacillation and

haggling at that critical moment might be fatal. Then he was aware of Rubén's crazed shouts close at hand and, turning his head, saw him some ten yards off, his face half-sunk in the water, waving one arm, begging, "Miguel, brother, come here, I'm drowning, don't go away!"

He stopped perplexed, motionless, and it was suddenly as if Rubén's despair were kindling his own. He felt himself recovering his courage; the rigidity in his legs was diminishing.

"I've got a cramp in my stomach!" Rubén shrieked. "I can't go on, Miguel. Save me! For the sake of what you love most, don't leave me, brother!"

He floated toward Rubén, and he was about to reach out to him when he remembered that drowning persons often manage to grab hold of their saviors like pincers and pull them under, and he kept clear, but the screams frightened him, and he had a presentiment that if Rubén drowned, he would not reach the beach either, so he turned back. A couple of yards from Rubén, who looked like something white and shrunken that sank and surfaced again, he cried, "Don't move, Rubén! I'm going to tow you, but don't try to hold onto me. If you hold onto me, we'll drown, Rubén. You're going to keep quiet, brother. I'll tow you by your head. Don't you touch me!" He stopped at a prudent distance, reached out his arm until he could grasp Rubén's hair. He began to swim with his free arm, making every effort to help himself with his legs. His progress was slow and arduous; it required all his senses; he scarcely heard Rubén complaining monotonously, suddenly uttering terrible cries, "I'm going to die, save me, Miguel!" or being shaken by retching. He was exhausted when he stopped. He supported Rubén with one hand; with the other he traced circles on the surface. He breathed deeply through his mouth. Rubén's face was contorted with pain, his lips pursed in an unusual grimace.

"It's just a little farther, brother," Miguel murmured. "Keep trying. Answer me, Rubén. Yell! Don't be like that!"

He slapped his face sharply, and Rubén opened his eyes; he shook his head feebly.

"Yell, brother," Miguel repeated. "Try to stretch out. I'm going to massage your stomach. It's just a little farther. Don't let yourself give up."

His hand groped under water, found a hard ball beginning at Rubén's navel and occupying a large part of his belly. He rubbed it many times, slowly at first, then harshly, and Rubén cried out, "I don't want to die, Miguel. Save me!"

He began to swim once more, dragging Rubén this time by his chin. Each time a wave overtook them, Rubén choked, and Miguel shouted to him to spit. He went on swimming, not stopping for a moment, closing his eyes at times, encouraged because a sort of confidence, something warm and proud and stimulating that was protecting him against cold and fatigue had sprung up in his heart. A stone scraped one of his feet, but he merely cried out and went on faster. A moment later he stopped and put his arms around Rubén. Holding him pressed against himself, feeling his head supported on one shoulder, he rested for a long time. Then he helped Rubén to turn onto his back and, supporting him on his forearm, forced him to stretch out his legs; he massaged his belly until the hardness began to yield. Rubén was not screaming now; he was making a great effort to stretch out completely, and he rubbed himself with his hands too.

"Feel better?"

"Yes, brother, I'm all right. Let's get out of here."

An inexpressible joy filled them as they came in over the stones, bending forward to face the undertow, insensitive to the spiny sea urchins. In a little while they

saw the edge of the cliffs, the bathhouse, and finally, now
close to the bank, the Sharpies standing in the women's
gallery, watching them.

"Look," Rubén said.

"What?"

"Don't tell them anything. Please don't tell 'em I
screamed. We've always been good friends, Miguel. Don't
do that to me."

"Do you think I'd be such a stinker?" Miguel said. "I
won't say anything, don't worry."

They emerged shivering. They sat on the steps surrounded by excited Sharpies.

"We were about to send condolences to your families,"
Tobías remarked.

"You were in for more than an hour," the Scholar
said. "Tell us, how was it?"

Speaking calmly, while he dried his body with his
undershirt, Rubén explained:

"It wasn't anything. We went out to the breakers and
back. So, we're Sharpies. Miguel beat me, by just a stroke.
Of course, if it'd been in a pool, he'd have made a fool of
himself."

Congratulatory slaps rained on the back of Miguel, who
had dressed without drying off.

"You're getting to be quite a man," Melanés told him.

Miguel did not answer. Smiling, he was thinking he
would go to Salazar Park that very night. All of Miraflores
would already know from Melanés' account that he had
won that heroic test, and Flora would be waiting for him,
her eyes shining. A golden future was opening out in front
of him.

Translated by MARY E. ELLSWORTH

Manuel Puig (b. 1932) was born in General Villegas, a small pampas town in Argentina. As a child he became addicted to the (mostly American) movies that changed daily at the local movie house. After secondary school in Buenos Aires he tried studying architecture and philosophy, but was drawn to film and eventually went to Europe, especially Rome and Paris, where he failed to find his niche in European filmmaking. Eventually he ended up in New York City, where for three years he worked at Kennedy Airport. At this point, having tried writing scripts, he found himself writing a novel and in 1965 he finished *La traición de Rita Hayworth (Betrayed by Rita Hayworth)* which in December of that year, in manuscript form, was a finalist at the Seix Barral contest. Three years later the first edition of the novel was finally published; its reception was disappointing. His second novel, *Boquitas pintadas (Heartbreak Tango)* was published in Buenos Aires in 1969 and became a bestseller there. The following selection is a chapter from that novel, which was written as a serial. The chapter stands up well as a short story.

As David Gallagher has written about *Heartbreak Tango*, "What Borges has done for the detective story, Puig has done for the sentimental popular novel." On the one hand, the serial form is a vehicle to show the unbridgeable "gap between the dazzling world of the media and the reality of small-town mediocrity"; and yet, just as Borges' stories function on one level as detective stories, "so Puig forces us to share and believe in the impossible passions of Nélida Fernández and her friends."

A third novel, *The Buenos Aires Affair*, was published in Buenos Aires in 1973.

A Meeting

Episode Thirteen from *Heartbreak Tango*

> Her eyes of blue did open wide,
> my timeless grief she understood,
> and with a snarl of woman scorned
> said life plays tricks and left for good.

(from LePera's tango "She Returned One Night")

It happened on an autumn afternoon. The trees that grew along that street in Buenos Aires bowed low. Why? Tall apartment houses on either side of the street blocked off the sun's rays, and the branches spread obliquely, as if pleading, toward the middle of the road . . . seeking light. Mabel was on her way to a friend's house for tea, she raised her eyes to the aged treetops, she noticed that the strong trunks bowed, humbly.

Perhaps a vague omen seized her throat with a silk glove, Mabel held a bouquet of roses in her arms and inhaled the sweet perfume, why did she suddenly think that autumn had come to the city never to leave it again? The front of the apartment building seemed luxurious, but the absence of a rug in the entrance reassured her: the building where she was very soon to live counted on just that decisive element to define its rank. Then again the elevator had a mirror, and she checked her makeup through the fine veil of her black felt headpiece, adorned with bunches of cherries, made from cellophane. Lastly she adjusted the fox tails wrapped around her neck.

Third floor, apartment B, in an upswept hairdo and with so much shadow around her eyes that her friend Nené seemed somewhat aged when she opened the door.

—Mabel, how good to see you! —and they kissed each other on either cheek.

—Nené! What an angel, why the little darling is already walking! —she kissed the child and caught sight of her friend's younger son in a playpen—And the baby, what a cute face!

—No . . . Mabel . . . they're not cute at all, don't you think they're a bit homely? —the mother spoke sincerely.

—No, they're adorable, so chubby, with their little turned-up noses, how old is the youngest?

—The baby is eight months old, and the big one over a year and a half . . . but fortunately they're boys, right? it doesn't matter much that they're not cute . . . —Nené felt poor, she had nothing to show but two ungraceful children.

—But one after the other . . . you didn't lose any time, did you?

—You know, I was afraid you wouldn't have a chance to see me, how are the preparations going?

—Well, it's a madhouse, and I'm not even getting married in a long gown or having a party! . . . Your apartment looks so nice. —Mabel's voice crackled with hypocrisy.

—You think so?

—Of course I do! as soon as I come back from the honeymoon you'll have to come see my little nest, and for sure, my apartment is little.

—I'm sure it's a dollhouse. —Nené answered while placing the fragrant roses in a flower vase and admiring them— I'll bet you forgot to bring me a picture of your fiancé.

Both thought of Juan Carlos's perfect face and for a few seconds avoided looking each other in the eyes.

—No, what for, he's just a runt . . .

—I'm dying to meet him, you're not marrying him for nothing, smarty. He must be a very interesting man. Show me the picture of the runt . . . —before finishing the last sentence Nené already regretted having said it.

—Such comfortable chairs. No! no, dear, don't touch my stockings!

—Luisito! You're going to get it if you don't stop . . . here, I'll get you a cupcake. —and Nené went into the kitchen to heat the water for tea.

—So you're Luisito, and what's your little brother's name? —Mabel smiled to the child searching his features for some decisive similarity to Nené's husband.

—Mabel, come, I'll show you the house.

Meeting in the kitchen the two couldn't escape the incursion of memories. All those afternoons spent in that other kitchen of Nené's, while outside the dusty wind of the pampas blew.

—You know something, Nené? I'd like a maté, like in the old days . . . how long has it been since we've had maté together?

—Ages, Mabel. Not since the time I was Miss Spring more or less . . . and here it is April of '41 . . .

Both were silent.

—Nené, one always thinks the past was better. And wasn't it?

They were silent again. Both found an answer for that question. The same answer: yes, the past was better because then they both believed in love. Silence followed silence. The dying light of dusk entered the window and tinted the walls violet. Mabel wasn't the hostess, but she couldn't stand the melancholy any longer, and without asking permission she turned on the light that hung from the ceiling. And asked:

—Are you happy?

Nené felt that a shrewder opponent had attacked her by surprise. She didn't know what to answer, she was going to say "I can't complain," or "There's always a but," or "Yes, I have my two sons," but she preferred to shrug her shoulders and smile enigmatically.

—It's easy to see you're happy, you have a family that not everyone . . .

—Oh, yes, I can't complain. What I'd like is a bigger apartment with a full-time maid, but to have one sleeping in the living room is more trouble than it's worth. You should see the work these kids make me. And now that winter's coming and they start with the colds . . . —Nené preferred not to mention her other complaints: that she had never set foot in a night club, that she had never traveled in an airplane, that her husband's caresses were not for her . . . caresses.

—Why they're healthy little things. . . . Do you go out a lot?

—No, where am I to go with these two always crying or going weewee or doing duty? Have kids, you'll see what it's like.

—If you didn't have them you would want them, so don't complain. —Mabel, two-faced, figured that the routine life of mother and wife wasn't what she wanted either, but was it by any chance better to remain single in a small town and continue being the target of slander?

—And you, tell me about yourself . . . do you want a lot of kids?

—Gustavo and I have agreed not to have children until he graduates. He has a few more courses to go but he never takes them. I'll have to see to that. . . .

—What was it he's studying for?

—A Ph.D. in economics.

Nené thought how much more important a doctor in economics could be than a public auctioneer.

—Tell me about Vallejos, Mabel.

—Well, I don't have any fresh news, I've been in Buenos Aires more than a month, getting ready.

—Is Juan Carlos still in Córdoba? —Nené felt her cheeks blushing.

—Yes, it seems he's better. —Mabel looked at the blue flame in the gas stove.

—And Celina?

—Fair to middling. What's there to talk about, she went the wrong way, that's all. You know fooling around with traveling salesmen is fatal. Don't you listen to any serials in the afternoon?

—No, is there anything good on?

—Yes, a marvelous drama! at five, don't you listen to it?

—No, never. —Nené remembered that her friend had always been the first to discover the best movie, the best actress, the best leading man, the best radio serial, why did she always let her get one step ahead?

—I miss a lot of episodes but when I can I put it on.

—What a pity, today you'll miss it too. —Nené wanted to talk at length with Mabel, bring back old memories, would she dare to bring up the subject of Juan Carlos again?

—Don't you have a radio?

—Yes, but it's after five already.

—No, it's only ten to five.

—Then we can listen if you want. —Nené remembered that as hostess she must entertain her guest.

—Yes, marvelous! You don't mind? We can talk just the same.

—Sure, it's fine, what's the play called?

—*The Wounded Captain,* it has four days to go and next month they're going to do *The Forgotten Promise.* Want me to tell you about it from the beginning?

—Yes, but afterward don't forget to tell me about Fanny. How's she doing?

—Just fine. Well, I'll tell you the beginning because it's almost five and otherwise you won't understand a thing, and I'm sure you'll keep listening to it from now on.

—But hurry then.

—Well, it's during World War I, a captain in the French army, a young man, from a very aristocratic family, falls wounded somewhere on the German border, and when he comes to in the trenches he finds himself next to a dead German soldier, and hears that the place has fallen to the Germans, so he takes the uniform off the dead man so that he can pass for a German. And what's happened is that this whole region has fallen to the Germans and they march toward one of the villages around there, and pass a farm, and go in and ask for food. The farmer is a thickheaded, brutish peasant, but his wife is a very beautiful woman, and gives the Germans everything just as long as they keep moving on, but then she sees him and recognizes him. It so happens that she had been a girl from a village near the castle where the boy lived, and when he was just beginning his military career and would come home to the castle for holidays he would always meet her in the forests, she was his first love.

—But what kind of girl was she? Was she a good girl or the kind that sleeps around?

—Well, she had been in love with him since she was little, when he'd escape from the castle to go swimming in the brook and they'd gather flowers, and when she grew up she probably gave in to him.

—Then tough luck. If she gave in.

—No, in his heart he really loved her, but since she was a peasant girl, he had to give in to his family who wanted an arranged marriage with a girl of noble birth like him. But Nené, weren't we going to have maté?

—Oh, with the talk I forgot, the tea's already made, but you want maté, don't you? and does he love the aristocratic girl or not?

—Well . . . she's a young girl who is also very in love with him, and she's very refined, he must like her. Let's have tea, forget about it. . . .

—But he can only truly love one.

Mabel preferred not to answer. Nené put on the radio, Mabel observed her and it was no longer through the veil of her hat but through the veil of appearances that she was able to see Nené's heart. There was no doubt about it: if the latter believed it impossible to love more than one man it was because she hadn't succeeded in loving her husband, since she had certainly loved Juan Carlos.

—And he goes back to her for convenience sake.

—No, he loves her in his own way, but really, Nené.

—What do you mean in his own way?

—Well, for him his country comes first, he's received many medals. And then came a part when her brother-in-law, a traitor, you get me? her brutish husband's brother, who's a spy for the Germans, comes to the farm and finds the boy hidden in the barn and the boy is forced to kill the spy and buries him at night in the orchard, and the dog doesn't bark because the girl has taught him to love the wounded guy.

"—LR7 Buenos Aires, your friendly station . . . presents . . . the 'Afternoon Radio Play' . . ."

—Meanwhile I'll serve the tea . . . the kids are hungry.

—Yes, but you have to listen, let me make it louder.

A melody on violin shed its first few notes. Then immediately the music's volume decreased and made way for the finely modulated voice of a narrator: "That cold winter morning, from his hiding place in the loft, Pierre could see the crossfire of the first shots. Both armies were confronting each other just a few miles from the farm. If he could only rush to the aid of his comrades, he thought. Suddenly there were noises in the barn, Pierre sat motionless in the hay loft."

"—Pierre, it's me, do not fear . . ."

"—Marie . . . so early."

"—Pierre, do not fear . . ."

"—My only fear is that this is all a dream, that I'll wake up and not see you anymore . . . there . . . against the light in the doorway, behind you dawn's rosy air . . ."

—Mabel, don't tell me there's anything more beautiful than being in love.

—Shsh!

"—Pierre . . . are you cold? The fields are covered with an icy dew, but we can talk freely, he has gone to town."

"—Why so early? doesn't he always go at noon?"

"—It's that he's afraid of not being able to go later on, if the battle spreads. That's why I've come to change your bandage now."

"—Marie, let me look at you. . . . Your eyes are strange, have you by chance been crying?"

"—What things you say, Pierre. I don't have time to cry."

"—And if you did?"

"—If I did . . . I would cry in silence."

"—As you've just done today."

"—Pierre, let me change your dressing, there, that's it, so I can remove the herb-soaked linen, we shall see if this coarse country medicine has done you any good."

"Marie proceeded to remove the bandages that covered her beloved's chest. Just as a battle broke out on the fields of France, so did two opposing forces strive in

Marie's heart: more than anything she wanted to find the wound healed, as the joyful conclusion of her cares, though she had no faith in the healing power of those paltry rustic herbs; but if the wound was healed . . . Pierre would leave the place, he would go away, and perhaps forever."

"—This bandage has gone around your heart so many times, does it not hurt when I take it off?"

"—No, Marie, you can never hurt me, you are too gentle for that."

"—What nonsense you're saying! I still remember your screams the day I washed your wound."

"—But from your lips, Marie . . . I have never heard complaints. Tell me, how would you feel if I died in battle?"

"—Pierre, don't talk that way, my hands tremble and I might hurt you . . . I just have to remove the herb-soaked linen and that's it. Don't move."

"And, unbandaged, the decision of Destiny, lay before Marie's eyes."

A lively and modern musical theme came on the air, followed by a commercial announcement describing a dentifrice of lasting and hygienic action.

—How do you like it, Nené?

—I do, the story is lovely, but she's not too good. — Nené was afraid to praise the actress's work, she remembered that Mabel didn't like Argentine actresses.

—Why no, she's very good, I like her. —Mabel replied, remembering that Nené never did know how to judge movies, theater, and radio.

—Did she give in to him for the first time in the barn or before when she was still single?

—Nené, before! can't you see that it's a love of many years?

—Of course, she can't have any illusions about him because she already gave in, because I thought that if she hadn't given in before when they were very young, and in the barn he was wounded and nothing could happen, then he would come back to her more eagerly.

—That has nothing to do with it, if he loves her he loves her. . . .

—Are you sure? What can she do to get him to come back to her after the war?

—That depends on the man, if he's a man of honor or not. . . . Quiet, it's beginning.

"Unbandaged, her destiny was written before her eyes. Marie saw with joy, with amazement, with sorrow . . . that the wound had healed. The ointment had produced the desired effect, and Pierre's robust nature had done the rest. But if Marie decided . . . that scar could open again, she had only to gently stick her nails into the new and tender, still transparent, skin which joined both edges of the deep wound."

"—Marie, tell me, am I healed? . . . why don't you answer?"

"—Pierre . . ."

"—Yes, tell me quickly, can I rejoin my troops?"

"—Pierre . . . you can leave, the wound has closed."

"—I'm on my way! I shall join my men, and then I shall return and if it is necessary fight him hand to hand . . . to free you."

"—No, never, he's a brute, a vile beast, capable of attacking from behind."

—Mabel, why did she marry such a terrible husband?

—I don't know, I missed a lot of episodes, it must be because she didn't want to stay single and alone.

—Was she an orphan?

—Even if she had parents, she'd want to make her own home, no? now let me listen.

"—How can you be so sure you are going to return?"

A lively and modern melodious theme came on the air, followed by a commercial for a toilet soap made by the same company advertising the already praised dentifrice.

—I'll kill you, Nené, you didn't let me listen, no . . . I'm only kidding. Look at me eat this cream puff! boy, I'm going to get fat!

—And Fanny? how's she doing?

—Fine, she didn't want to come back to work at our house anymore, she doesn't even look at me now, after all I did for her . . .

—And what does she live on?

—She takes in wash, at her shack, with her aunt. And the neighbor's wife died, he's a farmer with his own land, and the two women cook and take care of his kids, they get by. But she's ungrateful, Fanny is, those people, the more you do for them the worse they are. . . .

The narrator next described the state of the French troops. They were surrounded, they would gradually weaken. If Pierre joined them he would only increase the number of dead. But the astute captain thought up an extremely daring scheme: he would wear the enemy's uniform and sow confusion among the German lines. Meanwhile Marie confronted her husband.

—Would you be capable of such a sacrifice, Mabel?

—I don't know, I think I would have opened his wound, so he wouldn't go back to fight.

—Of course if he realized he'd soon hate her forever. There are times when you're up against the wall, right?

—Look, Nené, I think everything is written, I'm a fatalist, you can break your head thinking and planning and afterward everything comes out the opposite.

—You think so? I think that you have to play it to the

hilt, even though it's once in your life. I'll always regret not
having known how to play it to the hilt.

—How, Nené? by marrying a sick man?

—Why do you say that? why do you bring that up
when I was talking about something else?

—Don't get angry, Nené, but who would have thought
that Juan Carlos would end up like that?

—Does he take better care of himself now?

—Are you out of your mind? He spends his life chasing women. What I can't figure out is how come they're
not afraid of catching it.

—Well . . . maybe some of them don't know. And since
Juan Carlos is so handsome . . .

—It's because they're all dying for it.

—What do you mean?

—You should know.

—What? —Nené had the feeling that an abyss was
about to yawn open, she reeled with vertigo.

—Nothing, I guess then you . . .

—Mabel, what are you talking about?

—I guess then you didn't have with Juan Carlos . . .
well, you know what.

—You're terrible, Mabel, you're going to make me
blush, of course there was nothing. But I don't deny that
I loved him, as a boyfriend I mean.

—Come now, don't get like that, how edgy you are.

—But you were trying to tell me something. —Vertigo
had taken over, she wanted to know what there was at the
bottom of those abysmal depths.

—Well, it seems that when women have something going
with Juan Carlos they never want to give it up.

—That's because he's so good-looking, Mabel. And
so endearing.

—Oh, you don't want to understand.

"—If the French troops advance, we'd better leave here, woman. And faster with those bundles of hay and those molds of cheese. Each day you're clumsier, and now you even tremble with fear, blockhead!"

"—Where will we go?"

"—To my brother's house, I don't understand why he hasn't been back here."

"—No, not to his house."

"—Don't argue with me, or I will fetch you a blow upon your face, and you already know what a heavy hand I have."

—She lets him beat her! What a jerk!

—But Mabel . . . she must do it for her children, doesn't she have children?

—I think so. I'd kill anyone who dared hit me.

—How disgusting men are, Mabel . . .

—Not all of them, dear.

—Men who beat women, I mean.

The narrator took leave of the listeners until the next day, after interrupting the scene full of violent threats between Marie and her husband. The musical background followed and lastly another word of praise for the above-mentioned toothpaste and soap.

—But Mabel, what is it you're saying about Juan Carlos that I don't want to understand? —Nené continued playing with her own destruction.

—It's that women don't want to let go of him . . . because of things that happen in bed.

—But, Mabel, I don't agree. Women fall in love with him because he's good-looking. All that about bed, what you're saying, no. Because to tell the truth, once the light goes out you can't see if your husband is handsome or not, they're all alike.

—All alike? Then Nené, you don't know that there are

never two alike. —Nené thought of Doctor Nastini and her husband, she was unable to establish comparisons, the moments of lust spent with the detested doctor had been fleeting and undermined by inconveniences.

—Mabel, what do you know, a single girl . . .

—Why, Nené, all my friends from school are married now, and we confide in each other completely, my dear, and they tell me everything.

—But what do you know about Juan Carlos, you don't know anything.

—Nené, you don't know the reputation Juan Carlos had?

—What reputation?

Mabel made a crude movement with her hands indicating a horizontal distance of approximately fifteen inches.

—Mabel! now you're really making me blush. —and Nené felt all her fears violently confirmed. Fears that she had harbored since her wedding night. What she would have paid to forget that vile gesture she just saw!

—And it seems that has a lot of importance, Nené, for a woman to be happy.

—My husband told me it didn't.

—Maybe he took you for a ride. . . . Silly, I'm pulling your leg, that's not what they told me about Juan Carlos, I only told you that to pull your leg. What they told me was something else.

—What?

—I'm sorry, but when they told me I swore I'd never, never tell anybody, I'm sorry.

—Mabel, that's not nice. Now that you began, finish it.

Mabel was looking in the other direction.

—I'm sorry, but when I make a promise I keep it.

Mabel cut a pastry in two with a fork. Nené saw that the fork was a trident, two devil's horns grew out from

Mabel's forehead and under the table her winding tail curled around the leg of a chair. Nené made an effort and sipped some tea: the literally diabolic vision vanished and the hostess suddenly thought of a way of partially returning the blows dealt during the reunion and, looking her straight in the eyes, she asked abruptly:

—Mabel, are you really in love with your fiancé?

Mabel hesitated, the brief seconds she took to answer betrayed her game, the comedy of happiness was over. With profound satisfaction Nené confirmed that they were talking from one humbug to another.

—Nené . . . what a question . . .

—I know you love him, but sometimes one asks silly questions.

—Of course I love him. —But it wasn't true, Mabel thought that with time she would learn to love him, but what if her fiancé's caresses didn't make her forget the caresses of other men? what would her fiancé's caresses be like? for that she had to wait until their wedding night, because finding out before implied too many risks. Men . . .

—And you, Nené, do you love your husband more now than when you were engaged?

Tea, without sugar. Pastries with cream. Nené said that she liked boleros and the Caribbean singers who had introduced them. Mabel voiced her approval. Nené added that they really got to her, the words seemed written for all women and at the same time for each in particular. Mabel affirmed that this happened because the boleros said many truths.

At seven Mabel had to leave. She regretted having to go without seeing her friend's husband—kept at the office for business matters—and therefore without appraising how much he had been disfigured by the many pounds acquired. Nené inspected the tablecloth, so difficult to wash and to iron, and found it clean, without a stain. Then she examined the satin chairs, they didn't have stains either, and she immediately proceeded to place their respective covers on them.

Mabel went out on the street, night had already fallen. As she had planned, she would take advantage of the free time before dinner to see the show windows of an important department store located in Nené's neighborhood, and compare prices. Mabel reflected she had always been so organized, she had never wasted time, and what had she really achieved with all that calculation and precision? Perhaps she would have done better to let herself get carried away by an impulse, perhaps any man who passed her on that street could give her more happiness than her dubious fiancé. And what if she took a train to Córdoba? in the mountains there was the man who once had loved her, who had thrilled her as no one had. On that street in Buenos Aires the trees bowed low, both day and night. What useless humility, it was night, there was no sun, why bow? had those trees forgotten all dignity and pride?

As for Nené, she finished placing the covers on the chairs and cleared the table. Folding the tablecloth she discovered that a cigarette spark—Mabel being the only smoker—had made a hole in the cloth.

How careless, how selfish!—Nené mumbled to herself, and she would have liked to thrash on the floor, to utter a heartrending cry, but in front of her two children she could only raise her hands to her ears to still the haunting voice of Mabel Sáenz: " . . . and it seems that has a lot of importance. Nené, you don't know the reputation Juan Carlos had? . . . silly, I'm pulling your leg. What they told me was something else . . . but when they told me I swore . . . I swore . . . I'd never, never tell anybody. And I only told you that other thing to pull your leg, Nené. WHAT THEY TOLD ME WAS SOMETHING ELSE."

Trees that bow day and night, lovely embroidered linens that a tiny cigarette spark can destroy, peasant girls who fall in love one day in the forests of France and who fall in love with someone whom they shouldn't. Destinies . . .

Translated by SUZANNE JILL LEVINE

Abelardo Castillo (b. 1935) was born in San Pedro, a small Argentine town in the province of Buenos Aires. During his teens he wrote many poems, which he later burned, and finished his first play, *El otro Judas* ["The other Judas"] when he was twenty-two. In 1959 the unpublished play received a first prize from the journal *Gaceta Literaria.* In 1959 he founded a literary magazine called *El grillo de papel* ["The paper cricket"] which was closed by the police after the sixth issue. He started a second journal in 1961, *El escarabajo de oro* ["The golden beetle"], which is still being published. In 1963 his *Israfel,* a play in four acts based on the life of Edgar Allan Poe, won the first prize of the Contemporary Latin American Dramatists' competition in Paris. It was published in 1965 and produced with great success in Buenos Aires in 1966. Three plays were published in one volume in 1968: *A partir de los siete* ["After seven o'clock"], *Sobre las piedras de Jericó* ["On the stones of Jericho"] and *El otro Judas.* He has finished another, *Salomé,* and *Sobre las piedras de Jericó* is being readied for production. His novella, *La casa de ceniza* ["House of ashes"], written when he was twenty-one, was published in 1968.

His first short story collection, *Las otras puertas* [1961, "The other doors"]—which includes the following story—received the distinguished Casa de las Américas prize and has gone through several printings. Most of the stories in it, some of the stories in a second collection, *Cuentos crueles* ["Cruel stories, 1966"], and most of the stories in a new collection, *Las panteras y el templo* ["Panthers and the temple"] were gathered in one volume in 1972 as *Los mundos reales* ["The real worlds"]. He regards all of these earlier stories as part of "The Real World," whereas the stories he is writing now are about Hell. The main character in the more recent stories, a dipsomaniac, appears also in Castillo's as-yet unpublished novel, "El que tiene sed" ["He who is thirsty"], except that in the stories the character is older and has had much more to drink. A constant reviser (the stories change with each edition), Castillo has been working on the novel since 1962. He is considered one of Latin America's finest new writers.

Ernesto's Mother

Whether Ernesto found out or not that she had returned —why she had returned—I never got to know, but the fact remains that, not long afterwards, he moved to Tala, and we didn't see him more than once or twice that summer. It was hard to look him in the eye. It was as if the idea Julio had put in our heads—because the idea had been his, Julio's, and it was a strange idea, disturbing, dirty—made us feel guilty. Not that one is a puritan, no. At that age, and in a place like that, no one is a puritan. But precisely for that reason, because we weren't, because we didn't have a trace of purity or piety and after all we were pretty much like almost everybody else, the idea had such a disturbing quality. Somehow it was dark, cruel. Attractive. Above all, attractive.

It was long ago. The Alabama was still there, that place by the highway just outside the town. The Alabama was sort of a harmless restaurant, harmless in the daytime, at least, but after eleven p.m. it turned into a rudimentary nightclub. It stopped being rudimentary when the Turk decided to build some rooms upstairs and bring women. He brought one; one woman.

"No!"

"Yes. A woman."

"Where did he get her?"

Julio adopted that mysterious attitude we knew so well —because he had a particular brand of gestures, words, inflections, which characterized him and made him enviable, like a modest provincial Brummel—and then, lowering his voice, he asked:

"Where's Ernesto?"

I said: out in the country. Ernesto, now and then, spent a few weeks at the farm in Tala. This he had been doing since his father had refused to return to town because of what had happened with his wife. I said: in the country, and then I asked:

"And what's Ernesto got to do with this?"

Julio lit a cigarette. He was smiling:

"Do you know who she is, that woman the Turk brought?"

Anibal and I looked at each other. I remembered Ernesto's mother now. No one spoke. She had left four years ago with one of those theater groups that tour the small towns: loose woman, my grandmother said at the time. She was beautiful: dark and ample, I remembered. And she wasn't that old, maybe forty or so. Who knows.

"A whore, huh?"

There was a silence and it was then that Julio stuck that idea between our eyes. Or, perhaps, we'd already thought of it.

"If it weren't his mother. . . ."

That was all he said.

Who knows. Maybe Ernesto did find out, because, during that summer, we only saw him once or twice—later, they say, his father sold everything, and nobody ever heard of them again—and the few times we saw him, it was hard to look him in the eye.

"Guilty of what, man? After all she is a prostitute, and she's been in the Alabama for six months now. And if we're gonna wait until the Turk gets another one we'll all die of old age."

Then he, Julio, added that all we needed was to get a car, go, pay, and that's it, and if we didn't dare go along he'd find somebody else less chicken, and Anibal and I couldn't let him call us that.

"But she's his mother."

"His mother! What kind of a mother? A sow has babies too."

"And she eats them."

"Of course she eats them. So what?"

"And what's that got to do with anything? Ernesto grew up with us."

I said something about the times we used to play together; then I started thinking, and someone, aloud, expressed my thoughts exactly. Maybe it was myself:

"Remember what she was like. . . ."

Of course we remembered. We had been remembering for months: she was dark and ample, not at all motherly.

"Besides, half the town's been there already. We're the only ones. . . ."

We: the only ones. The argument had the strength of a provocation; her return had been one as well. And then, filthily, everything seemed easier. Today I think—who knows—that, if it had been just any woman, maybe we wouldn't even seriously have considered going. Who knows. It was frightening to say it, but, secretly, we were helping Julio to convince us; because the shadiness, the infamy, the monstrous attraction of it all was, perhaps, that it had to do with the mother of one of us.

"Keep your dirty mouth shut, willya?" Anibal said to me.

One week later Julio assured us that that same night he'd get the car. Anibal and I waited for him on the boulevard.

"Maybe he chickened out."

"He probably didn't get it."

I said it, I remember, almost contemptuously; but in a way it was like a prayer: maybe he chickened out. Anibal's voice was strange, indifferent:

"I'm not gonna wait for him all night; if he's not here in ten minutes, I'm leaving."

"What would she be like now?"

"Who, his . . . the woman?"

He almost said: his mother. I saw it in his face. But he said the woman. Ten minutes are long, and then it was hard to forget the times when we used to go play with Ernesto, and she, the dark and ample woman, asked us if we'd like to stay for milk and cookies. The dark woman. Ample.

"This is rotten, you know."

"You're scared," I said.

"Not scared; something else."

I shrugged. "Usually, all of them have children. Someone's mother she'd have to be."

"It's not the same. We know Ernesto."

I said that that wasn't the worst. Ten minutes. The worst was that she knew us, and that she would look at us. Yes. I don't know why, but I was convinced of one thing: when she'd look at us, something would happen.

Anibal looked scared now, and ten minutes is a long time. He asked:

"What if she throws us out?"

I was about to answer when my stomach tied into a knot: down the main street, knocking down the minutes, came the roar of a car with no muffler.

"It's Julio," we said in unison.

The car took a boisterous curve. Everything about it was boisterous: the high beams, the horn, the exhaust. It lifted the spirit. The bottle he brought also lifted the spirit.

"I stole it from my old man."

His eyes were shining. After the first swigs, our eyes were shining too. We went down Poplar Street, towards the railroad crossing. Her eyes also shone when we were kids, or perhaps it now seemed to me I'd seen them shine. And she used to wear make-up, a lot of make-up. Lipstick, especially.

"She smoked, remember?"

We were all thinking about the same thing, because I hadn't said this; Anibal had; what I said was yes, that I remembered, and I added you gotta begin somehow.

"How long before we get there?"

"Ten minutes."

And the ten minutes were long again; but now they were long exactly the other way around. I don't know. Maybe because I remembered, we all remembered, that afternoon when she was cleaning the floor, and it was summer, and when she bent down her dress had separated from her body, and we had nudged one another.

Julio stepped on the gas.

"After all, it's a punishment"—your voice, Anibal, wasn't convincing—"a revenge in Ernesto's name. That'll teach her, the bitch."

"Punishment! Are you kidding?"

Someone, I think it was me, came out with a gross obscenity. Of course it was me. The three of us roared with laughter, and Julio stepped on the gas some more.

"What if she has us thrown out?"

"Don't be an ass. The minute she gets on her high horse, I call the Turk and raise such hell that they'll get their joint closed down because of inconsiderate treatment of the customers!"

There weren't many people in the bar at that hour: some travelling salesmen and two or three truck drivers; no one from the town. And, who knows why, this made me feel bold. Unpunishable. I winked at the little blonde behind the counter; Julio, in the meantime, was talking to the Turk. The latter studied us for a few seconds. In Anibal's defiant look I saw that he too felt bold. The Turk said to the little blonde:

"Take them upstairs."

The little blonde climbing up the stairs: I remember her legs. And how she swung her hips while she climbed. I also remember I made some indecent remark, and the girl retorted with another, which (maybe because of the brandy we'd had in the car, or the gin at the bar) struck us as very funny. Then we came to a room, neat and impersonal, almost withdrawn, where there was a small table: the waiting room of a dentist. I thought maybe we're going to have a tooth pulled. I mentioned it to the others:

"Maybe we're going to have a tooth pulled."

It was impossible to keep from laughing, but we tried not to make noise. Things were said in very low whispers.

"Like in church," said Julio, and again we thought it was wildly funny; however, nothing had been as hilarious as when Anibal, covering his mouth with his hand and with a kind of snort, added:

"What if the priest comes out of there?"

My stomach was aching and my throat was dry from

laughing. I think. But suddenly we sobered up. The guy
who had been inside came out. He was a short, chubby
little fellow, like a little pig. A satisfied little pig. Pointing
to the room with his head, he rolled up his eyes, lascivi-
ously bit his lip, and he was repellent.

Then, while the guy's footsteps were still audible as he
went down the stairs, Julio asked:

"What's the matter?"

We looked at each other. Until that moment I hadn't
realized, or hadn't let myself realize, that we'd be alone,
separated—that's it: separated—in front of her. I
shrugged.

"I don't care. Anyone."

From behind the half open door we could hear water
running from a faucet. Lavatory. Then silence and a light
that fell on our faces: the door had opened completely.
There she was. We stared at her, fascinated. The half-
open robe and the afternoon of that summer when she
still was Ernesto's mother and the dress had separated
from her body and she was asking us if we wanted to
stay for milk and cookies. Except that the woman was now
a blonde. Blonde and ample. She smiled a professional
smile; a smile vaguely corrupt.

"Well? . . ."

Her voice, unexpected, shocked me: it hadn't changed.
Something, however, had changed in her, in her voice.
The woman smiled again and repeated "Well," and it
was like an order; a hot and sticky order. Maybe that's
why the three of us stood up. Her robe, I remember, was
dark, almost transparent.

"I'll go," mumbled Julio, and he stepped forward, determined.

He managed to take two steps—no more than two. Because then she looked us full in the face, and he at once
stopped. He stopped who knows why: out of fear, out of

shame perhaps, or out of revulsion. And that was the end
of everything. Because she was looking at us; and I'd
known that when she'd look at us something would happen. We stood motionless, nailed to the floor; and upon
seeing us like that, hesitating, with who knows what kind
of look on our faces, her countenance slowly, gradually,
began to change, until it acquired a strange and terrible
expression. At first, for a few seconds, it was perplexity
or incomprehension; but then she appeared to have obscurely understood something, and she looked at us with
fear, tortured, questioning. And then she spoke. She
asked if something bad had happened to him, to Ernesto.
  Closing her robe she asked it.

Translated by ANNEMARIE COLBIN

José Agustín (b. 1944), whose full name is José Agustín Ramírez, was born in Guadalajara, Mexico, in the state of Jalisco, which also produced Juan José Arreola and Juan Rulfo. His father was a pilot for Mexicana Airlines. Like many teenagers, he listened to rock music and was a devoted fan of Elvis Presley. He also joined a theater group and began to write plays. In 1960 he attended the Circulo Literario Mariano Azuela. He began to write short stories. His first short novel, *La tumba* ["The tomb"], was published in 1964 when he was only twenty. It portrayed the nonconformist, amorous activities of well-to-do teenagers in Mexico City, who rebel against hypocrisy and meaningless conventions. A second novel, also dealing with contemporary adolescent experience, came out two years later: *De perfil* [1966, "In profile"], a longer work that critics praised, although some have criticized the writer's preoccupation with adolescence. During this time he paid the rent partially with grants from the University Center of Cinematic Studies and from the Mexican Writers' Center. He studied film at the National University and drama at the National Institute of Fine Arts (where he later offered a course in the history of theater) and the National Association of Actors. Meanwhile, he has produced a prodigious amount of work, especially for so young a writer. His works include a book on rock music, movie scripts, reviews, songs, plays, translations, and a book of short stories. In 1969 he published *Inventando que sueño* ["Inventing that I dream"], a book of four narrative "acts," and more recently the experimental *Abolición de la propiedad* ["Abolition of property"], which mixes cinematic and narrative forms.

Walter M. Langford, writing about Agustín in *The Mexican Novel Comes of Age*, says that "brash and outgoing by nature, [Agustín] has more than once been referred to as 'l'enfant terrible' of present-day Mexican letters. With Gustavo Saenz (four years his elder) he has spearheaded the youngest crop of Mexican writers, which is sizeable, serious, talented, and articulate—to say nothing of unabashed." The following story is one of several included with the title novella in *La Tumba*.

Mourning

She vaguely remembers her mother's death. In the first place, the figure of her Aunt Berta stood out. With incisive words she chose the mourning clothes, and her glacial glances were met with everywhere. Before her mother died, Baby never took her Aunt Berta into consideration: an extremely thin lady, who spoke little (to scold), continually complaining of the disorder in Baby's family.

Once she heard her:

"They can say what they like, but what Cecilia"— Baby's mother—"is doing with *that girl* is unspeakable—" The aunt took a sip of her punch and went on, "—Naturally, Cecilia has always been a little 'touched.' She was very lucky to marry so *well*, but since Christian's death, Cecilia and that girl are going from bad to worse. What a bright idea to put her in that school . . . what do you call it?"

"Helena Herlihy Hall," Teresa said precisely. (She always wanted to study there.)

"Yes, *that* one." Another sip of her drink.

Now then, it surprises Baby that she'd never heard her aunt say, "If I were to bring up that girl, with me she'd always be on the right track," et cetera. Therefore it does surprise her, even more, that when her mother was dying, she begged her Aunt Berta to take charge of bringing her up and ("Damn her!" Baby spits on the floor) administering her inheritance.

Her aunt said on another occasion:

"It seems to me very harmful that they call her Baby . . . I don't know, it's a frivolous, senseless name."

On the other hand, it always delighted her that Baby's father was named Christian, because of its being a very masculine name ("The old clown!" Baby remarks), very musical and so Christian ("I'd like to vomit," she adds). To Baby her nickname didn't matter, nor her father's name ("Leave me in peace, and you can call me what you like," Baby says emphatically, blowing an unusually large puff on her cigarette): she's already used to it now.

Baby was twelve years old when her mother died. She cried more from surprise than from grief. She remembers how she was taken in hand by Aunt Berta: her dry, bony hand, her rosary dangling. At the interment Baby wept a great deal, clinging to her aunt's black skirt. The bony hand reached out to rub Baby's head, before she was captured by the rest of the family in their desire to console her.

But neither did she hear her aunt say, "Now that she's in my care, this girl is going to learn what decency is," or anything of the sort. Simply Baby, confused, saw how they took care of her clothes, and almost without realizing it, she found herself a boarding-school student at Motolinía, where her cousin Teresa was studying.

"I did all the mean things that occurred to me," Baby laughs. "I encouraged Tere to smoke, to wear stockings, to spend time contemplating the streets of the Colonia del Valle. If the filthy nuns didn't expel us, it was because of the esteem in which they held Doña Berta. *Ay tu,* those depraved nuns were the same as my aunt."

Look at Baby: laughing unkindly, she prevails upon Tere and the other girls, and they invite a new teacher. "Just a little cool drink, so you don't feel alone here. After all, we're nearly the same age." The teacher has just finished her studies and is on trial at Motolinía. She notices immediately that the drink is almost pure rum, but she feels so terrified that she drinks without saying a word. Finally she runs all over the school.

"You thieving nuns, you pay me four hundred pesos, and I work like a mule, God will punish you, you witches!"

In front of the primary school girls she raises her dress and shows her bloomers.

"That's embarrassing, *señorita!*"

Baby applauds.

Furious, the mother directress complained in front of Doña Berta, and Baby received a very detailed letter ("You're fiendish the fact that I'm not there you're corrupting your cousin our family name cast off my sister Cecilia would die of shame you haven't any breeding"), and she punished her by forbidding her to go out on weekends ("What a joke, I've *never* gone out on one weekend," Baby explains, and she adds: "Though it scratched, when I went to the bathroom, I wiped myself with her letter.") She scolded Teresa, too (on a lesser scale). Teresa is Aunt Ester's daughter and has always studied at Motolinía.

Baby finished her business course (at age seventeen because she did not take college preparatory), and her aunt could not find excuses to prevent Baby from living in Acapulco, where her family resides.

In Acapulco, Baby refused to work or to study anything else. She had to live with her aunt, and only on weekends did she see Tere, who was working as a secretary at the Hotel Caleta.

She would get up very late. Her daily cigarette before breakfast resulted in making her aunt neurotic. She begged them to buy her a car, but since they did not give in to her, she threw a tantrum and practically appropriated the shabby Hillman which had belonged to her mother and which they had out cruising for fares. Every day, even in the off season, she would go to the Condesa, where the boys gathered.

Baby got along with all of them, but she could tolerate only Jorge's conversation.

"He's stupid," she said, "but amusing."

In her house they accused her of being incorrigible, impudent, a chippie, et cetera, but the truth is that Baby was pretty much of a puritan. Admittedly, she kissed Jorge now and then, but,

"That doesn't count," Baby says gaily.

She went to parties, she often stayed up all night, and she replied with monosyllables to her aunt's scoldings. She smoked Raleigh filter-tips and drank vodka martinis. Nevertheless, she could never get out of nine-o'clock mass (Sunday after Sunday).

There came a moment when she stopped speaking to her aunt, and all mutual communication was by means of the servants and relatives.

From time to time, Tere stuttered and told her to improve her relations with her aunt.

"Look, Tere, you're half a mental defective, but I *like* you, so you close the sewer that you have for a mouth and don't ever mention that harpy."

"What you said, Baby!"

Inexorably, Aunt Ester prophesied once a week:

"Baby, you're sinning against the law of God and St.

Peter and St. Paul. You have to make peace with Berta, you're killing her, don't you understand that?"

"Now, that's enough!" Baby exploded once. "Either stop bothering me, or I'll kick you. What if I don't understand? Don't you understand that she's robbing me of my money, that she's wicked, that she gave my mother who-knows-what so they'd give her power over me? I vomit on the old wretch. I'd like to bury my nails in her eyes and gouge them out and throw them on the ground and stamp on them!"

Calm down, Baby.

Baby had the habit of walking on the beach, alone, on days when there were not many people. In one vague moment she allowed herself to sit down.

Baby made little piles of sand and automatically threw them into the sea.

"Listen, Aunt," she said to the sea, "you can't fool me so easily. You're used to running the whole family, but you aren't going to be able to do it with me. Just let me tell you. I've already found out *everything*. You poisoned my mother. You poisoned her. When she was dying, you forced her to sign that filthy paper that gives you parental authority and the management of my money. My *mamá* was all worked up, she was clawing at her throat, she saw you without being able to believe you were capable of murdering her. Because, that you did. You murdered her. Now you want to kill me. I've really found out everything, haven't I? Why do you keep silent, stupid? Deny it if you dare. With me you won't be able to!"

Baby spit into the sea.

"But you ought to imagine what she told me once," Baby specifies, her eyes on the bedspread, a bit pale.

With great coldness, Berta said:

"Look, *niña*, I've done everything possible for us to

get along, but I haven't been able to. You're possessed of the devil. I don't want to know anything about you. I can't let you have your money until you're twenty-one—"

"Aha?"

"—you know that. It's only a year and a half now. During that time, do you want to go to the United States, or where would you like to go?"

"Yes, but just till the money is mine. Until then, go away and leave me in peace."

"What a cynic, wasn't I?" Baby comments. "Besides, at that time I was having my period. I couldn't go to the beach because the Kotex would be noticed. I didn't want to see anyone. I was ex*cept*ionally angry."

Jorge, Malena, Chupeta, Rodolfo, Tomás and Baby went to the Rebozo. Tomás is the son of the municipal president and considered himself the big Don Juan of Acapulco. He took Baby to dance, while Jorge watched them coldly, waving his glass and making the ice tinkle.

In a little while Baby returned, frowning. Tomás smiled and took Malena off to dance. The combo had been playing a rhumba for the last eight minutes. Baby finished her vodka martini in one swallow. Jorge approached.

"What's the matter, Baby?"

"Nothing."

"Did Tomás say anything to you?"

"No."

"Did he hold you tight?"

"We always dance like that."

"Did he take hold of you below?"

"No."

"Look, are we spending the night together?"

"No."

"Come on."

"Leave me in peace, you clown."

Jorge began a very long, detailed story about his

parents: they wanted to put him to work. Bored, Baby went out to the beach.

"This doesn't remain like this, aunt," she said to the sea.

"Now I didn't know what to do," Baby explains, while the nurse hands her the orange juice. "Now I was fed up with everything . . ."

When Aunt Berta died (a heart attack, the doctors diagnosed), the surprise was general. Berta seemed strong, gnarled, with a lot of life in her yet. The wake was held in her house, and Baby refused to leave her room. Every five minutes an aunt, a cousin knocked on her door. "You've got to be there. Come on out. God will punish you."

"Go to hell!" Baby mumbled, pale, huddled at the head of her bed, not sleeping, hearing the sounds of the people attending the wake. All of Acapulco came.

On the following day.

She simply left her room and, behind her, the aunts and cousins watched her, gossiping safely.

"Somehow, it didn't matter to me," Baby explains, smoothing the sheets. "They could say whatever they liked without its mattering to me."

Idiots, she told herself, they're nothing but a bunch of idiots.

She put on a black bikini and a red blouse and went past the window, so they could see her. There, she realized she didn't know what to do. I'm going to the beach. She walked to a telephone booth. Coin in the slot, rings, a sleepy voice.

"Jorge?"

"Yes, who is it?"

"Baby."

"Hell, Baby, don't bother me now. What a time to call!"

"It's quarter after twelve."

"It's *awfully* early."

"Will you go with me to the beach?"

"Look, didn't your aunt just die?"

"Of course she did."

"Aren't you going to bury her today?"

"I know that. But it's okay, if you don't want to, no matter. *Ciao.*"

"Wait, don't get mad."

"Then you'll go with me?"

"Yes."

She began looking for a taxi. It occurred to her to take the Hillman, but she would have to return home. Suddenly Tere overtook her. Baby cursed the Acapulco taxis. ("They're never there when you need them," Baby says.)

"Don't be *difficult*. You have to go to the funeral."

"In spite of what you're doing, Tere, I like you. You'd better stop."

"Do you realize what you're doing? Last night you weren't at the wake. Right now my *mamá* and Aunt Cruz are already saying the worst."

"Then let them say it, sweetie. I hope their funerals happen soon, and I won't go, either."

"Then you don't intend—you really don't intend to go to the funeral?"

"No. See the blouse I put on? I'm going to the beach. Don't you want to come?"

Tere stood there motionless while Baby got into the taxi.

Jorge didn't mention the subject, and she could do no less than be grateful to him. On the beach they met the boys ("Of course, they were surprised to see me," Baby recounts, looking at a bottle of medicine), who asked some questions. Baby answered evasively.

They went into the restaurant, where they all ordered beer and she, a vodka martini "criminally dry, please."

The combo was slapping with its imitation of the surf, but nobody became demanding.

"Look, Baby," Tomás remarked, "we're going to celebrate your new wealth with a surfing dance."

Baby wasn't disturbed about it all and, frowning, got up to dance. Tomás danced, showing off, not condescending to look at Baby. Some tourists took photos and remarked, "These guys are really hot shots." Baby felt tired out when Jorge said the same thing as usual.

"Let's not deny it, the rich women have moved away from Acapulco. Where are the lovely times when there were little tramps even under the tables? We're getting old already . . ."

"Old your mother!" they cried.

In view of that, Jorge told about his vicissitudes in his new job as bellboy at the Presidente. He almost turned sad. Jorge has known Baby since childhood.

"Jorge," Baby insists, "is a defective, too."

She went down to the beach. She watched the waves breaking over her feet with repressed violence. The need to walk a lot ("until I got tired") took possession of her. She went beyond the frequented areas; she walked and stopped only when she found the beach cut off by some rocks. She sat down. Her fingers played with little piles of sand and, smiling bitterly, she tossed them onto her legs. I don't want to think about anything, now I'm free, now I'll get away from my filthy family, I'll be whatever I like, I'll be able to learn what I like, I prefer being alone, I'll be able to live quietly, live calmly . . . But she didn't feel calm; she was on edge with her nerves; the water that lapped at her feet made a martyr of her.

"I felt bad because, when I got up, the sand had stuck to my blouse, to my bikini and my legs," Baby smiled, playing at putting the top on and off the medicine bottle.

Afterward she felt angry because some fellows were looking at her persistently, from a distance. She walked a few steps and sat down again, sinking her head on her knees, feeling that her eyes were tickling and that she would end up crying.

"You crazy old girl, stop making a dunce of yourself," cried Jorge, but he repented at once. "Forgive me, Baby," he said as he came closer.

The idiot.

Together they went back to the restaurant, where the others had already left to go to Tomás' house. They all drank like crazy. ("I stayed in a corner, sitting on the floor, with a glass in my hand," Baby says.) She refused categorically to dance, and by her cutting jokes she made everyone who wanted to be with her keep his distance.

Baby was discovered to be quite drunk when Tomás climbed onto a table.

"Listen, Rodolfo has just talked to me from jail. They grabbed him prisoner, that silly kid, for offenses to decency. It's up to us to get him out, right?"

Tomás confronted someone who appeared to be a judge.

"We know, friend, by what maneuvers of high politics they locked up our long-legged Rodolfo Radilla, and we've come to demand his immediate freedom."

The apparent judge replied that young Radilla had to pay a thousand-peso fine ("A thousand pesos!" they all groaned) because he was caught right on the beach committing moral misdemeanors with a little girl who had succeeded in getting away.

"Now, that was very bad," Baby explains. "I remember only that Tomás threatened to tell his *papá*."

Unwillingly, the judge gave Rodolfo his liberty: he was received with applause and fanfares. Baby, perfectly drunk, had not let go of her glass.

"I propose a toast, can you imagine?" says Baby, smiling with a modest blush, still with the medicine in her hand.

Baby followed them to their cars and sat between Tomás and Rodolfo, who said to her:

"Look, didn't your aunt die?"

She looked into his eyes, her mind scatterbrained, blinking wetly, until she could finally say:

"Yes, I have to go to the funeral."

"Yes, I did say that," Baby admits, looking at the sheets.

She begged them to stop the car, and she got out into the street, staggering, with a desire to vomit.

The burial was already over, and on Aunt Berta's grave there were numerous bouquets of flowers. Baby didn't know what she was doing there. Seeing the earth piled up, odorous, with the cheap flowers on top, with the awful crowns forming an aureole, she felt nausea.

"I swear I couldn't hold back," Baby whispers, clutching at the sheets. The nurse stations herself at her back.

She tried to contain herself without succeeding, and she vomited for a long time on the flowers. ("I vomited like a mental defective," Baby says precisely). Afterward she sat on the ground, mumbling to the grave:

"Dear aunt, now that we're *en familia*, explain it all to me."

And she sat there on the ground, waiting for her aunt to begin the conversation.

Translated by MARY E. ELLSWORTH

Further Readings

The selected reading list that follows will no doubt need revising as new works are written and translated and others go out of print. Libraries should have at least these basic works, as well as some of the other titles to be found in the biographical sketches before each story. Because of space limitations, bibliographical information is kept to an absolute minimum. Get current price and publisher information from *Books in Print* or *Paperbound Books in Print* in your library or bookstore, if not from the Center bibliographies listed below. If your library doesn't have a title, ask them if they can order it or borrow it on interlibrary loan. Most bookstores will take special orders.

Reference and Criticism

Only general works are listed here. Every library should have them, and some are in paperback. Most of the biographical and background information in this volume was drawn from the titles on this list, including the special issues of *Review* and *Books Abroad*. The most interesting and readable books to start with are probably those of Guibert and Harss and Dohmann, as well as Franco's *Modern Culture of Latin America*.

Anderson-Imbert, Enrique, *Spanish-American Literature: A History*, 1963. Encyclopedic, although not quite up-to-date.

Franco, Jean, *The Modern Culture of Latin America: Society and the Artist*, 1967, and *An Introduction to Spanish-American Literature*, 1969. Good surveys.

Gallagher, David P., *Modern Latin American Literature*, 1973. Analyzes the work of Vallejo, Cabrera Infante, Borges, García Márquez, Vargas Llosa, Neruda, and Paz.

Guibert, Rita, *Seven Voices*, 1972. Interviews with Neruda, Borges, Asturias, Paz, Cortázar, García Márquez, and Cabrera Infante.

Harss, Luis and Barbara Dohmann, *Into the Mainstream: Conversations with Latin American Writers*, 1967. Focuses on Carpentier, Asturias, Borges, Guimarães Rosa, Onetti, Cortázar, Rulfo, Carlos Fuentes, Márquez, and Vargas Llosa.

Schwartz, Kessel, *A New History of Spanish American Fiction*, 1972, two volumes. Has more recent listings than Anderson-Imbert.

Books Abroad (published by the University of Oklahoma at Norman) has published special issues on Borges, García Márquez, and Paz, and provides regular information and reviews of new publications all over the world, including Latin America.

Review (published by the Center for Inter-American Relations, 680 Park Avenue, New York, N.Y. 10021) has published special issues on Borges, Cabrera Infante, Cortázar, Donoso, Paz, Puig, and Severo Sarduy, and covers Latin American writing regularly in three issues a year. The Center has also published several useful bibliographies of Latin American publications, including *Latin American Fiction and Poetry in Translation*, *Caribbean Fiction and Poetry in Translation*, and *Latin America Books: An Annotated Bibliography for High Schools and Colleges*.

Studies in Short Fiction published a special issue devoted to the Latin American short story in Winter 1971.

The University of Chicago "Folktales of the World" series has published *Folktales of Chile* and *Folktales of Mexico*.

Short Story Anthologies

There are several excellent collections of poetry and of West Indian fiction, and some older short-story anthologies which may be in the library, but which are probably out of print now.

Carpentier, Hortense, and Janet Brof, ed., *Doors and Mirrors,* 1972.

Cohen, J. M., ed., *Latin American Writing Today,* 1967, and *Writers in the New Cuba,* 1967.

Colford, William, ed., *Classic Tales from Spanish America,* 1962.

Donoso, José, and William A. Henkin, eds., *The Tri-Quarterly Anthology of Contemporary Latin American Literature,* 1969.

Franco, Jean, ed., *Short Stories in Spanish* (a Penguin parallel text), 1966, and *Spanish Short Stories,* Vol. II, ed. Gudie Lawaetz, 1972.

Grossman, William L., ed., *Modern Brazilian Short Stories,* 1967.

Levine, Suzanne Jill, trans., *Triple Cross,* 1972. (Includes the novellas *Holy Place* by Carlos Fuentes, *Hell Has No Limits* by José Donoso, and *From Cuba with a Song* by Severo Sarduy.)

Howes, Barbara, ed., *The Eye of the Heart,* 1973.

Jones, Willis K., ed., *Spanish American Literature in Translation,* Vol. II (since 1888), 1963.

Onís, Harriet de, ed., *The Golden Land,* 1948.

Torres-Ríoseco, Arturo, ed., *Short Stories of Latin America,* 1963.

Yates, Donald A., ed., *Latin Blood: The Best Crime and Detective Stories of South America,* 1972.

(Among the older titles now out of print are *Fiesta in November,* ed. Angel Flores and Dudley Poore, 1942; *New Voices of Hispanic America,* ed. Darwin J. Flakoll and Claribel Alegría, 1962; and *Prize Stories from Latin America,* sponsored by *Life* Magazine, 1964.)

A Basic Collection of Novels

Perhaps "minimum list" would be more precise, as many important titles are omitted for lack of space, including some titles mentioned in the biographical notes, especially the collections of writers like Arreola, Borges, and Paz, who specialize in shorter forms. Many major novelists haven't yet been translated into English but probably will be in the next few years; the *Review* mentioned earlier is one of the best sources of information about new translations. Teachers should be aware that several of the novels listed are more complex or experimental than others and might be difficult for some students.

Alegría, Ciro, *Broad and Alien Is the World,* and *The Golden Serpent*

Amado, Jorge, *The Two Deaths of Quincas Wateryell, The Violent Land,* and *Gabriela, Clove and Cinnamon*

Arguedas, José María, *Deep Rivers* (to be published soon)

Arenas, Reinaldo, *Hallucinations*

Asturias, Miguel Angel, *El Señor Presidente*

Azuela, Mariano, *The Underdogs* and *Two Novels of Mexico*

Cabrera Infante, Guillermo, *Three Trapped Tigers*

Carpentier, Alejo, *The Lost Steps* and *Explosion in a Cathedral*

Castellanos, Rosario, *The Nine Guardians*

Cortázar, Julio, *Hopscotch* and *The Winners*

Donoso, José, *The Obscene Bird of Night*

Fuentes, Carlos, *The Death of Artemio Cruz* and *The Good Conscience*

Gallegos, Rómulo, *Doña Bárbara*

Galindo, Sergio, *The Precipice*

García Márquez, Gabriel, *One Hundred Years of Solitude,* and the story collections

Garro, Elena, *Recollections of Things to Come*

Guimarães Rosa, João, *The Devil to Pay in the Backlands*

Güiraldes, Ricardo, *Don Segundo Sombra*

Icaza, Jorge, *The Villagers (Huasipungo)*

Lezama Lima, José, *Paradiso*

Lopez y Fuentes, Gregorio, *El Indio*

Machado de Assis, Joaquim María, *Epitaph of a Small Winner, Dom Casmurro,* and *Esau and Jacob*

Onetti, Juan Carlos, *The Short Life* (to be published in 1974)

Puig, Manuel, *Heartbreak Tango* and *Betrayed by Rita Hayworth*

Queiroz, Rachel de, *The Three Marias*

Ramos, Graciliano, *Barren Lives*

Rego, José Lins do, *Plantation Boy*

Rivera, José Eustacio, *The Vortex*

Roa Bastos, Augusto, *Son of Man* (London: Gollancz, 1965; not yet published here)

Rulfo, Juan, *Pedro Páramo*

Vargas Llosa, Mario, *The Green House, The Time of the Hero,* and *Conversation in the Cathedral* (1975)

Yañez, Agustín, *The Edge of the Storm*

SHORT FICTION
that does not fall short of
EXCELLENCE